To Nisha

C000263435

My HEART SINGS your SONG

Saz Vora

Saz

2021

A beautiful love story. It is modern and global in thought, yet fiercely Indian at heart.
Nik and Reena are unforgettable characters. They will stay with me for a long time to come.

Sarah Ismail, Editor, Same Difference.
www.samedifference1.com

Saz recounts her personal journey tackling topics such as generational conflicts, economic privilege, cultural issues and gender politics with the backdrop of Bollywood. She has a unique style of blending striking themes with her favourite songs, giving the readers a gentle feel of life and laughter after dealing with heartbreak and loss. Highly recommend these enjoyable reads.

Dr Pushpinder Chowdhry, MBE, Festival Director,
UK Asian Film Festival
www.ukaff.com

About the Author

Saz Vora was born in East Africa and migrated with her family to England in the 60's to the Midlands, where she grew up straddling British and Gujarati Indian culture. Her debut duet My Heart Sings Your Song and Where Have We Come is a story in two parts about love, loss and family, the second book in the series is based on true events that has shaped her outlook on life's trials and tribulations.

Please visit her website, where you can read her blog and sign up to her newsletter where she will share, missing scenes, recipes, playlists and all things book related.

Website **www.sazvora.com**

BY THE SAME AUTHOR
Where Have We Come Book Two
University Reena & Nikesh Duet

Note from Saz

The spelling used in this book is British which may be strange to American readers, but NOT to those living in Australia, Canada, India, Ireland or the United Kingdom. This means color is colour. I hope this is not confusing and will not detract from your reading experience.

The Gujarati words used in this book can be found in the Glossary at the back.

MY HEART SINGS YOUR SONG

Copyright © 2020 by Saz Vora

www.sazvora.com

Book Cover design by Mita Gohel

Author photograph by Gulab Chagger - creativeplanets.com

ISBN: 978-1-8381465-0-4

First edition. January, 2020.

10 9 8 7 6 5 4 3 2 1

Dedication

To my husband, my soul mate. When I think of all the times we could have met, it is a miracle that we finally fell in love in Leicester. I love you always and forever.

To our second son, come home, I miss you. Joking apart, I am so glad to have you as my son. You've made me very happy.

To our youngest son, I admire your resilience and perseverance. I am very proud of what you've achieved.

My Heart Sings your Song
Song
Book One

"Why are you afraid? We are in love and haven't stolen anything."

Translated lyrics from "Pyar Kiya To Darna Kya" Lata Mangeshkar, Shakeel Badayuni.

To enhance your reading experience, you can listen to my soundtrack on Spotify

My Heart Sings Your Song

Prologue

Summer 1974

MRS CHAMPNESS IS blowing her whistle in the playground. The sun is beating down, its heat burning my exposed arms. I have been waiting in the school car park since eight o'clock this morning, excited to be going on a school trip.

"Come on girls, line up for registration." We form a line in alphabetical order. I'm standing between Vicky Saunders and Lorraine Taylor. Everyone is talking about the trip to Woburn Safari Park. It is a celebration for successfully completing our first year at Upton Grammar School for Girls.

We've been allowed to wear our own clothes and, like everyone else, I'm wearing a pair of flared jeans with a top. Mine is a cheesecloth blouse with elastic on the waist. Others wear similar blouses or graphic T-shirts. I'd argued with my father about the amount of money I wanted for the trip. He insisted that he could not give me the same amount as my friends as the trip had already cost him enough already. In the end, I'd raided my piggy bank and had enough money to buy a Curly Wurly, a packet of crisps and a small souvenir.

The trip down the motorway is noisy. The coach driver has Radio 1 on and we all sing along to the songs as loudly as we can. We arrive at Woburn Safari Park at ten o'clock and wait in the winding traffic for what seems like days to get into the park. When the coach eventually parks up, we are instructed to go for a toilet break before we start our tour of the park. As we pile out of the coach, a boisterous bunch of boys fall out of the bus next to us, each shouting and running to the toilets.

Vicky and I are in the long queue that has formed outside the ladies' toilets. Next to us is a smaller line for the gents' toilets. Waiting behind us is Mrs Champness who asks which animal we are most looking forward to seeing.

"I want to see the elephants, Miss," I say.

"And why is that, Reena?" she asks.

"I love elephants. Did you know that they live in family groups and live a long time? I watched a documentary about it by David Attenborough on the TV."

Vicky butts in, "My favourite are the monkeys. Can't wait to see them, Miss."

Just then a group of girls standing behind us also start to say they like monkeys, too.

Mrs Champness laughs, "Well, we're definitely going to see a lot of monkeys, girls."

* * *

VICKY IS WAITING FOR ME outside by a small seating area. The boys who'd come off the coach are also waiting around in small groups of three and four. I'm with Lorraine and we gather in a huddle. Vicky is giggling and gesturing over her shoulder to one of the boys who has been glancing at her and smiling.

We try to look at him without giving him any idea that she might be interested in him. The boy has an olive complexion and curly-hair in the style of Marc Bolan. He is wearing a pair of flared dark blue jeans and a pale-yellow T-shirt with a rainbow on it.

"What do you think? Isn't he handsome?" she asks us.

"Yes, I suppose he is," I reply.

"I fancy the blond-haired one by the bench," Lorraine adds. "What about you, Reena? Which one do you like?"

"Oh, I don't …"

"It's not about having a boyfriend, Reena. Which one do you fancy?" Vicky adds. I don't understand why every time they come across boys, they get girly and giggly. Sometimes I despair and wonder why it is so important to have a boyfriend.

I see another boy approach the group. He has a slightly darker complexion than the curly-haired one and has a haircut like Donny Osmond. The boys turn towards us and stand, arms folded in front of their chests, smiling at us. Vicky and Lorraine giggle, covering their mouths. I stand taller and give them a stern stare in return. The curly-haired one whispers something to the boys on his left and right. They nod and step towards us in unison.

A stocky, tall, balding man in a tweed jacket and brown trousers shouts from beyond the seating area.

"Boys, time's up. Back on the coach!" They stop in mid-stride and turn to head for their coach.

Vicky and Lorraine give them a shy wave and the curly-haired boy shouts.

"Meet you in the playground later!"

"Okay!" she shouts back and then turns towards us and says quietly, "Ooh, he likes me," and giggles.

We all climb back on the coach and begin our safari. I watch the elephants look after a baby elephant and I try to sketch them. Those of us that sit at the back of the coach have a great view of the monkeys in their enclosure. We watch as some monkeys try to steal the windscreen wipers from the car behind us. The driver's face turns beetroot red and he waves his arms as the monkeys climb onto his car bonnet.

For lunch we all head for the playground and the grassy area, Vicky and Lorraine filled with excitement at meeting the boys.

The boys' school have decided to sit in small groups by the fence, and straight away I see the three boys we had met earlier. I slow down as I'm not sure I want to go to sit with them. Luckily Mrs Champness shouts for us to sit on the benches.

"I hope we're not going to be supervised all the time," Vicky mutters grudgingly while grabbing my arm.

The boys keep glancing towards us and smiling as we eat our lunch. Some of the girls are giggling and waving back at them, some ignore them like I do.

A whistle blows, "Girls, can you tidy up your mess. You now have the rest of the afternoon to explore the park. Meet you all at the coach at three o'clock."

Groups of boys and girls merge, girls blushing and giggling, boys strutting and preening. It is almost like watching the peacocks from the grounds.

Vicky and Lorraine link arms with me and we set off to queue for the train that circumnavigates the park. They discuss when we should go to the play area and whether the boys will notice that we've got on the train. It is only when the train goes around a bend that Lorraine sees them in the last carriage and begins to wave to them to get their attention. Wherever we go, we find that the trio are following, so, after a lot of looking back and giggling from Vicky and Lorraine, and a lot of ignoring from me, we find ourselves in the playground. It is full of the usual equipment you would find in a park playground, swings, slides, a seesaw, climbing frames and roundabouts. I join the queue to climb the stairs to the slide and, when I slide down, the boy with the Donny Osmond haircut is standing at the bottom.

"I've never seen long legs like yours before," he says. I'm surprised. I expected him to be Italian, and didn't expect the hint of an accent that reminds me of my father's. He certainly doesn't look Indian. I flick my hair off my face and turn away from him. I hate my legs; they are long and thin and my gait is slightly knock kneed. I pretend that I'm too good for him. I run to a roundabout occupied by some other girls and join them, my chin jutting into the air.

Vicky and Lorraine join me and tell me that the curly-haired boy is called Gino and he has introduced his two friends to them. I am told that the boy with the

Donny Osmond haircut likes me and wants to buy me a Coke.

I'm not impressed by these boys; I can buy my own drink, so I decline, telling Vicky and Lorraine that I'm not thirsty and that I want to do some sketching in the playground. Vicky and Lorraine sigh and comment that I'll never get a boyfriend if I keep behaving like this. They walk away, their arms entwined with the three boys and they all head to the cafe. The one with the Donny Osmond haircut glances back and gives me a small shy smile that I ignore.

It's 2.45 p.m. I'm waiting in the queue for the toilets and see him leaning against the trunk of a large oak tree. I find myself hoping that he will be gone before I come out so that I won't have to encounter him when I walk to our coach.

As I adjust my eyes to the bright sun, I release a sigh of relief since he is no longer there. It is only when I reach the tree that I see him again. He has moved and is standing with his shoulder leaning against the trunk. He moves towards me.

"I didn't mean to hurt you. It was meant to be a compliment. I like your long legs," he apologises as he walks by my side. I accept his apology with a nod and smile at him. I gasp. I've never seen eyes the colour of golden sand on an Indian boy before. He smiles at my reaction. I look ahead, focusing on the coach, hoping that he won't say anything else to me. He is far too close for my comfort and his stride matches mine. The short walk to the coach car park seems like a marathon.

We reach my coach and he repeats his apology, smiling

bashfully at me.

Ram Katha 1979

THE SUMMER AFTER MY O-LEVEL exams is hotter and longer than normal. I've found a job with the help of Divya Ba. I have taken a day off as I'd promised her that I'd go with her to Wembley for Ram Katha. The mandir has organised a day trip on a coach and she's asked me if I would volunteer and go with her.

I call her Ba, but she isn't my grandmother; she's the lady who gave my parents shelter when they first arrived in Leicester. I've never known my grandparents on either side. Daddy never talks about them. All we have is a set of black and white photographs in the front room and an old photograph album. The snippets of information my brother Amit and I have learnt about them are from Divya Ba.

She was a childhood friend of Dadima, Daddy's mother.

She told us about Dadima's hard life. At first, we had thought that she'd embellished the tales of loss and hardship, due to her love of Bollywood films. But, when we asked our father about his childhood, he would hint at the poverty and then quickly change the subject.

Divya Ba had told us that my grandfather had died in mysterious circumstances when Daddy was a child and that Dadima had raised her son and daughter, working as an ayaa and cook for some wealthy Indian families in Nairobi. I have a vague recollection of my Dadima passing away. Daddy had arranged bhajans at the mandir and we had taken the black and white photograph off the wall. I remember thinking that it was odd. We had lined up by the exit doors at the end of the bhajans and Daddy had cried when Divya Ba hugged him.

When we asked her about our mother's parents, her eyes would water, and a sense of sadness would wash over them. My brother, Amit, and I had decided that we wouldn't ask her again. We love Divya Ba; she would bring us sweets from the corner shop when she picked us up from school and she was always dropping off nasto and food. Without Divya Ba I'm sure Daddy wouldn't be able to work.

The sun is just rising, the sky is filled with differing shades of crimson. The quiet of the morning is interrupted by the noise of the milk bottles clattering against each other in the milk floats and the familiar hum of the engine as it idles while the milkman delivers fresh milk to the terraced houses.

I have put on a saree. I love wearing sarees; they help me connect with my mother. My favourite memory of my mother is her getting ready to go out. Most of the time she wore a light shirt and dark trousers, but I remember the vibrant colours and the feel and the scent of the silk fabric she used to let me wrap around myself.

I've decided to wear a printed orange saree that Divya Ba gave me for my 16th birthday.

I knock on a navy-blue front door on the terraced street. A small, rotund woman with gold-rimmed glasses opens the door. I say small in comparison to me; she reaches my chest and I'm not that tall. She pushes a large black canvas bag immediately into my hand. She turns back to the front room and picks up her brown handbag and a thick cream cardigan.

"It's too hot. You don't need two cardigans, Ba."

"I can't go out without this." She pulls at the cardigan draped over her arm.

She closes the front door and we walk up to Narborough Road and the coach stop.

"What was your first week working at Roop Lila like, Dikri?" she questions. She's always questioning. Sometimes I get fed up and only answer with an "all right." But this morning, I'm open to the inquisition.

"I like it. Mayur Bhai and Rohini Bhabhi are so nice to work for. Do you know they have a masi who cooks lunch for everyone? She made limbu sharbat every day because it was so hot last week."

"They are good people. I told them that you're only looking for a summer job. I also told them that Naren's children are too clever to work in shops for the rest of their lives. Mayur was a bit reluctant, but Rohini was very persuasive and convinced him." I smile at her and think she knows me well. I adore the sarees, the materials and all the carved statues and puja stuff they sell. It is a great place to work. The smell of the cloth, wood and joss sticks is unbelievable. I don't know what it is about sandalwood and silk, but it makes me feel comfortable.

"The other day, this lady walked in and bought a £300 saree. I know because Rohini Bhabhi asked me to write up the receipt. I can't believe anyone would spend that much! She'd said she was buying it for her daughter-in-law's birthday present."

Divya Ba nods in agreement at my astonishment. That

amount of money is half my father's monthly salary.

We reach the bus stop and nod to the other people waiting.

"Lalita, how are you feeling?" Divya Ba turns to a tall skinny woman.

"Much better Divya Masi. The fever has gone – just feeling a bit weak."

"You shouldn't have come," she reprimands.

"I couldn't miss it. He's not coming back for a few more years."

I loved going on these trips. Amit and I have been on so many day trips with the mandir and with Divya Ba. I guess we are a good substitute for her grandchildren. They live in San Francisco and Toronto and she only sees them when her sons collect her for a visit.

The mandir has organised social trips and religious trips to all sorts of destinations that could be covered in a day. We've been to a lot of seaside resorts, theme parks and major cities and towns up and down the length and breadth of the United Kingdom.

On these trips, the women would bring bags full of food and flasks of tea to distribute to everyone and the kids would bring sweets, crisps and fizzy drinks. We'd usually start to eat the sweets and snacks as soon as we joined the motorway and afterwards, sing songs and dance down the aisle. On our return home the coach driver would put on an old Indian film on the VHS which we would all strain our necks to watch on the two small TVs, one mounted in the front and the second halfway up the coach.

The trips were the best respite from the long, tedious summer holidays.

I'm waiting with Shruti. She is two years older than me and is excited about going away to university in September. I ask how she chose where to go. She explains that the only place she could go to was Manchester. I ask why and she says her mother's cousin lives there. I bristle with indignation and reply that I would go wherever the best course was. She shakes her head, her eyes full of pity.

The blue and white coach pulls up and we wait for the old people to get on. As we enter through the door, the driver greets us with "Kem cho?" the Gujarati greeting meaning how are you. We giggle; he is English. "How did he know what language we speak?" I ask Shruti, my eyes wide in astonishment. She looks at me with the same expression and shakes her head.

We head to the back seat to sit with all the other teenagers.

There is a hierarchy as to who sits where on these journeys. The front seats are for the mandir committee, and their husbands or wives. The next set of seats are for the really old people, the grandparents. The middle seats are for families with younger children and the back seats are for the teenagers. Very few twenty-somethings come on these trips. I know this because some of the people who volunteer at the mandir stopped coming as soon as they turned twenty.

I know everyone on the coach; I've spent a lot of time with them. It makes me happy to be part of the community. I like helping in the kitchen, playing with children, serving people. I like the calmness of the spirituality associated with the beliefs of Hindus. I learnt this from my father. He might not practise all the customs and rituals, but he does give a good discourse on the philosophy of Hinduism.

***

WE ARE GIVEN A WHITE BIB printed with the words 'Leicester Hindu Sanatan Mandir Young Seva Group'. Many other people have volunteered to help at the Katha, we have been tasked to help with serving food. This is the biggest gathering of Hindus in the UK. The organisers have estimated that at least ten-thousand people will be coming to Wembley Arena today. The attendees are coming to listen to Morari Bapu tell the epic tale of Rama, the Prince of Kaushal and his trials and tribulations as he rids the world of the evil Ravana.

We are told to go to the dining area and get some refreshments before the doors are opened to the waiting crowds. The place is full of men, women and children dressed in jabo pyjamas, sarees, and churidar kameez. The summer sun accentuates the colours and I get the impression that I'm not in England. It's like a scene from a Bollywood movie, the establishing shot before the hero and heroine start dancing at a Hindu festival.

"Shruti, Bharat, Pankaj, Akash, Asmita and Reena, can I put you in the VIP dining room? You'll help Prakashbhai and the ladies to feed Bapu and his guests."

"Hai Ram. I'm so excited we'll get to meet Bapu today."

I nod to Bharat; he is so excitable and has started to say "Hai Ram." Who does that? He's only seventeen years old. I've heard some grandparents say it, but he was born in Leicester, not some village in Gujarat.

A man, five feet ten inches tall, dark-skinned, bald, with a salt-and-pepper goatee beard, beckons us to a spot. He is wearing a white jabo pyjama and keeps pushing up a pair of Gandhi-style glasses that slip down his long nose periodically.

"It's an honour for Leicester Hindu Sanatan Mandir to be put in charge of this job. I want you all to be proud of the honour. And nothing, nothing must go wrong. You will all need to look for jobs. I'm not going to tell you what to do. That's not my way."

Everyone takes a deep breath. We all know that all Prakash Bhai does is shout out jobs for us to do, he just can't help it.

The morning serving had gone well; Bapu hadn't arrived so there were fewer people. There were a couple of hitches, but once the VIPs had left, we were given a detailed breakdown of serving etiquette and told how to improve for lunch. The tidying up was left to the other volunteers and so we headed into the arena.

One of the advantages of being a volunteer is that you get to sit at the front. Bapu always makes sure that these seats are for the sevaks. We sit on the floor in front of the dais where the musicians, gurus and main organisers are gathered.

The Katha isn't my favourite tale of Vishnu's avatars. I love Krishna Leela, but Morari Bapu's telling of the tales is captivating. He has a knack of relating the tales to modern dilemmas. I'm pleased to be part of this Hindu community in the UK; I know the numbers have grown recently and, somehow, I feel I belong.

***

THE DINING ROOM HAS BEEN rearranged. Breakfast had been set up for twenty people, but the lunch setting is much bigger. The room is set for at least one hundred people; the tablecloths have been changed from white to orange, the dining plates are large stainless-steel thalis with small katoris. Even the glasses are stainless steel.

As we line up to welcome the VIPs, Prakash Bhai walks up to give us a few words of encouragement.

Bapu walks through the double doors and, as he passes us, his palms held out in salutation, he tells us that he is proud to see so many young people committed to Seva.

We wait for everyone to pass, as I turn towards the serving table I am stopped in my tracks by a voice.

"Excuse me."

I turn towards the voice. Standing in front of me is a boy in a pale-yellow silk jabo pyjama. He is slim built with dark brown, layered hair. On his forehead, there is a red tilak.

"Hello, where should my sisters and I go to eat?"

"You can sit anywhere." I point to the tables as I reply.

"I don't think so," he frowns. "Motaba, Kaki, and Guruji usually sit with the VIP, and we usually go to the other dining rooms."

I ask him to wait and I go to ask Prakash Bhai, who is waiting by the access door to give his orders to the kitchen staff.

I can feel his gaze. His eyes remind me of the golden

yellow of a lion's eyes. I exhale. My lungs demand more oxygen and I take a deep breath. Those same eyes are watching me as I walk back to where he is standing awkwardly. He must have noticed that he is staring because he suddenly starts to look intently at the wall behind me.

I tell him that all his family has a place here and that he and his sisters should go sit. He thanks me, not making eye contact, and turns on his heels. I watch as he gestures to his sisters. The one in the green churidar kameez is taken aback, but the other one is more confident and leads them to sit at the end of a set of tables.

When everyone is seated, we start to serve the food on the plates. We are given the dry food to serve. Prakash Bhai had told us that hot shaaks and dalls were not suitable for children to handle, that job was for the adults.

Once all the different dishes have been served, we are given the task of serving water and chaas and prepare to collect the empty plates. I am standing by the washbasin. It is my job to pour water over people's hands.

The boy and his sisters are one of the first groups to finish and have come to wash their hands.

He holds my gaze. Those eyes are amazing. They have golden shards coming out of the black pupils. His head leans in as I pour the water.

"Why would you volunteer to do this?" he whispers in my ear.

I say "Jai Siya Ram," trying to stop the anger from rising.

My work in the community is important to me and these jobs are some of my favourites. Some people volunteer, but will only do the job of making food, greeting, serving. They won't do any of the cleaning tasks as they think it's dirty. I'm indifferent about clean or dirty, what's the difference? They are just jobs that need to be done.

I watch him go up to Prakash Bhai who directs him to the water serving stations. I'm shocked. I didn't expect him and his sisters to pick up the jugs of water and start topping up the stainless-steel glasses for the guests. I hear a man sitting next to Morari Bapu.

"Bapu, these three are Sarladevi's children."

"Reena, can I have your slop bucket?"

Bharat is standing before me. I pick up the bucket from under the table and hand it to him.

I glance across and the boy and his sisters are lining up to touch Bapu's feet, taking it in turns and waiting with their palms together in salutation.

Once Bapu has given them a blessing they continue doing their Seva.

At the end of lunch, the rest of the VIPs line up after Bapu to go back to the arena. On his right is an elegant woman who, I have learnt, is known as Sarladevi and that boy is her son. I can see him walking behind Bapu next to the Guru and he is listening intently to what Bapu is saying.

Bapu stops and walks to the hand-washing table.

"This is the most important job in this room, Beti. Your Seva will be rewarded."

I smile and bow my head in salutation to Bapu. When I look up, I see the boy nodding sheepishly and a small lopsided smile appears on his face as his golden eyes twinkle. My breath catches.

One

Late September 1984

I COULDN'T GET RID OF the ache that rested like a stone on my chest. I was not sleeping properly, waking up with a panic that made me gasp for air.

I had worked at Roop Lila again that summer, trying to keep my mind off what I had done. Even my brother, Amit, and his wife, Smita Bhabhi, gave me time to myself. Smita Bhabhi silently provided me with food and cups of tea in my room when I came home from work. The walls in our house were thin, so they probably heard from their bedroom the sobs I couldn't control. They asked me if they could leave me alone tonight. I loved them both for not asking me why I was so sad and told them they should have a life.

My father came home later than usual. I could tell straight away he wasn't happy. His expression darkened, and he had a look of determination to obliterate whatever had brought it on.

"Shouldn't you be studying?" he asked angrily as he saw me slumped on the sofa.

"I'm taking a break today," I replied, pulling my aching body up to get out of his way.

"No, sit. I want to talk with you." He slung his jacket on his favourite armchair and stood at the sideboard, reaching for a bottle. He filled a small tumbler with the golden liquid of Johnnie Walker, his favourite tipple.

"Do you know a Dolat Mehta?" His eyes, as dark as the night, burned into me. "I've just had to hear his pompous ramblings on how university has made some people reach above their class. And how he knows of a family whose son was besotted with a girl who was dirt poor and should have been brought up better. Do you know who that family is, Reena?" His voice rose. "Do you want to know their name?"

I fixed my eyes on the carpet. I didn't want to know, but I was positive he was going to tell me. He was in a dark mood, and I preferred to listen than to face the consequences of arguing.

"The late Ramprakash Raja, that's who. I've told you to stop being friends with that boy. You ignore me; you carry on behind my back. You do not respect me." His knuckles turned white from holding the glass too tightly. "When will you learn, they are indulging their son. You are never going to be suitable." He picked up his glass of whisky and gulped it down.

I was shocked Dolat Mehta could have said this and I found myself wondering how he knew my father and why he had chosen to say this now.

I recalled the times I'd met him at Nik's. He was arrogant and highly opinionated, one of the rich

Indians who thought too highly of themselves and took advantage of their privilege.

It brought back all my misgivings about wealthy Indians, and I was glad I wouldn't have to see him again.

"I'm sorry, Daddy; I've stopped seeing him."

My father pursed his lips. He wanted to say more but saw the hurt in my eyes. I walked out and ran up the stairs, flinging myself on the bed. Hot angry tears flooded my eyes.

I had been stupid. I'd let him get into my heart. He was just like all the other privileged types with a use-and-abuse-them attitude.

I had seen them before, the boys at my brother's grammar school. They'd played a complicated game of conquest with girls from my grammar school. It was always the same, a little bit of skirt from the other side of the track. They would then go off to university promising to keep in touch. The girls were left devastated, waiting for a letter, a phone call or any morsel of hope, their dreams shattered. Mills and Boons had a lot to answer for with so many girls of my social class. No one wanted a working-class girl in their family. The wealthy wanted to grow their wealth, not deplete it.

Nikesh Raja was the same. As soon as it became complicated, he disappeared. His fake love was a tick on his must-do list before he settled down with a suitable girl from an equally wealthy family. My head told me I was right, but my heart hoped he was different.

* * *

I RECOLLECTED THE DAY he came to see me earlier in the summer break, too late to support me. I had gone up to the bedroom; I couldn't tolerate the happy faces on the TV. It was just too much, too soon. The emptiness in my heart filled my core, blackening everything. I resented other people's laughter.

I knew it was the right decision to make. I was in my final year at university, and I promised myself I would fulfil my ambition to be a producer. I thought Nik supported me. He should have let me make up my own mind. After all, it was my body. If he hadn't cut the conversation in anger, I might have considered my options. But he'd done what he'd been brought up to do. His papa had warned me he wasn't responsible.

Someone rang the doorbell; I peered at the alarm clock. I wondered who would come visiting at this late hour. I had been staying at Umi's that week; I couldn't face going back home and having to deal with my family. They knew nothing about the choice I made. I'd told them I was spending some time with Umi to keep her company while her father was away at a conference. The conference part was genuine, but it was only for a few days, and her father had returned. He kept patting my head as he walked past me; he sensed something was wrong.

I heard murmurs in the hallway and recognised one of the voices. My heart was in my mouth.

There was a soft knock on the door, and Umi stepped in and sat on the bed. "Nik's come to see you."

"I don't want to see him. Tell him to go away," I whispered.

"I think … you need to speak with him. He won't go away. He's got that stubborn face on."

I turned my body over in the bed and said, "I can't do this … not now."

"I'll stay with you, I promise."

Umi helped me get out of bed; my body felt too heavy to lift by myself.

She pulled a sweat top over my head and helped put my arms through the sleeves. She wrapped her arm around my waist to prop me up, and we walked slowly down the stairs.

I felt his eyes before I saw them. He was standing at the bottom of the staircase with his hands in his jacket pockets. His hair was dishevelled; there was three days of stubble on his face, and it seemed as if he hadn't slept for days.

His eyes lingered on my stomach, and as I stepped onto the bottom stair, he moved forward to reach for my hand. I clenched my fists together. I didn't want him to take them in his.

I glanced up to his face through my fringe and saw his eyes were studying me, trying to gauge my mood. The golden shards in his eyes had lost some of their lustre.

"What do you want, Nik?" I asked through clenched teeth, my hands clenched into tight fists.

"Please, let me explain, Ree." His voice was rough and low.

Umi drew me closer to her.

He locked eyes with Umi. "Umi, can I please take Reena outside to talk?"

"It's not up to me. Ree has to want it."

He glared at both of us, his face tightened into a taut

expression.

"I won't leave until you listen to me."

"Go home, Nik. I don't want to hear what you have to say."

He stood with his hands stuffed in his pockets. I had seen the stance before, but he faltered, as Umi's father's head popped into the hallway.

"What's happening girls? Come and sit down."

Defeated, he turned back to the front door.

"I'll wait for you in my car," he said.

Umi's father watched the three of us with a quizzical expression.

"We're going upstairs, Dad; I don't think Nik will disturb us anymore. Goodnight."

We climbed to my room, and I headed for the window. Umi followed me and we both watched silently.

My legs felt like jelly and I clasped the windowsill. Umi guided me back to the bed and told me to lie down. She sat, stroking my head in silence.

The time on the alarm clock was 12 o'clock, midnight. I told Umi to go to bed, and she lifted the curtain to peer outside and confirmed to me that he was still waiting in the car.

I tried to sleep, lying in the darkness, hoping he would get tired of waiting and go. I heard Umi's father come upstairs and the house finally became still; the time on the alarm clock read 1.30 a.m.

I pulled the curtain slightly to take a glimpse of the car and he turned his head up to match my gaze. I stepped back. He had a sixth sense when it came to me. *So why hadn't he come earlier?* He knew I would have wanted him with me! My rage shouted back at me.

The time slowed; minutes felt like hours and hours felt like days. I rested on my bed. Sleep had deserted me.

At 6.30 a.m. I heard Umi's father unbolt the front door and beckon to Nik. "Come inside, son, I'm making tea." I caught the sound of the car door shutting and I heard muffled voices from the kitchen. I'm going to have to speak to him, I thought, exhausted.

"Someone, help me! PLEASE HELP! HELP! HELP!"

"Ree, Reena wake up."

I was in Nik's arms; he was stroking my hair and whispering, "It's all right, you're safe; I have you." I could taste the tears in my mouth and felt them trickle down my neck and I realised I was awake.

Umi appeared at the door, wiping her face with her hand and yawning. She stepped back onto the landing. "How did he get inside, Dad?"

"I let him in. Come with me, Honeybee," her father quietly instructed.

I pulled away from him, determined to keep a distance between us. His eyes filled with hurt.

He sensed the change in our relationship and his shoulders slumped as he shuffled to the bottom of the bed. We sat silently; I did not have the voice to express my feelings. The golden sparkles in his eyes dulled. I wondered, *was he hurting for the same reason I was?*

Umi brought up some hot drinks. She placed the mug in my hand and handed Nik his and said, "You look like shit, Nik. You both do. You need to talk and sort this out."

I held the mug in both hands, firstly to feel the warmth and secondly to prevent him from clutching them. I was scared I would not hold my resolve if he touched me again.

"I … I'm sorry … I should have been with you."

"You let me down, Nik. You're too late … You should have come on Tuesday." My voice gave way and I gulped back a sob.

The dream. What have I done? I sobbed and my whole body convulsed as the last vestige of any moisture in my body flooded through my eyes.

He reached to comfort me, and my hand held his chest to push him away.

"Go, Nik … I can't forgive you. I can't forget what I've done. Every time I see you, I'll feel the shame. We don't have a future together any more. I was wrong to even think we did."

I saw the tears trickle down his cheek. I wondered if he was crying because of me or because of what I'd done. "I love you. Please give me another chance … I promise I'll never let you down again."

I shook my head slowly. "I can't forget what has happened. You have to leave me."

I let him hold me and kiss me but when I couldn't respond his kisses stopped. He rested his forehead on mine. Our breath mingled, shallow, gasping. He was crying.

He pushed himself off the bed and stood with his hands hanging by his sides.

"I will always love you, Ree. Always have, always will. Without you my heart is empty."

I wished he had said it that day. I closed my eyes, not wanting to see him leave.

He said goodbye to Umi, and her father, and I watched from the window for one last time as he walked to his car. He had shrunk. His shoulders were hunched, and his steady athletic stride had been swapped for halting steps. He opened his car door and turned to the house. Our eyes met for one last time.

My heart broke into tiny fragments. It would never be whole again. I thought he was the only one for me.

My mind wandered to Fresher's Week in my first year at Warwick. The day I met Nikesh Raja and how my life had changed because of him.

Two

September 1982

I FORCED MYSELF TO WAKE UP. Wake up Reena! Wake up, Reena! Wake up!

My heart was thumping against my chest. I was gasping for breath. I opened my eyes and focused on my surroundings. Where was I? Nothing was familiar to me. I began to panic again and I felt a trickle of sweat run down my back. I sat up and willed myself to calm down. Suddenly I remembered where I was. I didn't want my newly-made bed to become soaked with sweat, not on the first night I slept in it. I glanced at the alarm clock; it was 6 a.m. It was too early to get out of bed, but I knew I wouldn't be able to sleep.

I dreamt of the white box again and the feeling of dread. Sometimes I shouted for my mother; sometimes I felt the claustrophobia of the hot room. Most of the time I woke up crying.

I changed into my jogging bottoms and headed out; the sky was navy-blue, and the sun hadn't risen yet. Rather than go for a run, I decided on a walk around the campus. I knew of the lake and made my way down the path leading to it. I came to a bench and sat to watch the sunrise. It was a peaceful time; there was a light breeze and bulrushes rustled as they brushed against each other. There was no one out at this time of the morning. It was too early in the term for returning revellers and for early risers. Although my day had started badly, the morning was unusually warm for late September and the sound of the grasses and the morning chorus was calming my nerves as I made a note of the place by the water, my new sanctuary.

It made me feel at home and calmed me down. I was used to walking by the River Soar that ran near where I lived in Leicester. Rivers and the sound of water soothed me and reminded me of my childhood days of lingering and drawing by the river at home. I sat by the lake until I heard people begin to stir and walked back to my room in Rootes Hall. The halls of residence had a shared kitchen which made perfect sense as I couldn't afford to buy food from the canteen every day. That would undoubtedly have made university life difficult for me. I had a student grant for the rent and living expenses, but it didn't cover everything.

However, I made my mind up to go to the canteen for breakfast. I had decided that the only way I was going to make new friends was to eat at the canteen for at least a week. It would deplete my already meagre funds, but I was hoping to get a job to help me live away from home.

"Oops," I said when I bumped into one of my housemates as I approached the kitchen door.

"What the fuck!" The girl adjusted her hold on her

mug of tea.

"Sorry, are you okay?"

Ignoring me, she walked away from me, shaking her head, and stepped into a doorway further along the corridor. *That's a bit rude*, I thought to myself. She didn't spill her tea and I did apologise.

I made myself a cup of tea and went back to my room to get ready for the day.

It took me ages to decide what I was going to wear, having already discounted three outfits. I admired myself in the full-length mirror.

I was wearing a pair of sky-blue trousers that skimmed my ankles, a white T-shirt and a carnation-pink cashmere V-neck cardigan which didn't make my breasts look too big. My long hair was swept back in a high ponytail. I had a full fringe that covered my forehead and I had applied red lipstick on my cupid-shaped lips. To complete the whole homage to the sixties, I had put on my black patent shoes with a tortoiseshell buckle. At the age of sixteen I had discovered charity shops had cheap, good-quality clothes that I could adjust and wear to keep my wardrobe fresh. How else would I have been able to afford fashionable clothing? We had a limited budget for clothes in my family.

Before stepping out of my room, I checked my face in the mirror; my pale skin is flawless, and a tinge of pink blush sat on my plump cheeks. My nose, small and almost button-like. I do not have any Indian traits; even the colour of my hair has an undertone of Auburn running through it. My eyes are huge for my small, round face. They are as rich as the soil in winter;

stained with the colour of dark chocolate, my pupils black and large. My dark lashes are thick and long. They say the eyes are the windows to the soul: mine show every emotion. That morning they showed the gnawing anxiety I was carrying with me.

I glanced to my right before I stepped out into the narrow corridor.

"Hello, I'm Umi."

She was holding her hand out to me. It was the same girl from earlier in the morning. My first instinct was to ignore her and walk away, but I reminded myself I was going to try to make friends.

I inhaled, and shook her hand and replied, "Hi, I'm Reena Solanki."

"Are you Indian?" Her expression was full of surprise; her eyebrows had risen, and two frown lines had appeared on her forehead.

She expanded, "It's just you don't look Indian. Your skin's a bit pale and you don't have the nose. Is your mum white?"

I had heard the implied meaning so many times, it was wearing thin, but I was shocked she would say it to my face. She had Indian features: the dark skin, the long nose, the almond-shaped eyes, the voluptuous body; she stood at five feet six inches tall which was unusual for Indian girls.

I'm five feet two inches tall and among some of the girls from the Indian community at home, I was always defined as the tall girl.

"I am Indian. I promise," I smiled.

She released a chuckle, grabbed my arm and said, "Come, let me buy you breakfast. You are going for breakfast, right?"

Her naturally soft, curled black hair is her crowning glory; it cascaded down her back. It is not the same colour as mine, as sometimes in the light you can see a red tint in my hair.

Her black hair showed a hue of dark blue; I wondered if she dyed it. I didn't mean to stare. She whispered, "No, it's all natural."

As we climbed down the stairs, I asked, "Is Umi short for anything?"

She replied, "Yes, my name is Urmila Yadav."

The canteen was housed in the Rootes Social Hall, a concrete and glass structure built at the same time as the other Warwick University campus buildings. It could be entered from the north by the student halls or from the south through University Street.

The ground floor was completely encased in glass and the levels were held up by concrete stilts. The dining hall was laid out with row upon row of long tables with wooden chairs on both sides.

The clock on the wall read 9.30 a.m. and the room was already bursting with students. The queue for the food was long but moved quickly. There was a large lady with dyed platinum blonde hair asking people to move out of their vacant chairs and barking orders to the cleaning staff.

The serving area was laden with cereals, bread, fruit, and soft drinks. I picked up a tray and Umi and I stood at the hot food bar to fill our plates with a full English breakfast. We both declined the gloopy baked beans and took a couple of slices of hot buttered white toast. There were a couple of women serving tea and coffee from large urns. I opted for tea and Umi asked for a coffee with hot milk.

The queue to pay was as long as the queue for the food. Umi started to eat her toast, moaning about the lack of tills.

I was impressed with the way she could hold her tray with one hand and eat with the other. I didn't have the confidence to do the same.

We searched for a place to sit in the crowded dining hall. Umi pointed to the furthest row, near the back windows. "Come on, Reena, before someone takes the seat." She swiftly walked to the end of the long room.

There were two vacant chairs opposite a bunch of people whose backs were to us.

I concentrated on keeping the cup of tea and the glass of water from sliding across the tray.

Suddenly my tray jumped out of my hand and a sausage, a rasher of bacon, six button mushrooms and a fried egg flew upwards. The tray miraculously landed back in my hand; I gripped it as if my life depended on it. The plate and a dollop of ketchup were still there as the food landed in slow motion. I began to pray, please, please don't land on anyone. I won't make friends if I keep throwing food at everyone. The shattering sound of the cup of tea and the glass brought applause from everyone in the vicinity. I was mortified. I wished the floor would open and swallow me up.

"I'm so, so, so sorry. Are you okay, are you hurt?"

Standing in front of me among the shattered glass and ceramic was a pair of expensive Italian brown leather shoes. My eyes slowly rose up; he was wearing a pair of dark-blue jeans, a light-blue button-down Oxford shirt and a tan leather bomber jacket. His eyes were exquisite; they were the colour of burnt toffee, with bright golden shards that radiated from huge black pupils. My breath caught and, when I tried to speak, my voice failed me.

"What the fuck! Didn't you see us? What do you think you're doing?" Umi was ranting at him.

He lifted up both his hands, palms out to her and apologised again.

The fake platinum blonde was already by our side, asking us to move so she could clean up.

We both moved out of the way of the broken crockery and he guided me gently to a clean area by placing his hand on my elbow. He stood in front of me.

"Please, let me buy you another breakfast. It was my fault entirely. I shouldn't have lifted my arm up without checking."

He wore his luxuriant hair long; a short fringe fell on his broad forehead framing his handsome face. His toffee coloured complexion glistened from recent exposure to the sun.

"No, it's okay," I croaked. I was sure I had seen him before, but couldn't recall where.

My eyes rested on his lips; they were full and of equal proportion. There was a small indent on the top lip. My mind began to wonder what could have caused it. It was a very faint, barely noticeable scar.

"No, I insist. Please, let me. Do you want me to get it for you?" Concern was visible on his face.

I shook my head in reply. "I can get it." He insisted on coming with me and walked by my side as I went back to the queue.

When I reached for the tray, he took it from me and released a soft sigh. He waited with me while the staff served me again. I added a dollop of ketchup to my plate. I placed it on the tray. He asked for a coffee for himself and asked me what I wanted to drink.

"May I have a tea, please? Thank you," I replied quietly.

We queued to pay, and he introduced himself.

"Hi, I'm Nikesh Raja."

He had perfectly straight white teeth, his smile slightly lopsided.

"Hi ... I'm Reena Solanki." I tried to raise a small smile, but failed miserably. I averted my eyes, looking at my feet and concentrated on the streak of ketchup on my shoe.

When we came back to the table, Umi was chatting with some other people and Nikesh put my tray next to hers and went back to sit at his seat. There was a plate of half-finished breakfast waiting for him. He set it aside and reached for his cup of coffee on my tray. Umi was laughing with Nikesh's friend and smiled up at me.

"Reena, meet Peter. Can you believe it, these guys are doing Law too." She was pointing to everyone else sitting at the table. They all shouted out their names and raised their hands as an introduction. I was reminded of school again. Finally, Nikesh waved at Umi and introduced himself.

I was so mortified at my accident that I blocked out all the talking, concentrating on my breakfast, cutting up the sausages and bacon into small pieces. It took a long time for me to eat. I chewed my food at least ten times before I swallowed. It was a habit I developed over time; my father would always refill my empty plate quickly. So, to stop him, I had learnt to take small mouthfuls.

"Come on, boys and girls! Make space for the next lot!" Ordered the platinum blonde. The future lawyers scraped back their chairs. Nikesh smiled at me and loitered briefly by his chair, then turned to catch up with his friends. Umi waited for me to finish my cup of tea.

Umi and I began to tease out information about each other's lives. We had both lost our mothers; her mother passed away when she was eleven years old and she, too, had been brought up by her father and a friendly neighbour. But that was the only commonality between us.

My father worked in a factory; her father was a maths teacher in an affluent school.

I loved to cook; she didn't know how to cook.

I went to the mandir a lot; she hadn't been since her mother's death.

I told her about my older brother; she told me she was an only child.

Leaning against a windowsill in the narrow corridor of our halls was Dick; his legs were crossed at the ankle, revealing the worn soles of his blue suede Chelsea boots.

He turned towards us, and snapped the book shut, using a postcard to mark the page.

"Hey, Reena. Thought I'd come and see if you want to go to registration together."

He stopped. His eyes roamed over Umi who was holding my arm and laughing at how Nikesh had looked so uncomfortable at the mess he had made of my breakfast.

I introduced Umi. He held out his hand and said, "Hi. Richard Downs."

I was surprised as he introduced himself as Dick Downs to me.

"So … What's so funny?" He asked us and we told him why we were laughing.

He scrunched his brow together and we told him he wouldn't understand, it was an Indian thing. "Sounds a bit racist to me," he shrugged as I opened my room to retrieve my documents.

We waited for Umi in the corridor and headed back out. The campus was full of new students heading to registration. There were bunches of students waiting on the benches, sitting on the grass verges, leaning against walls and buildings. Dick and I were both in the Arts faculty, Dick was studying English Literature and I was studying Film and Television Studies. We were heading for a huge marquee that had been put up in front of the Student Union building.

Umi needed to find the Social Science faculty. She took out her introductory pack and confirmed she, too, had to go to the same place as us.

The enormous marquee was full of students queuing at numerous tables placed along the sides. Their faces were full of anxious excitement. A couple of third-year students with badges and clipboards were pacing inside the entrance. A brunette with a breathy voice asked us what faculty we were from and instructed us to register on our courses at the tables which had large bright yellow signs with course names printed on them. She pointed to an area where single tables had been arranged into four-by-four rows and explained that was administration.

The wait to register was unbearably long and I envied Dick, who had brought a book to read while he waited. I was given some more documents to take away with me and I was instructed to show proof of address, my birth certificate and my grant documents to the administration team. I took a detour to where Dick was still waiting to register and I told him I was heading to administration and would meet him outside. I saw Umi talking and laughing with a couple of people in her queue. I wished I had her ease of talking to anyone. I decided I would find her after I had shown my certificates.

The queues were moving much faster at administration and I headed to one with the least number of students. I felt uncomfortable; the tables were small and spaced closely. I tried to make myself as small as possible. I had already touched a couple of people and it made me uneasy.

I handed my certificates to a plump Afro-Caribbean lady with a friendly face. She scrutinised my documents and took the sheet I collected at registration.

"Date of birth?" she asked, looking up at me.

"25th September 1964," I replied

"Happy birthday for tomorrow," she added.

"Thank you," I said and collected my documents. As I pushed back the chair to stand, it knocked into someone. They had been eavesdropping. How rude, I thought indignantly.

"I've never met anyone born on the same day as me."

It was the guy who knocked my breakfast tray. I gasped. He raised his left eyebrow and smiled his perfect smile. I raised a tight smile, but inside I was cross he shared my birthday.

I had a sense that I had met him before, but the name wasn't familiar to me.

October 1982

I HAD SPENT THE AFTERNOON in the library wasting time looking for books for my essay on the World Cinema that had already been signed out by eager classmates; I was desperate to find a copy of a book about Satyajit Ray and India's Parallel Cinema. Unlike many of my classmates, I couldn't afford to buy all the books from the reading list and I hoped I would find at least one to get me started, before I had to beg and borrow them. My morning had been spent in Coventry, distributing my CV in the search for a job to support me. The bright and cold late October day started off optimistically. I had managed to get a lift from a new classmate, Steve, who was heading in to visit his grandmother who lived in Hillfields, so had saved on bus fare. He also spotted me waiting at the No.12 bus stop on the way back, so a win-win for my limited purse. Steve and I parted company by the bus interchange as I had wanted to start on my assignment and he had decided he should go back to halls for an afternoon nap.

At 6 p.m. I decided I'd worked hard enough and

struggled to put my new folder of notes in my old leather satchel, a cherished birthday gift that went with me everywhere. The library hadn't been too busy. It didn't have as many bodies in it as usual, but the long tables were full of books left unattended by students. It was a territorial marking ritual I'd observed while on my morning jog around the central campus. I had seen many of the second-year students heading into the library armed with books. It was only after the third day of my circumnavigation of Library Street and University Street that I realised the same students were heading back without books to their rooms.

The Student Union building located in the central campus of Warwick University was a modernist building built in the 1970s and housed the bank, a coffee shop, the NUS help desk and the student bar.

I felt the eyes before I saw them; my stomach began to fill with bile and the contents of a ham and cheese sandwich and Coke I'd had half an hour before began to swirl. The acrid taste of bile and half-digested food hit my mouth. I swallowed the feeling down, gasping for air to help ease the nausea. Why was this happening now? I had always had trouble with crowded places, but, at this time of the evening, the Student Union wasn't crowded. Besides, I needed to get some money out of the National Westminster Bank, and I'd promised to meet Dick here, too. I waited for an interminable time for the cashier to dispense the cash; I gave the teller a weak smile and grabbed the notes. Instead of opening my purse, I decided to put the money straight into my coat pocket.

"Come on, Reena, get a grip," I scolded myself with an inaudible whisper. My lungs filled with air, but this did nothing to dispel the uneasiness. The more air I inhaled, the greater my urge to expel the contents of my stomach. I felt the anxiety in every pore of my being.

When I had an anxiety attack, my senses would heighten, and I knew when someone was watching me. What should I do? Should I stop and search for whoever is watching me, or should I leave the building? I mouthed to my myself.

The rush of adrenaline initiates the flight or fight response in most people. My usual instincts were to get away from what was making me uneasy. In this case, it was the concrete-encased building of the Warwick University Student Union. Turning around quickly, I took long strides, hoping I didn't look like a panicked victim being chased by an invisible monster in a horror movie. I headed in the opposite direction to the set of floating stairs that led to the top-level to the Student Union bar.

I grabbed at my dark-olive parka coat, wrapped it closer to my body and fixed my gaze on the doors. The glass facade of the building was open to the elements on two levels; each exit was through glass double doors. The roof was taller on one side; constructed of rectangles around a rhomboid, it pointed upwards to the top floor bar. My eyes were drawn to a Warwick crest sticker, beyond which I could see the darkness of the night had closed in.

It's not far. You'll soon be safe, I told myself silently.

My hand pulled at the handle at the same time as a tall,

blond-haired man; our hands met and I flinched from the touch.

"Reena! Why are you heading out of the Union?"

Relief flooded into my core. Dick Downs's broad smile filled his entire face; his eyes, the colour of azure, twinkled with a query. We stood on the threshold while people tutted and muttered as we blocked their way. Dick grabbed my elbow and casually steered me back into the building. We walked up the wooden stairs set in the middle of the Union and entered the bar area. Suddenly, I felt it again; someone was watching me, and it wasn't Dick's gaze that had me panicked. I resisted the urge to run and called on all my inner anger. Who are you and what do you want? I shouted inside my head.

I scanned the coffee tables against the concrete walls. The occupants were sitting in groups of three and four, all engrossed in conversations with newly-found friends, no-one was looking my way. Who in this building was watching me? I searched the faces, looking for minuscule twitches to reveal their secret. Nothing. My investigations failed me, not a tweak. Perhaps I had wound myself up for no reason, exaggerated the anxiousness. I was nervous about the weekend. I told myself that's what it was, my fear of going home.

"So, what do you think? Shall I get the tickets?"

"What? Sorry, tickets for what, Dick?"

"Reena! What's the matter with you?" Realising Dick had been trying to have a conversation with me, I pulled all my focus back to him as we climbed up to the top level.

"Let me get the drinks. Your usual?" I enquired.

The bar in the Student Union was full of recently legalised drinkers who were on a path to discovering their alcoholic limitations. Thursday wasn't as busy as the weekend, but it was still bustling with every hue of the student fraternity. I tried to attract the barman's attention, by edging into a gap. A bleached-haired postgraduate approached, smiling. "Can I help?"

"Can I have two pints of lager and a packet of cheese and onion crisps?"

"Can I see your ID please?"

I swung my bag to the front and reached into it for my purse. This happened to me all the time. I had been eighteen for over a year and nobody believed me.

He took it from me and scrutinised it, holding it up to the light. You would have thought I was committing a major crime; it was only a couple of pints of lager for heaven's sake. He returned the ID card back to me with a smile.

"Righty oh. Two lagers and cheese and onion crisps, one pound and eighty pence, please." I handed him two crisp one pound notes and waited for the change. I quickly slipped the packet of crisps into one of the large pockets in my coat. As I turned with the pints in each hand, I felt someone standing too close for my comfort. My eyes spotted a pair of expensive-looking black shoes. Doesn't this guy realise he's invading my space? And why is he just standing there? Can't he see I am armed with drinks?

I set my face with an indignant expression and glanced up, adding my usual "Excuuuse Me!" in my best school ma'am voice. In front of me was a tall Indian man. His left eyebrow lifted up, and his soft broad lips slowly smiled. His golden eyes drifted to the two pints, revealing a glint of mischief.

"Why would a girl like you drink lager? If you were with me, I'd buy you a Martini, something sophisticated."

"Ah, but I would never be with you," I whispered into his ear, making sure to keep my eyes focused on his. I was not going to let him intimidate me. I knew his type: privileged, spoilt, wealthy Indians. What was his name again? Rikesh? Pritesh? Oh yes, Nikesh." His eyes flickered first and broke the deadlock. He nodded his head slightly and stepped aside.

A trickle of sweat ran down the back of my neck as the heat rose in my body. I felt my cheeks redden and hoped he didn't notice. He chuckled quietly and I turned towards the long bar against the glass windows, my eyes desperately seeking Dick. I spotted his hunched back sitting next to an empty stool. Pausing to steady my nerves, I took a deep breath and inhaled the acrid smell of cigarettes in the confined space.

I was surprised I made it across the room without spilling a drop and put the pint down gently. Dick asked, "What's wrong?"

"It's okay. I'm fine. Just some bloke," I said nodding towards the bar.

"You're on edge today. Nervous about the weekend?" he questioned.

Considering I had only met Dick a few weeks ago, he really did seem to have a true understanding of my moods.

Dick and I met at the bus stop at Pool Meadow in Coventry. He had helped me with my suitcase as we boarded the bus up to Warwick University. As we travelled to the Warwick campus, we had quickly struck up a conversation; making me feel comfortable straight away. We had realised that day we had a lot in common; our passion for old black and white films, '60s fashion, art and photography.

"Reena, what's the matter with you today?"

My thoughts were interrupted by Dick's concerned voice, as his gaze fixed on me. "That's the second time I've asked you if you want me to get a ticket for the special screening of *Gone with the Wind* for you?"

"Sorry. Just worried about tomorrow and my daddy. You were there when my brother Amit told us he isn't coping with me being away?"

"Umi's coming with you, isn't she?" I nodded.

He took my hand and said, "I'm sure he'll be happy to see you and won't even remember your argument. Come on. Drink up. I'll buy the next round."

Dick didn't know that my father held onto his hurt and wasn't quick to forgive.

Three

Late October 1984

IT WAS THE SIXTH DAY OF NAVRATRI, the nine-day dance festival to celebrate the power of Durga. I was going home to Leicester.

I loved going to garba, but it was also a sad time; my father drank heavily and didn't come to the festival at all. When we were younger, it was Divya Ba who insisted my mother's favourite time of the year should be celebrated, not mourned. I lit a small divo for my mother in the morning to remember her life. It was difficult, as my memories of her were only vague. My brother, Amit, had a few more and had told me of the times we'd been to Navratri at the mandir and how she used to hold me on her hip and twirl around and around the central shrine.

I had woken in the morning with a start, sweating and crying. I didn't remember what the dream was about, but, looking back, it would have been the recurring dream of the white box.

I had persuaded Umi to come with me for the weekend. I needed support. It was the first time I was going home since I left. When I told my father, I had accepted the offer from Warwick University, he had been cross and upset. The worst argument we had was the day I left for Freshers' Week. My brother, Amit, had gone to Leicester University to study dentistry. I think he chose to stay at home because he felt responsible for me and didn't want me to deal with my father's issues alone.

Amit is only four years older than me, but he seems much older. He has taken on the responsibility of looking after us. My father drifts in and out through his mood swings and alcoholic stupors.

We had taken the 1.15 p.m. bus from Pool Meadow to Leicester and reached the Narborough Road stop by a quarter to two.

As we entered Grasmere Street from the bridge over the River Soar, I knocked on Divya Ba's door and waited. A plump but tiny old lady opened the door. "My Reena, you've come home." She beckoned me into the house through her sitting room.

Umi and I stepped into the room. The furniture had been placed against the wall; a small 1960s cloth sofa set, a dark-wood coffee table, with a matching display cabinet full of china plates, trinkets and photographs of her children and grandchildren. She also had pictures of my family, one from when I was a baby and a recent photo of us at Amit's graduation.

"Who's this, Dikri?" She turned to ask.

"This is Umi. She's my new friend from university."

"Kem cho, Ba?" Umi replied in Gujarati.

"We thought we'd come early to help with the cooking," I added as she smiled at us.

"You're a good girl. First, have you eaten today?"

I told her we'd eaten lunch but wouldn't mind a drink and we headed into the back room.

In the back room, there was a small TV, two armchairs, a dining table with a drop leaf, chairs and a small coffee table.

She had portioned the vegetables and herbs into stainless steel bowls on the table in readiness for chopping. There was an aroma of cardamom, nutmeg and boiling milk wafting from the kitchen. She headed into the kitchen to stir the dudhpak, which was reducing in a large pan on the stove. "Go get some juice from the fridge," she turned to me.

The kitchen was neat and tidy. I reached for the glasses from the open shelves by the sink and filled them with orange juice.

"Can you make the masala for the bhinda? Your masala is so much better than mine," she said as she entered the kitchen.

Umi asked, "Can I do anything?"

"Yes, Beta. Can you wash the mug ni dall? Usha loved it so much she would make twice as much so she could eat it for two days in a row," Divya Ba replied.

I took the masala tin and headed back to the dining table. "Can I put on a film, Divya Ba?"

"Yes, which one are you going to put on?"

"*Guide.*"

"Ah … good choice." She started to sing R.D. Burman's "Aaj Phir Jeene Ki"; her voice as good as

Lata Mangeshkar's.

I poked my head back into the kitchen and saw Umi turn to me, her jaw slack.

We have done this since I was young; she loved listening to Lata Mangeshkar and Mohammed Rafi and would take us to the Natraj on Belgrave Road to watch Indian films. Umi and Divya Ba joined me in the back room and, while preparing my mother's favourite meal, we watched Dev Anand and Waheeda Rehman's controversial love story of two people who break society's rules.

Once we finished all the preparation, we headed back to the kitchen, listening to the dialogue on the TV. Divya Ba told us what to do. Umi kept asking questions and started to write notes in a little book she had taken out of her handbag.

"What are you doing, Umi?"

"I can't cook, so I'm making notes. My dad will be surprised when I cook this for him."

"You don't have a mother?"

"No, she died when I was eleven. My dad does all the cooking, mostly English food."

"So, you'll find this food spicy?" Divya Ba said with concern.

"No, no, we have Gujarati food. We go to Wembley to eat and we sometimes get a tiffin from the lady down the road."

"Reena cooks really well. You must learn from her." Divya Ba nodded, understanding why I'd made a friend of Umi. It didn't take long to make the meal and we left the frying for later at my house.

"Okay, Divya Ba, we're going home. I'll come help

with the food later," I told her as I gave her a hug. She returned it, kissing me on the cheek.

"I'm so proud of you Dikri. University suits you." She gave Umi a hug and said, "If you want to learn any more about cooking, come to my house any time."

✳ ✳ ✳

UMI HAD UNPACKED HER OUTFITS and hung them up in my wardrobe and we were both sleeping head to toe on my single bed.

"When does your bhabhi come?"

"I think she arrives at five or sixish."

"What is she like?"

"She's lovely, constantly checking we're all okay. She really loves my brother."

"Did they study together?"

"Oh, no. She went to Nottingham … Her parents are like your dad; they don't object to daughters going away to university."

"Are they having an arranged marriage?"

We chatted about their introduced courtship. I explained to Umi that Amit and Smita had met a couple of times before they decided on getting married.

"She's a dentist too, right?' Umi asked.

"Yes, they'll probably have dentist babies, too." We both started to laugh hysterically at my silly joke.

"Hello. Is that you, Reena?" I heard a familiar voice.

"It's Amit, he's early. Come on, Umi," I said as I jumped off the bed and headed for the stairs. We ran downstairs to find my brother waiting in the dining room, his arms outstretched. I rushed into his arms. He almost lost his balance.

"Woah, you've put on weight." I punched him playfully on his arms and he gave me a bear hug.

"Missed you, Sis. How's uni?" he asked me as he pushed me to arm's length.

"Stop it, Amit. You only saw me on my birthday." I punched him again.

"Ouch." He faked an injury by rubbing his arm.

"Hi, how are you?" He leant in and kissed Umi on the cheek.

Umi told him she was looking forward to meeting his fiancée and going to the garba over the weekend. He informed us we would be going to the Sanatan Mandir with Divya Ba that night, but he had bought tickets for Navratri at De Montfort Hall with a group from India for Saturday night.

"I'm picking up Smita from the station. Do you want to come?" Amit asked.

"Yes, please. What time does her train come in?" I replied, clapping my hands with glee.

"She'll be here at 5.30. Go and get your coats."

Leicester Railway Station was a Victorian building on the London Road. Amit was chattering away to Umi about spending his first Navratri with Smita and how excited he was that she was coming to stay with us. I watched my brother; he was nervously running his hand through his thick black hair. He wore it long and it curled up naturally above his shirt collar.

My brother is thin, but not skinny; he has defined muscles across his back and biceps. He resembles my father; his square face has the same prominent forehead and the same thick arched eyebrows. His cheekbones are high, and he has a small prominent chin. His complexion is slightly darker than mine, the colour of white coffee.

His round black eyes were searching the noticeboard for information on what platform the London train was arriving on. He doesn't smile often; I think it is to do with the burden of responsibility he carries for my father and me.

Smita Gohel is the same height as I am; she has an hourglass figure and it is fuller than mine. She wears her straight black hair exceptionally long and loose; it was pushed back off her face by a hairband. She wore subtle make-up, kohl and eyeliner that flicked up in the outer corner. Her large eyes are brown with black flecks. Her full lips were painted a pale coral.

She was wearing a royal blue coat with black buttons, a pair of cream stirrup pants and high-heeled black court shoes. As she approached the turnstiles, she caught sight of Amit and smiled brightly from ear to ear. Her teeth were perfect, white and straight; she was an excellent ambassador for her profession. Amit ran up to her, taking her bag. I saw a rare smile on my brother's face. A warm sensation filled my stomach as I, too, began to smile, and they stepped into a matching stride. He pointed, lifting their entwined hands towards Umi and me, as she asked him something.

"Hello, Reena. How's uni? All you expected?" Her voice is slightly high-pitched, like Marilyn Monroe in *Some Like It Hot*. She has one of those voices, the type that never loses its girlish tone.

"Hi, Bhabhi. Meet my friend, Umi." She shook Umi's

hand and greeted her with a smile.

***

"WAIT! WAIT!" DIVYA BA shouted from the kitchen.
I was surprised that Amit opened the front door; we usually came in through the back. I never thought my brother would put on airs and graces with Smita.

"Come in Reena and Umi." She urged us into the front room. Smita and Amit waited outside in the cold. We followed Divya Ba into the kitchen. She had prepared a large shallow stainless-steel platter with red sindoor powder and flower petals.

"The kettle is boiled. Can you fill this up and add some cold water to make it comfortable," she directed me. "Not too much, though. Umi, can you get the white cloth. I've put it on the table." She added some oil and a drop of perfume and I carried it to the waiting couple.

"Smita Dikri, you're going to have to take off your shoes."

Smita was giggling, holding onto Amit's arm as she slipped out of her shoes, standing barefoot on top of them.

"Umi, can you lay the cloth on the carpet. Reena, take the puja plate and put a tilak on your bhai and bhabhi's forehead. Put some rice on the tilak … now, put a piece of gaur in their mouths. Smita Dikri, you step into the platter and then step out on the cloth, right foot first."

We watched as Smita's first steps into our home as a future daughter-in-law were traced on the white cloth for prosperity.

She touched Divya Ba's feet, and she blessed her by placing a hand on her head. My Divya Ba reached for a cellophane-wrapped present on the coffee table. It was a bright-yellow silk saree. "Welcome home, Dikri." She kissed her on both cheeks.

We sat down in the front room, our coats still on, as the gas fire warmed up the room.

"So, how long are you here for?" I asked Smita.

"I've taken a few days off. I go back home on Tuesday."

Amit was caressing Smita's knuckles with his thumb. "I'm going to take her to all the garba in Leicester," he said, his eyes smiling.

"Can you girls come and help me get the food from my house?" Divya Ba was putting on her coat in the lobby by the back door.

She had noticed that Amit and Smita would need time alone. They had only been engaged since the summer and had spent very little time together. As the date for their actual marriage approached, both sets of parents relaxed a little and allowed them more and more unchaperoned time together.

We took longer than needed to bring the pans from Divya Ba's house and by the time we came back, the table had been laid and Amit and Smita were sitting on the settee in the dining room holding hands and talking.

The key turned in the back door and my father entered the lobby as I was reaching for the kadia to fry the puri and bhajia.

He took off his coat and asked, "You got home safely?"

"Yes, Daddy. I've brought a friend with me."

"New friend? University has made you less shy." He

smiled at me. He walked to the dining room. "How do you do. I'm Reena's father."

"Kem cho, Kaka. My name's Urmila Yadav. Everyone calls me Umi," she replied in Gujarati. My father's expression softened. Umi had called him Kaka, the word for paternal uncle in Gujarati.

"How are you Smita? Was your train journey good?" He turned to Smita.

"It was fine, Daddy." Smita stood up and touched my father's feet. As he blessed her, Amit handed him a small gift-wrapped box that he gave to his future daughter-in-law. She opened it to find a gold chain with an Omkara pendant. Amit asked to put it on her; she lifted her thick hair as he closed the clasps behind her neck.

"Thank you, Daddy. I love it." She smiled at my father, and he smiled back.

"Let me wash and we can start to eat." He glanced at the dining table. "I know you want to go to the garba tonight."

"Kem cho, Divya Masi? Have you made Usha's favourite food today?"

"Yes, Naren. These girls came early to help me."

"Did you?" He raised a sad smile at Umi and I. My mother's death anniversary was a difficult day for my father. I do not know how my mother passed away, but I am aware of the guilt he has carried since her death. For the rest of Navratri he would not go to the garba or the mandir. He would listen to music from films he and my mother watched before they came to England. He would drink into unconsciousness and Amit would be responsible for putting him to bed. During

Usha Solanki's Favourite Meal

·Bharela bhinda
sautéed spicy masala stuffed okra

Chuti mag ni dall
lightly-steamed split mung bean lentil cooked with mild spices

·Bateta tameta shaak
potato and fresh tomato curry

Waatidall na bhajia
ground black-eyed pea and split mung beans fritters

·Topra ni chutnee
fresh-ground coconut chutney

Kadhi
thick spicy broth made from gram flour and natural yoghurt

·Baath
plain boiled rice

·Dhudhpak
thin and creamy milk dessert with rice, sugar and cardamom

Puri
deep fried small rolled flatbread made from wholewheat flour

Gajjar no sambhaio
Gujarati-style stir fried carrots and green chillies

Papad
fried thin crispy bread made from lentils flour

the festival, we became the parent and my father became the child who needed to be taken care of.

I entered the kitchen and Smita came behind me. "Let me make the puri, Reena?"

"No, not this time. Go sit, Bhabhi. You are our guest today," I replied, waving my hand at Umi.

"I can't roll round puri, Reena," Umi whispered.

"Don't worry I'll roll … you fry." I reassured her quietly. We made a pile of puri and then we made the bhajia and took both bowls into the dining room. Divya Ba had ladled out the heated food in serving bowls and they waited for Umi and me to bring in the hot puri and bhajia to start serving our dinner.

We ate the food thinking of my mother, the conversation full of recollection of her life and her knack for making even the most common ingredients into delicious food.

Divya Ba talked most of the time; my father's eyes glistened as he listened to tales of my mother's short life in England.

When we came back at midnight, we found my father asleep in the armchair in the sitting room with an empty bottle and an ashtray full of cigarette ends on the side table.

"Daddy, Daddy." Amit gently tapped my father's face to wake him up. Smita and Umi stood by my side. My father slowly opened his eyes.

They focused on me and he asked, "Usha?" Confusion and joy visible in his eyes.

"No, Daddy. That's Reena," Amit gently reminded him. His face dropped at the realisation his wife was no longer with him. Smita and Umi squeezed my hands in sympathy. People have always said I take after my mother and when I wear Indian clothes my father's eyes cloud over and his furrowed brows deepen as he sees the resemblance.

Amit took my father up to his room and we helped Smita make a temporary bed on the settee for Amit. He was sleeping downstairs while Smita visited. I had brought down the spare bedding from my father's bedroom earlier in the evening and had left it in the dining room.

Amit came downstairs dressed in his pyjamas.

Umi and I said goodnight to Amit and Smita and walked up to my bedroom.

When I opened the door to go to the bathroom, I saw Smita stepping lightly down the stairs in her nightgown. I smiled to myself, thinking my brother and his fiancée would be up for a while.

***

UMI AND I WERE RESTING IN MY BEDROOM. Smita and Amit were sitting in the front room and my father had gone out to the pub. We had eaten a big thali at Bobby restaurant after going to Belgrave Road with my brother and his future wife to choose sarees, jewellery and shoes for their forthcoming wedding.

My door opened. Smita poked her head through. She had a friendly face, open and inviting. She asked, "What are you girls wearing tonight?"

"I'm wearing this, Bhabhi." I held up a purple and yellow striped chaniya choli and Umi showed her the parrot-green and maroon chaniya choli.

"Can you come and help me choose what I should

wear?" she asked us.

My brother's room was bigger than mine and he was sifting through his wardrobe looking for his outfit. He pulled out the pale blue jabo pyjamas and Smita pointed to two sarees laid out on the bed, a royal blue and cream silk one and a pale mint-green silver-embroidered chiffon one.

"Good, we've been discussing which saree Smita should wear." Amit greeted us as we entered the room.

"Don't tell them which one you like, Amit."

He smiled. "Okay I won't, but I know they'll pick my choice."

"I think the blue one's not right for tonight. Wear the mint green, Bhabhi."

"What about you, Umi. Which one would you choose?"

"I agree. I'd wear the mint green."

"Did you give a secret signal?" Smita teased Amit, grabbing his hand and giggling.

* * *

The queue outside De Montfort Hall was full of people in bright festival clothes, the women dressed in sarees or chaniya choli and men dressed in jabo pyjamas.

They had set up some ropes like the ones at airports to wind us in a zigzag style across the square rather than create a long queue down Regent Street.

The October night was chilly and there was a smell of damp in the air. Amit had arranged to meet some friends and was looking over people's heads to search for them.

"Hey, Ashwin!" he shouted at a walnut-complexioned man walking up from University Road. Ashwin and Amit had known each other since grammar school, and he was also engaged to be married and had brought his fiancée, Darshana to the garba. The friends and their fiancées talked about their upcoming weddings with excitement.

My feet began to go numb from the cold as the queue progressed slowly. I should have put on shoes and not my flimsy sandals, but I always felt strange wearing shoes in Indian clothes. I started to hop from one foot to the other.

"Are your feet cold?" Umi asked. "What's wrong with wearing shoes?" She was lifting her long skirt to show me hers.

Smita smiled at me, "It won't be long." She grabbed my hands and started rubbing them to take away the chill. She'd probably rub my feet if I let her, she was so caring. I was glad my brother had found someone who cared for him.

"Hello, Umi." We all turned towards the voice.

"Hello, Peter. What are you doing here?" Umi asked in astonishment.

"We've come to the garba," he added, turning to Ravi. "Did I say that right?"

"Yes. Hi, Umi and … Reena?" Ravi confirmed and questioned at the same time.

I hoped the ground would swallow me up and spit me out far away. The last time I met these men was when I emptied my breakfast tray by their table. I tried to raise a smile, as Umi asked them how they'd found out about the event and who else had come from Warwick.

"Hello, Umi." His rich, dark brown voice was raised in

greeting behind me.

"There you are." He said as he spotted his friends in the winding queue. "Took me ages to find a parking space."

"Hello … Reena." He made his way to our side and was staring intently into my eyes, his head bowed.

"Hello, Nikesh," Umi replied. She introduced my brother and Smita, explaining to Amit that they studied Law together.

"Hello. Peter Macauley, and this is Ravi Patel and Nikesh Raja." Peter held out his hand to my brother and Ashwin, after pointing to Ravi and Nikesh.

Amit and Ashwin stared at them sternly. The blood rushing to my head stopped me from fully hearing my brother's replies.

" … a lift from my father—"

My heart was pounding

" … walk back home as we live close by—"

Nikesh was standing so close, I felt the tension in his body as he told us about his search for a parking space and the one-way system.

"Where did you find a space in the end?" my brother asked him.

"I found a space by the prison," he replied.

"Oh, that's near where we live. Parking during Navratri is always difficult."

"Why is that?" Nikesh questioned Amit.

"Lots of people come to Leicester for Navratri," Amit replied.

The queue moved and Nikesh joined his friends. He told us he would meet us inside.

I was hoping we wouldn't, besides, the hall was

enormous; it was unlikely we would meet again.

I prayed we wouldn't meet up again. Nikesh Raja made me feel uneasy, his natural charm and the way he talked to everyone like he had known them all his life. I found myself wondering if that's what you get when you grow up with money. I didn't want to be part of his crowd. I had seen them playing pool in the Student Union, at the cinema, in the pubs enjoying themselves, always in the company of well-groomed girls, hanging on their words.

The live band consisted of two female singers and one male singer; the songs were some old ones we all knew off by heart and some new ones with unfamiliar lyrics composed to Bollywood tunes. Our coats and shoes had been put into the cloakroom and Amit had found someone who would take care of our dandiya while we danced the garba. There were six huge rings around the shrine of the nine manifestations of Durga. We had danced in the outer circles for an hour. Smita motioned to one of the rings that had energetic young people twirling and whirling to the music and we joined it.

I felt someone watching me and tried to find who was scrutinising me.

My stomach clenched; Umi saw my euphoric expression drop to dread.

"Do you want to go out?" she shouted over the music. I nodded. Amit watched us leave and gestured he would come out with us. I shook my head and mouthed that I needed some air, grabbing Umi's hand. We headed to an open door to get some fresh air. A short, stocky man bumped into me. "Do you mind?"

Umi yelled at him.

"No, I don't mind," he said, as he stood too close to me. We moved away and he moved closer.

"What's the fucking matter with you!" Umi shouted.

"Look, mate, they are not interested." Nikesh Raja grabbed the man's arm.

"You can have the gobby one," he winked at Nikesh. "She's too tall for me. I'm interested in the light-skinned one."

Nikesh's face darkened and he pulled himself up to his full height.

"Is there a problem here?" Peter approached us from the hall.

Nikesh was scowling at the pock-faced man, who had shrunk and was trying to make himself small. "Okay, okay, mate." He put his palms out in apology and skulked away.

"Are you two all right?" Nikesh's eyes scanned Umi and me to check.

I was taking long deep breaths to get oxygen into my bloodstream. I wanted to run away from there, back home, safe in my room, away from the crowds. I liked going to the mandir for garba; it was smaller, and I knew everyone who was there. Enormous functions filled me with dread and worry. It's always been like that for me.

"Thanks, Peter," he nodded. "Can I get you something to drink?" He was talking to us calmly, but his eyes had become fiery, like kindling ready to ignite.

Umi asked for some water for me and he walked to the drink table and came back with two glasses. He held up a glass to me and gently said, "Drink this Reena. It will make you feel better." I gulped it down and he handed me another.

"What's going on here?" Amit strode over to us holding Smita's hand, his eyebrows knitted as he glared at Nikesh and Peter.

"It's all right, Amit. We had some unwanted attention and these guys came to our rescue," Umi explained.

He grabbed my hand, "Next time, wait for me. I'm not letting you two out of my sight. There are quite a few troublesome types from out of town here tonight." He was trying to stay calm, but his shoulders hunched up. I knew my brother meant Nikesh and Peter in his classification. Anyone of the opposite sex who gave me any attention was a problem for my brother. He was overprotective of me. I was the only girl in my school who went to the 6th Form leavers' disco with my brother. I didn't mean to sound ungrateful, but when all the girls, even the Indian ones, came with dates, it made me the centre of attention.

I could still hear the remarks ringing in my ear; she thinks she's too good; a bit high and mighty with her raised chin; brother's always hanging around; maybe she's been caught with her knickers down. She wears those weird old clothes; who would want to ask? No one would dare to ask her when her big brother's looming.

That was one of the reasons I wanted to go away to university. This was England in the twentieth century. I should be trusted to make the right choices. When he had come to uni to surprise me for my birthday, he had spent a great deal of time interrogating Dick about our relationship. Luckily Dick wasn't attracted to me, and we had a brother–sister bond. My brother soon realised he had an ally.

Someone who would protect me.

"Was he from here?"

I stared up at my brother.

"Reena! Was he someone you know?"

I shook my head.

"We're all dancing together for the Dandiya Raas," he commanded.

"You're so bossy," Smita giggled at Amit, raising a bright smile.

"Sorry, I'm trying not to be, but … " He pulled her towards him, and reached his arm around to Umi who was by her side.

*** *** ***

"Strange meeting the guys today," Umi said as we were head to toe on the bed, trying to calm down after an evening of dancing.

I wondered why I felt I had met Nikesh Raja before. Before Warwick. The cream jabo pyjamas he had on seemed familiar. I had a vague memory of meeting him somewhere or sometime.

I was humming to the tune of "Ek Vanjari Jhulana".

"Do you know all the words?" Umi brought me back to the room. I started to sing.

She laughed, "You're not as good as Divya Ba." I closed my mouth tight.

I found myself thinking about how many times I had bumped into Nikesh Raja this year. Counting one, two, three; his eyes, his face, the way he stood kept invading my thoughts as I dozed off.

Four

Early December 1984

I REALISED I HAD OVERSLEPT. I told myself off for my excessive drinking the night before with Dick and his friends from Drama Club.

I quickly grabbed a tea and a piece of bread and butter and headed to the library. It was a Thursday and the library was going to be packed. I hated going to crowded places, but I needed to use the reference section extensively for my end-of-term essay on early Hollywood cinema.

The library was in a square building with glass windows on one side and rows and rows of long tables. When I walked in, every single table was occupied with students working and quietly chatting with their peers. I scanned the room for space; all I needed was one chair to be empty to begin my research. I spotted an area and decided to head towards it. As I approached it, a large female student in a multi-coloured tracksuit stepped out from the shelves and occupied it. I was ready to abandon all hope of finding a seat when my eyes rested on a table at the back of the room. There was a whole table free with a lone student whose back was towards me; I exhaled and took brisk strides towards the seat. Still upset with myself for sleeping in, I swung my satchel off my shoulder and slammed it on the table. The noise resonated through the building and the librarian, a grey-haired woman wearing a loose blouse and a grey A-line skirt scowled at me while placing her index finger to her mouth. I sheepishly apologised to the adjacent tables and to the guy who was already sitting at the table.

It was him; my heart was in my mouth. He smiled his utterly lopsided smile and I could see a spark light up in those amazing eyes. His gaze lingered on my face for a fraction longer than necessary. He seemed to realise he was staring and began examining his textbook as if his life depended on it. I moved my satchel from where I had placed it and put as much distance between us as was possible at the table.

The sound of a freight train filled my ears. How could it be? I wondered. There wasn't a railway station anywhere near the campus. Suddenly it dawned on me: it was my stomach that had made the noise. I had been so engrossed in my research that I had not noticed it was lunchtime. Most of the tables were empty and the occupiers had left their folders and books out ready to return to once their lunch break was over.

I checked the only other occupant who hadn't gone to get lunch. Why was he still sitting there? I peeped through my fringe, hoping he hadn't heard. I saw his lips trying to force the smile off his face. I wished the ground would swallow me up; he was the last person I wanted to enjoy my dilemma.

My head felt hot suddenly, and I yanked the hairband out to shake my long hair loose.

"Yeh reshmi zulfein ..."

Did he just quote from Laxmikant Pyarelal's "Yeh Reshmi Zulfein". These silken hair, these intoxicating eyes? His eyes met mine. My treacherous heart began to sing.

I grabbed my satchel and ran out of the library to the annoyance of the librarian.

Christmas break had started in dribs and drabs. Eventually, I was the only one left on my floor at the halls. I had managed to get a job at the Warwick University Art Centre working at the ticket office to help my depleted bank balance. That year, the City of Birmingham Youth Orchestra was playing all seven Sibelius symphonies in a session over the holiday, and they needed extra short-term staff. I didn't mind staying behind; I worked in the evening and studied in the library during the day. They paid well too, so I wouldn't have any worries for the spring term, besides, I wanted to buy an expensive wedding present for my big brother.

After eating my usual breakfast of porridge, cooked the Gujarati way with cardamom, milk and sugar, I made up a couple of ham sandwiches and headed out to the library. I couldn't really work in my room; I got distracted easily by my music and I would spend too much time thinking about what I wanted to cook for dinner.

I wanted to get acquainted with my reading for the spring term. I'm always much happier when I know what's coming ahead. It makes me feel better. I have never been good with new situations. I was pleased with the autumn term grades and my exams. I wanted to make sure the spring exams went well too.

The library was still reasonably busy; many of the third-year students were still on campus finishing off their dissertations. "Good morning," I nodded to the librarian, a rotund woman who had the tendency to wear flowing skirts and cheesecloth shirts even in the winter.

I headed for my usual spot, a table farthest from the entrance; I liked to place myself in one of the chairs facing the room. It allowed me to periodically check on the clock above the entrance door and also see people coming in and out.

I used my coat as a cushion to support my lower back and settled down to making notes from my books on the next unit. I continued to work steadily and when I looked up, it was ten to ten. My eyes drifted across the other occupants along the rows and rows of seats and I saw him sitting with a Walkman in his ear, writing something, stopping and referring to notes on various cards he had arranged around himself. To his left, there was an auburn-haired woman who kept tapping him on the shoulder to ask questions. The seat on his right was empty. On the long table next to his, there was a group of blondes, and I observed them peeping at him surreptitiously from under their coiffed fringes.

He was wearing a light-grey crew neck jumper with a white shirt underneath; his tan leather bomber jacket was draped on the back of the chair.

A mousy haired woman walked up to the table and placed herself opposite the auburn-haired woman; they exchanged a greeting and he continued to work on his writing. What was wrong with these women? I was seething with anger. Why would you place yourself in these situations? Yes, he's good looking, yes, he's smart, yes, he's wealthy, but come on ladies, women burned their bras for equality a decade ago.

He must have felt my hate, and stared directly at me. I averted my eyes by examining my notes intently.

"Hi, Reena," he stood by my side, "What are you doing here during the holidays?"

I flustered and I stammered out my answer. "I'm … I'm working at the Art Centre … two birds … one stone," pointing to my books.

The young woman sitting two seats away watched us and ran an appreciative eye over Nikesh Raja.

He nodded in approval at my answer and raised a small smile. I felt I had to ask him the same question as the silence between us lengthened. He stood nonchalantly by my table; my neck strained from looking at his face. "And you?" I asked.

He explained quietly that he was working on a group project for which he needed a rough outline by the beginning of the term. He added that he couldn't work at home as it was chaotic because of his brother's Christmas Eve engagement.

He waited expectantly as I fixed my gaze intently on my notes. "See you around then." He turned to walk back to his table.

I watched him walk back, my eyes raised through my fringe. The jumper accentuated his broad shoulders and back. The blondes on the table next to him smiled up at him and blushed as he smiled back at them. He sat back down, watching steadily with those eyes, put on his headphones and continued to write.

I wished my work colleagues, Debbie and Simon, goodnight and stepped out of the side door of the Art Centre. There was a chill in the air, the type you get when the temperature drops, and the air was full of static. I drew my coat closer and pulled up my hood. I forced my gloved hands into my coat pockets and walked back towards Rootes Hall.

The area around the Art Centre was busy with people waiting for minicabs or waiting in queues to get on the minibuses they'd travelled in. I was on door duty and had the sublime experience of listening to the performance. The performers piled out into the cold night air joking with each other, pleased with how the concert had gone, and holding onto their instruments like cherished loved ones.

I saw him leaning on the concrete wall; he smiled at me and started walking towards me.

A vague memory stirred. My heart skipped a beat.

He stopped inches away from me and I forced my eyes to his face, wondering whether his eyes were hazel or gold.

"Hey, are you going to be okay walking back to halls?" asked Joe, a postgraduate student who had just walked past me. His eyes darted towards Nikesh.

"May I walk you home?" Nikesh asked quietly.

"I only live over there." I pointed towards my halls, returning the smile.

"Yes, I know, but there are too many unsavoury characters around at this time of the night."

"They've just come out of a classical music concert," I chortled.

He turned his head to gaze at the crowd of middle class, middle-aged people, quietly discussing which rendition of Jean Sibelius's symphonies they liked best.

"I confess." He gazed intently into my eyes. "I wanted to walk you home."

We walked in silence to my block; he stood in front of me at the entrance and studied my face with his striking eyes. I'm sure he noticed my breath catch; my heart was thumping so loudly that I was silently praying he couldn't hear it through my thick coat. I could feel his warm breath on my skin, and we said nothing for what seemed to be an eternity.

"Goodnight, Reena. Sweet dreams." He turned, and I watched him walk back to University Street.

My legs felt like they were going to buckle under me. I grabbed the balustrade and climbed up to my corridor. I took off my coat, dropped it on the armchair, and flung myself on the bed. My heart stopped crashing against my chest as I counted, one, two, three, four, five, six, seven … I knew of his reputation with women. I had seen him with plenty.

I told myself off for not being stronger and reminded myself to be careful as I recalled the party we had gone to at his house in November.

* * *

"COME ON, REENA. It will be great. They have a lovely house in Coventry, so I've been told. And they are going to have a bonfire and fireworks. I love fireworks. Let's go, and Peter said we don't need to bring anything. Come on, how many times have we actually gone anywhere this term without paying for our food and beer?" Umi pleaded.

I could tell Umi was developing a crush on Peter and I couldn't blame her. He was polite, well-groomed and attentive. He spoke with one of those posh voices, the type you expect to hear on the BBC. I had met him a couple of times when she asked him to help with an essay. It was a shame he was living with Nikesh Raja and Ravi Patel. They were typical of the wealthy Indians I didn't like. I had explained this to her, and she too agreed the Nikesh and Ravi situation wasn't great, but they weren't as bad as some.

"Can we take Dick?" I'd asked after she'd spent the whole evening wearing me down, while I was making dinner with her in the kitchen.

"Sure. He said bring friends … that means more than one, right?"

Peter lived in an unusual student house; for one thing, it was new, in a quiet cul-de-sac, had an attached garage, and was in a posh part of Coventry.

We ordinarily were invited to second-year students' houses, and they were the usual Victorian terraces, bought up cheaply by landlords, with no heating and hastily-constructed downstairs bathrooms, much like my own home except we had gas fire heating.

We'd taken the bus into Cheylesmore and got off at Black Prince Avenue. We had decided it was wrong to come without a gift and brought a bottle of Blue Nun, which we thought would be an appropriate gift for the son of Nigerian judges.

The door to the house was open. We stepped from the porch straight into a red room; the curtains had been drawn and a red lightbulb had been put in the single pendant shade, casting a red hue. One wall was painted a dark brown and stuck on it was a happy birthday banner. The room was heaving with people. There was a DJ set up in one of the corners playing '70s Motown.

"Look, there he is!" Umi let go of my hand and shouted back at us, as she pushed herself to the door leading to another room. I held on to Dick's hand tighter in the hope that he would stay with me and not abandon me too. I hated going to these things: too many people, not enough space. We battled our way through the crowd and followed her.

The furniture that would have been in the front room had been moved to this room. There was a dark-brown G-plan sofa with matching armchairs. A rectangular dark-wood dining table had been pushed against a wall and was laden with food. In one of the corners, a large coffee table was covered in a red cloth and unopened gifts and cards were placed on it.

"Hello, Reena," Peter greeted us, waving his hand.

"Hi, Peter," I said.

He held Umi's hand in his; she was gazing up at him. Umi was five feet five inches tall and Peter was at least a head and shoulders taller.

He turned to Dick. "Hi, I'm Peter, the birthday boy" and shook his hand. Dick handed him the wine bottle wrapped in tissue paper.

"Dick Downs. Happy Birthday. Thanks for inviting me."

I handed him the birthday card. "Happy Birthday, Peter." I gave him a kiss on his cheek.

"Thank you for the present and card." He took his gift and walked to the coffee table. When he came back, he told us the drinks were in the kitchen, pointing to the serving hatch, and asked us to help ourselves to the food.

All the time we were talking, I felt I was being watched. A wiry Indian man with a round face, hook nose and sullen eyes came up to us. "Peter, aren't you going to introduce me?"

"Sure, Jay. This is Umi, her friend Reena, and their friend Dick."

"Pleased to meet you. I'm Nikesh's oldest friend, Jayesh Dattani."

As he spoke his pointy chin jutted out and his chest puffed up as if it was a badge of honour. He had a thin moustache above his small upper lip and extremely dark eyebrows which seemed odd in comparison to his thin receding hair that was cut short at the side and a little bit too long at the top. He was wealthily dressed; his Pierre Cardin shirtsleeves were rolled back at the cuff to expose a gold bracelet on his right wrist and a gold Seiko on his left. He wore a gold signet ring on his left pinkie finger. His black eyes wandered up from my shoes to my head, and then he leant in and said, "You've got a funny taste in clothes." I was taken aback. Even if he thought this, no reasonable person would say that the first time they met you.

"It's not funny mate, it's eclectic," Dick said, squaring up to him. The top of Jay's head reached Dick's eyes.

I took a long time deciding on what to wear that night. Umi had flung on a pair of faded jeans and an orange jumper. I'd told her she'd be roasting in it and she should reconsider. She lifted her jumper to show me a cream camisole. "If it gets too hot, I'll take it off," she'd said defiantly. I opted to wear a tartan A-line skirt that rested just above my knees. The colours on the skirt were orange, red, dark green and yellow. I'd tried on so many tops that Umi had fallen asleep waiting; in the end, I eventually settled on a red fine-print long-sleeve shirt and a pair of bright-orange tights with my brown school brogues.

Jay apologised, muttering, "I thought the latest fashion was tight skirts and boxy tops." He took out a small cigarette case and offered us a cigarette; Dick and I declined and when Umi took one and asked for a light, his eyebrows rose a little in shock. Dick grabbed my hand and turned, "Nice meeting you, Jay," which he yelled over his shoulder as we strolled to the table full of food.

There were two large pans of curries: one chicken and one mixed vegetable, vegetable samosas, sheek kebabs, a big bowl of salad and packets of pitta bread. We each took a paper plate and began to load our plate with food. Umi was still talking with Jay and Peter; I had just got to the end of the table when the double

French doors to the garden opened, letting in some much-needed fresh air. Nikesh Raja stepped in with a long-legged blonde girl, clinging to his arms, giggling uncontrollably, an effect of drinking too much. He laughed and was taking a puff from the Davidoff cigarillo he was holding in his free hand. He saw me and stopped, loosening the girl's grip on him. Jay was by his side in seconds relieving him of the well-dressed blonde; she was wearing a navy-blue sweater dress, boxy and loose at the top and tight at the hips. She had a red-velvet hair band in her perfectly layered, shoulder-length hair. Nikesh quietly instructed, "Fetch her some water, Jay. Hello, Reena. Can I help you with your plate?" I blushed as I remembered the canteen incident.

"I'm fine, thank you," I replied as I headed to a spot on the sofa, vacated by Jay, and told Dick to squeeze in beside me.

Nikesh walked to Peter and Umi, who were in the line that had formed by the food table. I watched as he picked up a plate, put his cigarillo in his mouth, and used the freed hand to take some food. He inhaled through his mouth and exhaled from his nostrils, the smoke misting over his lips; I was mesmerised by the way he smoked.

Sometime later that evening, I found myself wedged on the sofa with Jay and Ravi; I was drinking beer straight from a bottle and Ravi teased me on my choice of drink and said for an Indian girl I was not ladylike. I'd retorted that he had no idea what Indian girls were like, as he hadn't made any effort in getting to know one. Ravi Patel was well built, five feet nine inches in height with dark cropped hair; he wore the same uniform as the other men who lived in the house. He smoked continuously, using the final embers of his last cigarette to light the next. He'd smiled at the remark, lifted his bottle up and mumbled, "Touché."

Dick and Umi were in the dance room and I wasn't drunk enough to join them, but I aimed to get in the room soon. Jay kept telling me about some girl that Nikesh had fallen in love with, his first love. A lovely girl; blonde-haired, English, her father was a banker. He repeated he hadn't recovered from their break-up yet. I wasn't sure why he felt he had to tell me. I wasn't sure why it made me upset. I stood up abruptly and yelled, "What Nikesh Raja does, has done or will do is none of my business!" When I turned to the door, he was leaning against the doorframe, his arms crossed, and his eyes burnt their fiery embers at Jay.

As more and more people filled the front room, my feeling of claustrophobia increased. To get some respite for my weary heart, I had moved to the stairs, as it was the least occupied place.

"Come on, Reena. Come back and dance."

Dick and a tall, slim brunette called Jean had come to tempt me back into the red room. I told them I needed to cool down and climbed up to the bathroom.

The coolness of the water on my face helped my body relax. I stared at myself in the mirror, glad I hadn't worn mascara. I took one final deep breath and unlocked the bathroom door. The door to the adjacent bedroom opened simultaneously; a squeaky and whining nasal voice was pleading with someone. Nikesh Raja was prying himself out of the arms of a blonde. Not the same blonde he was with earlier, this one was about my height with a huge chest, the top buttons on her white blouse undone, revealing a lacy bra.

"Come on, Katy. Let's go downstairs."

He saw me standing there, rooted to the spot, my jaw slack. Two different women on one night: I couldn't believe what I was seeing. He was a Lothario, a womaniser. I had watched the BBC's *Casanova* and had a measure of his cloth there and then.

* * *

I wondered whether I was wrong in the conclusion I had drawn, or whether my heart was playing tricks with my mind. I fell asleep thinking what made my heart skip when I saw him. I also told myself that I needed to be careful, after all, he was one of the rich, privileged Indians I didn't trust.

He waited for me after every performance for the rest of the week. We walked to my halls; we talked about our favourite music, books and films. He occasionally asked about my family and revealed details of his. And as we arrived at the entrance to my halls, his eyes studied me intently. I knew he wanted to say something, and I waited for him to build up the courage.

"Goodnight, Reena. Sweet dreams." He turned and I couldn't help watching him walk back to University Street.

Saturday night the performance finished later than planned. I also had to count the float, so by the time I was ready to come out of the Art Centre, I was an hour late. My eyes automatically went to the spot where he waited for me. My heart stopped. He wasn't there. I was overwhelmed by the lack of him. Then the realisation edged its way to the front of my mind. Of course, he's not here. Most people went home on Friday, I thought to myself. The campus was considerably empty during the day. He could have said he was going home. What did I expect? These people don't have to justify their actions to me, I told myself to mask my disappointment.

I pulled at the zip of my parka and dragged my feet despondently towards my room. My heart felt like someone had pulled it out and was using it as a football. My head was telling me to get a grip. I stopped to cross University Street.

"Reena, Reena!" a voice called. I searched up and down the street. I couldn't see anyone. I took in my surroundings. I saw that the car parked on the opposite side of the road had its driver's window open.

My heart jumped for joy; he was waiting for me, and he hadn't gone back home. He crossed the road and rushed towards me. "It's too cold to stay outside today and when I heard you were running over, I thought I'd wait in my car." He turned and pointed to the car.

I smiled up at him; I tried to force myself to stop grinning like a lunatic.

"Can I take you for a drive tonight?" he asked, placing my hand on his arm.

I nodded at him and asked, "Where are we going?"

"I'm going to show you the Christmas lights," he grinned.

His car was an Alfa Romeo Alfasud Sprint; I was surprised it was not the usual red paint that most men opted for, but a metallic-silver one. It was only a year old, unlike my father's L-registered Hillman Avenger. He rushed to the passenger side to open the door for me and waited for me to sit and then sat in the driving seat.

"Seat belt on, please," he ordered, and he reached for the glove compartment. An electric current passed between us as he brushed my thigh. He stopped; his head was lower than mine and his eyes sparkled as they smiled up at me. He had felt it too.

He grabbed a cassette box, opened it and put the cassette in the player.

The small clock on the dashboard read ten past eleven. "Main Shayar to Nahi" came on and I yelped and clapped my hand to my mouth; it was the music from my favourite film *Bobby*. He smiled at me, started the car, and drove down Kenilworth Road.

He turned the volume higher as we drove into Coventry and started to sing; his voice was fantastic. He could easily be mistaken for Shailender Singh. I closed my eyes, and instead of imagining the face of Rishi Kapoor, I saw Nikesh Raja's. I wondered at this man, what else is he good at? We listened to the *Bobby* film soundtrack and I wondered where the Christmas lights were. He left the ring road, drove past the glass entrance of the Sports Centre and parked the car in Bayley Lane. We walked up the steps of the Coventry Cathedral, admiring the stained-glass windows of the modern rebuild, and the ruins of the old, and headed down the cobble path to Broadgate. The doors to the foyer of Leofric Hotel opened and a group of thirty-somethings in party wear spilt out onto the square. More Christmas party revellers were walking out of pubs and restaurants. We stood by the statue of Lady Godiva and admired the twinkling lights of the huge Christmas tree that had been put up in Upper Precinct. Nikesh pointed to a bench and said, "Let's wait for Peeping Tom." We sat and waited for the hands of the clock to meet at twelve.

"Dick and I will be volunteering at the Oxfam shop over there next term," I told him, pointing to Hertford Street

"Is that where you get all your clothes?" He turned to me, raising his left eyebrow.

"Yes, mostly. Do you get all yours from Savile Row?"

He laughed out loud; a group of partygoers glared at him. He was shaking with mirth.

The bells rang twelve times and Lady Godiva rode out totally naked on a horse; in an arched window above, a man held up his hands to his eyes.

"A lesson for men who look upon naked women, when they are told not to," I told Nikesh.

"Enough. Our eyes will be destroyed too," he said as he grabbed my hand and stood up. I laughed at him as we ran back to the car, hand in hand. When we got to the car, he stood in front of me gasping. He must be really unfit, I thought and then I saw his smouldering eyes linger for far too long on my lips. I felt the sensation of lips on my lips.

He inhaled. "Right let's see Papa's magical lights." He opened the passenger door for me and waited for me to get in. I smiled up at him. I had been smiling since he called my name from the car.

We drove past the ruins of Swanswell Gate listening to the *Bobby* soundtrack and the Alfasud joined the Coventry ring road.

"The first time I saw them, I was eleven years old. Look at the lights, Reena. Aren't they magical?"

I was confused. All I saw were the yellow streetlights.

"Come on, use your imagination."

He drove anti-clockwise, past Whitefriars and, as we approached the Coventry Railway Station exit, he took the underpass. His face filled with a wicked grin. He drove around the Coventry ring road six times in total, three times anti-clockwise and three times clockwise.

I lost my inhibitions and joined him in singing Anand Bakshi's "Main Shayar to Nahi".

We sat in the car for an hour, neither of us wanting to leave, both of us making small talk. He glanced at his watch, "It's late, Reena. I'll walk you to your room."

We walked hand in hand back to my room and he stopped at the entrance.

"Can I take you out for dinner tomorrow night?"

"I'm working tomorrow night," my shoulders dropped. "I'm sorry, I've opted to work every night until the twenty-first."

"Can I take you out for lunch then?" I smiled a yes.

He lifted my right hand to his mouth and brushed his lips on my knuckles.

My heart danced in my chest. I forced myself to take a breath.

His eyes met mine, the gold shards glittered, and he swept my face with scrutiny. I held my breath; I felt he wanted to kiss me, as his eyes lingered on my mouth.

"Goodnight, Reena. Sweet dreams." He reluctantly let go of my hand and turned around to walk back to the car.

Every inch of my being wanted to stop him. I wanted him to turn back and take me in his arms and kiss me like the couples you see in the black and white Sunday afternoon films on TV.

He turned around and shouted, "Go in, Reena." He was walking backwards, his hands in his jacket pockets, watching me standing still. "I'll call for you at twelve."

Five

I HAD BEEN UP FOR HOURS from the anticipated excitement of having lunch with Nikesh Raja.

I was not really sure how we had arrived at this day. I had seen him around the campus with groups of women in tow. Why had he picked me? I was certainly not his type. But he made me feel whole. My anxiety attacks lessened when I was with him. It felt like I had known him all my life. There were times when I was thinking about something and he raised the subject.

Every piece of my clothing was out of my wardrobe. I was sure he would take me somewhere smart for lunch. I only had two decades of clothing in my wardrobe and nothing new. Either sixties smart or seventies smart. I pulled out a green paisley-print dress with a round neck and long sleeves with ruffle cuffs. I teamed this with a boxy cream short jacket from the sixties. I placed my 1950's Liberty poppy-cloth bag in bright pink next to my black square-toe court shoes. The other outfit was a pair of very wide seventies high-waist purple trousers, teamed with a silver-grey rayon tie-collar blouse and an unlined cardigan jacket in chocolate and lilac geometric print that I'd made from an old 1960's fabric. For this outfit, I'd set aside a tan-leather double-handled handbag and a pair of brown high-heeled ankle boots.

I must have tried both outfits on at least twice. Each time I stood in front of the mirror, I saw the inadequacies of my body shape.

The dress clung to the little pouch of flesh under my belly button and the sleeves made my skinny wrists even skinnier. The short cream jacket drew the eye to my waist.

The shirt with its high collar made my neck look short and the trousers made my hips too broad. I put on the longer jacket; at least it disguised them.

I opted to look like a turtle. As I was going to be eating lunch, the dress would definitely be worse afterwards. I had washed and dried my dark-brown hair straight, put some blusher on my cheeks, black mascara on my eyelashes, and applied a thin film of red lipstick too.

I asked him up and met him at the top of the stairs; he was wearing a pair of dark-navy trousers with black brogues, a light-blue shirt and a navy pinstripe double-breasted jacket. I was glad I'd dressed up. Nik walked up the stairs, his eyes studying my outfit slowly from top to toe. "Good choice, you look very sophisticated. Do you have a warm coat?"

"Oh!" my mouth opened, my eyes lowered. I didn't expect him to come into my room. The place looked like a bomb had hit it. Should I invite him in; *should I ask him to sit in the kitchen?*

He saw my panic. "I'll wait in the kitchen," he pointed with his hand. I had two coats, a parka and a 1970s beige woollen long coat with brown fake-fur collar and a missing belt. I rummaged through my box of belts and grabbed a men's brown PVC belt and put it in its hoops and threw it over my shoulder.

He was standing with his hands in his trouser pockets looking out of the window. He turned, smiled, and strode swiftly to my side, grabbed my left hand, and placed it on his forearm. In my heels, I almost reached his neck and could smell tobacco, musk and sandalwood – the scent of Davidoff Cool Water.

He drove down the A46 towards Stratford-upon-Avon and we listened to a mix tape of 1970s music. Stevie Wonder was singing about sunshine and life.

I found myself wondering, was this the beginning of a love that has happened before? I felt like I had known him for a million years. My thoughts of eternal love were interrupted by his voice. "Hope you're hungry; they do an amazing Sunday lunch."

The White Swan was an old half-timber Tudor house. He held the black arched door open and we walked through into a wooden-panelled reception hall with a large fireplace. The receptionist welcomed us.

"Good afternoon," she smiled. "How can I help you?" Nikesh informed her of our lunch reservation at one o'clock in their restaurant. He helped me take off my coat and handed it to the cloak girl. The low ceilings were painted white and there were large wooden beams everywhere. The diamond-shaped leaded windows let in very little light and lamps had been placed in corners to provide lighting that reflected the ambience of the building in Tudor times. We walked into a smaller room buzzing with discreet chatter. There was fireplace in the room too; above it were three oval portraits of Tudors: a red-haired woman, a young boy and a fat man wearing a flat hat. We were taken to a table for two in one of the nooks and the waiter presented a wine list to us with a maroon leather-bound menu.

"Do you drink wine?" Nik enquired as he lowered the wine list.

My breath caught, and I nodded a yes. He pulled the menu up to shield his eyes and ordered a crisp white wine after asking my preference.

We both ordered the chestnut soup for starters and I ordered the roast pork with all the trimmings. Nikesh ordered the Christmas lunch.

The sommelier arrived and asked him to taste the wine; he took a sip and suggested it had oxidised. The waiter poured a sip into his tasting cup. "Sorry Sir, I'll fetch another bottle." He nodded at Nikesh with approving eyes.

I supposed he'd never had someone in his teens, or for that matter an Indian, telling him this.

"How could you tell?" I leant forward and whispered behind the sommelier's back.

"It tastes a bit too acidic."

"Where did you learn that?" I was impressed.

"I have a friend, Gino, whose family owns a wine bar," he shrugged. "His dad is always making us taste wine."

The sommelier returned with a different bottle and Nikesh tasted it again and nodded.

I took my glass and he raised his and said, "Saluti."

"Do you speak Italian?" I asked and he laughed.

"No, only a few words I've picked up from Gino."

I was beginning to feel like I was with someone a lot older than nineteen.

The waiter put the plates with roast meats and trimmings on our table and brought several dishes of vegetables and a gravy boat.

"When did you start drinking wine?" I asked as I filled my plate with mashed potato, sprouts, parsnips and roast potatoes. I poured far much more gravy than I intended on the mash.

He watched me filling my plate and then began to do the same.

"When I was thirteen," he replied, filling his plate with the vegetables.

"Thirteen, isn't that illegal?" I quizzed.

"Gino's dad is Italian; they give their babies watered-down wine," he replied. "So, when did you start?"

"Oh, I started on my 16th birthday. My father introduced me to rum and blackcurrant." I pulled a face.

"Interesting choice of drink." He lifted up his knife and fork.

"Does your father know you eat meat?"

"Does yours?" I replied. My voice came out slightly harsher than I wanted it to.

I was sick of people expecting me to behave in a certain way. I had had this conversation with Divya Ba and the ladies at the mandir often. Gujarati girls don't drink, Gujarati girls don't eat meat, and Gujarati girls don't leave home to go to university. When I eventually met his gaze, I saw the hurt.

His eyes moved down to his food and he continued to eat his lunch. The tension prolonged in the silence.

"Sorry, I'm just fed up of being told what I can and can't do."

"No, I'm sorry. I don't know any Gujarati girls who eat meat." He paused, his eyes narrowed, and fine lines appeared in the corners. "Well, they might do, but not admit it to me. It's good. I don't understand why men can eat and drink and women can't."

"So, your sisters don't eat meat or drink, but your brothers do?"

"Oh, my sisters and my bhabhi drink wine, that's allowed, but Motaba is not pleased."

For pudding, Nikesh had a Christmas pudding and I chose an apple pie.

"You don't like Christmas dinner?"

"No, I do, but I'm going with my father for his work's Christmas dinner on Wednesday night and then I've got a Christmas party with my brother on Thursday and we have Christmas dinner on Christmas Day. I think I need to pace myself," I raised a smile.

"You'll be going home on Wednesday?"

I told him I planned to be home by lunchtime.

"Are you being picked up?"

"Oh no, I'll take the coach from Pool Meadow." I wanted to ask him when he was going home but hadn't dared to ask; a small lump came to my throat. So, I changed the subject. "Is your brother's marriage arranged?"

"Yes and no," he replied.

I frowned.

"Suresh and Ashveena have been seeing each other secretly for a couple of years. Her parents are our family friends, and then Kaki was told the secret and she suggested it to Motaba."

"Does everything have to be approved by your motaba?"

"Yes, pretty much everything."

He took out a cigarette case and asked, "Do you mind?"

I shook my head. The waiter came up to the table and presented a lighter. He discreetly blew the smoke away from me as he savoured the tobacco.

"When did you start to smoke? Not at the same time as drinking, I hope?"

"When I was fifteen, some of my friends dared me to smoke in the playground. I got suspended for two days. Why don't you smoke?" He raised his left eyebrow, mocking me.

I thought about how my father's coughing fits made me feel and the fear that came of losing him too. "You know it's bad for you?"

"I know. I'm trying to reduce them down; I used to chain smoke cigarettes and have moved to Davidoff Club Cigarillo to cut back."

He could tell I wasn't convinced of the strategy. "No, honestly, I only have a couple of these a day," showing me his cigarillo as an exhibit.

* * *

He asked for our coats and slowly wrapped me in mine. He was standing behind me and I inhaled the scent of him; I heard him sigh and felt embarrassed that I had heard. I moved away, busying myself with the belt around my waist.

He pulled out his left elbow. "Shall we go for a walk by the river?"

The cold winter sun was low on the horizon, the air was crisp, and I was glad of the warmth from my coat. Nikesh and I zigzagged our way to the River Avon and ended up in a grassy area; even in winter the garden was full of tourists.

On our left was the Royal Shakespeare Theatre. The red-brick and zinc-pointed roof of the rotunda was bathed in the sun.

"Have you been inside the theatre?" I asked Nikesh.

"Yes, we came on school visits for *A Midsummer Night's Dream*, *Julius Caesar* and *Macbeth*. What about you?"

"I took A-level English. My teacher loved Stratford."

"Why didn't you choose English as a degree?"

I started to explain that I wanted to work in film and television production and told him about how I'd met Jane, my mentor. I was so engrossed in what I wanted to do for a career that I hadn't noticed we had walked across the river to Bancroft Garden.

He took me to an empty bench and we sat down. He was a good listener, asking me questions when he didn't understand. I realised I was talking too much and apologised. "You know why I want to work in film and television: what made you choose law?"

"Didn't have many choices, really. My papa thought it would help the business."

"Didn't you know what you wanted to do?"

"To be honest, I know I want to work in the family business. And I wanted to come to university. Law seemed a good option."

I wasn't surprised; this was usually the norm for Indian families, even my brother chose to be a dentist because my father wanted him to do something in science.

"My family has a computer parts business, my older brother studied Accountancy and my middle brother studied computer science. My kaka manages the business and my papa networks. Well, I call him my kaka, but he's really my father. We all live together. My papa is my father's older brother."

"Oh! So how many real brothers and sisters do you have?"

"They are all real, Reena. I haven't made them up." He raised a smile.

"If you want to know how many biological siblings I have, then I have an older sister."

"So, your brothers and one sister are also your cousins," I confirmed.

"What about you? Do you have cousins?"

I told him my father had an older sister who lived in India, who didn't have any children and we knew very little of my mother's family and what we knew was that she had a brother who we had lost touch with.

"Do you remember your mother?"

"No, I was only three years old and have vague feelings and memories. Sometimes I smell something that reminds me of her. Sitting by water reminds me of her a lot. I think she must have taken my brother and I to the River Soar by our house."

"Do you know what happened?"

"No, my father doesn't talk about it. I used to ask

when I was younger, but I've stopped. I think my father blames me for my mother's death." He squeezed my hand, sensing it was upsetting for me. He put his arm around my shoulder. I leant into him. His gesture relieved the knot in my stomach that had developed as I thought of my mother.

"It's not your fault, Reena. You were only three. I think your father probably misses her."

We sat in quiet contentment. I wondered if he had lost someone too, to understand how I felt. I rested my head on his shoulder and watched the swans glide gracefully on the river. Nikesh wasn't as I expected. He didn't have the same arrogance of other wealthy Indians I had met before; even his friends Jay and Ravi display their wealth like a badge.

The garden quietened as the coaches of tourists left; the winter sun almost descended. "What time do you start work?"

"Six o'clock." I lifted my watch up to peer at it.

When I came back to my room, I changed into my uniform, opened my diary, drew hearts on 19th December and wrote up what we had done. I turned the page and wrote, 'Make dinner for NR.' I was on the doors tomorrow and had asked him to come for an early dinner.

When he dropped me off that evening after work, he gave me a slow, soft kiss. My heart stopped in mid beat and I tingled from top to toe.

I fell asleep reliving the moment over and over again.

Six

WHEN I WALKED INTO THE LIBRARY on Monday morning, Nikesh was sitting at his usual table, but instead of using his note cards and folders, he was reading a book and making notes. I stood near his desk and asked him where his friends were. He explained they had finished their project research and had gone home. I stood there longer than I needed to absorb the information. If they've finished the work, why is he still here? I wondered.

"There's plenty of space on this table, Ree. Take a seat." I was slightly confused by what he'd called me.

"You don't mind me calling you Ree?" he asked, smiling.

"Only if you don't mind me calling you Kesh?" I returned the smile.

"I would love that or any other name you wish to call me," he whispered quietly.

I sat opposite him. It was the same view I had all week, but I could make a closer observation.

"So, what are you doing?" I asked.

"I thought I'd follow your example: read up on my units for next term."

Sitting closer allowed me to observe the neatly arched eyebrows and I wondered if he plucked them. I studied the chiselled cheekbones on his square face; his long nose is slim, with a slight point. His beautiful eyes pointed upwards when he concentrated on a problem. We sat studiously keeping the pretence of working when all we wanted to do was talk to each other. Occasionally I glanced at him, hiding my eyes under my fringe, lingering on his wonderful face. I knew I was going to have to sketch him. I was making plodding progress and I scolded myself under my breath.

"Sorry, did you say something?" he asked.

I shook my head; a smile developed on his face until white teeth shone from ear to ear. "Do you want to go for a coffee?"

"Yes, I'd love one."

We left our books on the table and walked hand in hand past the librarian; her eyes drifted to our entwined hands and she smiled. We grinned back at her like naughty children caught causing mischief.

Nik held a tray with two cups of coffee in his hand; I stood with him in the queue to pay. I wanted to be near him as much as possible. I was relishing the time with him.

We sat next to each other in a booth, our fingers entwined as we waited for the coffee to cool.

"What's on the menu tonight, Ree?"

"You'll have to wait and see. You eat anything, right?"

I teased him.

"What do you mean anything?" Tiny crow's feet appeared on the edge of his eyes.

"Fish, meat, etcetera. You're not allergic to anything are you … Nik?"

"Wow, when you say my name, it's so sexy," he breathed in my ear. I suddenly felt hot. I felt my cheeks heat up and I concentrated on my coffee.

We quenched our thirst as slowly as we were able, extending the opportunity to hold hands as long as possible. On our return to the library, I was able to concentrate, as Nik had placed my legs between his under the table to keep us connected.

At 12.30 p.m. I began to pack up my books, and his eyebrow rose questioningly. I told him I was going to Coventry market to pick up fresh ingredients.

"Can I take you in my car?"

"It wouldn't be a surprise if you come with me," I replied and I stood up and gave him a quick peck on the lips and almost ran out of the library. I took a quick glimpse back from the door and saw him grinning back at me, his finger tracing his lips.

The intercom rang as I was lighting the candles in some old wine bottles. I had changed into a pink paisley-print silk shirt with dog-ear collars, a pair of black drainpipe trousers and my black square-toe court shoes.

I rushed to the stairs and watched him come up. He smiled, holding up a pack of Foster's and a bunch of cut flowers. He had gone home and changed, and as he unbuttoned his coat I saw a white shirt, brown trousers and a cream cable knit jumper.

He stopped at the top where I was leaning against the bannister, handed me the flowers and kissed me on the cheek. I felt like I wanted to giggle, but suppressed it. I took his hand and walked him into the dimly-lit kitchen.

"You've made Indian food!" It was not a question, more of a surprised statement.

"Yes, why?" I was startled at his reaction.

He shrugged his shoulders "I … I thought you'd make something … English."

A retort surfaced to my lips; I bit it back. No, I was not going to get angry.

"Ah but my Indian food might not taste good," I teased him.

"Where are your glasses, or are we drinking from the can?" he enquired, holding up the lager. I pulled out two tall glasses from the cupboard and handed them to him. He sat with his back to the window and began to pour them.

I had prepared the menu after checking what was available at the market for my meagre budget.

I plated up the kebabs and turned on the grill before sitting down. Nat King Cole crooned about falling in love. I watched him take a bite of the kebab, waiting for the signs of changes in his expression as the spices tingled his taste buds.

"Oh … God, this is amazing!" His eyebrows raised and his mouth was open.

My head lowered; I had been observing him through my fringe. A small smile lifted my lips.

I knew I was a good cook. I had had an abundance of practice. It took my father a long time to recover from

Reena & Nikesh's Dinner Date

Mutton kebab
spiced cubed mutton cooked on skewers under the grill

Dahi phudina ni chutnee
mint and yoghurt chutney

Murgi kari
Gujarati-style chicken curry

Sabji dall
mixed vegetable and assorted split lentil stew

Quick naan
*unleavened flatbread made with baking powder and plain flour
cooked under a grill*

Baath
Plain boiled rice

Tameta dungali kachumber
chopped tomato and onion salad

Peaches with kesar cream
peaches with saffron-infused cream

the death of my mother. Divya Ba helped my father as much as she could. She would bring us food to eat and make sure we washed when we were very young. She would even look after us until my father came home from work. But on the weekends, it was my father's turn and all he did was cry and drink. It was only when Divya Ba found out that my father couldn't cope that she decided to teach us to be self-sufficient. Most of it fell on poor Amit. He was both a mother and father to me. Slowly I took some of the burden off him. When I turned eight, I became the cook and Amit took the responsibility to shop, wash and clean.

Then Divya Ba became ill; she was diagnosed with diabetes. I was ten years old and my father changed: he started making dinner and keeping the house clean. I was glad for Amit; he needed the break. I loved those times; he would show me how to cook a new dish. When I asked him who taught him to cook, he talked about how my mother was a fantastic cook, and that her food was so good that you would lick the skin off your fingers to keep the taste in your mouth. But I hated seeing the sadness in his eyes and I would change the subject. I took to cooking easily. It helped with my anxiety, the method of chopping, measuring, waiting for the chemical changes in the ingredients.

My father says I have my mother's magical touch; I just know what to add to give food a particular flavour.

"What have you put in here?" He lifted up a piece of kebab.

"Secret family recipe. My father would kill me if I told you."

I cleared away the empty plates and washed and dried my hands. I grabbed a piece of dough from a bowl under a damp tea towel.

"Do you want me to help?" I felt his warm breath on the back of my neck. My skin heated and I pointed to the pans on the hob.

"You can take the pans to the table."

He lifted the lid of each pan and nodded in approval as he checked their contents.

I rolled out the piece of dough into a large circle the size of a dinner plate and did the same with another, placing both on a sheet of greaseproof paper on the worktop.

"What are you making?"

"Naan."

"How can you make naan without a tandoor?"

"Watch." I placed the dough circles onto a hot baking tray under the grill. When the heat hit them, small bubbles rose, and the bread eventually browned.

I placed the naan on a wooden breadboard and took it to the table.

Nik was grinning. "I've never seen that before."

I opened a small metal tin and asked, "ghee?"

"You make your own ghee?" His eyebrows lifted in astonishment. "You do know you can buy it?"

"Yes, but it's expensive and when you're on a limited budget." My lips pursed. I didn't want to tell him about my struggles with money.

I had tried to create a thali for our main meal: a large plate, two small bowls and a small saucer. I filled the bowls with the chicken curry and vegetable dall; I filled the saucer with boiled rice, folded the buttered naan in half and added a small helping of chopped tomatoes and onions on his plate.

He was like a small boy who had discovered a secret den; the joy on his face filled the whole kitchen with light. "You've made my favourite food. How did you know?"

I threw him a knowing look. I didn't know. I had cooked what I liked to eat, but I was not going to tell him. It was my secret. He ate eagerly, tearing his naan and dipping it into the curry and the dall. I liked that he ate with gusto and had a good appetite. I had placed a spoon next to his plate, but he hadn't bothered using it: he was using his hands, picking the food up with his fingers and using his thumb to flick the morsels onto his tongue. When he tasted the salad, he stopped, chewed slowly and asked, "What have you put in it that makes the tomatoes so sweet and the onions so hot?"

I raised my eyebrows and smiled.

I made him another naan and topped up his bowls of curry and dall. He licked his fingers. I was happy; he liked my cooking.

He stood up, took the dishes to the sink and started to rinse them.

"Wait, we still have dessert."

He turned to me. "You've made dessert too?"

"Well, I haven't made it." I took out a glass bowl of tinned peaches and a milk jug from the fridge.

He sat back down and waited for me to bring it to the table. I picked up two bowls and filled them with the peaches, handed one to him, poured the single cream on top and handed him a spoon.

He peered at the pale-yellow cream. "You've put kesar in it."

"Damn, you've discovered one of my secret family recipes."

He laughed and ate his peaches with saffron cream.

"I'm full," he leant back in his chair. "I'll have to stay here all night … I can't possibly move." He patted his stomach. He asked for permission to smoke and turned around to search for an ashtray. I held it in my hand, standing briefly by his side. He pulled me onto his lap, put his cigarillo on the ashtray and gave me a kiss. I could taste the tobacco. I don't like cigarette smoke, but I loved the taste of it in his mouth.

"Oh, God, you're incredible," he whispered breathlessly as we pulled apart.

He insisted on helping me clean the kitchen. He washed the dishes as I dried.

"Do you cook?"

"Only the basics. I can make a good English breakfast, beans on toast, cheese on toast. I can make the basic bateta nu shaak and mug baath. Ravi does most of our cooking and we get rotli from a masi who lives a couple of doors away."

"Does Peter eat Indian food too?"

"Yes, when we make it, and he cooks some Nigerian food, so we manage. Mostly we eat what's sent by Motaba; she usually has Suresh drop off a batch of food, all vegetarian."

"What! She sends your brother up just to give you food?" My jaw dropped.

He chortled, "No, Ree, my brother comes up fortnightly to Birmingham and Jay's parents come up often, so she sends food with them."

I had stopped drying the dishes. I was stunned his motaba cared so much for him to do this regularly. The tape stopped and I turned it over and pressed play. Nat King Cole continued to sing "The Very Thought of You."

"I don't listen to Nat King Cole, but I'm going to start. You have some strange tastes in music —" He studied my outfit, his eyes lingering over my body, " — and eccentric taste in clothes, Reena Solanki."

I was flustered by the long slow stare and lifted up my watch hand. I hadn't told him the tape was my brother's favourite song collection.

"I have to change into my uniform. Do you want to sit here or come sit in my room?"

"Can I come to see your room?" he asked hesitantly.

I asked him to take a seat anywhere and picked my uniform from my wardrobe. "I'll be back soon." I rushed to the bathroom to change. Conflicting thoughts raced through my mind. I shouldn't have asked him to my room, I scolded myself. He'll want something from me; I know I'm not ready for that. But inviting him to my room sent all the wrong signals. I'm going to have to explain to him, "I'm not that type of girl," I told my reflection. Calmed myself down by washing my face in cold water and headed back to deal with the consequences.

When I walked in, he was looking through my sketchbook; I must have thrown it on the chair earlier that morning. He held it open at a drawing of the lake. "Are these your drawings?"

"Yes," I answered warily. People reacted differently to

my drawings; they had a polarising effect, and you either loved them or hated them.

"They're beautiful, disturbing but beautiful. When do you get the time? You work, and you are studying in the library all the time."

"I draw when I can't sleep," I replied quietly.

"Why can't you sleep?" he asked, worriedly.

"I have bad dreams when I'm stressed."

He opened his arms wide, his eyes filled with concern. "Come here," he wrapped his arms around me and squeezed me slightly. I felt the warmth of his body against mine. His body heat was at least a degree higher than mine. "Any time you feel stressed or upset, come to me Ree. I'll deal with it."

He lifted my chin and brushed his lips against mine; it started as soft and tender, a small press of the lips, a little exploration of the tip of my tongue, and continued to deepen to my core, the intensity opening every nerve in my body. I began to feel his urge to make it more. I tasted the hunger. I responded and knew I would lose myself in the moment. I pushed at his chest and tried to draw away.

"What's wrong?"

"I'm sorry," I gasped.

"Am I your first boyfriend?"

"You're my first kiss," I said, my voice barely audible from the feeling I was struggling to comprehend.

"What!" He pushed me back at arm's length, scrutinising my face. "You're joking, right?" His eyes flickered like millions of candles. I shook my head slowly. "How has anyone resisted the urge to kiss you, Ree? You're clever, you're talented, you're beautiful, you have great style, and you are an amazing cook. Were you living in a nunnery?"

"No." I shook my head, "I have an older brother and father who are very protective."

"Get your coat, let's go for a walk. When do you start work?" He was heading for the kitchen collecting his camel coat and scarf; I had a feeling he wanted some fresh air.

"Got your keys?" he asked when I came into the kitchen. He reached for my hand and we walked hand in hand to University Street. We sat on a bench opposite the Art Centre.

"I'm not going to lie to you. I want you. I'm finding it difficult to keep myself away from you." He inhaled slowly, "But … I promise, I won't force you to do anything you don't want to do."

I thought of the times I had seen him at the pub crawls holding up some drunken girl on his arms, or he and his friends checking the women out when they entered the room. I felt a fist punching my stomach. He would soon get fed up. I was sure there were plenty of girls who would give him what he wanted. But I wanted him to like me, to choose me. My heart ached when I thought of the other girls he had been with.

"Did you hear what I said? I promise I'll wait for you to tell me when."

I took in what he had just said to me. He liked me enough to stay with me. My heart sang with joy.

"I've had too many girlfriends to count. I started when I was thirteen years old."

"Did you … you know … with them?" I asked.

"No! Not when I was thirteen, but yes, I have. I don't

want you to think I do that with every girl I go out with … I'm not like that. I met a girl when I was fifteen … I thought she felt the same about me. I guess she was my first love … but she went away. Then I did something I'm not proud of … for a month or two with loads of girls. I wasn't interested in long-term relationships and wanted to forget the hurt. You're different. I've never felt like this before. I … I really have fallen for you."

He saw the dismay in my eyes. I had pulled my hand away when he'd said she was his first love. I was disappointed I was not his first love. Why was I feeling jealous? I hardly knew him. He pulled my chin with his fingers, "Look at me." I kept my eyes closed; my emotions were difficult to hide, my eyes would reveal the hurt. "Please," he implored.

When I gazed into his eyes, they glistened with moisture and I said, "I like you too, Nik. I'm just not ready for that." I scanned his face for any sign of rejection.

He planted soft small kisses on my face, eventually kissing me longingly on my lips and we kissed and cuddled until it was time for me to go into the Art Centre.

He walked me to the entrance and said, "I don't want to leave you tonight."

"You can't come in here without a ticket." I pointed to the foyer.

"Wait, I have an idea," he strolled to the ticket desk. He walked back, smiling and waving the ticket at me. "Where's this seat?"

"Lower circle," I said.

"Where's your door duty?"

I pointed to the upper circle.

"Can you swap with the person on the door?"

"I'll try." I walked across to talk to the woman on duty. I turned back to him and nodded.

His face lit up and a huge grin ran from ear to ear.

He stood next to me as I checked tickets for the concertgoers.

"I just need to make a quick phone call." He leant in to give me a kiss and headed to the phones. "I'll see you soon." An elderly couple tutted as he disrupted their progress.

The auditorium was filling up and the lights dimmed. I was concerned he hadn't come back. I glanced across to the other doors. I swatted the thought away. He knew where I was standing. I began to panic.

The conductor walked in and took a bow. The audience raised an applause. The lights dimmed further; it was my cue to close the doors. I glanced at a single empty seat. I pulled one door closed and reached for the other. "Hi, sorry took longer than expected." His eyes had lost their sparkle and were dull. He composed himself and grinned at me.

"Right, where do I sit?" I walked him to the seat. He whispered, "I'm going to imagine you're sitting next to me and I'm caressing your arm to the music." I shivered as the hairs on my arms stood on end.

He apologised as he stepped towards his seat and purposefully held his programme up to hide his wicked grin.

I headed back to the door for latecomers. The auditorium was dark, and I placed myself so I could watch the door and watch him. It was too dark to see his face, but I could see his outline.

During the interval, he stood by my side.

"That was amazing. I loved it. I've never heard Sibelius. I think number two is my favourite so far. What about you?" I glanced at him quizzically. "It's a date, Ree. We have to make small talk in the interval."

"You cheapskate. You didn't even buy me a ticket!" I exclaimed.

He shrugged, "Not my fault you have the best job. You can listen to City of Birmingham Youth Orchestra every night."

I beamed at him. "I'm glad you like it, but I also work out there and in the bar," I said, pointing to the lobby. "So, it's not every night."

"Okay, but you were here tonight … Tell me, which one is your favourite symphony?"

"I'll tell you later."

"Does that mean your favourite's coming up?"

The lights dimmed; he lingered by my side and then took my hand, turned it over and brushed his lips on my wrist. Wretched goose bumps rose again.

My duty that night entailed picking up litter after the concert, usually ticket stubs and discarded programmes. As I brought my black bag into the lobby to pick up any other litter, I saw him sitting at the bar talking to Debbie. She was smiling as she cleared the glasses.

"Come on, mate, you'll have to wait outside. I need to lock up!" Simon yelled, jangling his keys.

"It's all right, Simon, he can go out the side door, Reena's nearly finished," Debbie added.

I stepped from the staffroom with my coat and

handbag. Nik stood up, turned and said, "Thanks, Debbie. Goodnight," striding towards me, fixing his eyes on mine. We walked out into the cold night; a glittering of frost had formed on the trees.

"Tell me ... which one of Sibelius's symphonies is your favourite?"

"I like number three; it reminds me of the fairies rising from their sleep as the night draws in and I also imagine the creatures on the forest floor working industrially to decompose leaves. I like number seven too; it fills my mind with autumn colours and the early morning sun hitting the leaves, reds, coppers, golden and yellows," I replied.

"Very descriptive, he smiled. "I like number two the best. It's the type of music you hear in cathedrals; the grandeur of the brass instruments remind me of pageantry. I enjoyed the whole concert. They were different but not different enough to be jarring."

I gawked at him, overawed. I didn't think he'd have any knowledge of orchestral music. Not many Indians do and he hadn't grown up in England.

He stopped. "I did go to a private school. They make us listen to this stuff all the time," and he smirked.

We reached the halls of residence. "Can I come up. I can't bear to go yet ... it's too cold to stand outside tonight." I hesitated. "We can sit in the kitchen and finish the lagers," he added, his stunning eyes imploring.

"Okay." I took his hand and led him up the stairs to the kitchen.

He stood awkwardly by my side while I opened the fridge and filled two glasses. His breath caught my ear. I let out a small sigh. I was being very stupid. I had told him I was not that kind of girl and I was sending mixed messages again.

He asked me to sit next to him at the table. We sat silently. I could sense he wanted to say something and was finding it difficult to tell me. "I've got some bad news." He was nursing his glass with both hands.

My mouth felt dry. Even after taking a sip of cold lager, the liquid burnt my throat.

"I have to go to Manchester tomorrow. Motaba wants me to pick something up for Suresh's engagement. I'll have to leave early and I'm not sure I'll be back to pick you up after work. I'm here on Wednesday. Will you let me take you home in my car?"

I felt relieved. I didn't know what was going through my mind, and it certainly wasn't that. I found myself thinking about his request. What if someone saw him dropping me off and told my brother, or even worse told my father. But I didn't want that day to be the last time I saw him. "Only if you come for breakfast on Wednesday morning?"

"I won't say no to breakfast. If it's as good as dinner, I'm in for a treat." His face filled with his lopsided smile.

"I might not be good at making English breakfast," I teased, and he took my free hand and held it to his lips, placing tiny kisses on each knuckle. My breath stopped. He pushed up my shirt sleeve and moved up my arm.

"Promise me you'll get someone to walk you home. I don't want you to walk back alone." He frowned into my eyes.

I closed my eyes and savoured the kisses. He pulled at my shirt collar and worked his way up to my neck. "Promise me, Ree," he whispered. I nodded, unable to speak.

Seven

I WOKE UP FUZZY AND WARM; my dreams had been about soft kisses and Nikesh Raja. My lips were bruised from the intensity of the kisses from the night before. The past eight days had dispelled all the myths I had of wealthy and privileged Indians. I enjoyed his company and had learnt I should not jump to conclusions.

I made the most of the library for the final time in the holiday and spent the morning finding books I could reserve, the librarian sending me to shelves I wouldn't ordinarily have gone to. I was looking forward to my new units.

I left before lunch to finish my packing. I spent time arranging my clothes for the two Christmas dinners I was going to with my father and Amit and chose to only take clothes I needed for the break. I ate some chicken and rice, leftover from the dinner I had cooked for Nik, and changed into my uniform.

As I walked back to the Arts Centre, I thought I saw

Nik standing at his usual spot and my heart skipped with joy. When I looked again, he wasn't there. My heart sank. How can anyone miss someone so much so quickly? It was impossible. I understood how my father felt, listening to songs from *Tumse Achha Kaun Hai* over and over again on his record player. The song tells of a lover's yearning to live hundreds of lives with the woman he loved. The meaning of the lyrics made me think about how Hindus believe in reincarnation and spending many lifetimes together as eternal lovers. I didn't believe in reincarnation, but I felt Nik and I had met in another lifetime.

"Your man's very gallant, always waiting for you after work," Debbie told me as I came back into the lobby with the black bag. "He's been waiting for half an hour, so I let him in. Poor boy would have frozen to death out there tonight. Feels like snow's coming."

He was standing by the tall glass windows, his hands in his coat pockets, watching for me to come out of the auditorium. My heart was in my mouth; just seeing him made my knees go weak. His long strides brought him in front of me in seconds.

"Hi," he whispered.

"Hi," I replied. We both grinned at each other, our smiles beating the Cheshire cats in the biggest smile competition.

"Oh, give me the rubbish and be gone. Have a lovely Christmas, Reena, Nik. See you in the new year." Debbie handed me my coat and handbag.

"Thanks, Debbie. Merry Christmas and a Happy New Year to you, too!" I shouted back to her as Nik took my hand and we strode briskly out into the night.

"I couldn't stay away any longer … I missed you so much. I know it sounds stupid. But I really did," he began and I smiled up at him. "Do you know the song from that Shammi Kapoor film —" and he started to sing, "Janam janam ka saath …" his voice just as good as Mohammed Rafi.

I suppressed a gasp. He stopped. "What?"

He tried to make eye contact, but I forced myself to keep my head down and glanced away from him. How could that happen? *Was he a mind reader?* I had only been thinking about the same song earlier. How could he feel the same as I do? I shook my head.

"Tell me, what are you thinking?"

The air was crisp and cold; frost was forming on the grass and the moon had disappeared behind a thick cloud. The only light was the yellow streetlights on campus as we stood facing each other.

I eventually built up the courage to talk. "I was thinking of the same song earlier today, Nik."

He picked me up and swung me around. "I'm so happy, so, so happy. You missed me too!" He was shouting and I laughed from the exhilaration of flying in his arms.

He headed for the kitchen, but I stopped him. He searched my face.

"I … I'm still not ready —" I said as I pulled him to my room,"— but the kitchen isn't comfortable." I took off my coat. "Do you want something hot to drink, or will this do?" I pulled out a half-full bottle of whisky from my wardrobe.

"You drink whisky?" he said, shaking his head. "You're full of surprises! You're … er … unique. Do you have ice?"

"Of course!" I replied and headed to the kitchen to fetch the glasses and ice.

When I returned, he had taken off his coat and was gazing intently at a portrait on my bookshelf.

"Is this your mother?" he asked, turning to me as I walked in. I nodded, "I thought she was — " he paused.

I stood by his side, looking at the pastel portrait of my mother on her wedding day.

"I drew it as a close study for my O-level art; the oil painting is in our front room."

"You are just like her. No wonder your father's protective," he remarked.

My eyes coated with moisture. "I still don't understand why she isn't here, Nik. Why she left us —"

"She didn't leave you; it was just her time to go."

"Do you believe that?"

"Yes, I'm positive." He picked up the glasses and handed mine to me. We clinked our drinks. "To your beautiful mother, and her even more beautiful daughter." He pulled me down on his lap as he sat in the armchair. He sipped his drink and observed my face carefully as I drank mine.

"Enough?" He took my glass and placed it on the desk. "I need some kissing and cuddling time." He began to explore the small curve in my lower back, running his warm hands up to the back of my neck into my hair. I leant into his touch, my eyes closed, and I couldn't suppress the moan escaping from my mouth. I opened my eyes in shock; his eyes were full of desire and he raised a wicked smile.

"That's better. Kissing you is necessary to help my heart sing again. To fill the hole that has grown." His words said what I'd felt. Every cell in my body wanted to kiss him, touch him, fill the hole that had grown in my heart, too. I became braver and started to stroke his chest and we explored each other's bodies and continued to kiss to make up for the time we were apart.

When we kissed. I loved the feeling of his lips on mine; he pulled away and I felt bereft. He sighed.

"I have to go home and pack … " Desperation filled his voice. "Unless … you want to come with me?"

My heart wanted to say yes, but my head was saying no. I felt safer in my own room. He saw the conflict in my eyes. That was the trouble with my eyes: they revealed my emotions too readily.

"I'm teasing you," he raised his beautifully arched eyebrows. The shards of gold twinkled, and a wicked lopsided grin drew across his face.

"Besides, you need to sleep. I'm coming for breakfast, so you'll have to be up with the larks. What time do you want me to come?" he asked as he pulled on his coat. "Oh … " He pulled out a small card with handwriting on it and handed it to me. "It's my family tree. You were confused about who's who in my family; this explains everything. I want you to know everything about me and my family." He pulled me towards him, his soft lips filling me with a deep longing.

"Good night, Ree. Sweet dreams." I walked with him to the stairs and kissed him again. I couldn't get enough of his lips.

"I missed you Nik. See you at 9.30," I whispered in his ear and nudged him down the stairs. He stood at the bottom, clasping his heart with his right hand, pretending it was breaking. I laughed.

"Good night, Nik. Sweet dreams."

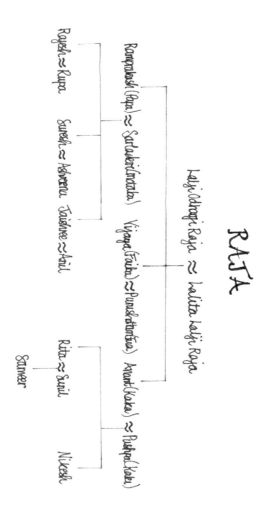

I DECIDED ON A SOUTH Indian breakfast dish, upma. I remembered it from my childhood days when Divya Ba would come around with it steaming hot and savoury. We would eat it with natural yoghurt. The soft spiciness of semolina, the crunch of the fried cashew nuts and the cold tang of the yoghurt always made my mouth water. I hoped Nik liked it as much as I did.

The intercom rang. I found my heart singing: he was early! I had a feeling he would be and anticipated his arrival. The upma was steaming in the pan on a low heat; the Indian-style tea was simmering on the stove. I ran to the top of the stairs to see him; he was flicking snowflakes off his head and shoulders.

"Is it snowing?"

He smiled and nodded as he climbed up two stairs at a time and took me in his arms. "Good morning, did you sleep well?" He kissed me with longing before I could reply. My heart stopped. He inhaled deeply. "Can't smell a fry up?"

"You're early!" I jokingly exclaimed.

"Couldn't wait to see you again. You haven't answered my question. Did you sleep well?"

"Not too bad, but I had instructions to get up at sunrise."

"Instruction?" He laughed. "Oh yes, last night. If only I'd known you'd take cooking breakfast so seriously, I'd have been here like a shot. Do you know how agonising it was to wait for the time to pass?"

I took his hand and led him down the corridor to the kitchen. "When did it start snowing?" I stopped and stared out of the window.

"Just as I drove into campus. It's beautiful." He was grinning like a child. He turned to me, pulling me into his arms. "We don't get much snowfall that settles down south. I love it! Can we go make a snowman before we go?"

I grinned back at him. I love the snow, too. One of my earliest memories is of snowflakes falling on my face, and my mother laughing with my brother.

We stepped into the kitchen; his eyes searched the room for any signs of preparations for breakfast. "Do you want me to help? It's one of my specialties."

"I've made something else," I said, pointing to the stove.

He inhaled. "I can smell tea and something spicy?"

"I've made upma. I hope you like it?"

"Upma? I … I, where did you learn how to make upma?"

I strained the tea into mugs and filled the plates with upma. I told Nik to fetch the yoghurt from the fridge. He sat down at the table and saw the soft, pale yellow bejewelled mound. "You've added cashew nuts, too?"

"Yes, Daddy insists I have nuts every day."

"That's the first time you've called your father, Daddy."

I averted my gaze; my eyes moistened. "I miss him a lot … Nik."

"You're going to see him today." He reached across and squeezed my hand.

He took a spoonful of upma and yoghurt and put it in his mouth.

I waited apprehensively as he chewed and swallowed. "It's amazing, just like you. Where did you learn to

117

make it?"

"Divya Ba and Tarla Dalal obviously."

"Who's Tarla Dalal?"

"A very famous Indian cook. Amit gave me her cookbook."

"Is Divya Ba your grandmother?"

My eyes rested on his hand and he released it reluctantly.

"Divya Ba has helped my father raise us. She is an old school friend of my father's mother. Dadima passed away when I was ten. Nanima died before I was born. So, is she my dadima? Yes, I guess she is. She used to pick us up from school when we were young and keep us at her home until my father finished work. She's an excellent cook; she's taught me most of the Gujarati food I cook, and I've picked up some of the other vegetarian dishes from the ladies at Sanatan Mandir."

"Sanatan Mandir?"

"I go and help out in the kitchen when we have functions."

He shook his head. "How do you make time for all this? I'm just exhausted from studying."

"And partying," I added.

He held his heart gesturing I had wounded him. I raised my eyebrow. "Time is relative."

He put the mug of tea to his lips.

"I haven't put any masala in it."

"You don't like it?"

"No, reminds me too much of being sick. Daddy makes us drink masala chai when we get colds in the winter." I faked a shudder at the thought of it and he laughed.

His legs had entangled mine under the table and he was holding my left hand, his thumb caressing my knuckles. His body heat was definitely higher than mine. I was flustered.

After breakfast, we stood by the window. Snow was falling rapidly and had left a thick blanket of white over everything.

"Can we go out? Do you have to be home by lunchtime or any time after?"

"Let's go build a snowman." I smiled up at him.

The grass in front of the halls had a pristine white coat of snow. We ran and gathered as much snow as we could to make a heap. He ran to find some more, and I stopped him. "No, let's roll this to make it bigger."

He rolled the ball around the lawn and I made a smaller ball. I pointed to the small ball and asked him to lift it on the larger ball. Instead of rolling it to me, he ran to pick up the small ball. I laughed uncontrollably. "It's easier to roll that here!"

He laughed, too, grinning at me. "Never built a snowman before."

"What!" I exclaimed.

"Not much snow in London when I arrived."

"Let's find some pinecones for his eyes." We searched through the campus, holding hands and giggling like little children.

We found three pinecones, an old tennis ball and a lost scarf.

We admired our creation. "Wait here. I'll be back … want to get something from the car." He pointed to the road on the side of Rootes Hall. I searched for other objects to decorate the snowman, found an old traffic cone and put it on his head.

He was waving a camera at me. "I have to take a photograph!" he shouted as he ran back. "Papa's going to love this! You've made it even better," he said as he approached.

He started to take photographs. "Go on, stand by the snowman."

I hesitated. He pulled me to the snowman and started snapping away. My mittens were soaked through, but I was not cold. The snow continued to fall, creating a magical world of white.

"Can you drive in this, Nik?" I was beginning to get nervous.

"Yes, the motorway will be clear. Don't worry." He took my hand and we headed back into my halls to thaw out and dry our sopping wet gloves on the radiator.

* * *

THE M69 HAD BEEN GRITTED and he drove slower than the speed limit.

"Haven't driven in snow before," he said, concentrating on the road. His knuckles were white on the steering wheel. I tried to lighten the mood by singing out of key to the mixtape of '70s Motown we were listening to. The eerie glow from the snow on his face heightened my anxiety. He was chewing at his lower lips, and his eyes narrowed as he concentrated on the road.

Once the snow stopped falling, he relaxed his grip on the steering wheel, but he was still concentrating intently on the road. The worst part was when we had to overtake a slow lorry. The spray from their huge wheels coated the windscreen and the wipers creaked and stopped, struggling to clear it. Nik's eyes darkened and his jaw tightened as he drove past it slowly. I held my breath, too, willing for time to speed up.

"Can you turn the radio on?"

We listened to the news reports; the country had been hit by a snowstorm overnight and everything was affected. Rail disruptions, burst water pipes, and power cuts.

"Do you have to go home tonight?" I asked, unable to disguise the anxiety in my voice. I hadn't wanted him to drive home on his own. I wasn't sure what my family would say when I told them he was staying with us, but my need to keep him safe was stronger than my fear of them.

"Yes, I do. I've stayed up here for far too long."

I wanted to tell him I was worried, and he should abandon the car in Leicester and go home by coach or train, that it was too dangerous, and he was too precious to me.

As soon as we reached Leicester, the roads were clearer, and the sun had come out.

"You're going to direct me, right?"

I told him to take the Narborough Road exit.

"How far from De Montfort Hall do you live?"

I gawked at him. "I remember your brother saying you didn't live far," he said.

We pulled up into Grasmere Street. I was thankful the snow had kept everyone inside their homes, and it was deserted.

We sat in the car and listened to the engine cool down. I glanced at the clock. No one would be home until six o'clock, and the least I could do was offer him a hot drink.

"Come in," I said.

He frowned. "Are you sure?"

"Yes, come in, Nik."

He took my bags out of the boot and waited by the front door. I headed to the alleyway next to the front room.

"We use the back door," I told him and added, "when it's wet." I don't know why I said that; we always used the back door. The only people who knocked on the front door were Jehovah's Witnesses. We stepped into the small lobby between the kitchen and bathroom. We took off our boots. We had coat hooks in there, too, but I took his coat and told him I would dry it out on the heater.

I watched him survey the surroundings, checking for any sign of disdain, as we walked through the kitchen into the dining room.

"Where do you want me to put these?"

"Just leave them there." I pointed by the sofa in the dining room. "I'll take them up to my room later."

"Aren't you going to show me your room?" He smiled, raising his wicked eyebrow. My heart skipped. I placed his coat on the clothes rack that always sat by the heater in the dining room and turned on the gas fire. I walked to the front room and asked him if he wanted tea or coffee, as I turned on the gas fire in there, too.

"Can you make me a masala chai? I think I need it."

"You can turn the TV on if you want," I suggested as I headed for the kitchen.

My house was so small that you could have a conversation from the kitchen to the sitting room by raising your voice. He told me the portrait of my mother was even better than the pastel in my room.

When I came back into the room, he was gazing at the photographs on the wall behind the sofa, grainy black and white images of my grandparents, each with a sandalwood garland. I put the tea tray on the small wooden coffee table and stood by him.

"The one in the dapper white suit who looks a bit like Clark Gable is my nana."

"So that's from whom you get your sartorial elegance," he teased and I blushed.

"The portrait of the man with a handlebar moustache is my dada. My nanima is the lady who has her head covered and my dadima is the lady with grey hair. Daddy says he can't ever remember her with black hair," I said as I pointed to the portraits on the wall. He pulled me towards him, and my breath caught.

"Not here, Nik," I said as I pulled away.

He laughed, "No-one's here to see us." My eyes drifted to my grandparents.

He raised his hands palms up at me. "Okay, okay, but it's going to be difficult," he whispered. I felt his warm breath on my neck. We sat on the sofa and I poured the tea into our best china cups.

He took a sip, "You've put fresh ginger in it, too. I love fresh ginger in my tea. How do you know what food and drink I like? Have you been speaking to my family?"

I smiled up at him taking credit for what my father does when he makes tea when it's cold. But it was quite strange that I somehow made food he loved. I pulled a face as I drank my masala chai. "You really don't like masala chai? So why are you drinking it?"

"Because you wanted it," I replied, raising a small smile.

He finished his tea and lifted his watch hand. "I have to get going."

"Can I make you sandwiches for the journey?"

He shook his head. "I've made some sandwiches for the drive home."

"Oh … can I make up some more tea to take with you?"

"Not sure I'll be able to drink it while I'm driving."

I switched on the TV. "Let's watch the news before you go to … to check on the snow."

"Okay as long as you sit closer to me. I'm not happy with this gap." He tapped the space between us on the sofa.

We watched the news; the lead story was full of pictures of motorway jams and travel disruptions. I held on to his hand tightly as the newsreader spoke to the reporters in different location.

"Can't you take a coach home?"

"There's hardly any snow in the south and the M1 isn't bad, they've just said that. I'll be fine, I promise."

"Will you call me when you get home?"

He pulled me to him, lifted my chin and kissed me softly. "Don't worry, I'll be extra careful."

I asked him how long it would take him to get home and he told me he'd be home by four-thirty. I clung to him, afraid to let him go.

"Before I go, I have something for you." He pulled me back into the dining room, took his coat and headed to the back door. I waited for him by the door; he was holding something behind his back. "I have a present for you," he said as he presented a rectangular box, wrapped in striped green and red wrapping paper, with a white ribbon bow.

I closed the door as I took it from him. "I haven't got you anything," I apologised.

"I just wanted you to have this." He took out a smaller package wrapped in the same paper from his coat pocket. We went back in the sitting room. I unwrapped the larger present carefully; I wanted to reuse the paper for something else. "A Sony Walkman? It's far too expensive, Nik."

"Nothing is too expensive for you, Ree. Besides you'll need to listen to the tape in private." He pointed to the other gift. I struggled to save the wrapping paper on the smaller gift.

"How much Sellotape have you put on it?"

"If I'd known you save wrapping paper —" he said, shaking his head "— I would have wrapped it with less tape."

"A mixtape and … batteries?" I questioned.

"Wasn't sure you'd have any at home. Listen to side B first."

I thanked him and promised I would get him a gift when I saw him after the break.

"Not sure I'll last until January. Might have to see you before then." He groaned and I watched his expression shyly through my fringe. He pulled me to him and we held each other. "Right, I have to go. Unless you want me to stay and meet your family," he teased.

We held hands until we reached the lobby; he kissed me and dipped me just like the photograph of the sailor in Times Square. I felt giddy from the experience.

He released a deep sigh. "I have to go." He nuzzled my neck and inhaled. "Want to remember your scent. One more kiss and then I'll go," his kiss was full of longing. I didn't want him to leave either, so I wrapped my arms around his neck as if my life depended on it. We held each other as long as we could. "I have to go." He pulled my hands apart, and he kissed my forehead. I held his hand as he stepped out of the house. His eyes drifted to our entwined hands. "You have to let me go." My heart felt like it had been wrenched out of my chest.

"Listen to the tape … I'll call you when I get home." I watched him close the back gate, then rushed to the sitting room. I lifted the net curtains and saw him climb into the driver's seat. He saw me, wound down the window and mouthed, "I miss you already." He puckered his lips and sent an air kiss. I found myself blushing; it was only a puckering of lips, I told myself. I gave him a shy wave.

He pulled away, honking his horn. My eyes darted left and right checking the street and exhaled with relief that no one had seen him.

I took my bags upstairs and dumped them in my room. I was excited to listen to the mixtape. I lay on my bed and listened as the first song on the tape resonated through my ears and I lost myself in the meaning behind the Hindi song lyrics, "Pal Pal Dil Ke Paas."

The words translate to 'you are near my heart for every single moment. You call this life a sweet thirst.'

I closed my eyes and listened to the compilation of Bollywood songs. All the songs were about love and longing and how the separation between the romantic leads was unbearable.

I felt the back door close and my eyes rested on the alarm clock. It was only 4 o'clock.

"Hello, Reena, are you home?" my father shouted.

I climbed down the stairs, the Walkman on my shoulder and the headphones around my neck. I walked to the door of the kitchen as he was putting his coat on the rack in the lobby.

"Had to let the baheno go home early today; the snow is causing a lot of problems with the buses."

My father was a foreman at a clothing factory. He always called the ladies who worked there his sisters.

"Can you make me some chai? I'm frozen." He walked past me straight to the front room, never once glancing at me. The tension between us had not eased since I left for university. I turned the tape in my Walkman and prepared masala chai the way he liked it, lots of ginger and lots of sugar. The Partridge Family and David Cassidy melodiously declared his love.

My heart had stopped and climbed into my mouth; I gasped for air. *What was Nikesh Raja trying to say?* We didn't know each other well enough; nine days was far too short. How could he feel this way so soon? I sang along quietly; contentment filled my soul as I realised I felt the same. I couldn't believe we had only been seeing each other for nine days.

I strained the chai in a mug, took some nasto out on a small side plate and brought the tray of snacks and the hot drink into the sitting room. My father was in his usual armchair; it faced the TV and was placed to the right of the gas fire; a small table was by its side. The TV was on, but he wasn't watching the Christmas film. He was thinner than my last visit, his face held a perpetual frown, and his lips were a thin line. His eyes finally rested on me.

"Don't come running to me for money when your grant runs out. You shouldn't squander your money on expensive cassette players. You have a perfectly good one in your room."

"Daddy it's fake. I got it from the market." I prayed my face didn't betray me. I was ashamed. I had never lied to my father.

The telephone rang. "It's for me." I picked up the phone.

"Hi, I'm home safe. Did you listen to the tape?"

"Yes."

"Did you like it?"

"Yes."

"Is your brother in the room?"

"No."

"Is your father there?"

"Yes."

"Can I call you tomorrow?"

"Yes."

"Ten o'clock in the morning?"

"Yes. Thanks for letting me know, Nikky."

"Oh, I like being called Nikky." He paused. "Say it again, Ree." His voice was soft and breathless.

"Take care. Bye." A trickle of sweat dripped down my neck.

"New friend?" my father asked. He had calmed down. I nodded and I rushed back upstairs saying, "I've got to unpack, Daddy."

Eight

I HAD BEEN UP SINCE SIX O'CLOCK, even though we came back after midnight from my father work's Christmas party.

I dreamt of Nik and our time in Bancroft Garden, and had begun a sketch of a couple sitting on a bench holding each other, watching the swans glide elegantly past.

My father shouted up to tell me the bathroom was free. I ran downstairs; he was making our usual breakfast of warm porridge, Gujarati-style. Amit took the teapot into the dining room. The clock above the fireplace read eight o'clock.

"Good morning, Reena. Did you have a good time last night?" Amit smirked.

We had both been subjected to my father's works dinner before, the women loud and constantly grabbing our cheeks muttering, "beautiful children, so light-skinned, too clever; I can find a family for a good marriage." Because my father was a widower, they felt they had to care for us; this was usually in the form of Tupperware boxes of food they prepared especially for us. My father teased them mercilessly, telling them that his cooking was better than theirs; they would gaggle like geese at his taunts, but insisted on bringing him Indian snacks. Last night was no exception. I brought back a Santa sack full of nasto; we were going to get fat on the fried snacks over the holidays.

However, last night, the conversation was all about my going to university. What a brave thing to do. How lucky I was to be allowed to go away from home. How could my father cope with being so far away from me? I told them Coventry was only half an hour away and if boys could go away to university, why couldn't girls do the same? "So headstrong," they said to each other, when I rebuked them. My father had become drunker and drunker as the conversation progressed. At the end of the evening, I had to ask for help from one of the husbands to bring him home. Amit had put him to bed, as was his job most days and, yet again, we were subjected to my father's inability to control his alcohol consumption.

I filled a bowl with the remaining porridge from the pan and sat in my usual place, opposite my father. For someone who had completely passed out from too much alcohol, my father was remarkably bright and fresh.

"Good morning, Reena." His gaze fixed on me.

"Good morning, Daddy. Good morning, Amit," I replied nodding to both of the men in my family. They are almost identical in appearance. The only noticeable difference is my father's skin hangs loosely around his thin bones and Amit's body is muscular. I know my father looked much healthier when he was Amit's age; I had seen the photographs of him with his friends and my mother, always smiling, playing badminton or cricket in sports whites, or at the beach in his swimming trunks. They have the same shaped face and the same shaped eyes, my father's rheumy, my brother's bright and sparkly. For someone who was only fifty, his eyes were ancient; they reflected the pain he had suffered and was still suffering. His hair had started to grey at the sideburns and gave him a distinguished air; it was slicked back off his face with Brylcreem. He always wore a white shirt and tie, and in the winter, he also wore a woollen waistcoat under his jacket.

Amit was wearing his usual uniform of V-neck jumper and dark trousers; I couldn't remember a time when he didn't wear a V-neck jumper in the winter. Sometimes he would wear a shirt underneath it and at other times he would wear a polo neck; that day he was wearing a cream polo neck.

"What are you going to do today, Reena?" asked my father.

I told him I was doing the laundry and ironing, and he nodded in approval.

"Are you going to Amit's Christmas party tonight?"

"Yes, she is, Daddy," Amit replied, "and we won't be back until the early hours of the morning; we're going to Baileys after dinner."

"Do you want me to make you dinner, Daddy?"

"No, I'll get fish and chips from the chippie." My father smiled at us.

It was ten to nine; the kitchen was clean, and I had sorted the dirty laundry into lights and darks while I listened to the mixtape. I sat anxiously waiting by the telephone for Nik to call me as he had promised. Time was playing tricks on me, and the hands hadn't moved in what felt like an eternity. What if he realised I was not the right girl for him? What if he got swept away with the romance of it all? What if he wanted something more and he knew I couldn't give this to him? What if he had changed his mind? What if. What if. What if. My stomach clenched as I thought of all of the reasons I was not good enough for him.

The shrill sound of the telephone relieved me of my what ifs. I looked at the clock and noticed it was five to ten.

"Hello." I clutched the telephone, waiting to hear his voice.

"Hello." His reply made my stomach churn; a field of butterflies fluttered inside.

"Hello." My voice was low.

"Hello, my darling. Did you sleep well?"

"Yes, and you?"

"I dreamt about you and our lunch date."

My heart leapt into my mouth. "What … did you say?"

"I dreamt about our lunch in Stratford."

I was speechless. *How could we have had the same dream?* It was as if we were one soul. I calmed myself down by repeating in my head: Soul mates are not real; soul mates are not real.

"Are you okay?" I heard the concern in his voice.

"Yes."

"Is your brother there, or your father?"

"No."

"So why aren't you talking?"

"Sorry, it's just … " I took a long deep breath and willed my heart to slow down.

"Did you miss me?"

"Yes, it's been odd."

"Good odd or bad odd?"

"That depends. Good odd because I miss you, bad odd as it's only been twenty hours and thirty minutes since you left. It's all a bit too fast."

"Why fast? I think it took too long for us to meet. As for missing me, we can change that. Listen, Peter is throwing a New Year's Eve party at his house. Why don't you come down for it?"

"I can't. Amit's coming down to spend the new year with Smita Bhabhi."

"Oh, and you don't want to leave your father alone?"

"It's better if one of us is here."

"So, how was last night? You were at your father's Christmas party, right?"

"Oh, it was okay."

"Okay, what happened?"

"Nothing. Just the usual. Something always triggers Daddy's mood."

"Do you want to tell me, or shall we change the subject?"

"Change the subject."

"Is it snowing there?"

"No, but we still have snow on the roads."

"There's nothing here. It melted during the night. Do you think our snowman's still alive?"

I laughed. "Snowmen aren't living things," I told him.

"Course they are. Don't you know anything, Ree?"

I smiled.

"Did that help?"

"Yes."

"Do you remember what I told you? Any time you feel stressed, come to me."

"So, how's the preparation for the engagement going?"

"It's madness here; Motaba is walking around with endless lists of jobs to do. Kaki and Rupa Bhabhi have taken the day off and are helping to prepare the mithai. I've got to go and buy exotic fruits and nuts. My sister, Jaish, has the job of making sure everything is wrapped up beautifully."

"What time does it start?"

I loved listening to his voice, and I imagined the way his hands moved as he talked, the way he tilted his head sideways when he spoke of his motaba, the lopsided grin.

"We have to be at the hall before ten for breakfast and the actual ceremony can't start until twelve."

"Why twelve?"

"It's the most auspicious time when the planets are aligned according to Guruji."

"Why do the planets need to be aligned?" I was confused.

"Motaba is a stickler for that sort of thing; she wouldn't let me come up to university until she checked the best day and time."

"We never do that. When Amit got engaged, we just drove to Woolwich and took our gifts to Smita Bhabhi's house and they drank some sweet milk."

"Dolat Masa would never do something as simple as that. He has booked Wandsworth Town Hall. Tell me, what do you have planned for this afternoon?"

"Very boring stuff really, laundry and ironing, then I have an appointment at the beauty salon."

"Beauty salon? Are you having your hair done for tonight's party?"

"No, I need to get other things done."

"What are you having waxed?"

"Nik!" I blushed, wondering how on earth he knew about waxing.

"I have two sisters and Jaish is always moaning about what women have to do to remain perfectly groomed." He inhaled. "I look forward to the day when I can examine your perfectly groomed body."

"Stop … you're embarrassing me."

"Why is it embarrassing? I'm telling you the truth."

"Stop! I'm going to put the phone down if you continue."

"Okay, okay. I'll stop. Are you looking forward to the dentist's Christmas dinner?"

"Yes, it will be fun. I'm not happy about going to Baileys after, though."

"What's Baileys?"

"It's a nightclub; Amit has arranged it. We're going to meet up with some of his old school friends."

"You didn't tell me that before? I thought it was just dinner."

"I didn't know."

"Will there be eligible bachelors there?"

I was holding on tight to the phone thinking what right did he have to talk to me like that?

"I don't know Nik … they allow all sorts to come into nightclubs," I retorted.

"But your brother's friends are going to be there."

"So … I've known them for ages."

He released a long sigh. "I'm not happy about you going to a nightclub. I can't protect you if I'm not there."

"I'll have my brother with me, Nik. No one will get near me, and it hasn't happened before, so it won't tonight."

"This is going to kill me. I'm not sure I can wait until the third of January."

"Nikesh are you still here?" I heard a woman's voice.

"I'm going soon, Motaba. Just finishing this phone call. What time can I call you tomorrow?"

"Any time after eight thirty in the morning, but aren't you going to be busy tomorrow?"

"How about the afternoon? What time can I call you?"

I told him that I was picking up the turkey crown from the butcher's at lunchtime. The silence expanded as he tried to think of a time to call me. "What time do your brother and father come home from work tomorrow?"

"Daddy's factory closes at lunchtime and my brother's practice closes at four … you can call me in the evening; no one's at home tomorrow after six. They'll be out until eleven."

"All right I'll call you at nine o'clock. Promise me one thing, promise you'll be safe tonight?"

"I promise, don't worry. Say goodbye, Nik."

"Bye, Ree. Dream of me tonight, I know I will of you."

I held onto the phone, waiting for him to put it down. One, two, three, four … my heart calmed down.

"Put the phone down." He sighed.

"You first."

"No, you first. You, you, you." He sang the lyrics of 'Mujhe Kuchh Kehna Hai'. "Your favourite film. I'll call you tomorrow. Bye … miss you … say goodbye."

"Goodbye, Nik … miss you." I took a deep breath and put the phone down.

The phone rang straight away.

"Hello?"

"Hello, forgot to ask did you enjoy the tape?"

"Yes."

"What's your favourite song?"

"I have two, 'Likhe Jo Khat Tujhe' and 'Can't Smile Without You'."

"My favourite's 'Pal Pal Dil Ke Paas'; you are near my heart every single moment," he sighed. "Think of me when you listen to the songs, kissing and holding you."

"I think of you all the time, can't help myself."

"I … " I could hear him breathe. "Speak to you tomorrow evening, bye."

I held the phone and listened to the tone. Time stopped as I found myself thinking I, what? I miss you; I like you. I want to be with you. I love you, and please let it be I love you. I was falling in love with Nikesh Raja. I had watched enough Bollywood films and read enough books to know of the emotions I was feeling.

Christmas Eve morning was bright and crisp; we had caught a light flurry of snow when we came home from Baileys in the early hours of the morning. I was tidying up the breakfast things after spending a long time drinking my second cup of tea and the telephone rang. I wondered who could be calling so early in the morning.

"Hello —"

"Hello … " My heart was in my mouth,

" — had to speak to you this morning, wanted to make sure you got home safe." His voice was hushed.

"How are you calling me? Aren't you at Suresh's engagement?" I asked.

"Yes, I'm at a phone box. We're waiting for breakfast, so … I sneaked out. How was the nightclub? Did you meet anyone?"

"No, spent all the time dancing with my brother and his friends. Do you know what it's like when overprotective men surround a girl?"

"Good, I'm glad you were protected."

"What time did you get to the hall this morning?"

"We had to leave at seven-thirty, as that was the best time to leave. So, we've been waiting."

"Okay, you know I'm safe. You should go back in."

"Tell me you dreamt of me."

"Can't remember what I dreamt of last night, had a bit too much to drink."

"I dreamt you were at the engagement with me."

I thought, I wouldn't have wanted to be with him. I doubted if his family would approve of me.

"Ree, did you hear me?"

"Yes, I was thinking about you at the nightclub. Do you dance Nik?" I couldn't recall a time when I saw him dancing at the parties.

"What a lovely thought. I'll have to dance the slow dance with you, Barry Manilow singing your favourite love song. I can't make you change your mind about

New Year's Eve?"

"I'm not coming to Peter's party — " I found myself recalling an argument with Umi about it when she left and I was fed up of having to justify myself " —told you yesterday, can't leave Daddy."

There was a pause. "Just the thought of you and the slow dance … " He inhaled deeply. "I have to go. I'll call you tonight and you can tell me what songs we could dance to when I take you dancing. I keep thinking of you, Ree; it's like you've become a part of me. Every thought is you," he crooned. My heart somersaulted. I exhaled slowly. How could something so encompassing happen so quickly? I thought of the Nat King Cole song and wondered how anyone could fall madly and deeply in love in days. But that was make-believe, life was never that simple. Life was complicated.

"Say something. Do you feel the same?"

I thought about our time together all the time, how I smiled at tiny things that reminded me of the days we had spent together. Even my brother had given me worried glances.

"I see you everywhere," I spoke quietly into the handset repeating the next line of the lyrics to the song he had just sung to me.

"My heart has stopped," he gasped, "I … like you, Reena Solanki. I like you a lot. Goodbye, call you later."

I held the phone and listened to the tone, waiting for my heart to stop racing.

A few minutes later, the phone rang. I picked it up, ready to tell him off.

"Hello!"

"What's the matter, Reena?"

"Hello, Daddy, had a couple of prank calls." Another lie I had told my father.

That evening he called at 9 p.m. as promised to tell me how he imagined me by his side. I could hear the longing in his voice and told him how I wanted to be with him too.

Christmas day was long and tedious. I wasn't as cheerful as usual, and my father and brother were confused. I loved the songs on the radio, but they brought with them moments of sadness and moments of happiness, the memories of my time with Nik. I was trying very hard not to show how I felt, by fixing a smile on my face, but my eyes kept giving me away and my family were puzzled at my duplicity.

On Boxing Day, I waited impatiently for Amit to get off the phone, pretending I was expecting a call from a friend who I had agreed to help with a film production. More lies to add to my already full repertoire.

The holiday dragged; I spent more and more time in the front room. My father commented on the number of telephone calls I was getting. My heart filled with joy when I heard Nik's voice; we wasted time talking about trivial things to keep each other on the telephone.

The telephone became my only tether to Nik, to keep me sane, to help me survive. We spoke for hours when the house was asleep, secretly communicating without our families' knowledge.

Amit left on New Year's Eve to spend the new year

weekend with Smita. I envied his relationship and his ability to openly display his happiness at spending time with the woman he loved. I wished I had agreed to go to Peter's party; I resented my father who had kept me at home. I knew he would come home drunk and his friends would put him to bed, and I would be the adult who dealt with his guilt of enjoying a night out without my mother.

I spent most of New Year's Eve afternoon preparing the mutton biryani we ate for dinner. While I cleaned up in the kitchen, my father changed out of his work clothes for his night out at the Indian Queen.

"Are you sure you don't want to come, Reena?" he asked as he pulled on his coat.

"Yes, Daddy. I need to do some reading before term starts," I said. I was losing count of the little lies I'd accumulated over the Christmas break.

My father hugged me; he had put on Old Spice and the spicy aroma filled my nostrils.

The coffee table was set up with a glass of my usual tipple for a celebration, gin and tonic, bowls of crisps and roasted peanuts. I had brought down a blanket and my sketchbook. It was seven thirty, and I found myself thinking of the times Nikesh Raja had crossed my path, the various times I had seen him around campus; in the library, the Student Union, in the canteen. When I had judged him as the typical Indian playboy who had some girl hanging off his arm. I was cross with myself to have held such a view. His absence made me jittery; I couldn't stay inside for long, or outside for long. My heart hurt from the longing I was experiencing. Could this be love? Is this how you felt? I asked myself. I had nothing to compare it to; I had no one to ask.

The shrill ring of the telephone made me jump; my heart pounded. The time on the clock was eight thirty. My thoughts drifted to where Nik should be at this time; he should be travelling to Peter's. It can't be him or can it? He had called me before outside our agreed time.

"Hello," I smiled into the phone.

"Hello, Sis. You sound happy. Was Daddy in a good mood after I left?"

"Amit … you got there safe and, yes, he's good." I made myself focus on my brother's voice.

"What are you planning to do tonight?"

"I have some reading to catch up on," I replied guiltily. I hated lying to my brother, but I knew he wouldn't approve of my relationship with Nik.

"God, you're such a swot. Put the reading down and grab yourself a drink."

"I have it all laid out, don't worry. I'll make sure I'm reasonably tipsy before the night is out."

He laughed. "Not too much, drinking alone is a bad habit to get into — " There was a pause as we both thought of our father.

"Give me the phone, Amit." I heard Smita Bhabhi in the background.

"Oh, yes, sorry honey, I'm passing it to Smita, I'll call you in the morning."

"Hello, Reena. It's a shame you didn't come down with Amit. We're going to Trafalgar Square tonight with my friends. Watch the TV news tonight."

"Okay, I'll watch. Make sure you get near the

cameras."

"So … do you have any news for us?"

"No. What do you mean?"

"Just thought you'd want to tell us something — "

I felt my head getting warmer, my cheeks blushing. I thanked the gods she couldn't see me.

"— you know you can call me any time and talk to me, don't you, Reena?"

"Yes, Bhabhi." My mouth felt dry. How did she know? Had Amit eavesdropped on my conversations with Nik?

"So, you'd tell me if something was happening."

"What have you planned for tomorrow?" I changed the subject; I was not ready to tell her how I felt about Nik.

We continued to talk about their excitement of spending a full weekend together and how Smita and Amit were meeting up with friends. I was happy for them. I thought my bhai and bhabhi were the luckiest people in the world. They were in love and spending the new year together, the first of their future life as a couple.

The incessant ringing woke me from a blissful sleep, and I tried to drown it out with a cushion. I had already drunk two glasses of gin and tonic as the realisation of the long hours waiting for his call dawned on me. The television wasn't interesting; listening to music hadn't soothed me. The songs brought images of his face, and sketching was impossible. I had curled up under the blanket and thought of Nik and our time together and fallen into a dream.

My eyes focused on the sideboard and the telephone wasn't there. I searched for it. If it was him, he would hang up soon. I panicked. I couldn't breathe. In my haste to find the phone the coffee table toppled, sending the empty glass and bowls onto the floor. My eyes rested on the vibrating, shrill sound of the brown Bakelite telephone as my glass rolled to it on the carpeted floor.

"Hello," I croaked.

"Are you okay, Ree?" I checked the time.

"Just dozed off."

"Hello, my darling."

"Nik! It's too early to call me. We were going to count down together. Call me five minutes before midnight."

"Don't you want to be in my arms and give me a kiss?"

I inhaled. "Yes I do, but you're in London … and I'm in Leicester, so we'll have to make do with the telephone. Peter's parents won't be happy if they see this charge on their bill. Call me later."

"What if I'm not at Peter's?" I listened for music or people chatting, "Are you dressed or are you in your pyjamas?"

"I'm dressed." My heart was thudding in my chest; my mind was racing, and I did not dare let the thought surface to my consciousness.

"I'm at the phone box at the bottom of Grasmere Street. Come and meet me, or can I come to you?"

"What?"

"Do I come to you or will you come to me?"

"How did you get here?"

"Easy really. I got in my car and drove up the M1."

"I'll meet you in the park across the bridge. Divya Ba

lives at the bottom of Grasmere Street," I said, unable to contain my excitement.

"Okay, I'll move my car and meet you there. Don't be too long. Can't wait to see you."

My heart was bursting through my chest. He was in Leicester on New Year's Eve.

I raced upstairs to put on a pair of warm tights and grabbed the new woollen hat and the matching mittens Divya Ba had made me as a Christmas present. I walked down Ullswater Street. The streets were empty; most people were either out to celebrate or watching television. I kept my head down, hoping I wouldn't meet anyone I knew.

He was leaning against a tree at the entrance to Bede Park; the butterflies in my stomach jumped somersaults in celebration at seeing him. I had seen the stance before, and a distant memory surfaced to my mind of another time and place.

I was shielding my eyes from the brightness of the sun. A boy with a Donny Osmond haircut was leaning against a tree, and he gave me a bashful smile. Another memory pulled at my subconscious, and I remembered the voice, and the eyes, the familiar way he leant in to talk and the magnificent smile.

I stopped from the sudden realisation that I had met Nikesh Raja before. The first time was when I was in my first year at grammar school on a school trip to Woburn Safari Park, and the second time was when we were at the Ram Katha in the summer of 1979.

He ran towards me and lifted me in his arms and whispered, "I've missed you so much. I couldn't bear it any longer." He asked me as he put me down, "Why did you stop?" His arms held me tightly.

"Just the shock of you … here." I hadn't wanted to tell him that we had met before. My mind was filled with nonsense about destiny, fate and chance meetings with soulmates. We stood opposite each other just holding hands; the park was quiet except for the sound of the River Soar. It was my favourite place and it would be full of the memory of that moment. He began to fill my face with kisses and moaned that he couldn't kiss my neck because of my scarf.

"Let's go somewhere else. It's too cold out here."

We walked back to the car, holding hands, not caring if anyone saw us. He asked me where we should go. I found myself wondering where we could go to at this time of the night. It was New Years' Eve: we would not find a place to sit and talk. I wanted reassurance he was with me and held onto his arm. I was uncertain that I was awake, perhaps I was asleep in my front room.

"Let go of my arm, Ree." He smiled at me as he lowered me down into the passenger seat. As soon as the car started, he took my hand and only let go when he needed to change gear. He was driving back towards the motorway. I thought he was going to take me back to Coventry to his student house and I didn't care. I needed to be with him; the time I was away from him was nothing compared to how I felt in his company. My heart sang; my vision was sharp, my lungs filled with oxygen. I felt alive, every nerve in my body charged. He turned onto the M1 north exit and looked at me, the golden shards dancing in his eyes, "I know of a place." He lifted my hand to his lips and kissed my palm. My body shuddered, and he laughed out loud and shouted, "You missed me too!"

After a short drive, he pulled into the service station at Leicester Forest East and parked in the car park. He leant across, pulled my car seat back and down and did the same with his, and we reclined facing each other.

"Let me look at you." His eyes lingered from the top of my head to the bottom of my feet. He unzipped my coat and opened it up to examine me again. I could feel the heat rise in my body as his eyes stopped at my throat, my chest, and my thighs as I imagined his hands stroking me, kissing me. The frown lines softened as he filled with the sight of me.

"I've missed you so much. Don't do this again. I'll never agree to be this far away from you. I love you and I've loved you since the first time I saw you. My life away from you doesn't have the same shine. I think of you all the time; I'm on tenterhooks. I can't stay inside for long and I can't stay outside for long. I've hardly slept. Tell me you feel the same, tell me you love me too."

My heart skipped; I couldn't believe someone like Nikesh Raja was in love with me. The feelings we both shared were the same, even his explanations sounded like how I felt.

"I love you, Nik. I don't understand it … I've hated not being with you every day … It's been nineteen days since you walked me to my halls." I found myself thinking that it was far too short a time. "It feels like I've known you all my life."

"It feels longer than nineteen days. I've never felt like

this before; it's as if you live in my heart. There's a line in 'Pal pal dil ke paas' - even my heart sings your song - that's how I feel about you." He leant in and kissed me with longing and desire. I returned the kiss, the gear stick preventing our bodies from touching.

"Damn it, let's go get a coffee. I'm sure they are open." He pushed his seat up, stepped out of the car and opened the passenger door. As he pulled me up, he pressed his body against mine and kissed me again; my legs felt weak and I clung to his neck.

We nursed our coffees for hours whispering, kissing, touching. We heard the cheers from the staff at midnight and kissed each other smiling in the knowledge we would spend more of the new year together. He told me how he had told Peter what he was going to do and how Peter had slapped him on the back and had said, "about time."

I told him about my earlier conversation with Amit and Smita and that I was sure my brother suspected I had met someone. He suggested a double date, but I told him I was not sure I could tell my brother yet. He asked me why and I lied saying my brother was protective, but the truth was, I was worried Nik would soon tire of me. After all, I was not the type of girl he usually hung around. All my insecurities came to the surface. What if he did tire of waiting? I was certain I was not ready to take our relationship to the next level. We sat inside for as long as we could, even when our coffee cups were empty.

He pulled me towards a building beyond the car park as we headed back to the car. I stopped; he smiled. "Come on. We'll find some shelter; the car's not good for what I want to do to you."

My breath caught, I was not ready for what he had said, and I held him back. He saw the panic in my eyes. "No, not that. I promised I'd wait."

We found ourselves leaning against a wall away from prying eyes.

He opened his coat and mine and our bodies touched through our clothes. His hands caressed my back and lifted to the back of my neck. He moaned, "Why did you have to wear a polo neck?"

"Didn't know I was going to be seeing you," I replied in between the kisses that took my breath away.

He frowned into my eyes. "Well, if the neck isn't available, I'll have to find something else." He pulled my jumper up and kissed the tops of my breast; the cold air created goose bumps and an electrifying sensation all over my body.

"Now that you're my girlfriend, Reena Solanki, I think a bit of heavy petting is allowed."

I had never felt like this before; he had released an urge in me I had never known before. I had read the articles in *Cosmopolitan* and knew enough about arousal.

He parked by the industrial laundry on Rydal Street; we were holding hands and listening to a tape of Nat King Cole, crooning about "L-O-V-E." I asked him why he was listening to Nat King Cole and he replied, "I met this amazing girl, who has strange taste in music. I wanted to know why she likes him so much."

He cleared his throat. "I told my parents about you."

"What ... why would you do that?"

"They knew there was something wrong; I was behaving like an idiot. They want to meet you."

"I ... think it's too soon," I told him.

"No, it's not. I've known for so long you would come

into my life. I've been waiting for you. I know you don't believe me. I thought I was in love, but that was nothing compared to what I feel about you, Ree. The days feel like weeks when I'm away from you; my heart slows down. It doesn't belong to me anymore. Think about it, we could go down for a weekend."

I gulped back the fear and changed the conversation. "When are you coming up to Warwick?"

"I can go up tonight if you want me to. When are you going?"

"You have to go home and rest. Promise me you won't drive up again tonight, Nikesh."

"Are you telling me off?" His eyes smiled at me.

"Yes, I am. I'll be there Sunday morning. My daddy's dropping me off. I'll see you on Sunday afternoon."

"I like bossy Reena. Your wish is my command, my lady," he teased as he mockingly bowed his head and kissed my knuckles.

"I have to go home … Daddy will be home soon." It was two o'clock in the morning.

He sighed. "Do you have to? I can't bear it," he groaned.

"It's less than twenty-four hours," and Nat King Cole sang "The Very Thought of You."

He pulled me into his arms, and we kissed for one last time. He said, "I love you, Ree, always have, always will; without you, my heart is empty." The words seeped into every cell of my body. How could he feel this, so soon? I asked myself.

We prolonged the goodbye by holding onto each other as long as we could. His eyes searched my face and I saw a frown and his glorious eyes wrinkle at the edge. "Tomorrow," I whispered, and his face filled with a smile.

"Yes, it's only tomorrow." He opened the door for me

and helped me out.

"I'm going to follow you in my car and wait until you're safe inside," he told me.

My words choked; I nodded instead. I didn't want him to go. I found myself feeling tearful and tried to breathe through the iron clamps across my chest.

"What's the matter?" he asked as he saw my eyes glisten and I forced my tears back. "Nothing," I whispered. "Just … I love you so much."

He opened his left palm, held my left palm to it, entwined his fingers and said, "Did you know there's a vein in your palm that's connected to your heart? Now our hearts are joined as one." His golden eyes were full of pain.

"Go. I'm coming." He released my hand, walked to the driving seat and followed me slowly in his car until I reached the alley in Grasmere Street. The house was quiet and cold, and I ran to the front room, turned on the light and lifted the net curtains to let him see I was safe inside.

I watched his car drive up the street, and hot tears streamed down my face. The hurt from the separation stabbed at my heart. I couldn't believe how intense my feelings were for him. "Even my heart sings your song." It felt as if my life had turned into a Bollywood film.

Nine

July 23rd, 1983 – Morning

I WAS WOKEN BY THE RINGING of the phone and I focused on my bedside alarm; it was early morning. The time blinked at me like a warning – 7.30am. Muffled footsteps approached my room and there was a knock on my door.

I pulled myself out of bed and wondered who could be calling me at this time of the morning. Suddenly, I was frightened, and thoughts of my family filled my mind. Has something happened at home?

I rushed to the phone, apologising to Umi's father. "Sorry, Shashi Kaka."

I had been staying with Umi during the summer break, as Jane had offered me a job at her production company in Soho, London.

"Ree … please … it's Papa."

I heard his wretched sobs.

"Nik, what's happened?" There was a silence at the end of the phone as he tried to control his emotions.

"He's … he's gone … I need you. I can't … he's gone."
My heart ached for him; I heard the loss and the pain
and promised him I would be there as soon as I could.
When I turned around, Umi had climbed down the
stairs and was waiting, her arm crossed, stifling a
yawn.

"Nik's papa has died. I have to go to him," I told her.
She nodded, understanding that even though Nik's
papa wasn't his father, he was still important to him.
She walked to the kitchen, and I followed, numbed
from the news.

"Dad, can I borrow the car? Nik's papa has passed
away, and he needs us."

"Of course, you can, Honeybee."

He always called her that, even when he was angry.

She hugged him. I wished I had the same relationship
with my father.

We were eating breakfast when the phone rang again.
Umi went to answer it; I strained my ears to listen.

"Thanks, Peter. What time will you be here? Okay,
we'll be ready."

She walked to the door. "That was Peter. He's picking
up Ravi and will come to get us, too. Won't need the
car, Dad," she said to her father and kissed him on the
cheek.

We buzzed at the gates of Shakti Bhavan at nine
o'clock.

Peter parked near the stable block, where several other
cars were parked up.

We walked to the front door of the house; the
Bhagavad-Gita was reciting on the sound system.
People had taken off their shoes under the covered

porch and we had done the same.

He was waiting, his head lowered, his shoulders stooped, at the double doors that led to the family room. I ran to him; I couldn't help it. I didn't care if anyone saw me doing it. I wanted to take him in my arms and comfort him. He held on to me like you would hold on to a raft in a shipwreck, sobbing into my shoulders. Then he saw the others standing behind me and moved me to his side. Umi gave him a huge hug and said, "We're here for you, Nik."

Peter held out his hand and then changed his mind and hugged him instead.

Ravi hugged him. That was the first time I had seen Ravi demonstrate any form of physical contact with anyone.

We went for a walk to Nik's favourite place, all five of us, holding hands, sometimes in a line, sometimes in a row.

We sat on the dry grass; the sun was streaming down; the heat had risen. It was going to be another sweltering day.

He started in halting waves recounting the events of the morning.

"We were woken up by Motaba, shouting and banging at the main bathroom door at six in the morning. We couldn't get the door open from the outside; we had to get Manu Kaka to take out the hinges. He had a massive heart attack. Our GP and the ambulance came at the same time. Papa's not been well since his return from Kenya. We should have taken better care of him. He said he was fine and that it was a summer cold. He didn't even go to see Anousha in the hospital when she was born, saying he didn't want to give her his cold. I should have persuaded him to go to the doctors."

"It's not your fault." I squeezed his hand.

"But he listens to me. I was busy going to see Anousha; I should have insisted."

"There are other people in your family, Nik. If they thought he was ill, they'd have made him go see a doctor. It's not your responsibility," Ravi comforted.

"Are Bhabhi and Anousha still at the hospital?" Umi asked him.

"No, no, they came home yesterday. Papa was so excited. He held Anousha from the moment she first came into the house until she finally had to go to bed at night with Bhabhi. Motaba was so cross, telling him he was going to spoil the child by holding her all the time."

"He got to meet her – that was nice," Peter said to give him some solace.

"Yes, but he won't see her walk and babble like he's seen Sammy and she won't know her dada." He had started to sob. Umi and I held his hand tighter, and Peter reached his arms around Umi to rest it on Nik's shoulder.

We stayed until the evening; the house filled with the Gita chants. We went to see Anousha in the cottage by the stables. Nik's haunting eyes lightened as he played with his niece. He wouldn't let me go with Peter, saying he would drop me home. I protested; I told him he needed to be with his family and promised to call him later.

When I called that evening, the conversation was full of sadness and loss. He repeated his usual "Goodbye,

I love you, Ree. Always have, always will; my heart is empty without you." I told him I loved him more than life itself and promised to speak with him after the Prathna they were holding every evening.

* * *

"REENA." I RECOGNISED THE VOICE. It was Nik's mother. I glanced at my watch; it was seven thirty in the evening. The daily prayers that were being held at Shakti Bhavan were scheduled to start at eight o'clock. It's a custom for Hindus to hold prayers and read from the Bhagavad-Gita for thirteen days to help the soul move on.

"Yes, hello, Kaki. Is everything okay?"

"No, Beta – do you know where Niku is?"

I had spoken to him last night and remembered every word of the conversation.

He'd said, "My heart aches. I miss him so much, Ree. How can you miss one person so much? He was always there for me. When I needed help, he would know it and understand how I felt. Not my father, it was always Papa. Have I told you that when I was young, he was the one I would get into bed with when I woke from a bad dream? Not Kaki, not Motaba, but Papa. He would pick me up, and we'd go to the kitchen to drink Ovaltine, and he would tell me stories of his travels in Africa. I would sit on his lap, and eventually, fall asleep. When will the pain stop? I can't bear it."

I couldn't say anything to comfort him, because his pain brought back mine. All I could say to him was that he would get better with time. It was too soon to feel happy.

"Reena?"

"Sorry, I spoke to him on the phone at nine last night, Kaki. He was upset."

"Did he say anything to you about going away?"

My heart was in my mouth when I told her he didn't.

"Do you know of any place he would go?"

"When did you see him last?" I had asked her, keeping my voice calm, although my mind was conjuring up images that broke my heart. What if he had hurt himself?

"He left in his car at ten. We just thought he might have come to see you."

"No, he didn't; if he had I would have … " My words choked in my throat.

"If you can think of anywhere he might be, please, please let me know. I'm worried. Goodbye, Beta. I'm sure I'm just being overprotective; he'll walk back through the front door any minute."

I was alone in Umi's house that night; her father had gone out with some friends, and Umi was at her circuit-training class. Where could he have gone last night and why hadn't he gone home? The first person I called was Peter: he asked me to call Ravi, and he said he would call Jay.

When I called Ravi, he told me about his friend Gino whose father had a wine bar in Rickmansworth; he thought that perhaps he'd gone to stay with him. I took out the telephone directory and searched for wine bars in Rickmansworth. There were two. One called Giuseppe's and another called Luciano's.

While I was searching for anything else that sounded

Italian, Umi opened the front door.

I told her about Nik's disappearance and the phone call from Shakti Bhavan.

"Have you called his house in Coventry?" she asked.

The phone rang, rang and rang. I held on and prayed for him to pick it up; eventually it cut off. The phone rang immediately after I put it down.

Peter was on the other end. "Hello – just spoke with Jay's mother. Nik went there last night."

I sighed with relief. "Thank God. Is he all right?"

"No, he isn't there any more. They both left last night."

"Does she know where they went?" I asked, hoping she knew exactly where they were, but my heart sank at Peter's answer.

"I'll call Jay's house in Birmingham. You call Dick, maybe he's heard from them?" he said as he hung up.

I called Dick and told him what had happened, and he asked, as he always did, if I wanted him by my side. I told him I was fine and would call him if he needed to come down. I began to dial the numbers for the wine bars I had found in Rickmansworth.

"Hello, may I speak to Gino?"

"Sorry, there's no one by that name here."

"Do you know of Gino, your boss's son perhaps?"

"No, sorry, my boss is called Paul and he doesn't have children yet."

"Hello, may I speak to Gino?"

"Hold on. Gino, there's someone on the phone for you."

"Hello, my name's Reena. Is Nik with you?"

"Hello, Reena. I've heard lots about you. Pleased to finally meet you even if it is on the phone. He was here last night till closing. Why are you asking about tonight?"

"His family is worried about him. He left home last night and hasn't come back yet.

Was he alone last night?" I had known the answer but wanted confirmation.

"No, he left with Jay. Oh shit, he's such an idiot — with Nik losing his uncle — I'm gonna kill him when I find him."

"Do you know where they are?"

"Yes, let me confirm it first. Can you give me your number and I'll call you back?"

I finally let out the breath I was holding and started to cry; big, fat tears rolled down my face. My legs gave way, and I flopped down on the floor, my back against the front door. I was so worried he had done something awful, and I hadn't noticed his plight. I felt guilty. I had let my pain hinder me from helping him deal with his. I made a promise to myself that I would never let him down again. I would try to be stronger for him for as long as he needed to recover from the loss of the man he loved like a father.

We sat in the hallway waiting by the phone to hear for any news of where Nik and Jay might be. When it rang Umi picked it up.

"No, it's Umi — a friend — yes." She indicated to me to find a pen. I pulled out a pen from my handbag. She wrote down the name and address on the note pad. "Thanks, Gino." She put the phone down. "Found him. He's staying in a hotel in Watford," she said out loud, and her shoulders relaxed.

Then I called Shakti Bhavan.

"Jai Shri Krishna. My name's Reena. Can I speak to Kaki, please?"

"Reena, it's Rita."

"Oh … hello. I've found Nik. I'm going to fetch him and bring him home. Can you tell Kaki."

"Thank you, Reena. We were so worried. He's done this before, you know."

I wondered what had triggered his disappearance last time and where he had gone.

When Jay opened the door of the hotel room, his eyes darted from Umi to Peter and then finally rested on mine. A fleeting look of resentment ran through them, and the smile on his face disappeared. Umi pushed past him. "Nik, Nik. Where is he, Jay?"

She turned when she hadn't found him in the room. I overcompensated by breathing too much, and mumbled, "I'm going to fall," turning to Peter. He grabbed me as I blacked out.

"Ree, Reena. My love. I'm here, I'm here."

Nik was holding me in his arms. He hadn't shaved, and his beautiful eyes were bloodshot. I was on the bed in the hotel room; his back was against the headboard, my head resting on his arms. I concentrated on those eyes. "Nik." I called his name softly and smiled. "I was so worried, I thought … " I let out tears I was holding in and held onto him tightly. He lifted my face up to his and said, "I'm sorry, my love. I didn't mean to worry you. I wasn't thinking." And he began to dab at my tears with a tissue.

I pulled myself up and saw Umi. She was staring angrily at Jay, who had sat down on one of the chairs by the window. He opened a brand-new packet of cigarettes and began to light one, ignoring her glares. On the table between them there was an empty bottle of vodka and several cans of Coke, the ashtray was brimming with cigarette ends. A blue carrier bag full of beer cans and packets of crisps sat on the TV cabinet opposite.

Peter was sitting on the edge of the bed, his back to us, looking down at the floor. His clenched fists held the bedcover. He turned his head slowly towards Jay and said quietly, "What are you doing, Jay? Don't you know the family is grieving?"

"I know the family better than you, Peter. Don't lecture me. I'm helping my best friend."

"This isn't helping," Peter pointed to the empty bottle and beer cans.

"I know what helps Nik and what doesn't. You only met him this year." He stood up and pointed, imitating a gun with his two fingers, his cigarette resting in between, contempt written on his face.

"Jay! Peter and Umi are my closest friends and if you hadn't noticed, Reena is my girlfriend. I love her … more than you could ever understand."

Jay glared at me, his dark eyes glinting with, I was not sure what – resentment, hatred, jealousy? "I'm going for some fresh air," he told us as he walked out of the hotel room.

I took Nik's hand and walked with him back to the house in Loudwater. We entered through the small kitchen; Peter and Umi were following behind. The atmosphere was strained when Jay came back into the room. We blamed him for letting Nik stay out, and for adding to his family's grief. He didn't want to come with us, saying he would make his own way home. We heard voices in the family room. All the heads turned to the door as it opened, and I led him into the room. He became a child. His head bowed. His shoulders slumped.

"Niku, my beta," his mother flung herself into his arms; I pulled away. Tears ran freely from the relief on his mother's face. Everyone from his family surrounded him, asking him if he was okay. The only person sitting down was Sarladevi. The petite, well-dressed woman sat rigid, in a simple white saree; her hair, usually neatly coiffured, was in a loose bun. The large red vermillion dot on her forehead was gone. She was no longer a married woman; she was the widow of Ramprakash Raja, the man who was the head of the Raja clan. Nik sped to her, ignoring everyone. He grabbed her hands as he knelt in front of her.

"Motaba, I'm sorry, I'm really sorry."

She began to cry and said softly, "You broke my heart more by disappearing, Nikesh. You're not a child anymore. Your papa would have been worried sick."

"I won't do it again. Forgive me, Motaba."

"You're my son; of course I forgive you." She kissed him on his forehead.

Nik's mother hugged me and said, "Thank you, thank you, Reena. You found him and brought him back."

"It wasn't just me," I told her.

She nodded. "But you knew where to look."

When we left that evening, Nik's mother asked if I would come to the daily bhajans they held at Shakti

Bhavan. I hesitated, unsure of Nik's motaba's reaction. She misread the anxiety and thought I was reluctant to travel up from London.

"I'll get Niku to pick you up from London, and you can eat with us," she had said, adding, "I just think you will help him deal with the loss."

Every day for the next five days I was picked up from Dean Street in London and taken to Shakti Bhavan. The drawing room furniture was re-arranged as it had been for the puja, when I first came to meet the family. We sang bhajan and read from the Bhagavad-Gita to help the family deal with their loss.

Jay came with his parents, the day after the incident. He saw me sitting next to Nik and sat as far away as possible. I saw Nik's eyes glisten with hurt as his best friend avoided him. We didn't see him again until the morning of the funeral.

The atmosphere at the house was strange. During dinner everyone cooed and laughed at Anousha, celebrating the small milestones babies have in their first few weeks. After the prayers, everyone was subdued and reflective, the memory of the family patriarch still fresh and raw in their minds.

One evening after the prayers, I was picking up the bhajan books in the hallway and I heard Sarladevi in the study.

"There must be something wrong with the alignment of her planets, Jagdish Bhai?"

"Sarladevi, I've examined her charts. Just a tiny misalignment in the ninth house; nothing to worry about." The Guru replied.

"I don't believe it. Look again: she came home, and my

husband dies. There must be something. I don't want her to be a risk to my sons or Anant Bhai." Her voice was angry. It had dawned on me that she was talking about Anousha. I wondered how an innocent child could be held to account for the death of her husband. I remembered the Guru's words from the puja, 'The beginning of your life was difficult, Beti.' I felt an immediate urge to protect Anousha.

"We can have a Sunderkand paath, but it can't be done until the third month."

I didn't like eavesdropping, but I had realised with Sarladevi it was the only way to understand how she really felt about you. She said one thing to your face and said something else behind your back.

After hearing the conversation, I began to notice all the little injustices poor Anousha experienced from her dadima. She hardly held her. When people commented on how beautiful she was, she reprimanded them and told them all babies were adorable. She wouldn't allow Rupa Bhabhi to bring her to the bhajans, telling her daughter-in-law to rest. She stopped Nik and Suresh from spending time with her, always giving them a small task to do when it was their turn to hold her.

The day before the funeral, I told Nik I would come to the crematorium with our friends. He urged me to come to the house, but I declined, telling him the last rites and prayers should be a family affair.

"But I need you with me," he pleaded, tears in his eyes. I took his hands in mine and spoke gently and softly. "You have to be strong for your motaba; she has lost her husband." I had seen the disapproval in the woman's eyes when he held me at the bhajans, when he couldn't cope. "I promise to be at the crematorium before you arrive." I took him in my arms and kissed him softly and earnestly, telling him with kisses I was always going to be by his side. We sat in the car for a long time afterwards, not wanting to let each other go.

***

I DREAMT OF A WHITE BOX and crowded places and woke with a start at six in the morning. It was far too early to get out of bed; the funeral was not until ten o'clock. So instead of disturbing Umi and her father, I took out my sketchbook and began to sketch Nik's papa from my memory; his laughing eyes, his ready smile, the way his head tilted to one side when he sat observing the countryside. I made a mental note to myself to go back to the ruin on the grounds of Shakti Bhavan again to make sure I got the essence of the space.

Peter and Dick arrived at 8.45 a.m. to pick Umi and me up. We had decided we would wear black after seeking approval from Nik's kaka. Traditionally at a Hindu cremation, everyone wore white. We arrived at the crematorium quicker than expected and walked to a small chapel where there was a reflection garden and some benches.

The sun was shining brightly, and the heatwave that had hit the country showed no sign of abating. Both of the boys were wearing black. Dick had managed to find a black jacket and was wearing a pair of tight black trousers and his black winklepickers; they wore white shirts with sombre ties. Peter was stunning in a

Hugo Boss suit. I had decided to wear a pair of black cropped pants from the sixties and a white, puffed-sleeve blouse with a round collar. I didn't have a black jacket, so I had picked up a black cardigan. Umi was wearing a cream sleeveless shift dress with a simple black jacket. We sat basking in the sun, our eyes protected with sunglasses.

"Hey, you look like a bunch of Benetton models," Ravi shouted as he approached us. He was also wearing black suit, his jacket flung over his shoulder.

The black funeral cars arrived, and the Raja family emerged from them, all dressed in white. The women dressed in pure white sarees and the men in white cotton jabo pyjamas. The first thing Nik did when he stepped out of the car was come up to us. He hugged everyone in turn and finally held onto me, silent tears rolling down his cheeks. I glanced to where his family were greeting the other mourners and his mother give me a small smile. Once he had calmed down, we walked in pairs to where the family had lined up to meet the mourners.

"You need to stand here." I pointed to a spot next to Suresh. His eyes were full of fear. "It's okay, Nik. I won't be far. You have to do this for your family," I said, my voice hushed so only he and Suresh could hear. His older brother drew him closer. Nik began to cry again. My heart ached, and I turned away, to hide my tears.

We stood at the back of the crematorium; the place was full to the brim. Everyone had turned up, all of their friends and family as well as business associates. The chapel could not accommodate everyone; many people waited outside while the simple ceremony was performed.

The Guru was wearing a white turban and read chapter two, verse twenty-two of the Bhagavad-Gita. The shloka was translated into Gujarati, and then he told everyone in English.

"As a person sheds worn-out garments and wears new ones, likewise, at the time of death, the soul casts off its worn-out body and enters a new one."

His melodious and resonating voice brought a calmness to the people seated in the front rows.

The family lined up outside, and the mourners walked past, palms pressed together, murmuring Jai Shri Krishna. We allowed everyone to line up first and waited by the side. Nik kept glancing at me, and I nodded at him reassuringly. Once everyone had walked past, we approached the family and he stepped away from the line-up and took my hand. I could tell he had found it difficult; his eyes had lost their lustre, the edges red from the tears.

"Have you seen Jay?" he asked me.

I shook my head. "I'm sure he's here. He'd want to be here for you."

We found Jay by the side of the chapel with a group of young people. He was wearing a white jabo pyjama, and they were a mixed group, male and female, some in black suits, others in smart, dark clothing. They approached Nik once he had moved away from his family. I stepped away, giving them space for their private grieving. A tall blonde woman with immaculate makeup, her hair styled like Farrah Fawcett-Majors in *Charlie's Angels*, took Nik's face in her hands and started kissing him on his lips. I was shocked; my stomach turned. It was such an intimate moment, even the people surrounding them were embarrassed. Jay turned his head to where I was standing and glowered directly at me, triumph in his eyes. How could he allow whoever she was to do that to him? He hadn't even pushed her away. He just succumbed to her kiss. I averted my eyes and fixed them on my feet, trying hard to force back the tears that stung at the back of my eyes. I felt someone wrap their arm around my shoulder and pull me to them.

"It's not what you think, Reena." I looked up at tall Mediterranean man with curly-hair; his voice sounded familiar, his eyebrows knitted together, his eyes full of regret. "She likes the attention. Hi, I'm Gino, we met on the phone." He raised a smile; his teeth were white, and both incisors were prominent and large. "Nik is a lucky man to have found you. You're beautiful." His deep dark-brown eyes explored my face. My mouth felt dry; I couldn't say anything, afraid a wretched sob would escape.

"Ree, Reena, my love." He took my hand in his. I didn't want to look at him. I tried to pull my hand away, but he tightened his grip.

"Sorry, Gino. Can I take her away from here?" Gino released my shoulder, and Nik pulled me inside the chapel. "I'm sorry, I didn't expect her to do that. I was surprised, that's all."

I pulled my hand away, and he released it as I walked to a pew and sat down. I began to cry, my mind filled with the number of times I'd felt inadequate, unwanted, unequal with the people he knew. What was the point? I would never be good enough, and soon he would tire of proving to them that I was. He belonged to one world, and I belonged to another. I could hear him breathe, inhale deeply, slowly exhale.

He gave me a fresh tissue, and I used it to collect the tracks of tears that poured out of my eyes. "This isn't going to work," I said, unable to look directly into his magnificent eyes, concentrating on the small indent on his top lip instead.

"Don't say that. You and I are meant to be together. I'm an idiot. I shouldn't have let Julie do that; she's a tease."

"Julie! That was Julie?" I shouted angrily at him. "Your first love: the one you took years to recover from?"

"Who told you it took me years?"

My mind recalled Jay's words. "He still thinks about her even after all these years."

"I told you how long it took me. A couple of months, that's all. I told you. Do you remember, after our lunch date, about all the one-night stands? I've been honest with you, Ree. I thought I was in love with her, but I was wrong. You are my first love. I love you, always have, always will. I've known it for so long. Please forgive me." His head fell, and he rubbed his forehead. "Please," his eyes pleaded. "I've found it hard this past week. Today was difficult … seeing him again." He sobbed. "I can't live without you … it will be too much to bear. It was just a kiss, nothing else. I'm sorry. I've done it again … I've hurt you." He held his head in his hands, his back bent.

I found myself remembering the times he had turned up to see me, the telephone conversations, the mixtape. The way my heart skipped every time I heard his voice. How I'd felt when we didn't know where he was earlier in the week. How I'd ached at the thought of losing him. I thought of his best friend, Jay, who had taken a dislike to his new friends and me. I knew that many women found him attractive; I saw them on campus. Even when they knew he was with me, they

169

stared longingly at him. Perhaps it was my jealousy that was making me feel that way. My heart ached for him as he sat with his head bowed, and I felt his pain. I reached for his hands and said, "I love you, Nik. Always will."

He smiled a thin smile. "Promise me, you always will."

I nodded and said, "Always."

He kissed me longingly, wanting to possess me, own every part of me. I felt the same, and we kissed until our need to feel loved was quenched.

"I could stay here with you forever, but we have to go. Kaki will have sent a search party for us."

When we opened the chapel door, we found Gino standing guard at the entrance. He turned around and took my hand, "Hello again, Reena Solanki. You've certainly made a big impression on Nik and his family. I'm looking forward to getting to know you. Come on, everyone has been gone for half an hour. Let's go and celebrate your papa's life." He placed my hand on his forearm, and we walked to the car park.

There were more cars parked at home than at the crematorium. The marquee was set up on the lawn. There were waiters serving fruit juice and water to the people milling around. A station was set up for people to wash their hands and faces. The women in Nik's family had changed out of their white sarees and were wearing sarees or salwaar kameez in muted shades of grey and brown. His motaba was dressed in a pale-cream saree with minimum jewellery and without the red dot on her forehead. She appeared older and a little frail. Nik's father had changed into a cream jabo pyjama and walked towards us.

"Ah, good, Niku. You'll need to go and have a shower and put all your clothes in the wash." He saw the reluctance in Nik's eyes. "Don't worry, Beta. I'll keep Reena safe." Nik headed to the house, and I said, pointing to the washing stand, "I'll go and wash my hands and face, Kaka." He seemed surprised.

"I was just going to instruct you Beta, but you already know."

I raised a smile and nodded.

"Come on, Gino. You have to wash your hands and face before we can eat or drink anything," I told him. As I explained about the Hindu burial service and the meaning behind the bathing and washing, Nik's father stayed close as he promised his son.

"But, why do we have to wash? I wasn't at the house this morning," Gino asked.

"In India, the mourners are exposed to the ash from the cremation. We're not exposed to ash here, but it's something Hindus still observe," I replied.

"Even I didn't know all that, Reena. Where did you learn that?" Nik's father said.

"My daddy told me." I replied confidently, knowing my father was an expert on Hinduism.

"I will have to meet your father; he's brought his daughter up very well," he replied. My heart stopped, and my mouth went dry. I was too frightened to think about my father's reaction when I eventually told him about Nikesh Raja and my relationship with him.

His father was as good as his word and stayed by my side until Nik returned. "Feeling better, son?" he asked him, and he nodded. His father took my hand and placed it into Nik's. "Told you I'd keep her safe and sound. Take Reena to get something to eat and drink." He pointed to the tea and coffee stands and walked back to mingle with the rest of the mourners.

Ten

September 1983

EVERYTHING CHANGED AFTER THE FUNERAL, and I recalled the day Nik had come back from his trip to India.

I woke up after having a delicious dream of sandy beaches and warm seas. A ray of sunlight was streaming through the gap in the curtains, pointing to the top drawer of my bedside cabinet. I opened the drawer and picked up the photograph of Nik taken by Dick at Amit's wedding.

"Hello, my love. Good morning." It had become a ritual; the first thing I did when I woke up was to take out the photograph hidden in the back cover of my diary and stare at his beautiful face.

Since New Year's Eve, when he had come to Leicester to tell me he loved me, we had spent a good deal of time together. He made a point of coming to see me in the morning before lectures and a point of wishing me goodnight. We had been on dates and spent as much time as possible together. I moved to London at the beginning of the summer holiday and met him and his family often; they knew I was his girlfriend, especially after the sudden death of his papa, the man who was the head of the household. After the end of the mourning period, Nik's brothers and his parents had gone to India to Varanasi to scatter his ashes in the Ganges.

Hindus believe the goddess, Ganga descended from heaven to earth in the form of the river and she flowed in all of the three worlds, heaven, earth and the netherworlds. Varanasi became a crossing point for the living or dead to reach Moksha. Those who could afford it waited until the time of Shradh to take the ashes of loved ones to the sacred site. Nik's family had gone as soon as Shradh started; they planned to visit Varanasi and feed the poor and hungry in the many ashrams. It had been challenging to communicate while he was in India. I missed talking to him, hearing his voice, seeing his face. But the wait would be over soon; he was due back and we would at least talk on the phone until we met again.

I had come back from my first holiday abroad. Jane had persuaded my father to let me go to Spain to her apartment in Marbella for a week. At first, my father was hesitant telling Jane I should come home and stop being a burden on other people. Amit and Smita Bhabhi had tried to persuade him, too, as had Umi's father that it would be a good experience for me. He was much happier once he learnt Jane had also asked Umi and cautiously agreed. My father insisted on paying for the flight and gave me some pocket money, even though I had been paid for my summer internship with Jane and didn't need his help.

University would start in a week and I was back home in Leicester after working in London in the summer. I had told Smita Bhabhi about Nik as the summer break started and she had spoken to Amit. He wasn't happy about the relationship, but he reluctantly accepted it, insisting on speaking with Nik. He interviewed him just like Nik's papa had when I met him, asking about his future career, where he could see himself in five years. What were his lifetime goals? Nik had joked that it felt like an interrogation. I laughed and told him at least I had a small family unlike his, who had asked me similar questions when I first met them in March.

I WAS MAKING DINNER when the phone rang.

"I'm back. Just landed, going home, showering and then I'm driving up to see you." I made him promise me he wouldn't come up straightaway. I heard him inhale, controlling the desire to drive up. "Okay, I'll come tomorrow. See you at our favourite tree at 12 o'clock. Make an excuse, any excuse. I'm coming earlier to take you away for our birthday. Somewhere alone, just you and me."

I told him I wasn't sure I would be able to convince my father and his voice came out harsher.

"I can always come to spend the weekend with you, no compromise. I've been away from you for two weeks. Two long, painful weeks. You have no idea how I missed you." He released the anxiety and said. "Please, Ree. Say yes … say you'll meet me? Bags have arrived — I'll call you tonight. Our usual time. Say it, tell me you love me and missed me too."

"I missed you, Nik. I love you, always and forever."

"I love you, always have, always will. My heart is empty without you."

When my bhai and bhabhi came home, they both frowned when they saw me sitting in the front room listening to my Walkman. Smita Bhabhi said something to Amit and they both smiled. After dinner, while tidying up in the kitchen, she asked quietly, "Is he back?" I grinned at her. "Aah … the long phone calls start again," she laughed.

I spent the rest of the evening smiling, thinking of the following morning, when he would be leaning against the tree, his hands in his trouser pockets, waiting and watching me cross the bridge as I walked up the path. The thought of him made my heart ache. I longed to be in his arms, to feel his soft lips on mine. I raised the courage to ask my father. He had taken to sitting in the dining room since I came back to allow me to spend more time with my brother and his wife.

"Daddy, can I go down to London tomorrow? I'm meeting up with some of my friends tomorrow night."

"So, it begins. You no longer want to spend your birthday with your dear old daddy. Friends have taken over." He peered at his whisky glass. My heart stalled. I felt the tears sting in my eyes. When he gazed up at me, he was smiling; I hadn't expected it and hugged him.

"I love you, Daddy. Thank you." And then I started to cry.

"What's the matter, Reena? Why are you crying?"

I shook my head at him. I didn't know why I was

crying. Had my longing to see Nik overwhelmed me, or was it because my daddy had finally relinquished the burden of being my protector?

I had observed little changes in his behaviour after Smita had become part of our family. She was good for him, always enquiring about his work, talking to him about his friends, his life in Africa. He had let go a little. For the rest of the evening I sat with my father, instead of watching TV with Amit and Smita. We talked about the time when we were children and our trips to the seaside, his love of swimming, the recipes we had developed together. I felt happy there was hope for our relationship to grow.

*** *** ***

I TOSSED AND TURNED ALL NIGHT, waking every hour and peeping at my alarm clock; time was dragging its heels. The dawn chorus took an eternity to arrive. I had gone up to my bedroom after Nik called and packed my bag several times, choosing outfits and discarding them, not knowing where we would be going or what we would be doing. We had arranged to meet with our friends in London for dinner on Sunday, but that was all I knew. It was going to be the first time I would be spending a night with Nik, sleeping in the same room, waking up together. I knew I could trust him, but I was nervous.

He saw me first as I turned onto the path and ran, his long legs traversing the distance in minutes. He picked me up and swung me around. I let my holdall drop and held onto him, burying my face into his neck. I inhaled him, taking his scent into my lungs, the sandalwood of his aftershave, the lemony scent of his body, the smell of tobacco I had become so accustomed to. I floated in the air, my feet dangling, his arms holding me tight. I felt his heart against my heart, both recognising what they missed, and our heartbeat synchronised. I was whole again.

"My love, my heart. I'm never going anywhere without you again." His voice was full of love and longing. Time briefly stopped, the sound of birdsong disappeared, and I only saw and heard him. I pushed at him to put me down and my eyes took him in, checking he had recovered from the pain of losing his papa and his heart had healed a little from his visit to India. When our eyes met, I gasped, my stomach flipped so many times, I felt I was on a relentless rollercoaster. His eyes were full of golden fireworks, his tanned complexion enhancing their colour. He took my hand, lifted my arm and twirled me around as if we were dancing.

"Is that a new dress?" I wore a short shift dress in a block design, mostly white with a royal blue and red rectangles and a black and yellow striped hem. I loved shopping in charity shops in London and had picked up the dress inspired by a Mondrian painting. "I'm going to die here and now. I'd forgotten how beautiful you are. Do you have a tan?"

He kissed my cheeks first and then lifted the hair off my left ear and kissed it and then my right. He lingered there and said. "Let's go before I do something in front of everyone." I hadn't even thought about the people in the park and peeped furtively at my surroundings. A man with a dog walked along the towpath, he was no one I recognised.

"Where are we going, Nik?" I asked him, as the car turned onto the M69 to Coventry. He held my hand as he drove. The Commodores, and Lionel Richie sang 'Just To be Close to You.'

"I can't drive down to London, yet. We're going to my house."

"Oh," I said.

He turned his head to me. "Do you want to go somewhere else?"

"No, I want to go to your house." I said thinking the same; I, too, couldn't bear the long journey down to London.

He stopped the car in the drive, stepped out to open the garage, and pulled the car in. "Leave everything. We're going to get better acquainted." He opened the passenger door. The front room was full of flowers, baskets, huge bouquets, small flowerpots, the sweet smell of roses filled the air. I turned to him, wrapped my hands around his neck and said, "When did you do this?" excited at the sight of my favourite flowers.

"I got here this morning and bought all the flowers from the florist in Cheylesmore. You deserve to live among roses, my love." Then he kissed me, softly at first; his kisses telling me how much he had missed me, how I completed him, and then with some urgency. I felt his passion build up. My body responded to his kisses and my stomach lurched. We kissed until our appetite for kissing was satisfied. I lingered in his arms, knowing this was where I belonged, resting my head on his chest as we lay on the sofa surrounded by roses, red, yellow, white, pink, orange and every hue in between.

A sound of gurgling and rumbling came from my

stomach, and he kissed me, "Hungry?"

I laughed. "Do you have food in the fridge?"

"The fridge is fully stocked, and we can survive here without stepping out until Sunday." He raised his wicked eyebrow and a chill ran through me. I pulled him to the kitchen. I knew his kitchen as well as mine. As our college year progressed, I had spent days with him, studying in his rooms, eating together, at times, only going back to my room to sleep. But there were other people in the house, then, not just the two of us. We savoured the proximity of our bodies and the opportunity to be alone, no one watching us or disturbing us. I began to imagine what our life could be like in the future, in our own home, cooking, cleaning, sitting together, and listening to each other's breath. We talked and we kissed as we filled each other in on the two weeks we had spent apart. When I told him about my holiday to Spain, he became cross and said,

"I wanted to be the first person to take you abroad. Damn Jane, how could she?" I laughed at him and kissed him for being cross. He questioned me on where we went and who was there; he asked if anyone had danced with me at the clubs. He wanted to know if I drank sangria and whether I liked it. He told me of his trip to Spain after his O-level results and how he got drunk on sangria and couldn't drink it again as it brought back memories of being sick.

"Hope you've brought something to wear for dinner? I've booked the Royal Court Hotel. I lied about being holed up for the whole weekend." He teased me. I lifted two outfits: a kameez suit I'd made from some georgette, printed with purple daylilies on a white background and a paisley print silk dress in grass green.

"White, always the white. Did you make it?" His voice came out as a groan.

"Yes, I was going to wear it instead of the dress but changed my mind."

"Glad you did. I would have had to kiss you heavily there and then in that outfit—" he'd replied, staring intensely into my eyes.

We were in his room. Earlier he had asked if I wanted to sleep in Ravi's room and when I told him I wanted to sleep in his room he had blanched.

"Are you sure?"

"Why? Don't you trust yourself?" I had teased.

"No, no, I do. I promised I'd wait." He had gulped out his words.

I had taken my outfits and hung them in his wardrobe, my clothes next to his. I'd taken my toothbrush and put it next to his. It all felt so right that this was where I wanted our relationship to go to next.

I had gone to the bathroom to change my clothes, and I walked in to find him shirtless, his back turned to the door, his muscles well-formed. I exhaled loudly. He turned and raised his wicked eyebrow, his eyes glinting. Instead of reaching for his shirt, he grabbed at my arms and pulled me to his body. He lifted my chin and kissed me, and for the first time, I touched his body without the restriction of a shirt. He pulled away, reluctantly and sighed. "You're going to kill me this weekend. I'm going to need all my strength not to ravish you. That and cold showers." His lips parted as he smiled.

The Royal Court Hotel was an old Tudor manor, and

their restaurant was busy with tourists and Coventry residents. Nik had booked a table for 7.30 p.m. We were presented with a menu and he ordered Laurent Perrier to drink. The waiter asked for my ID. I pulled out my Student Union card for proof of age from a small white clutch bag. We both smiled at this. No one believed I was eighteen; it had become a familiar request. We ordered from the à la carte menu.

When the main courses arrived, the champagne loosened my inhibitions, and I was feeding Nik with morsels of food from my plate. His eyes sparkled with happiness, as he tasted it, licking his lips. His legs encased mine under the table. He closed them as I raised the food to his mouth. I giggled every time he did that knowing he was teasing me with his actions; every morsel couldn't elicit the same reactions. Once our plates had been cleared, the waiter brought the dessert menu and we chose to share a Black Forest gateau. This time, Nik fed me, and I closed my eyes as the food was delivered to my mouth.

"If only that fork was my finger," he leant in to tell me quietly. I opened my eyes, glanced surreptitiously to the tables around us, checking no one heard.

After dinner, we walked around the grounds while Nik smoked his cigarillo. There was a chill in the air, and I wrapped my purple chundadi around me like a shawl. He pulled me to his side, his body a few degrees hotter than mine and I no longer felt the cold, even though my flesh was covered in goosebumps.

We could not keep our hands off each other when we got back to the house. He grabbed me by the waist, and we walked side by side up the narrow stairs to his bedroom. He closed the door and pulled me to the bed, and lay down facing me, fully clothed, looking hungrily into my eyes. I kissed him, pulling him closer to me; my desire had built to a crescendo, every hair on my body stood to attention. He felt my hunger, my passion, my desire, and pulled away.

"I'm ready," I said blushing at the thought of what we were about to do.

"What?" His voice rose a little.

"It's. When. I can't. Wait." I spoke in small breaths.

"Are you sure?" he quizzed. "One hundred per cent sure. I promised you."

"One hundred per cent sure, Nik. I knew I was when you left for India."

He stood up, pushing his hair off his face. "Shit, I don't … I have to get some condoms."

I smiled and rummaged through my holdall. "Nik," I said holding up a small rectangular box. He strode to where I was standing and kissed me, slowly, methodically, making sure he covered every inch of my face; he worked his way down to my neck and then kissed the tops of my breasts.

"I love this neckline; I'm going to enjoy taking your clothes off," he said as he ran his finger along it. I pushed his jacket off his shoulders, and it dropped on the floor. I began to loosen the buttons of his shirt, concentrating on every contour of his chest. I ran my hand through the hairs on his chest; he waited for me to finish and pulled his shirt off. His eyes were smouldering embers, the golden shards were on fire, and my stomach was full of butterflies knocking against its wall. He pulled at the hooks at the front of my dress and pulled it over my head. He grabbed the tie cord of my bottoms; the knot loosened, and they fell to my knees. "Sit down," he groaned as he knelt at the end of the bed and pulled them off.

"Oh, white. God … help … me." He said the words in short breaths. I pulled at his belt and zip and pushed his trousers down. He stood up and stepped out of them, hopping and pulling at his socks. He pulled me up and then twirled me around as he had done before as if we were dancing. My hungry eyes feasted on his long legs, his small hips, his flat stomach, his muscular arms, and his beautifully sculpted face.

I suddenly felt shy and covered my body unsuccessfully with my hands. I had worn a bikini in Spain and had not felt as conscious about my body as I stood with Nik in my white broderie anglaise bra and knickers. He laughed, "you're beautiful, my love. Let me see." He pulled my hands away.

"Can we turn the lights off?" I whispered.

"Oh no, I don't think so … I want to see every bit of your perfectly groomed body."

He pulled me towards him, and his kisses were full of lust and longing; he devoured me, possessed me, touching every part of me. He fell back on the bed and pulled my body on top of him. I could feel his arousal. "Oh God, Ree." He grabbed at me and pulled my legs apart and I straddled him. He thrust his hips and started to gyrate them. "A bit of reacquainting with each other first," he whispered. I shook my head, grabbed his hair and kissed him, my tongue exploring his mouth. "We've got plenty of time," he said as he slipped off my bra, continuing to move his hips. "Tan marks, I'm going to want to examine that a bit more," he said as he viewed me and began to kiss me along the parts of my breasts that were still pale. He kissed every part of my body; every sensor on my skin was alive, and I wanted him to claim me. I wanted to become part of him. He flipped me onto my back, and he was on top of me. "I want you to enjoy your first time." His voice was gravelly and sent shivers over my body.

"Please, Nik. I can't wait any longer." I pulled at his pants, pushing them over his pert backside. He pulled at my knickers and reached for the condoms. He pushed himself inside and we finally became one. My breath caught, and my heart raced, and he groaned and then I was lost. I felt tears well up in my eyes and I began to cry. The feeling of belonging to him overwhelmed me. He relaxed and rested on top of me, raising himself on his forearms; his exquisite eyes focused on mine and he frowned as he saw the tears.

"Did I hurt you?"

His eyes turned entirely golden, the light brown and sand shades had disappeared, and tiny lines appeared on the edges of his eyes.

"No, I … I'm just."

He pulled me to him as he lay down next to me and kissed me softly, engulfing me in his arms, our bodies entwined. "I didn't mean to hurt you, my love." His voice was hushed.

"You didn't." I kissed him back, telling him with kisses the tears were not from pain, but from the feeling of love that had engulfed me. The kisses were the best, soft, long and sweet, we just couldn't stop smiling and kissing. Eventually, we fell asleep holding each other, naked and entwined in each other's arms.

I woke up in the night, my throat dry, gasping for some water. Nik wasn't in bed with me. My eyes searched in the dim light for him and rested on where he was sitting. "What's happened?" I asked, pulling myself to sit to take a sip from the glass on the bedside table.

"You happened," he replied and smiled.

"Come to bed." I lifted the bedcover. I pulled myself on top of him and we made love again. My lust for him hadn't abated. I needed him to be part of me once more.

When I woke up again, I saw him watching me, and his eyes focused on my face.

"Good morning, my love." His lips brushed mine and my body awakened.

"Good morning, what time is it?"

"We don't have to worry about time, my darling." He threw the covers off the bed. I instinctively covered myself.

"Oh no, you don't. I'm going to want to inspect you a bit more." He scrambled off the bed and opened the curtains; sunlight streamed into the room. I blushed when I saw he was already aroused. "I can't believe Reena Solanki is naked in my room. I want to take a photo of you in my mind."

He stood at the bottom of the bed, lifted my foot and planted soft kisses, his tongue, leaving cool spots on my skin as the air touched it. I closed my eyes to savour the feeling as he worked his way up my body.

***

OUR SECOND YEAR AT UNIVERSITY was very different; most nights, I would stay with Nik in his house in Coventry. Everyone knew we were serious and one day we would marry. Our friends joked about it all the time, telling us we should elope, forget about our parents' approval. I had met all of his family and Nik had spoken with my brother, but we weren't ready for marriage yet. I knew I would spend the rest of my life with him, but we were too young, and the nagging doubt of our different social class gnawed at me. We lived a life of students, enjoying our freedom to do whatever we pleased. The holidays were stressful. I went to visit Umi often and used her as my alibi. Nik would turn up at the most unexpected times as the holiday dragged on, his need to be with me never fully satisfied until the beginning of term when we were back to seeing each other morning, noon and night.

In the summer break of our second year, Nik went to India as it was the first anniversary of the death of his papa. This time he called me every day at 8 p.m. My father wasn't happy about the phone calls but had worked out there was more to the relationship than just friendship. He told me repeatedly it would end in tears, as people like Nikesh Raja have their lives planned out for them. I wouldn't accept Nik's life was planned without me in it.

Summer 1984

THE SHOCK OF THE RESULT of the pregnancy test left me breathless. I was on the contraceptive pill and had been since our first mishap with a condom in the autumn term of our second year. I waited anxiously for the phone to ring. Time stopped, the minutes slowed to hours and my stomach clenched into a tight cannonball. I had picked up some brochures about unwanted pregnancy from the pharmacy and hidden them in my sketchbook so no one would come across them by chance. I read them over and over again, making a list of the pros and cons of the options.

The ringing of the telephone made me jump. I lifted the receiver to my ear.

"I've been worried about you all day, darling. Is something wrong?" These were the first words I heard from him as I picked up the telephone.

I was relieved; he had a connection to my feelings, and I thought this must be true love. I thought about the times when he turned up when I was dealing with an issue that upset me. I thought all was well and he would understand the decision I had come to and would be there to support me. I let the tension that had built up since the morning release.

"I'm pregnant, Nik." My voice came out as a whisper, knowing he would know what to do. But I was wrong. He ranted and raved about entrapment and how I had betrayed him. He told me he hadn't thought I was that kind of girl. He'd said he was too young and the third year at university was an important year for him.

I listened in shock; he hadn't even allowed me to say what decision I had come to. I thought we were a couple who took our relationship seriously. My father's words swam in front of my glistening eyes. 'People like Nikesh Raja have their life planned out for them.'

He stopped and the silence between us expanded. I heard him take long breaths to calm himself. My heart was deafening, and I held the telephone tightly to my ear. My throat burned and constricted, and my voice came out as a croak. "I've found a clinic in London and I'm going to book an appointment as soon as possible. I know how you feel about it. I'll write to tell you where and when."

"I'm sorry, Ree … I can't … " he said after a pause.

He hung up without his usual words of goodbye and

my heart broke. I felt the rip and clutched my chest to stop it hurting. It took all my strength to pull myself together, staring at the phone, willing him to call me again to tell me what he always did when we departed, the words that made my heart sing, the words that would help to heal the tear, but he hadn't.

I braced myself to go back into the dining room. My father put down his paper and stared at me. "I'm going to my room, Daddy. Goodnight," I said, pretending to be happy when my life felt like it was over.

He hadn't called me at our usual time the next day. When he called the following day, I held onto the hurtful words and turned them into anger and told him I would write with the details of where and when. My letter was short and to the point. I reminded him that birth control was never one hundred per cent safe and I thought we were in a committed relationship. I told him that I, too, didn't want to ruin my third year and it was more of a burden on me than him. I told him I was disappointed that he hadn't known how important my course was to me. I reminded him of the reasons he said he loved me. Finally, I said I loved him and felt betrayed that his love for me wasn't the same and hoped if he loved me a little, he would be at the clinic on the day to support me.

I booked to see my GP and I received a referral letter from him which allowed me to contact the Marie Stopes clinic in London.

Umi called and I broke down and told her everything. I was on autopilot, not allowing myself time to think about what I was planning to do and the consequences of my actions.

Eleven

Autumn term, 1984

AMIT AND SMITA INSISTED on dropping me back for my final year at Warwick University. The events of the summer left me drained of any emotion. I hated maintaining a happy face and pretending my breakup with Nik and the despicable thing I had done was okay. My friends were great and my bhai and bhabhi were attentive. Since my father had heard from Dolat Mehta, his anger bubbled to the surface for days, and he started to drink more heavily again. He made me sit with him and listen to him before my return.

"When you brought that boy home, I knew he would break your heart. The Rajas have a reputation, Reena, even when we were in Africa." He paused, nursing his glass, staring at the ice. "One of your mother's school friends worked for them. Before she started working there, we used to meet with her quite often at the hotel dances. She had a beautiful voice and would sing with the band. But once she started working for Ramprakash Raja, we didn't see her out at all. In

Africa, single young people who live in a hostel have a curfew. Every man and woman had to get back to their rooms by a certain time. So, when a young lady doesn't come home until the early hours of the morning, she gets a reputation." I realised then that my father had an inkling something had happened, something had tainted his daughter. He put down his glass and took me in his arms and told me. "Be careful, my daughter: rich people have different morals. We are usually the ones who suffer."

I spent the weekend slowly and deliberately taking my time packing and unpacking my clothes and leaving some of the brighter, beautiful clothes in my wardrobe. I was dreading going back to university and didn't arrive until late Sunday night. I knew I would have to see him. He would be on campus, at parties and in the library. We had planned to live together secretly, and I had agreed with Umi for appearances' sake, and visits from my family, I would take the smallest room in the house we lived in Leamington.

Umi, Dick and Feroza were already settled in and were watching TV in the shared sitting room. I popped my head in to say hello and Feroza came and hugged me with genuine warmth and affection. Umi had found the house for us in the summer of our first year. We had asked Dick and he'd asked Jenny, Saleem and James who he had met at Drama Club to make up the numbers. We found Feroza in summer term after Jenny, who used to live in the small room, moved out because Dick had broken up with her. It was a big house with two bathrooms, two small kitchens and reasonable gas-fired heating. Our landlord, Mr Singh, was surprised we were a mixed house share and insisted on installing bolt locks in our rooms. The kitchens and bathrooms became segregated: the boys used one and the girls used the other. We would occasionally go for a meal in the boys' kitchen when we wanted fried foods.

I had spent far too much time with Nik last year and vowed to make amends, making sure I spent more time getting to know my housemates just as well as Umi and Dick. I lay in bed and thought of Feroza, our new housemate, hoping that she wouldn't fall for Dick's easy charm. She was just his type, tall and slender with beautiful olive-coloured round eyes, her skin the colour of single cream.

I saw him leaning against the wall, his head down, his shoulders slumped. His hair was long and greasy; he was wearing a tracksuit and had grown a beard. At first, I didn't recognise him. He was nothing like the Nikesh Raja I met in the first year, adorned in expensive clothes, dressed to impress. I hid, I physically hid behind a tree trunk, making myself thin and small and watched him as Ravi tapped him on his shoulder to break his thoughts. He turned to Ravi and began to walk to the lecture theatre. Even his gait had changed: instead of long strides, he shuffled. My heart thudded in my chest, and I inhaled gasping for oxygen. I found myself thinking, if the sight of Nik is going to leave me in this state, how will I survive the year? After that day, I went to my lectures and headed home to my house as quickly as possible. I tried not to linger on campus for longer than I needed. I borrowed books from people and worked through the night, making notes, so they could work with them during the day. My life changed. The places I loved being – the campus, the lake and the library – I avoided. I behaved like a fugitive in a film, hiding from a pursuer. I went into Coventry and discovered the library at Lanchester Polytechnic. I found a job at Woolworths instead of working at the Art Centre.

Weeks passed and life became a little more tolerable. I controlled my heart. I told myself I'd made the right decision and that Nikesh was not my true love and fairy tale endings were not real life. He had sent me a mixtape of songs for my 21st birthday which I had left in my room at home with the Sony Walkman. I didn't listen to music any more. It didn't feel right to hear lyrics of love and loss when every cell in my body felt the loss keenly. I changed my clothes. I wanted to blend in, to disappear. I wore jeans, dark trousers and big baggy sweat-tops just like all the other women, instead of my quirky clothes. People noticed and made comments, asking me what was wrong; as an excuse I pretended I had put on weight and didn't have time to make and mend this year.

Peter and Umi had started to see each other seriously. They had briefly dated in the first year and broken up. They were one of those couples who kept drifting together and didn't mind that their relationship was one of mutual sexual consent. I admired how they could keep their friendship intact and envied them for their maturity. I knew they had met several times during the summer holiday and I was happy for them. I was glad to see they had finally realised that their relationship could be both. Umi disappeared to Peter's. He still lived with Nik and Ravi. When she came back from being with him, she would come and check on me sitting in my room, her face full of sadness. I wondered if the sadness was for the loss of the double dates we discussed endlessly, or something else she didn't want to share with me.

One evening I came back from Coventry and found Peter and Umi in the sitting room; they urged me to sit with them. I was reluctant. I had worked in the morning and had spent the day in the library researching for my essay and didn't want to sit and have a conversation.

"Ree, please sit. We have something to tell you," Peter implored.

My heart sank; the first thought that came into my mind was something terrible had happened to Nik. Even after what had happened between us, my mind and my heart betrayed me. Tears welled up in my eyes and I slumped on the sofa and began to sob. Umi rushed and took me in her arms, stroking my hair, and wet fat tears fell on my lap.

"What's the matter?" she asked.

"Has something happened to him?" I whispered.

"Who?" said Peter. "Nik?" He asked. I nodded. They both exchanged glances and Umi let out a small laugh of relief.

"I know you still love him. You're a mess and he's a mess."

I listened to Peter.

"Nik came to stay with me after the … He just sat and said it was his fault over and over again. I know the whole thing upsets him. He keeps blaming himself. But it wasn't all his fault. He left his hometown in India as soon as he got your letter. He was stuck on the train for four days because the monsoon washed away the tracks. Everything that could have happened to stop him from getting here did. He couldn't get a ticket back to the UK as the flights weren't available and when he did the flight was diverted to Birmingham. If the flight had landed in London, he would have been by your side at the clinic. He loves you … I can see that, I know it. Did you know I was the one who encouraged him to come to tell you how he felt?"

I nodded and remembered New Year's Eve.

"Please forgive him or … at least talk to him," Umi added.

"I can't … please don't." I didn't know how to process what Peter had just told me.

"But you love him … How long can you avoid him?" Umi replied.

"People get over these things … He'll find someone else and forget." My heart ached at the thought of him being with someone else, but I held on to my rage, *it takes two people to make a child*.

His words reverberated in my mind. 'I didn't think you were the type to trap me.'

We sat quietly for a while, Umi and Peter holding my hand. Eventually, I stood up, hugged them, walked upstairs to my bedroom and cried until I fell asleep.

***

HE WALKED TOWARDS ME, his head bowed, as I left the library. I stopped on the steps, building up my courage. I told myself I could not avoid this situation any longer. I would sooner or later have to deal with him being in the same place as me.

There were a group of first-year students playing Frisbee, shouting and running across the lawn. The Frisbee hit me on my shoulder. I screamed from the shock and my books flew out of my hands and fell down the steps. He appeared by my side, holding my arm.

"Are you okay? Did they hurt you?" His eyes were full of rage and fire. He ran up to the group and shouted, "You fucking idiots! You could have hurt her!" The first-year students stared at him and moved away, frightened by his outburst.

A ginger-haired man who came to retrieve the Frisbee helped to pick up my books. Nik strode back to the steps snatching the books out of his hands, and the man walked back to his friends looking anxiously over his shoulder as his strides lengthened.

"Are you sure you're all right?"

I could smell the alcohol and tobacco on his breath. I nodded at him and pulled out my hand to take back my books.

"Ree, please forgive me … " he implored. "I love you." His eyes were red; there were dark circles under them, and the golden shards had disappeared.

"Please, Nik … We have to move on. It's over."

His face dropped. "I can't move on. Please, let me explain."

I clenched my fist and made myself gaze directly in his eyes. "Sorry, I've made up my mind. Can I have my books?"

He reluctantly handed my books back to me and, for a moment, I remembered a time when he carried my books for me. He stuffed his hands in his sweatpants pockets and left me standing at the bottom of the steps as he walked across University Street to the Student Union.

***

AT THE END OF MY SHIFT at Woolworths, as I headed out of the staff room, I saw him again. He was leaning against the wall. He approached me hesitantly; my stomach was in knots, my heart paused, I was unnerved.

"Hi … "

His eyes dug into my soul, and I sighed; he heard it and shrank a little. His eyes cast down to the holdall I was carrying.

"I thought I'd … " his voice trailed off.

"Go home, Nik. Please don't do this to me." My voice was low. It was my mother's death anniversary on Sunday, and I was going home to spend it with my family.

"It's your mum's death anniversary. I thought I could give you a lift home."

"Please … not today … How many times do I need to tell you. I'm not interested."

I let the tears that were blurring my eyes run down my face. One of my colleagues walked towards me and asked if everything was okay. I nodded and thanked her. Nik pulled out a handkerchief from his trouser pocket and handed it to me. He took my bag and waited for me to walk towards the car park. I shook my head and said, "I'm going by coach, Nik."

"All right." His eyes searched my face and my heart skipped a beat. He turned towards Pool Meadow and we walked in silence to the coach station. I kept my distance from him by putting my hands in my coat pockets, jutting my elbows out, to stop our bodies touching. The sky was dark and cloudy; a cold freezing drizzle began to fall. I pulled up my hood to protect my head. He ignored it like someone accustomed to the rain and cold.

I asked him for my bag and he quietly urged, "Can I wait with you until the bus arrives? I promise I won't say anything."

The bus was due in fifteen minutes, but the wait was excruciatingly long. I could hear him breathing softly next to me, the warmth of his body, the smell of tobacco and musk of his aftershave that I loved so much. He had shaved, but, without the beard, his face was gaunt, and the circles under his eyes more pronounced. His cashmere coat hung off his shoulder. When the coach arrived, he took my bag and handed it to the driver. He watched me climb the steps on the coach and waited in the shelter for it to leave. I took out a book from my bag and pretended to read, trying my best to ignore him, taking deep breaths to stop my heart from beating so fast. The coach pulled out into Fairfax Street, and when I glanced back at Pool Meadow, he had moved out of the shelter and was watching for the coach to join the Ring Road. His hair was sopping wet from the rain.

***

I GOT OFF AT MY USUAL stop and walked up the main road to my house. I let myself into the cold house, and, instead of turning on the fire in the dining room, I headed straight to my room. I unclenched my jaw and released the tension I had held through the journey home. I began to cry hot, angry, sad tears. It is his fault we aren't together; he was the one who has not supported me in my time of need.

It was 4.30 p.m. and I realised my family would be home soon. I lifted myself off the bed and my eyes fell on a brown tattered envelope on my dressing table. I picked it up and scrutinised the unfamiliar postage stamps from India. Inside it was a blue, flimsy airmail envelope, and I held my breath: I recognised the handwriting. I tore at it, my hand shaking.

I had to put the letter down twice before I finished it. I had to let my eyes refocus several times as the tears blurred the cursive writing. I read the date over and over again to make sense of when he had written it. It was straight after the phone call. He had proposed; he wanted to marry me. I understood now why he was so depressed. I found myself thinking of how unlucky I was. If this letter had arrived when it was supposed to, I would have still been at home. I would have called him, we would have decided together, and the guilt that was gnawing at me would not have been my own. I know I would have forgiven him. My heart began to hum. I read the postscripts again:

P.S. We'll make great parents if you choose to keep the baby.
P.P.S. Please say yes, I can't wait for you to be my wife.
P.P.P.S. I've loved you since the first time I saw you.

He did try his best to support me; his love was just as strong as mine. What should I do? Should I call him, or should I wait until we meet face to face?

I reread the words – Reena Solanki, will you marry me?

The words of the Guru filled my ears: 'Your life will be full of hardship.'

25th July '84

My darling Ree,

I'm sorry, so so sorry. I think about what I said to you the other day and still don't understand why I said it. I panicked, my love. I shouldn't have put the phone down the way I did.

I know I upset you. I could sense your anger like an electric charge. I tried to call you straightaway. I'd forgotten to tell you how much I love you or my usual goodbye. You must believe this, Ree, I did try, at first. All the lines to the UK were busy and then my fua came in and asked me who I was calling so late at night. I know this isn't an excuse, but I need you to know.

I hate this distance from you. I shouldn't have come, but, my love, you convinced me that doing this would help me deal with my pain. I can't grieve for my papa, knowing you are alone and need me to be there for you. I love you, please forgive me. I'm in more pain than ever before, because I can't be with you.

I knew you needed me and what did I do? I ruined it; I went back to being a spoilt child.

I had wanted to tell you we were going to stay at a farm by the family shrine and would be feeding the surrounding villagers and I couldn't call you. But my stupidity has ruined everything.

We set off on the 22nd July at 4 a.m. to go to our family shrine. I had hoped to find a Telephone station to call you, but there was nothing on the way and then everything became impossible. You'll understand when I bring you here, my darling. I couldn't find anyone who had a phone. They must have thought I was a madman, taking them to one side and begging to use their telephone.

When we came back to Porbandar, I called you several

times in the hope that you'd be at home and when I finally got through, I heard your rage. I don't blame you, my love. I hope this letter will get to you to help you to make your final decision. I'm going to send it by express delivery. I will support you with whatever you decide. I await your letter about the dates.

Do you remember what I said on New Year's Eve, that I had always known I would meet you, that I'd been waiting for you to come into my life?

Reena Solanki, will you marry me?

I've wanted to ask in a romantic setting, but at least you have it written in ink.

I have wanted to ask for a long time, but the universe and a higher power has stepped in for my lateness. I should have told you on New Year's Eve that you are the girl who I will marry, but I was too scared you'd laugh in my face and tell me to grow up, so I didn't.

Marry me, your pregnancy is God's way of keeping us together, now no one can object.

Neither my motaba nor your father has an excuse to keep us apart. They have to agree to let us marry and spend the rest of our lives together.

I'm sorry for not saying that when you told me. I let nerves and panic get the better of me. I'm a terrible person without you by my side. I revert to being childish and self-centred. I am a better person because of you. Please know that. I will do my best by you.

I wait for your letter, please, say yes, please, accept my offer. I'm aiming to get home as soon as possible. You have my number here in Porbandar.

If you can't phone, I'll be waiting for you at the clinic. I promise I won't let you down.

I love you, Ree, always have, always will. Without you my

heart is empty.

Yours forever, Nik

P.S. We'll make great parents if you choose to keep the baby.
P.P.S. Please say yes, I can't wait for you to be my wife.
P.P.P.S. I've loved you since the first time I saw you.
My eyes focused on the bright red parcel on my bookshelf in the reflection of the dressing table mirror. I opened it and inside there was a note.

My darling Ree,
I am to blame for your hurt. My stupidity. I have lost the thing more precious to me than breath itself.
I thought after you'd received my letter you'd have understood, but I was wrong. Deeds are better than letters. I tried, I tried to be with you on that day. The date is engraved in my heart forever, Tuesday 14th August, the day I lost you and I lost our future. The universe is playing with us, playing with our hearts. Please listen to the tape, it isn't much, I know, but perhaps you'll know I ache as much as you. I'm sorry. I love you so much. These few weeks without your love have been the longest in my life. I can't eat; I can't sleep. I thought you felt the same as I do. I was wrong.
Just listen to the tape once and do whatever you wish with it afterwards. The songs and the lyrics will tell you how I feel, and I will always love you. I'm sorry I hurt you.
I wish I could be with you today on our 21st birthday.
I love you, Ree, always have, always will. Without you, my heart is empty.
Yours forever Nik

The weekend was exhausting. I didn't feel like going to garba but did to satisfy Amit and Smita Bhabhi that I was happier. My Divya Ba, Smita Bhabhi and I had prepared my mother's favourite meal for a late lunch–early dinner so I could get back to university at a reasonable time. Back at the house, I took my Walkman and listened to the tape Nik had given me.

***

I GLANCED AT THE FLOOR NEXT to my bed and that's when I saw Umi's feet. She asked me about my weekend, and I told her everything. I showed her the letter and the note and made her listen to the mixtape. She smiled when she read the letter and was visibly upset when she stopped listening to the tape.

"What are you going to do?"

I shrugged my shoulders and replied, "I don't know. I love him, but … " I let my voice trail, *but what?* Is my love enough; will I regret it when we face another crisis and he can't cope? Has what has happened changed him and, for that matter, me, too?

On Tuesday morning after my lecture he was waiting for me outside. I was confused – he had a lecture at the same time; I knew when he was on campus and when he was not. I used that knowledge to avoid him, so what was he doing here? He rushed towards me. I stepped back, and he lifted his palms in apology.

"Sorry, sorry. I heard you read my letter."

"Oh." I replied, and we walked down the stairs onto the path winding through the small grassy area near the Art Centre. The clouds parted and the pale-yellow winter sun shone on the bare branches of the oak tree. Although it was the first day of November tomorrow, it felt warmer than it had for some weeks. His gait had changed; he wasn't shuffling as he had been when I'd seen him the previous week. He kept turning his face to mine and the golden shards in his eyes were dancing. I was aware he was very close. He stopped under the tree and stood in front of me, blocking my way. Everyone skirted around us. He leant in, and whispered in my ear, the warmth of his breath sending a tingle down my spine.

"Say yes, Ree. I love you. Tell me you love me too."

My lungs stretched, screaming for fresh air. I gazed into his delicious eyes. I missed him. I missed him so much. He started to sing 'Tum Agar Saath Dene' from the mixtape. A group of female students walked around us giggling as he sang and gesticulated; his voice was as beautiful as before, just a little hoarse.

"Did you listen to the tape?"

I raised a small smile and averted my eyes, and he continued.

"If you look at me and keep smiling, I will keep looking at you and sing for you. Let's get a coffee." He took my hand and led me to the cafe in the social building. I pulled my hand away feigning that I needed to adjust my scarf.

He brought the coffee to the table and sat opposite me, gazing intently into my eyes. I kept my hands on my lap.

"What's wrong?"

"I … don't know … I missed you, but … I don't know what's next?"

Lines developed on the edge of his eyes, and he chewed at his lower lip.

"I know I hurt you; please give me time to make it up to you." He wrapped his fingers around my hand as I held my coffee cup and pulled them away once he saw the look in my eyes.

"I'm not ready for … us," I told him.

"All right … I like courting. Can I court you?"

I laughed. Why did I feel this way? Those eyes had me every time. A small part of me ached from the hurt and I was scared he would do it again. But this was the first time in a long while that my heart beat properly.

"Okay, courting it is then."

He sensed the reluctance in my voice and lowered his head fractionally.

"Thank you for the coffee. I have to go to a tutorial." I got up. He held onto my hand for longer than necessary, his eyes smouldering, and he raised his left eyebrow and tilted his head.

"Until we meet again, Reena Solanki."

My heart was jumping and bumping against my chest. I was afraid it would tear its way out. I tried to walk as calmly as I could to the door, feeling his eyes on my back as I left the building. What have you done? I told myself off for agreeing to his request, for not being stronger.

The next day he found me in the library and asked if I would join him for lunch. He waited for me after my shift at Woolworths on Friday, and he took me out for a drink at the Penny Black. We talked about our dissertations and how the workload had increased; we asked after each other's families – the one thing we needed to talk about we avoided. I wanted him to ask how I dealt with it, and I wanted him to tell me how he dealt with it.

Each time we met, he never tried to hold me or kiss me. After each meeting, he behaved like a Jane Austen gentleman; he brushed his lips on my knuckles and bid me goodbye.

Twelve

ON THE DAY OF PETER'S 21st birthday party. I woke up sweating and gasping at five thirty in the morning. It was too early to go for a jog, so I decided to finish the painting I had started in the summer. Almost two hours later I was finally satisfied that the portrait was finished. I changed into my sports clothes, leaving the paint to dry, and went for a run along the towpath of the River Leam.

He was waiting outside in the car. I knocked on the window and asked him why he was waiting. He lowered the window and said, "I brought you some breakfast." He lifted a shopping bag from the passenger seat. "Can I come in?"

I opened the door to the house and led him to the kitchen. He put the shopping bag on the worktop and emptied it. He had brought everything we needed for a full English breakfast, including a small loaf of bread. He reached for the frying pan and baking pans in the cupboards. He had done this before, and my mind drifted to last spring. He smiled at me and asked me to sit at the table. He worked with efficiency, turning on the grill as he opened the can of beans and emptied it in a saucepan and sliding two slices of bread in the toaster. He reached for the butter and oil from the wall cupboard by the cooker.

"Do you want fried or scrambled eggs?" he asked, holding up an egg.

"Fried, please."

He is good at making an English breakfast: the bacon just crispy at the edges, the sausages were cooked through and when he fried the eggs, he used the oil to baste the top to cook the yolk soft and whites firm, leaving the edges crispy. I ate slowly, making the most of the taste. He took big bites and gulped down his coffee, crunching on his toast periodically, dropping his fork on his plate with a clang. He was sitting opposite me, and that wasn't his usual place.

"Feeling better?" he asked once I'd finished. He leant over and took my hand. He knew I was anxious and had come to ease my nerves; there was that sixth sense of his. I smiled at him and thanked him.

"Can I come to pick you up tonight?"

I nodded.

"No, she's coming with me, Nik." Dick's voice was curt.

Nik turned in his chair towards him. "Just thought I'd pick you all up."

"Thanks for the offer, but we're fine." Dick leant against the doorframe with his arms crossed. Nik stood up. The air was charged as the two men glared each other out like two gunslingers in a Western. I broke the tension in the kitchen by picking up the plates and took them to the sink. He moved to the cooker and started to tidy up. Dick made a coffee and reached for a cereal box. He sat down at the table to eat his breakfast and watched as we washed up. He boiled the kettle again and refilled his mug.

"If you ever hurt her again, I won't be held responsible for my actions."

Nik's jaw dropped; I had never heard so much malice in Dick's voice; he was usually such a kind and gentle man, easy-going and amiable. "Do you understand?" His steely blue eyes fixed on Nik's.

"I promise I won't hurt her, Dick … I made a mistake." Dick turned and headed out of the kitchen. The door to his bedroom slammed and the house shook.

"I … I love you. I promise I won't hurt you."

He held my hands in his, and a tear rolled down his cheek. "I don't know how I can make you understand?" he added, defeated.

"I need time … I forgive you, I really do, but you hurt me more than you can imagine." My eyes filled with tears and he took me in his arms. I felt his body shake from the pain.

"I dream about us, the baby growing in your belly. We are happy and planning our wedding, nothing grand, very simple, the way you'd want it. All our family are involved, Motaba instructing everyone on what to do. Your father glaring at me for taking you away from him. I wish my papa was here; he would have known a way."

"Oh … sorry, don't want to disturb you … " Feroza walked into the kitchen and stopped.

I let go of Nik and said, "Good morning, Feroza. Meet Nik."

"Nik?" Her eyes darted across to mine. "Pleased to meet you." she held out her hand. "Feroza Khan, mathematics, from Birmingham."

Nik took her hand and said, "Nikesh Raja, law, from Loudwater. Are we on University Challenge?"

She laughed, turning her face up towards him and let out a small gasp.

He squeezed my hand. "We won't disturb you, Feroza. Is it okay if we leave the dishes drying on the sink?"

"Sure," she replied as she watched us walk up the stairs to my room.

"Wait," I said as I halted outside my door.

"We're just talking; can't do it downstairs." He pointed with his thumb.

"I just need to put something away." I headed to the easel and turned it towards the wall. "Come in!"

He walked in awkwardly and glanced around the room. His eyes rested on the small photo frame on my bedside table of us at Amit's wedding, smiling up at the camera. It had been there since last year and I couldn't bear to put it away. Recently, it had felt right to look at him before I fell asleep and when I woke up. He sat on the bed and pulled me to sit down beside him.

"Tell me everything. I want to know."

I rested my head on his shoulder and began to talk about what I'd done in the summer. How I'd found out and that he was the first person I'd told. About the anger after his phone call and how scared I'd been when I rang the clinic; the feeling of loneliness I'd felt. Breaking down when Umi called. Her support throughout the ordeal when it should have been his. How my heart broke as the wait for him became unbearable. My realisation that he wasn't going to support me. My dreams. The dreams that haunted me and made it difficult to forget because I lost a piece of my heart when I did what I had to do. I couldn't make eye contact. I spoke to him staring at Audrey Hepburn and George Peppard kissing on the poster of *Breakfast at Tiffany's*.

"I'm sorry, my love ... Would you have changed your mind if you'd got the letter?" he asked, his voice choking as he stared at my hand and stroked my knuckles with his thumb.

"I don't know ... I was sure we weren't ready for a child; it would have meant taking a year out. I love what I'm doing, Nik. I love you, but marriage and a baby are a big step. I wished we'd talked it through. I tell myself every day I had to make the decision I did."

"It's not your fault; you can't take all the blame for it. I was responsible, too. Perhaps we are too young for a baby, but I want to marry you, Ree. I've known for a long time. You do believe me?"

He took my chin and gazed into my eyes. "Say yes, Ree."

I slid my eyes away from his to break his gaze. My soul was conflicted. Was my love for him enough for me to forgive and forget?

"I believe you, Nik, but it's too soon after ... "

"After the pain I caused you." He finished my sentence.

We sat silently in my room holding onto each other, crying openly until the time on the alarm clock read 10.30 a.m. and he let out a deep sigh. "I have to go ... got jobs to do for the party."

We stood up; he rested his forehead on mine. I felt his warm breath on my lips as he said, "I love you, Ree, always have, always will. Without you, my heart is empty."

"I love you too, Nik," I replied. "My heart aches when I'm not with you,"

He smiled and his golden eyes sparkled like exploding fireworks.

We held hands as we walked down the stairs; the door to the bathroom opened, and Umi stopped short, slack-jawed and then slowly, a smile filled her face. We both gave her a bashful smile and I gave him a long kiss as he left. He skipped to the car and rolled down the window and shouted, "See you tonight, my love."

Umi sat in the armchair in my room

"Tell me everything. How, when, where. You've been naughty, keeping this a secret from me," she teased.

"You told him about the letter." I poked my finger at her chest, accusingly.

"Had to. Do you know what's it's like seeing the people you love in pain?"

Before I started to tell her everything, there was a knock on the door, and Dick poked his head through.

"God, that was long. Do you have any idea what I've been going through?" He flung his slippers off and flopped on my bed, his head resting on the pillow. I loved them both; they had been my support throughout the summer, taking it in turns to visit me and lift me from my gloom. At one stage, my father was seriously worried Dick was my new boyfriend until Amit put him right by telling him that we were friends and thought of each other as brother and sister.

***

UMI WENT TO PETER'S after lunch and the rest of my housemates agreed we'd be there for seven thirty.

When I came downstairs, Dick whistled and yelled, "Wow, you look stunning. Reena Solanki is back!" He threw a punch in the air in celebration.

James pulled me towards him into a hug. "You look lovely, Reena. You'll definitely make every hot-blooded man envious of Nik." He grinned as he pushed me away from him to admire my outfit. If you didn't know them, James and Dick could quite easily be mistaken for brothers, the only difference is James has chestnut-brown hair instead of Dick's dirty-blond. I had decided to wear my emerald-green pencil pants, a black Bardot-neckline top with bell sleeves and my black patent courts with the tortoiseshell buckles. My hair was styled in a homage to Holly Golightly, using a brooch as a hair accessory, and I had applied some make-up for the first time since that awful day.

Feroza was also impressed and, as we stepped out of our house, she took my arm and asked, "Where did you get the outfit?"

Saleem laughed and said, "Meet the real Reena Solanki, Feroza. She doesn't shop, she creates," which was a real compliment considering his unique, ethereal style, floaty shirts and ripped jeans that clung to his small, slim frame. There was no mistaking Saleem is gay and proud.

The DJ was testing the sound system as we approached the house. I saw Jay's bright-green Ford Escort parked outside the garage and braced myself. Jay had never taken to me and seeing me with Nik again was bound to cause friction. Dick took my hand and squeezed it.

"You'll be fine. I'm here." Dick and I stepped into the house in unison.

He was standing at the door leading to the stairs, watching for our arrival. Although the room was full of people, all I could see was Nik, and everything else lost focus. He was wearing a cream shirt and a pair of dark brown needlecord trousers, one hand in his pocket, the other holding a can of beer. I took a breath; he was in front of me. He watched Dick wearily, who gave my hand to him, a thin smile on his face. "Remember what I said," he said quietly.

"I won't hurt her, I promise," Nik blustered. He handed his can to Dick and placed his hand around my waist and guided me to the stairs.

"Let's go to my room." We both walked side by side on the narrow stairs. "Hope you've brought your lipstick, because I'm planning on a lot of kissing," he whispered.

I stopped. His eyes were questioning me, and I asked. "Nothing else, only kissing?"

"Yes, we're still courting ... aren't we?"

I caught my breath when I entered. The wall above the desk was full of photographs of us. Every photograph that existed of us as a couple. The pictures at the parties and reception we had gone to with his family, a copy of one I had on my bedside table taken at Amit and Smita's wedding. On his bedside table was the photograph he took of me when we made the snowman.

"I decorated over the summer." He pointed to the wall bashfully. "May I take your coat?" I started to pull at my coat, and he moved behind me. He gasped. "I've missed these shoulders." He planted a kiss on one and I shuddered. "Oh God, Ree, you set my senses on fire. The smell of you. The taste of you," he whispered as he planted small kisses on my neck, my collarbone, my shoulders. Eventually he turned me around and his mouth met mine, his tongue teasing. My body ached for him, but I was afraid. He sensed it and said through the kisses, "We've got plenty of time. I won't rush you. I'll wait."

He had said the same words before and I trusted him. He pulled me towards the bed, and we lay facing each other. He couldn't stop kissing me and his eyes creased at the corners. "Why did you start wearing those dreadful boxy sweat tops? I missed this the most, seeing you like this. You look amazing today."

"I couldn't wear anything nice … it felt wrong." The music was thumping through the floor.

"It feels okay now?" He asked his eyes sparkling.

"Yes, it feels right, now that I'm here with you."

"I love you, Reena Solanki," he said again, this time smiling and planting kisses on my eyes, my cheeks and my forehead, and we kissed. I loved his kisses and savoured the taste of him.

"Come on, let's go downstairs. You'll need to freshen up your lipstick, and I might have messed up your hair at the back."

I added a slick of red to my lips and pulled the stray strands up. I wet a tissue with spit and wiped the remnants of lipstick off his lips. The door opened.

"Nik, what are you doing in here?" Jay walked into the room without knocking and halted, his eyes darting to Nik's arms around my waist, to my hand resting on his chest, the other wiping his mouth. "Didn't know you were busy." He turned and closed the door.

We both looked back at each other and giggled like children caught with our hands in a sweet jar.

The party was in full swing when we went downstairs. The living room was full of people dancing and I waved at Dick who was dancing wildly with a tall strawberry blonde to Abba's 'Dancing Queen'as he always did when there was beer and music.

We walked hand in hand to the back room where the food was laid out. Ravi was sitting on the sofa with a plate of food in his hand and smiled up at us as we entered the room. Umi and Peter were sitting together in the armchair, sharing a plate. We queued at the table. "Shall we share a plate?" I glanced back at Nik.

"Only if you promise to feed me." He raised his eyebrow and grabbed my waist.

"Or you could feed me," I replied.

"I'd love to if you allow me to feed you with my hands … Oh the thought of it," he whispered in my ear. We reached the patio doors to the garden and Jay entered, his dark, beady eyes glaring at me, and he said, "Hello, Reena. I see you've wormed your way back into his life again."

"What did you say, Jay?" Nik grabbed his shirt collar. I tried to pull at him with my free hand. "Nik, Nik, please, stop," I yelled.

"I heard what he said. How dare he. You're my life!" Ravi wrapped his arms around Nik's chest, and someone pulled Jay back into the garden.

"I want him gone. Do you hear me. He's not welcome here," Nik shouted to Ravi.

I gave my plate to Umi and took his hands, standing in front of him.

"Look at me, Nik. Nik, please." His face had darkened and his eyes were full of fiery darts. Our eyes connected.

"It's okay. He's only protecting you." Ravi released him slowly.

I heard his heart quieten. I took him and our plate of food to the stairs. We sat silently until his breathing returned to normal.

"So … are you going to feed me with your hands?" I whispered and he grinned at me.

"Love to. Please may I?" He raised his left eyebrow.

The fireworks were spectacular; Peter had pushed the boat out and brought some impressive rockets. He and Ravi lit them in succession at the bottom of the garden, while we watched, standing by the house. The DJ put on a compilation of classical music by Wagner and Bach.

Nik was holding me, his arms wrapped around me; the temperature dropped, but I was warm and happy. Jay was nursing a Bacardi and Coke, glaring sheepishly at us from the side.

Nik avoided being in the same room as him all night. We spent most our time in the living room dancing, while Jay sat and sulked in the dining room.

When I was in the kitchen fetching more beer, I overheard a conversation by the serving hatch between Saleem and Jay.

"Don't I know you from the club in Birmingham?" Saleem asked.

"I'm not like you," Jay replied with contempt.

"I do know you, Jay. That's your name, am I right?"

"Piss off perv; I don't like men. I'm not who you think I am," he retorted.

"What did you say?"

"I'm not a faggot. I've never met you before."

"No one here cares, why hide it?" He paused. "Your loss." Saleem sighed and moved away.

I bumped into Saleem as he stepped out of the dining room. His big expressive eyes revealed the hurt, and I squeezed his hand.

It all made sense: the way he talked to me, the way his face lit up when Nik talked to him. The lack of girlfriends. The one-night stands he boasted about when he'd been clubbing. The sneering way he talked about women. How could I have missed it? When I first met Saleem, I knew he was gay, but he wasn't at the stage of accepting it. He struggled for a few months with his identity but had been out and proud since the end of the first year. His mother was upset at first and didn't speak to him for six months, but he is her youngest son, and eventually, his older sister persuaded her to accept him for who he is. Now his older brothers and the rest of his family have accepted him too.

But what had happened for Jay to think Nik was like him, too? Jay was the one who told me about Julie, Nik's first love, and how he was devastated by their break-up. He was always whispering in my ear about the countless other women Nik had slept with; his preference for blonde women. He was always telling me I was not Nik's type.

***

I RECALLED HOW JAY had turned up at Nik's on Valentine's Day in our first year. Nik had come to pick me up from my room with a bunch of pink roses. He had gasped when I had turned to get a vase for the flowers. The pale yellow, 1970s-style dress I was wearing was sleeveless with a round strap neck, exposed back, cutaway arms and a defined waist and tie belt.

We had finished a fantastic meal that Nik had cooked for us and he had pulled me to sit on his lap as we ate our pudding, a deliciously light mousse. He was running his hot hand on my back, watching my face for any reaction. I closed my eyes and parted my lips and then he kissed me.

"You're going to give me a heart attack," he groaned. "You're going to give every man a heart attack tonight. If I pull this, will it fall off?" His fingers were on my belt and I shook my head. "What a pity, it would have been a lovely Valentine present."

The cassette player was playing Sibelius, the tape of the City of Birmingham Youth Orchestra I had given him for a Christmas present.

"Happy?"

"Oh yes," I told him, even though my stomach was in knots. I had felt safe in my small room knowing I could shout if I needed help. Being in his house was new territory.

"I promised, I'd wait. I just wanted to make you dinner," he said, taking my hand. I saw the hurt in his eyes. *How could he know what I was thinking?*

"I feel I've known you all my life. I would never do anything to hurt you." He raised his glass, handed mine to me and said, "To the most beautiful woman in the world."

I took a long sip to give me courage.

"Let's go and find a place for my Valentine's present." We were interrupted by the sound of the doorbell chimes.

"Who could that be?" he said as he glanced at his watch. "Wait here," he told me as he walked to the front door and turned the music down.

"What are you doing here, Jay?"

"I thought I'd pop in to see you."

"On Valentine's day? I have a date." Nik's voice was sharp.

"Oh, sorry, didn't know you'd have company." The front door closed and I heard Nik direct Jay to the sitting room.

Nik walked back into the dining room, and he wrapped his arm around my waist. Jay shouted, "What a weird painting. Did a long-legged blonde sell it to you? I'd chuck it in the bin before anyone sees it."

"It's a Reena Solanki original, and I think it's beautiful." The tone was harsh and he pulled me closer to his side as we entered the room.

Jay's eyes rested on Nik's hand, clasping my waist.

He was holding my painting up, disgust on his face.

"Oh, didn't know your date is with Reena … I was expecting … "

"Expecting who, Jay?" Nik queried.

"Nothing … Hello, Reena. You're looking … nice." He raised a disingenuous smile.

The hurtful words and the fake smile on his face made my blood boil and I said, "Hello, Jay. No Valentine's date?"

Even Nik was shocked at the tone of my voice and blustered, "I … I'm sure Jay had plenty of offers … he's just picky. I'm making coffee, do you want some, Jay?"

"No, I want something stronger." He followed Nik into the kitchen.

I took a deep breath and wondered what it was about Jay that brought out the worst in me.

Thirteen

SINCE THE CHRISTMAS BREAK, I had seen Nik regularly. It wasn't the same relationship we had when we first started to date. I was cautious. I loved him, and he told me many times loved me. He routinely picked me up after work, and there were times when he stayed until the morning at my house share. I missed being with him; I missed the comfort of sleeping in his arms, so when I was anxious, he stayed. Umi and Dick joked incessantly about his lack of contribution to the household bills when they saw him at breakfast. He asked me to move in with him, and I'd made up some excuse or another to put him off. I was not sure I wanted to be in his house. I felt safer with my friends; I was not comfortable about the intimacy implied by living at his place.

We were in the library, at our favourite table near the back away from everyone else. Our legs entwined, as we continued to work on our coursework. Nik had his headphones on, and I could vaguely hear the beat of the music. Suddenly he stopped writing and stared at me with an intensity that burnt my skin.

"What?" I asked him.

He smiled. "Do you remember the song?" He leant in and quietly sang, "Yeh reshmi zulfein."

I felt the blush rise through my body and felt hot, as I remembered how he had said those words, that day in December.

"Please, Ree. Say yes. All I see is you and nothing else. It's driving me crazy. Let's spend the whole weekend together. Not these snippets. I promise, we won't do anything you don't want to." He whispered in my ear as he leant over the table.

He knew I was nervous about resuming where we left off and had not once forced me; he was, and has always been, true to his words.

I took a deep breath in. "Okay, I'll go with you."

"Where do you want to go? Brighton, Bournemouth, Isle of Wight?"

"Can't we go somewhere closer?" I asked anxiously.

"No, it has to be somewhere by the sea." He reassured me by leaning across and squeezing my hand. "I want this Valentine's day to be special."

***

WE ARRIVED IN BRIGHTON early on Thursday evening; he pulled into the Norfolk Hotel car park. It was built in the French Riviera revival style that was so popular in the Victorian era of hotel building. Not as big as The Grand, but it still had the air of grandeur with its cast-iron staircase and decor.

We waited for the car engine to quieten down and he raised a smile and stepped out to open the passenger door. Nik was nervous, his usual confidence slightly dented; his hand kept running through his hair, pushing it off his forehead. I understood his anxiety; I was also apprehensive and cautious. I took his hand and squeezed it.

We walked into the foyer of the hotel and the receptionist welcomed us. "Good evening, do you have a reservation?" she asked, ready to inform us that all the rooms were booked.

"Good evening. We have a room booked in the name of Nikesh Raja."

She hadn't expected this and cast her eyes down at the computer screen to hide her shock.

"Ah. Good evening, Mr and Mrs Raja."

My heart skipped a beat when she said those words.

When we had got back together, I had avoided the subject of marriage. He had proposed in the letter, but it was for the wrong reason. I knew as far as my father was concerned, he would rather I kept away from the Rajas. But, being called Mrs Raja made my heart fill with happiness.

"Do you need a porter, Mr Raja?"

Nik was back to his charming self, leaning on the counter, signing the book, confirming a dinner reservation. By the time he finished, she was purring up at him.

He took the keys, slung his suit bag on his shoulder, picked up my small suitcase, and pulled out his arm and said, "Shall we, Mrs Raja," a grin on his face. My stomach felt like a lead weight had been dropped in it, now we were actually here. I wasn't sure that it was a good idea, a bitter taste filled my mouth. I let the sudden happiness at being called Mrs Raja sink in to calm me down.

He dropped the bags when we entered the room,

pulled me into his arms and gave me a kiss, his lips soft and inviting. I kissed him back, wrapping my arms around his neck, wanting to extend the embrace forever.

We took it in turns to change into our outfits in the bathroom, the familiarity of our life together last year having not yet returned. I was still wary of taking my clothes off in front of him, aware my body had changed since the last time he saw me fully naked. Nik changed into a light-pink shirt and smart charcoal-grey trousers.

I'd spent days working out what to bring to Brighton in February. In the end I packed a couple of dresses and decide to wear a lapis lazuli Chinese silk dress I had altered to rest just above my knee. I put my hair up into a high ponytail and applied some light make-up. When I came out of the bathroom, he was sitting at the small table, nursing a vodka and Coke he had ordered up from the bar. He gasped.

"Oh, God, Ree, you're killing me." He held his hand to his heart. "That dress … it shows off all your scrumptious curves. I think I'm going to need a bit of fortification before we go down to the restaurant. You don't want me to embarrass you in front of everyone." He raised his wicked eyebrow.

I smiled at him shyly. I knew what he meant by fortification and walked to him and sat on his lap.

His hands roamed over the soft fabric of the dress, caressing me. I focused on the scar on his top lip. I wanted to kiss it. His eyes smouldered.

"Sorry, I'm going to have to smudge your lipstick."

We kissed, his hands pushing my dress up my thighs. I slipped my hand underneath his shirt.

"Stop," I gasped.

He moaned, and a deep sigh escaped from his mouth as he pulled my dress down, slowly smoothing it with the palms of his hands. I kept my eyes locked on his and slowly re-buttoned his shirt. He stood up and I unzipped his trousers and tucked his shirt-tails in; his hands moved to my bottom. He squeezed it and then released me and said, "Go touch up your lips," as he reached for a tissue from the box on the bedside table.

The restaurant was full, tables for two dotted all over, and Nik and I were escorted to ours. The waiter brought us the set Valentine's Day menu and asked us if we would like a sparkling wine to start with. Nik ordered a bottle of Laurent Perrier and we ate our dinner with ease, taking time to savour the taste of the food. He talked about his excitement at spending time with me. The thought of being in a hotel with no one to disturb us took me back to the September of 1983. A chill ran through my body and I shivered.

After dinner, we moved to the bar. We positioned ourselves in a small loveseat overlooking the promenade. We both drank Grand Marnier with ice. He held my hand, stroking the tops of my knuckles with his thumb absent-mindedly.

"I could do this forever with you, Reena Solanki," he whispered. "You complete me. Please tell me you feel the same," he pleaded.

"I love you forever, Nik." I said quietly.

Then it dawned on me. This is the truth. I do. There's no one else who makes me feel the way he does. *What am I scared of?* I picked up my glass and gulped it down, the corner of his mouth twitched, and a glint of anticipation flickered in his golden eyes.

I pulled at his hand; he stood up slowly. I led him up to our room, unable to speak, scared I might change my mind.

He opened the door. I took the Do Not Disturb card and put it on the door handle. I closed it behind me and leant into it for support. My legs were weak, my heart was thumping in my chest, my mouth was dry, and my body ached for him.

"Kiss me, Nik."

He pulled me up into his arms, wrapping my legs around his waist. My hands were in his hair. His lips hungered for me, to take back every ounce of me, all the parts he had known before, our bodies remembering. He turned and carried me to the bed.

"Wait." He frowned, small creases appearing on the edge of his eyes. "Are you sure?" He put me down.

I nod. "One hundred per cent."

The golden shards in his eyes sparkled and I pushed off his jacket; he unbuttoned the high collar of my dress and pulled it over my head. He stood back and his eyes roamed over my underwear. "Red?" It sounded like a groan, his heated eyes exploring my body slowly. He unbuttoned his shirt and unzipped his trousers, pulled out his wallet, threw it on the bed and bent down to untie his shoelace. I couldn't wait. I squatted down and started on the other; he laughed at my urgency. I pulled at his socks, stood up and pushed his trousers down his pert bottom, and my hands lingered. He pulled me to him and kissed my neck, my collarbone. I sighed and pushed him back. I stared lustily at his beautiful torso, the wide chest, the broad shoulders, the tuft of hair that disappeared into his boxer shorts.

He unclasped my suspenders and pushed me onto the bed. He took my red court shoes off, one after the other. He slowly rolled off my stockings, one leg at a time. I could not wait as he kissed my toes, deliberately and slowly. "Nik, please," I gasped, his lips travelling slowly down my legs. He stopped at the top of my thighs and he pulled himself on top of me, his arms holding his upper body up.

His mouth met mine, his tongue brushed against mine and he said, "But first some exploring," he grinned and I moaned, and then I savoured every flick of his tongue, the touch of his caress, the tiny bites he gave me.

My whole body was charged, the heat of his body adding to the intensity. The hairs on the back of my neck stood erect. I whimpered; he reached for his wallet and I heard a tear. He was inside me and I knew this was where I belonged, joined to him.

"I love you, Ree." I opened my eyes and saw that his eyes were on fire.

***

MY EYES FOCUS ON THE ORNATE ceiling and then I reached my hand out to where he should be sleeping. It was familiar, my search for Nik. A smile drew across my face, as I remembered what we did last night, the scene playing in my head like a movie. He was raised on one elbow, watching me intently. "Good morning, my love. I let you sleep in. I know you must be tired from last night." He grinned. I blushed and buried my head into his chest and we devoured each other again.

***

He was on the bed, propped up on pillows, his hands cradling his head, waiting for me to get ready, watching me with those incredible eyes.

He slid off the bed and strode over to me, bending down at the waist. His hands were on my shoulders; our eyes locked in the mirror.

"I've got to pick something up from reception. I'll meet you in fifteen minutes." He kissed my head, picked up his jacket and walked out of the room.

The lift doors opened, and I searched for him. He was escorting a blonde-haired woman in a dark-navy coat to the door; she shook his hand, and he gave her a kiss on her cheek. My stomach lurched, our eyes met, and he grinned. His long strides skipped across the polished floor, and he was in front of me. He took my hand. "Ready for breakfast?" he asked, and he pulled me to the glass conservatory where Valentine's Day breakfast was being served.

We ate silently. I was lost in thought at who the woman was and why he kissed her on the cheek. I recalled the scene in my head: she was wearing an expensive coat and had a designer bag over her shoulder. *Why are they always blonde?*

"You're quiet." His words interrupted my thoughts. "Are you regretting what happened?"

I lifted my eyes to his face. The creases around his eyes were back. *Do I regret what happened last night? Do I love him enough to deal with the women who can't resist his charm?*

"No regrets," I said softly and then added, "Very hungry," to justify my silence.

A grin filled his face. He took my hand, brushing my knuckles with his lips. A waitress walked past; her eyes darted at him and then at me. Envy flickered across her face.

* * *

THE ROYAL PAVILION is the most breath-taking piece of architecture I've ever seen. It's like a piece of vibrant India has been picked up and transported to grey England, the Mughal arches, the latticework in the stone, the onion domes, the tiny minarets. If it wasn't for the northerly wind and the thin winter sun, I would have been transported to the times of Shah Jahan and the dancing girls in the royal courts of India. "Do you like it?" Nik pulled me closer to him as we walked up to an ornate domed arch which held an inscription.

'This gateway is the gift of India in commemoration of her sons who, stricken in the Great War, were tended in the Pavilion in 1914 and 1915.'

"It's beautiful. I had no idea this was here! Did you know my mother's favourite film was *Mughal-e-Azam*?"

"Yes, you told me once." He smiled.

"I love watching the film with my daddy. Did you know the set for the dance sequence for 'Pyar Kiya To Darna Kya' is a replica of the Sheesh Mahal at Lahore Fort?" I stopped and put my arms around his neck and kissed him. "Thank you for bringing me here."

He took my hand and we walked up to a bench in the gardens and sat down to take in the view.

We watched an elderly Indian couple walk up to the entrance; the man was holding his wife's hand as he escorted her up the path.

Nik knelt in front of me. "Reena Solanki, I love you,

always have, always will. Will you marry me?" He held a small box and inside it was a ring.

I gulped back a sob and failed miserably as the tears flooded my eyes and streamed down my cheeks.

He handed me his handkerchief. "Is that a yes?" I blew my nose and then looked at him. Apprehension was visible on his face.

I pulled my glove off and offered him my left hand; he took out the ring from the box and held it with his right hand.

"Say it, Ree."

"Yes." My voice broke as more tears rolled down my face. He slid the ring onto the third finger of my left hand, the finger that signifies the linking of two hearts. I marvelled at how it fit me exactly. It was perfect, a square sapphire in the middle with two small diamonds on each side, set in a simple gold band; it was precisely what I would have chosen. It fit like it'd been made for my finger.

"How did you know my ring size?"

He pulled out a plastic ring from his wallet. "Do you remember this?"

I laughed and pulled him up. It was the ring from our friend's Christmas dinner in our second year. Nik and I had pulled a cracker together, and the ring was the gift inside. He'd put it on my finger, and we'd laughed at how it was made for me, and everybody clapped and shouted it was a sign. I wrapped my arms around his neck and kissed him softly and with trepidation. I've said yes, but now we have the task of convincing our families.

He sang in a soft, expressive croon from the second stanza from "Pyar Kiya To Darna Kya."

"Why are you afraid, my love? We are in love and haven't stolen anything."

"How do you remember the lyrics for these songs?"

"Natural talent," he murmured before he kissed me again.

We were on cloud nine; even the cold wind that hit us on the seafront when we walked back to the hotel did not dampen our mood. We made love again, this time slowly and sweetly. There was hunger and longing, but we had the rest of our lives together, so we savoured every moment. We didn't venture out for the rest of the day and most of Saturday. We ordered more champagne and food to sustain us from room service, nothing that demanded we sit at a table, all finger food we could feed each other in between the passionate love making. We couldn't help ourselves; staying confined to our room, we only wanted to be with each other, joined as one.

***

ON OUR LAST NIGHT IN BRIGHTON, I cajoled Nik into going out. I wanted to see more of the seaside resort and we drove down to Hove beachfront and found a small French bistro. The place was dimly lit with candles. We ate a wonderful meal of avocado with shrimps in Marie-Rose sauce, a terrine with thin Melba toast, a duck confit and a bowl of frites.

The Burgundy he had selected to drink with our meal warmed our insides, and we were on our second bottle. Nik stole a kiss.

"Nik! Nikesh Raja! What are you doing here?"

He stood up. "Jules? What are you doing here?"

I watched her as she leant into him a bit too easily and

he turned his head, so her kiss landed on his left cheek. He was still holding my hand and lifted me up.

"Can I introduce you to my fiancée, Reena Solanki."

She bristled. "Oh, hello." She held out her manicured hand and said, "Julie Ramsbottom. I think we met briefly at Nik's uncle's funeral." She raised a false little smile.

"When did this happen?" She turned her head to Nik.

"Yesterday. She finally said yes to me, yesterday." He smiled with his eyes and kissed the wrist on my left hand. "Join us. Let me get another glass."

She sat opposite me, and he turned to walk up to the bar; we watched him as he talked to the barman.

"Well, can I see the ring?" She asked after tearing her eyes away from him.

I showed her my left hand; she peered at the ring. "Didn't expect Nikesh Raja to buy such a small thing. No big diamond?"

"No, Ree likes understated jewellery. She's not into all that." He had slipped next to me and wound his arm around my shoulder.

"So why are you here, Jules. Weekend off?"

Her eyes rested on his hand caressing the top of my arm. I was wearing a cap sleeve black silk dress with a boat neckline. Goosebumps appeared on my arm.

"I've got a job at The Grand; it's a bit of a mess from the bombing, but I get a chance to manage some of the refurb work. So why aren't you staying at The Grand? I'm sure I would have seen you on the guest list."

I tried to breathe steadily; he'd told me she meant nothing to him. But she was his first girlfriend, the girl he made love to first and she was his type. She's blonde and quick to laughter. The rushing of blood in my ears stopped me from hearing anything as I sipped my wine. He was charming as always. She finished her wine and stood up, pulling at her tight black skirt to straighten it.

"Congratulations, Nik. Thanks for the drink. Got to go back to my friends." She pointed to a group of people sitting at the bar and walked away.

He turned to me, frowning. I averted my eyes. I didn't want him to see the hurt and the anger.

"That was funny," he said. "Didn't know she'd changed jobs." He filled my empty glass, and I took a big gulp of wine.

On our drive back to the hotel, I tried to ignore the gnawing ache that had settled in my stomach. He had asked me to marry him: why would he be interested in her? He seemed genuinely shocked to see her. *I'm just insecure,* I told myself.

When we stepped into the room, I pulled his coat off and reached for his head, pulling his mouth to mine. I wanted to possess him. I wanted him to know I was the only one he needed. I wanted him to show me he wanted me. I pulled at my dress zip and turned around for him to unzip me. I let it drop around my ankles and stepped out of it. I pushed him to sit on the bed. I pulled off his shoes and socks and lifted his pullover and shirt over his head. I unzipped his trousers and pulled off his pants with them. He was naked, watching me warily, his eyes locked with mine. I slipped off my knickers and reached for the condoms. He was aroused. I pushed him to lie on the bed and sat on top of him and took him. He belonged to me! I had the ring to prove it! I obliterated the image of Julie Ramsbottom from his mind and mine. I took a deep breath, and I flopped down next to him.

"Was that angry sex?" He raised himself on his elbow. I stared back at him, trying not to cry. I knew my eyes would give me away.

"I've told you before, you are my first love. She was my first sexual experience, but that's all."

A tear slid down into my ear; he kissed it and his lips caressed my cheeks and worked towards my mouth.

"I want make-up sex now, please," he said as he pulled at the clasp on my bra, and he pulled off my stockings and shoes. He slowly and deliberately kissed me, drawing me into his arms. This time we made love, revelling in each other, and he waited and lingered long enough for me to want him because I love him.

Fourteen

"DO WE HAVE TO GO?" I pleaded with him for the umpteenth time, as we came off the motorway and headed towards Loudwater.

I wasn't sure the people who lived there would welcome me with open arms after what had happened to Nik last summer. I remember the first time Nik had brought me to Shakti Bhavan

March 4th, 1983

THE ANXIETY I HAD FELT rose like the tide, as we drove to Loudwater after dropping Umi home. My mind was concentrating on the technique I'd learnt to deal with my nerves, repeatedly saying 'Om' and taking slow breaths.

Nik took my right hand and drew it up to his lips. "Don't worry, my love. They'll love you."

I smiled timidly up at him; my experience of high-society Indian families didn't agree with his. I had been at enough functions at the mandir to know how they treated people like me. We were just there to pander to their needs: 'fetch me water, where's my seat, take this away—'

We turned left into a winding country lane lined with foreboding trees on both sides. He stopped to allow a large black Land Rover to pass before he turned into a small turning; on either side was a small grass verge planted with primroses. We stopped at a brick wall, flanked by an ornate metal gate; beyond it there was a shiny-black tarmac road. On two identical stone pillars, there were marble plaques. Nik opened the driver's side window and pressed the buttons to open the automatic gates. I read the white marble house sign, SHAKTI BHAVAN, written in ornate-gold painted incision lettering. On the other plaque, there was an outline of Ganesh, to match the lettering. It was definitely a Hindu house.

As we drove further up the tarmac road, my jaw dropped, and a gasp escaped my lips. I knew he was rich, but not this rich. He chuckled under his breath and a shy smile developed on his face as he fixed his eyes straight ahead.

The house was gargantuan; the sun accentuated the red brick and the white-painted arched tall windows lined its face. In the middle, there was an ornate carved white stone portico, supported by two Georgian pillars. It all smacked of dripping wealth.

He turned left into the courtyard and parked the car outside one of the garages. He slid effortlessly out of the car and opened the door for me. I was glued to the seat. My eyes were anxiety-filled. He smiled, tilting his head to the right, lowering himself to my eye level; he gazed reassuringly into my frightened eyes. My heart was thumping uncontrollably inside my chest.

"You'll be fine, my love." He stood up and held out his

hand.

We walked through a rose-covered arched gate into a walled garden. I quietly thanked Umi for the wardrobe advice. She had suggested I wear my heeled red court shoes, and the rest sort of fell into place. I was wearing a spotted black and white T-shirt, a vintage silk scarf used as a belt and one of my least-faded pairs of Levi 501s that I had found in the Oxfam shop. I slowed down as I spotted a stream through a round window cut into the garden wall. Nik watched intently as my eyes darted from one view to another.

"Don't worry. I'll take you on a tour soon, but first we need to eat lunch. Did I tell you my motaba's kitchi and crispy bhajia are amazing?"

The rear of the house had an outdoor seating area below the central first-floor balcony, and he led me to a white door to my right. There was a set of full-height arched double doors; I counted them to help me calm down: one, two, three, four, five, six. *Who has six double doors leading out to the garden from their house!*

We didn't have one. I'd watched *Through the Keyhole* so I knew these houses existed. But to actually know someone who lived in a house like this caused my heart to race. *What have I done? Why have I fallen for this rich guy?*

"Jai Shri Krishna, Anu Masi."

I was surprised Nik had used the religious greeting. I hadn't expected it from him.

A small walnut-complexioned woman with salt-and-pepper hair was rinsing dishes in a large butler sink in the small kitchen. I had expected it to be more significant. I considered it small, but it was bigger than the kitchen we had at home. The walls on the left and right had full-height fitted cupboards. There was a five-ring burner and, next to the butler sink there was a dishwasher. A dishwasher! No one I knew had one of those; *what was wrong with washing dishes the old-fashioned way*? I thought, these people are way too rich for the likes of me; *I will never fit in.*

A breakfast bar made from dark wood jutted out. On the wall there was a bank of kitchen cabinets that housed two ovens, an American-style fridge and a big microwave. A huge table with chairs was positioned in front of it.

"Oh, Niku, you've lost weight." She dried her hand on the white apron she was wearing over a cream floral-print rayon saree.

He lifted her up in a bear hug and she chuckled, waving her index finger in mocking disapproval as he lowered her back to the ground.

She then turned to me and smiled, "Jai Shri Krishna, Beti."

I held my palms together in a salutation and replied, "Jai Shri Krishna."

"This is my girlfriend, Reena. Are they at the table?" he asked in Gujarati. She nodded in reply.

I inhaled and exhaled to get some oxygen in my blood as we entered the massive room with the plethora of double doors. Nik lightly pressed my back to reassure me. The room was divided into three different areas. Directly in front of me was a large dining table with twelve rosewood dining room chairs upholstered in cream damask silk. In the centre, there was a Villeroy and Boch crystal vase filled with pink flowers. I assumed they were from the beautiful garden we had just walked through. Above the table was an elongated spiral crystal chandelier set on a central polished chrome rod fixed to the tall ceiling.

"Nikesh, come sit; food is still hot," a woman's voice ordered.

Sitting at the gigantic dining table were two elderly people. The man looked up and a smile drew across his face. He had the same chiselled face as Nik, but it had filled out a little making the angles softer. I saw a flash of what Nik would look like in his old age. He was sitting at the head of the table in a large upholstered carver chair.

"Nikesh, my son, my son. Come, come and sit down next to me." He pointed to an empty place to his left. To his right sat a woman who didn't look as old as I had expected.

She picked up a small handbell and chimes sounded. Anu Masi walked in with two white dinner plates and two crystal glasses on a silver tray.

Nik moved his hand to hold my elbow and guided me to sit next to him. He waited for the plates to be placed in front of us and then he suddenly stood up, scraping his chair against the terrazzo floor.

"Sorry, sorry, we haven't washed our hands yet. Come, Ree."

Nik walked towards the double doors that led back into the house.

I stood up sheepishly, remembering to grab my handbag. I realised in the gesture that Nik was nervous too, and my shoulders relaxed a little. I would never relax completely in this place, it was all too big and grand for me. I felt like someone who was on a stately home tour and had somehow taken a wrong turn into the family living area.

The central atrium of the house was extraordinary, an enormous crystal cone chandelier hung from the top floor down the middle through the square cut out in the ceiling. The point of the cone directed my eye to the black grand piano placed in the centre; it reminded me of an arrowhead pointing to the furniture of importance. The walls were covered in tall mirrors in French gilt frames; there was a pink hue coming from the polished pink-marble floor. French gilt Louis XIV-style chairs upholstered in pale-yellow silk taffeta had been placed against the wall.

There were four identical dark-walnut doors with gold handles in the four corners of the grand entrance hall; the dark-walnut feature staircase was located by the side and centre: it, too, had gold rods with ornate finials.

There was a floor lamp-sized gold candelabra to my right with fresh candles; beyond it was a massive arched front door. A vestibule had been created by tall plant-holders and urns in front of the doors. This area had a French gilt la lune table with a cream telephone placed on it and a small padded yellow-and-gold bench sat next to it; even the piano stool was French gilt with a pale-yellow seat. The excessive use of gold intimidated me, why would you model your entrance hall on the Palace of Versailles?

It was a statement: 'look at what we have achieved. We're rich, and we're proud.' I hated all this materialism, and wondered why Indians covet it so much?

Nik pointed to a door to my right and told me I could freshen up in there; he headed to a door to the left.

I stepped into the marble-tiled cloakroom; the theme

continued, gold and marble. I took a deep breath and washed my face and hands in the washbasin. I told my reflection: *you can do this; they are people after all.* Where was the towel? I was ready to wipe my hands on my jeans when I saw a small wicker hamper, one side filled with neatly rolled white hand towels and the other had a discarded one. "What's wrong with using one hand towel?" I said to myself.

Nik was waiting for me on one of the chairs. He grabbed me around the waist and smiled, pulling me close, and planted a soft kiss on my lips. My stomach lurched and I pushed him away.

"Don't, someone will see," I whispered.

He raised his left eyebrow. He tried to reach for my hand, but I slid both of them firmly into my front pockets. He sighed and took hold of my right elbow.

I felt the scrutinising stare of the woman. Her eyes wandered from my shoes slowly up to my face; she glared straight into my eyes and held my gaze. I noticed her lips curl up, but only fractionally, then she smiled a professional, courteous smile you would give to someone who you met briefly at a social function.

"Motaba, Papa, may I introduce Reena. I'm sure Kaki has told you I was going to bring her."

"Haan, haan, Nikesh, sit down. Anu Ben's waiting to make garam bhajia for you."

"Jai Shri Krishna." I placed my palms together in subjugation. I had quickly decided this was the norm for this family and walked timidly back to the table.

She turned to Anu Masi and nodded. The servant walked silently back into the kitchen.

I observed the table, noting down all the dishes laid out for lunch.

Nik started filling up his plate and nodded to me to help myself. Nik's papa watched him silently, scrutinising his actions.

"You look tired, Beta. Have you been partying too much?" he chortled.

His laughter was warm and friendly. They share a loving bond that must be a lot of fun, I thought. I wished I could be as comfortable with my father.

The words made his motaba bristle with contempt.

"He's supposed to be studying, not partying. You better be studying, Nikesh!"

His shoulders slumped; he had turned into a small child who had just been told off for doing something untoward.

"He's just arrived, Sarla. You can tell him off later; let him eat in peace."

I warmed to the man straight away; he wasn't going to let his wife's disapproval of Nik's social life ruin his return home.

She tutted and continued to eat; she had kitchi and farsi puri on her plate. She was rolling the kitchi in small rounds and dipping them into the tel and the lal marcha lasun ni chutnee as she popped it into her mouth.

Anu Masi entered the room and placed a large bowl of crispy bhajia near us, along with a plate of dark-green circular spirals.

"Timpa!" Nik eyes darted up in surprise at his motaba.

"I found fresh leaves at the grocer's this morning. Your favourite, Beta, hey na?"

"You like timpa too, don't you, Ree?"

I nodded and remembered when I first made them for

Sunday brunch. I'd told Nik I was making patra and he hadn't known what it was. When he saw them, he told me he called them timpa. Although both of our families come from East Africa, we do have some strange and different names for the food we eat. I'd teased him that Ugandans were strange and my nickname for them was so right. Ganda in Gujarati means crazy, 'U Ganda' means 'you crazy'; he had laughed so much at my lame joke.

The fact his motaba had made his favourite food broke the tension. His papa asked me what subject I was studying at Warwick University and I told him.

"What kind of job can you do after that?" he asked.

I was used to this. Most Indian families expected their children to be doctors, dentists, pharmacists, optometrists, accountants, computer scientists or lawyers; or they expected them to study business studies.

I explained I wanted to work in television or film as a producer; his face was blank until I elaborated that I would research a documentary programme or script and then manage the costs, logistics and people who made it.

"Ah, you must be organised. Management needs organisation. Nikesh's mother is good at organising the business. My wife, Sarla, is also good at managing the home."

He patted his wife's left hand with affection. She smiled; this time the smile was genuine. She was an attractive woman when she smiled.

Sarladevi was a plump short woman. She was wearing a peach silk jacquard saree; the colour enhanced her coffee-with-cream complexion. Her dyed black hair was tied up into a French chignon. In the centre of her narrow forehead was a large vermillion dot. Her centre parting was coated with the same vermillion powder. Petal-shaped eyes, rested on an oval-shaped face, her irises jet black. Above the eyes were manicured eyebrows. She had defined cheekbones and a long slim nose, with a one-carat diamond nose stud. Her thin lips were pursed tightly. She certainly knew how to accentuate her best features, which I believed were her eyes. She had put kohl inside her eyelids and had drawn eyeliner on them. She was wearing a pair of gold-rimmed glasses which framed and exaggerated them. I continued to observe her, as I tried to eat my lunch of patra with ambli khajjur ni chutnee and crispy bhajia.

I felt totally inadequate. I didn't wear make-up unless I had to go somewhere special. I didn't even pluck my eyebrows. Umi said I was lucky I didn't have huge caterpillars for eyebrows, because I would look stupid with them on my face. She did tell me to put some lipstick on when we dropped her off, but I had forgotten on the drive up.

Around Sarladevi's neck were several gold chains of varying size and a short, pale, wooden tulsi bead to tell me she follows the Vishnu faith. The second chain was made up of black and gold beads with a paisley-shaped pendant, encrusted with diamonds. This chain was a sign of her married status, a mangalsutra. Finally, she was wearing a chain that dropped to her waist; this one had pearls, red-enamelled beads with filigree work and dark-green elongated Fabergé egg-shaped beads encrusted in the middle with small pearls. Her ears were strange. She had small earlobes but still managed to show off a large pair of paisley-shaped ear studs to match the pendant on her mangalsutra.

She and her husband had finished eating and were patiently waiting for us to finish. In my house as soon as we finished, we'd get up from the table and start clearing up. Anu Masi brought in a pot of tea and some floral teacups and placed them in front of Sarladevi. She asked me if I took sugar. I nodded and replied, "Three teaspoons, please." She explained as Ramprakash was diabetic, they didn't take sugar in their tea. Most Indians have diabetes, but they still eat bhajia and nasto. I think they don't believe fried food is fattening and don't relate it to diabetes. Besides, all East African Indians love their crispy bhajia.

She passed the teacup, and I took a sip. It was masala chai; this one had been brewed with fresh ginger, cinnamon, cardamom, cloves and some black pepper. Most families have their own blend, and the combination of spices differs greatly. My father makes a blend with cinnamon, fresh ginger and cardamom, which he made me drink in the winter.

I put the cup down and studied the bowls of food. Nik had demolished the whole bowl of crispy bhajia and timpa and was eating farsi puri like he would eat crisps, placing one at a time in his mouth. I saw his papa gaze at him with pride.

"Don't you eat at college, Beta?"

"I do, I do, Papa, but I love Motaba's food; I miss it. She's the best cook ever." His eyes rested on his papa and then on his motaba, his face lighting up with a huge grin.

She laughed like a bashful schoolgirl; it was quite delightful. With that small action, he had her wrapped around his little finger.

The dining table had been cleared when I came back from the bathroom. Nik and his family had moved to the end of the enormous room to sit on plush-velvet, upholstered Chesterfield sofas.

"Is everything ready for tomorrow?" Nik was relaxed and sprawled on one of the sofas. His long legs stretched out in front of him, his arms resting on his full belly.

"Haan, haan. All is well. Is your friend going to stay with us?" Nik's motaba enquired. She used the English word friend rather than the Gujarati one that translated to girlfriend.

"No, not tonight; she is staying with Umi in Harrow. They will stay tomorrow night. Can you sort a bedroom for them?" Nik replied.

"Haan, haan, I can. Who else is coming?"

"Jay, Peter, Ravi, and a new friend, Dick, but they can crash anywhere. You can give the girls a room over the garages if you don't have space."

"Na, na, it's fine. I'll find a room for them."

"Ah, here you are."

Nik eyes focused on me as I approached the seating area. I glanced to my left and my right looking for somewhere to sit. Should I sit next to him, should I sit on the other sofa or should I sit next to Sarladevi?

The Chesterfields were placed in a U-shape; a cream Persian rug with a delicate floral design was placed in the centre. The sofa Nik sat on was facing the marble fireplace. Nik's papa was seated on an armchair placed next to the fire. I felt there was a seating plan for this room, each person sitting in their designated seats. His motaba was sitting on the sofa on her husband's left; she had perched herself as close to him as possible.

Nik patted the space next to him to tell me where I should sit. I obliged but kept a gap between us for decorum's sake.

"So why aren't you staying tonight, Reena? You'll miss meeting Nikesh's kaka and kaki and my birthday dinner," Ramprakash asked. I could sense he wasn't pleased I was not staying.

"Happy Birthday for today, Kaka." I took a deep breath and continued. "Nik is taking me to meet everyone this afternoon. Sorry, I promised my friend I would stay with her tonight."

"Nik, Nik, oh, isn't that's what the tthodya call him, but you're Gujarati, aren't you? Call him by his name. It's Nikesh."

I shrank. I had just had a tongue-lashing from his motaba, and she didn't like me or approve of my English ways.

Nik stood up abruptly; a dark cloud danced across his sparkly golden eyes. He straightened and curtly replied, "I like being called Nik by Ree; it's only you and Papa who call me that! Everyone else calls me by my pet name, Niku. Jai Shri Krishna, we must be on our way." He pulled at my hand to take me towards the ornate entrance hall.

Nik's papa had stood up, his face full of thunder as he glared at his wife. He pulled at Nik's arm, and our eyes met; they were full of apologies. "Stay longer, Beta. I haven't really had a good chat with Reena yet."

The tension in Nik's body diffused as he heard his papa.

"Don't worry, Papa. You'll have plenty of time tomorrow. I've asked my friends to come early tomorrow to help with the set up." He, too, used the word friends instead of the Gujarati word.

I folded my palms in salutation, "Jai Shri Krishna," and followed him.

As I bent down to pick up my handbag and jacket, I took a surreptitious glance towards the sitting area. Sarladevi sat stern as a Victorian statue, her hands clasped on her lap. Ramprakash's face was filled with sadness, as he reached to pick up one of the newspapers that were stacked on the glass side-table next to him.

Anu Masi stepped out of one of the many doors in the ornate hallway. She was holding a silver plate arranged with small light brown penda.

She offered the plate to me. "Reena Beti, this is your first time at Shakti Bhavan. You cannot go without sweetening your mouth."

Nik smiled and grabbed two pendas; she laughed, he hugged her and said, "Thank you, thank you, Anu Masi, you're great." A big bright smile had filled his face.

I took a penda and said, "Jai Shri Krishna" before I placed it in my mouth.

The sun was still high in the sky for March as we headed straight back to the walled garden; he clasped my hand and took long strides heading back to the car. "I'm sorry, I don't think I made a good first impression," I murmured.

"No one can meet Sarladevi's high standards; you'll see more of it tomorrow. Come on, let me show you the grounds of Shakti Bhavan. I would have shown you the house — " He paused, " — tomorrow."

He peered at my feet, "Do you have your trainers in the car?"

I nodded.

"Let's go get them and I'll take you to my favourite place in the whole wide world."

As we approached the car, I was dying to ask questions. I had never seen a house as big in real life. I had never imagined anyone I would meet would live like that. They did say university life broadened your horizons. The first thought that came into my head was how much money could the house cost to buy and run?

When Nik had told me he was a Ugandan refugee, I'd assumed he was like some of the people I'd met at the mandir. The families who'd been allowed their clothes and fifty pounds as they left the country, they called their home. I know of affluent Ugandan Asians who came to the mandir in Leicester, but Shakti Bhavan was in a totally different league. As I laced up my trainers, I began to interrogate Nik. The questions came out in a stream. His face filled with trepidation as he started to explain.

"I didn't want you to say no. If I'd told you how rich I was, would you have gone out with me?"

I paused and thought it through. I probably wouldn't have. He was right, but this was unfair. I was falling for him, but I was also repulsed by the lifestyle.

"Tell me everything, Nik, no more secrets; you know all there is to know about me." I placed my hand in the crook of his arm. He led me to a path in between the garages.

"When we first came to the UK, we lived in a large

house in Harrow. Motaba and Papa had come in the '60s and thought they'd invest in a house as my brothers were expected to come to university here."

I raised my eyebrows, my eyes pointing to his shoes as we stepped onto the gravel and he smiled. "Ah, I'm going to have to get appropriate footwear, too."

We turned around and headed towards one of the garages. We entered a small store, through a door on the side. The wall facing us was made up of rectangular shelves and coat hooks. Some of the shelves had brass nameplates on them and pairs of Wellington boots or walking boots. Nik strolled to his shelf and sat down on a wooden bench. I gawked at the shelves.

"When you live in the countryside, you have to have wellies," he said nonchalantly.

He proffered his arm to me. "Right, let's go to paradise," and he continued to explain. He told me his papa was in Kenya when Idi Amin gave them notice to leave, so their exit wasn't as bad as some of the other Indians.

"Did I tell you Jay and his family lived with us for a short while? They only had their clothes and his mum's jewellery when they arrived." I shook my head; he continued.

"Papa had invested in quite a few businesses when we were in Africa; he still does. We help small businesses here and in Africa to set up, and we take a cut.

Kaka and my brothers run our electronic wholesale business called Nikesh Traders. We have a factory in Kenya that makes component parts which we export all around the world."

We strolled down a winding path towards the stream I'd seen when we first arrived.

"How much land do you have?" I asked.

"I don't know, Ree; that's something only Kaka knows. Lots, I guess. See the tree at the top of the hill? Just on the other side, there's a hedge; that's one boundary. We drove up from the front wall, that's the second. See the ruin?" He pointed to his left. "The edge of that is the third boundary." Finally, he turned me to the right where the stream continued to meander and explained. "See the gnarly tree that's almost collapsed over the stream. Just beyond there's a public footpath; that's the fourth boundary."

So much land. I had felt exhausted just thinking about the acreage. He grabbed my hand and began to run down to the stream. I felt suddenly overwhelmed by the joy of his bright face and laughed as we ran, my lungs filled with the country air.

We stopped at a willow tree, its roots in the stream, and Nik sat down. I was reluctant to sit on the ground. He understood my predicament, took off his jacket gallantly and laid it on the ground.

"My lady, your seat awaits you."

I giggled and sat; he wrapped his arm around my waist, pulling me closer to him.

I wished I had my sketchbook with me. I wanted to capture the moment, my senses amplified by the birds chirping, the ripple from the stream and the sound of insects buzzing. A light breeze rustled the leaves on the willow.

"Paradise," he sighed. "And I'm here with a beautiful pari." He pulled my chin and kissed me softly, just brushing my lips. My mouth opened to meet his. My stomach flipped; he was irresistible. I couldn't seem to quench my thirst for the kisses. The more we kissed, the more I wanted him to keep kissing me. I felt he was getting aroused. My breath caught.

I pulled away in panic. "No. I can't. It feels wrong."

He whispered. "No one comes here, that's why it's my favourite place."

I wondered how many other girls he had brought to this place? I knew I wasn't his first girlfriend and I knew about his reputation at university before we started dating. And he probably used the same words, 'beautiful fairy.' He lifted me to standing; my legs felt like jelly and I was grateful he wrapped me in his arms. I leant into him for support and rested my head on his chest. As I filled my lungs with air, I could hear the thud thud of his heart; he was also trying to calm his breath.

"Okay, I did promise, but wouldn't it be divine," he said quietly. "Let's go back to the car; you'll be able to explore more when we come home, next time."

I felt nervous and surprised he had included me as someone who deserved to be in this home and my heart warmed. I didn't understand how he could imagine me, Reena Solanki, a daughter of a factory worker, in his future.

I sat waiting anxiously in the car for him, clasping my hands so tightly my knuckles were turning white. *Why had I agreed to come to the party?* I could have made an excuse. I could have said I had to go home to see my father. He slid lithely into the seat, turning to face me; he took my hand and lifted it to his lips. Our eyes met. "That was the worst of it. Kaka and Kaki are pussy cats." He grinned, raising his left eyebrow. I hadn't believed it to be the case.

Fifteen

March 4th, 1983 — afternoon

"I THOUGHT YOU SAID we were going to the office?" I gasped in exasperation.

For the second time, Nik's idea of normal was different from mine. We had parked in the forecourt of a red brick two-storey commercial building in Rickmansworth town centre. The large black window front had the words Raja House etched into the glass. He took my hand and I walked reluctantly to the entrance door.

"Do you name all the buildings you own?" I asked him as I stared up at it. I saw a slight smile playing on his lips.

"We like to mark our territory." He pulled me closer.

There were three businesses in the building. He pressed the button for Nikesh Traders. My feet had grown roots; the built-up adrenaline had churned my stomach like the sea, and I dared not move, afraid my lunch would gush out.

"What's the matter?" He was holding the door ajar. I forced myself to take deep breaths, trying to add much-needed oxygen into my bloodstream. "Are you okay?" Concern filled his eyes.

"Okay! Okay! Are you insane, Nik? I'm not okay!" I replied through gritted teeth. He guided me gently to the side of the building.

The enormity of the wealth of his family overwhelmed me. I pushed against the wall to steady myself. "I can't believe you've kept this hidden from me," I muttered angrily.

"It's only a name," he shrugged, "and ... it's only money. We are people," he murmured, "just like you. I didn't think you were such a snob." His words hurt.

"Snob?" I smarted at his comment.

"You're a reverse snob, Ree. You are prejudiced to money. Please, give my family a chance. I want you to like us. I want you to —" he implored, his eyes, pleading " —love us."

Perhaps I was reluctant to like them because of my relationship with money. It's difficult when you don't have much. I knew he wasn't as bad as some of the rich Indians. I wouldn't be with him if he were.

"God, Nik, it's like a RK Studio film: rich boy, poor girl, and you know what happens next?" I took a breath and raised a smile.

A grin filled his face from ear to ear. "Ah, but in my family, there's no Lalita Pawar."

I laughed at the mention of the matriarch whose role was to cause mischief between the hero and heroine. I was not confident Lalita Pawar wasn't in this narrative. I was relieved; at least they didn't occupy the whole building.

***

NIK HAD GONE TO THE SMALL kitchen to make some tea and coffee. The woman who was sitting next to me on the cream leather sofa stupefied me. If I didn't know who I was with, I would have sworn it was Sharmila Tagore. Pushpa Raja was extraordinarily beautiful. Her round face was surrounded by softly curled, layered, dark-brown hair just touching her shoulders. A big fringe hung on her forehead to the left, over perfectly arched eyebrows. Her pink, painted lips were broad, and when she smiled, which was often, two deep dimples appeared on both cheeks. Her expressive brown almond eyes glistened and sparkled. Her nose was long and had a small bump on the ridge, and she wore a small diamond nose stud. She had a small red tilak on her forehead and a small dot of sindoor in her parting to signify her status.

I didn't know why I had expected her to be like Sarladevi, the closed stern expression, and the judgemental voice. She was completely the opposite. She was open and accepting. She had a warm, soft, lilting voice that made me want to confess all my sins. She was wearing an embroidered cutwork, navy-blue chiffon saree. Her jewellery was understated. She was wearing a double rope-pearl necklace with matching drop earrings and her mangalsutra was long with small black beads and a tear-shaped diamond pendant. On the one hand, she had a set of pearl bangles, and, on the other, she was wearing a gold Rolex Oyster watch.

I was envious of the whole look; she oozed elegance and good taste. I wondered how many heads she had turned when she was younger. She probably still turned heads, I had concluded.

Anant Raja was sitting opposite; he had inquisitive eyes and the same teasing lift of the eyebrow and good humour as his son. He put me totally at ease. Whereas Ramprakash, his older brother, was plump, Nik's father was slender. He was wearing a navy suit, with a red-dotted pocket square in his breast pocket. They had each taken it in turns to move the conversation along, asking questions about my course, my ambitions, my upbringing. It was very different from my early conversation with the two heads of the household. They had realised I was struggling with Gujarati and had switched to English, which made me feel comfortable. By the time Nik came in with a pot of tea, coffee and biscuits, I felt so comfortable that, when he sat down, I reached for his hand and squeezed it. When I realised what I had done and quickly took it away, they both laughed.

"Don't worry, Beta. We're happy to meet you." Nik's mother reassured me by patting my hand.

"Niku. She's just as you told us." She leant forward and clasped his hand. He grinned as he turned his face to me.

"So what's the plan for tonight. Is Reena staying with us?"

"No, Kaki, I'm dropping her off to Umi's after here. She'll stay tomorrow night."

"Hi, Niku. Saw the car. When did you get back?"

Approaching with her arms opened and a broad smile was a petite woman in a cream boucle Chanel suit.

"Hello, Kaka, Kaki, any tea for me?"

She was obviously one of his sisters, but I couldn't be

sure if she was his real sister. Extended families are a bit complicated and, as this one lived together, it was going to take me some time to understand who was who.

Nik jumped off the sofa and rushed to her, lifting her into his arms and swinging her around. She punched him jokingly on his shoulder and told him to put her down.

"Wow, you're looking fab. The new haircut suits you."

"Do you think so?" she asked timidly. "Just had it done." She turned her head to and fro to show it off. "Not sure Motaba is going to approve."

"Well, I love it. What do you think, Kaki?"

"It really suits you, Jaishu." Nik's mother nodded in approval.

She took the cup of tea proffered to her and sat down in the space vacated by Nik. After she had taken a sip, she placed it back on the coffee table and turned towards me. I saw her eyes linger over my face as if she were surveying a painting. Her mouth lifted into a broad smile and I recognised the eyes.

She was Sarladevi's daughter; her eyes were the same shape; one riddle had been solved.

"Sorry, I'm so rude. I'm Jaishree, you must be Reena." She held up her hand, the handshake was firm and confident.

Her new hairstyle was softly layered and long. She had a perfect figure; her hips and bust were of equal portion, and her waist was tiny. Her jacket was open, and underneath she was wearing an orange silk blouse, which enhanced her coffee-with-cream complexion.

"How did you meet? Tell me all?" she asked in her

husky voice.

Nik had gone to the glass-fronted office with his father. I was reluctant to tell her all, especially as Nik's mother was sitting next to me.

"Kaki, you have to go. Reena's not going to tell me anything if you're here." She waved her hand to send her away. His mother laughed and headed for the office.

"She's gone. Tell me. Was it love at first sight?" she asked conspiratorially.

I shook my head. *It was hardly that*, I thought, and my mind wandered to all the times I'd met him.

"Oh, forgive me. I shouldn't be so nosey; you can tell me later," she assured me by tapping my thigh. "Come on, come see the studio."

As I pulled myself to standing her eyes surveyed my outfit. I felt inadequate. I was not a match for either of these women on the elegance scale.

"Is that a Hermès scarf you have around your waist?"

I was quietly impressed she recognised it. I was not going to tell her it was damaged, and I had picked it up from the Oxfam shop.

"I like your style. I think we are going to be good friends."

* * *

FOOTSTEPS HIT THE TILED FLOORS as Nik walked into Belgrade Design Studio; we were at a drawing board with a set of mood boards of the interiors for the remodelling of the stables at Shakti Bhavan.

He smiled as his eyes observed us. "Are these the latest designs for Bhai's house?" His index finger pointed to the A2 cards arranged on the architect's drawing board.

"Yes, what do you think, Niku? I'm aiming for English country cottage with hints of Africa."

The studio walls were decorated with inspiration boards, photographs and sketches of Jaishree's creative touch at Shakti Bhavan.

"Have you met Bhai and Bhabhi?" she questioned. I shook my head in reply.

"That's why I'm here, Jaish. I want to take Ree to meet them."

"Oh, good. I need to take some samples to them too." She picked up a folder with wallpaper and material samples.

"They're downstairs." He pointed to the floor with his thumb, as he saw my confusion.

My face fell; I had hoped the building wasn't occupied by the Rajas.

"Safari Safari is Rupa Bhabhi's travel company. She runs her business from here, too."

Everyone seemed to be successful in this family. My insecurities surfaced like a dog gnawing a bone. *How could they like someone like me, the daughter of a factory worker? Rich people only marry rich people.* My heart tightened a little. Nikesh Raja would never want to be with me permanently. *Don't get too close, Reena Solanki, this can only mean one thing: heartbreak.*

"It makes sense to have us all in one building," he continued. "Ree, Reena."

I forced myself to look at Nik and exhaled; he extended his hand to me and kissed the soft underside of my wrist as he led me to the central stairwell.

The foyer of Safari, Safari was like a high street travel agent. Comfortable chairs had been placed against the wall; there were vast vistas of African landscapes, and there was a large pine coffee table strewn with a selection of travel brochures. A pine reception desk was positioned in one corner; sitting at it was a smartly dressed young blonde talking on the telephone. She smiled and waved at Nik. We walked through a double door into a glass-encased corridor. On both sides were small offices. The occupants sat on dark padded office chairs, and two equally comfortable chairs were placed on the other side of the desks. It was a busy day; most of the offices had clients in them. At the end of the corridor, there was a sizeable full-width room. The glass was obscured, revealing only the outlines of people inside. We stood at the entrance of the enormous room. Sitting at a huge white glass table was a woman in a royal-blue trouser suit; underneath her jacket, she was wearing a loose-fitting white blouse. On the other side of the desk, sitting on a black Bauhaus chair, was a broad-shouldered man; his hair was shorter than Nik's but still styled long. The large table had a computer and several telephones. Behind the desk was a set of shelves displaying awards and photographs. Jaishree had displayed the samples in front of them, and the woman was intently considering the fabric swatches.

Nik's brother was leaning forward and listening to the women as they lifted one fabric swatch after another.

"Bhai, Rupa Bhabhi, can we come in?"

"Niku, you took your time." His brother lifted himself up gracefully from the chair. For a tall man, he was very graceful. He reminded me of a gazelle. I shook the thought out of my head; the lack of oxygen had me thinking of exotic animals. The knot of anxiety I usually get in new situations was taking its toll on my sanity.

He resembled Nik; he was dressed in a dark grey business suit with a pale cream shirt and floral silk tie. "How do you do?" He took my hand. "I'm Rajesh." His eyes were chocolate brown, and he was slightly broader than Nik. They exchanged a look. I felt I had just been given a seal of approval from his brother.

"Bhabhi." Nik bowed slightly to the woman who was sitting at the desk.

His bhabhi tapped her left cheek with her index finger. He turned into a shy boy and blushed before he rushed to her side and planted a kiss.

"So," she paused, glancing at me. "Aren't you going to introduce me?" She laughed; it came out as low and rumbling.

I thought how lovely that he could feel comfortable enough with his brother's wife to do that. I was also mesmerised by the woman who radiated sunshine from her very core.

Her teeth were straight and white except for one crooked left incisor; her lips were disproportionate, the top lip thinner than the bottom. Her thick, long, straight black hair was parted in the centre and swept up off her forehead. She had the most striking hazel eyes. She didn't have any of the features you would expect to see in most Indians; there were tiny freckles that danced across the bridge of her long nose and upper cheeks.

She walked elegantly to where I had grown roots.

She leant forward and kissed me on both cheeks, gently holding my shoulders. She was wearing Chanel No 5. I recognised the scent.

"It's a pleasure to meet you, Reena, I'm Rupa."

There was no hint of accent to tell me she might be Gujarati. She spoke impeccable English like an aristocrat's daughter.

I quickly examined her: she was wearing discreet gold jewellery, and on her left ring-finger, there was a substantial oval ruby engagement ring encrusted with diamonds with a simple gold wedding band.

"Come, sit." She pointed to a square cloth sofa covered in grey slub linen. "Can I get you a drink?" She headed to a small fridge placed opposite the seating area.

"Raju, Niku, do you want a beer? I think its drink o'clock time." She lifted up her left wrist and tapped her watch.

"Beer, glass of white wine, Coke, Perrier or orange juice?"

I asked for an orange juice. My sugar levels were depleting, and I was feeling light-headed. Nik clasped my hand. "Deep breaths, my love," he whispered in my ear.

"I'll have a wine please, Bhabhi." Jaishree gathered up the samples from the desk.

I nursed the glass in my hand as I listened to the siblings chattering and I relaxed a little. At least I was not being asked about my life. Rupa hadn't contributed much to the conversation. Everyone's eyes focused on her when she interrupted.

"Raju. You know I don't want modern rooms, I want cosy rooms," she said, smiling amicably at Rajesh and Jaishree.

"Right, it's sorted Bhai. Bhabhi wants cosy and whatever Bhabhi wants Bhabhi gets."

They all laughed and admired Rupa with eyes full of

love.

I thought back to the conversation Nik and I had outside and admonished myself for my narrow-mindedness. Rich people were just the same as people like me, especially the ones I had met that afternoon.

* * *

"WHAT ARE YOU DOING NIK? Umi's house is that way!" I pointed my hand to my left as he turned into a broad street to the right. He pulled up next to a tree, making sure he was parked away from the prying eyes from the houses nearby.

"I know. We deserve a little 'kissing in the back row'," he teasingly sang while grabbing my hand. I blushed, but my body ached for his kisses and cuddles too. My heart skipped a beat as he silently pushed the car seat back and climbed into the back seat. I saw the seriously wicked grin on his face in the yellow light of the lamppost. He pulled me onto his lap and began to plant small kisses on my jawline, working his mouth up to my lips. I inhaled him, reassured by the spicy smell of his aftershave. I felt lost in his arms and conceded to his yearning lips.

Sixteen

March 5th, 1983

"WHAT THE EFF, NIK? Are you an Indian prince or something?" Umi exclaimed as she spun around. Peter laughed and thumped Nik on his shoulders.

Nik had buzzed us through the gate, and I had watched Umi as she had the same reaction to Shakti Bhavan as I did when I came the day before. When I told her of the enormous house, she had laughed it off saying I was exaggerating.

"How did you sleep, my love?" Nik's smouldering eyes rested far too long on my lips. "Can I have a kiss?"

I blushed; the place was full of people milling around. He was wearing a pair of dark-blue jeans and a short-sleeved light-blue polo shirt. I wondered why he wasn't cold. I felt goosebumps rise on my arms, and I was wearing a striped polo-neck jumper.

Umi stopped spinning, gawked at me and apologised. "Sorry, no one lives in a house like this." We both giggled in embarrassment, as she had just misquoted David Frost. Umi and I were from a different social group; we didn't associate with people from Nik's social group. Our families had to work for a living. Umi was better off than me. I was penniless.

Nik grabbed Umi's hand and mine and walked us up the path that cut the walled garden in half. Peter ran ahead. When we entered the family room from one of the double doors, we saw Jay, Ravi and Dick sitting at the dining table, their plates full, chatting with Nik's siblings.

The six-foot white Carrera marble worktop, in the kitchen area, was laid out with breakfast dishes. Nik took us to the sitting area; my mouth dried as I recollected the last thing Nik's motaba had said to me. "Motaba, Papa, Kaka, Kaki, may I introduce Umi; she studies law with me."

"Kem cho, you have a lovely house." Umi stood with her palms pressed together in salutation.

"Thank you, Umi. Very nice to meet you," Nik's mother replied. I saw a brief look of shock on Umi's face as she, too, recognised the similarity to Sharmila Tagore. Nik's motaba nodded and glared directly into my eyes, her stare digging deep into my soul, scorn written all over her face.

"Good morning. Jai Shri Krishna," I greeted the elders. "Good morning, Reena." Nik's papa and father spoke in unison, lowering their newspapers.

"Jai Shri Krishna, Reena. You've certainly made a good impression on the people you met yesterday," Nik's motaba retorted disapprovingly.

I wanted the ground to swallow me up; *why didn't the woman like me?*

Nik's mother threw me a sympathetic smile. I exhaled. Nik's body tensed, and he turned abruptly around. "Come on, you two, I'm starving."

Ramprakash's Birthday Weekend
Saturday Breakfast

Methi na thepla
*griddle fried wheat flour, gram flour with fenugreek leaves, rolled
thin bread*

Makai na pawa
Gujarati-style steamed spiced sweet corn and flaked rice

Khatti keri athanu
*raw mango pickled with crushed mustard seeds, salt, chilli,
turmeric and lemon*

Riawala marcha
green chillies pickled in crushed mustard seeds

Amba hurdar
*green yellow and white turmeric root pickled in salted water and
lemon*

Dahi
natural yoghurt

Toast
Butter, jam and marmalade.
Masala chai, coffee with cream
Chopped fresh fruits
Fruit juices

Anu Masi and another lady, who I learnt was called Bhavini, were waiting at the breakfast bar

"Can I get you toast, Beta?" Anu Masi asked, smiling. The door to the full-height wall unit was opened revealing a toaster and a huge microwave.

I declined and asked for methi na thepla, makai na pawa, adding some sour mango pickle. I asked for an ordinary cup of tea if it wasn't any trouble.

We had refilled our cups of beverage and headed outside to sit on the big terrace at a large outdoor table that seated at least twelve people comfortably. I was introduced to Suresh, who had the same shaped twinkling eyes as his father, but all his other features were a carbon copy of his mother, Sarladevi. Sitting next to Jaishree was an exceedingly tall, dark coffee-skinned man with a deep dimple on his chin.

Suresh was regaling the group with the tale of his friend, Anil, and his sister, Jaishree's, first meeting. How Anil and Jaishree had fallen head over heels in love and couldn't wait to get married as soon as Anil finished studying. A small ray of hope stirred within. *If Jaishree was allowed to marry a man of her own choice, I might be considered suitable.* I swatted the thought away like an annoying fly. I was not even from the same social background.

Umi and I exchanged a smile; we had never seen any couple touch each other so much. Everyone could see they were very much in love. I was surprised Sarladevi hadn't tut-tutted at them yet, as elders in our community always frowned upon signs of affection. Rajesh informed us of the list of jobs that needed to be done before the caterers arrived for the party. Dick and Ravi decided to go for a walk. A metal skeleton of a huge marquee was being erected on one side of the house for the event.

Suresh was recounting a particular weekend when his university friend had declared his undying love for his sister, laughing at the recollection. Suddenly they stopped.

"Nikesh, I've put Reena and her girlfriend in Jaishree's old bedroom next to your kaka and kaki," Sarladevi said. "And I have given your room to Savitaben and Dolatbhai."

"Oh, I thought we could stay in the rooms above the garages, Motaba."

"I'd give up if I were you, Niku. You know what happened when Anil came to stay in my first year?" Suresh chortled under his breath.

Jaishree became still and peered bashfully at her feet. Anil gripped her hand under the table. I wondered what they could have done for the rapid embarrassment in their demeanour.

"Na, na I have put the two sisters in there."

"Where have you put my boyfriends and me?" Nik sighed.

"You and your boyfriends are all sleeping in the cinema room. Can you fetch the girls' bags out of the car and put them by the lift, Nikesh?"

She turned to Peter and instructed in English, "Can you take your bag to the cinema room, please." She walked back into the house.

"Lift!" Umi's jaw had dropped to the floor. Luckily, Sarladevi hadn't heard the outburst.

"Come on, Umi, let's get the bags." Peter stood up and dragged Umi away; she gawked back at me, mouthed "lift" and rolled her eyes.

"Beta, can I take Reena for a walk?" Nik's papa was standing by the table. "Do you have suitable footwear for a walk in the country?" I showed him my feet. "Ah good," he nodded as he inspected my trainers.

A broad smile grew across Nik's face, and he replied, "Sure, Papa, but I think you have to ask her if she wants to go for a walk with you."

"Of course, Reena Beti. Would you like to take this old man out for his daily exercise?" There was a slight smile developing in his eyes.

AS WE WALKED TO THE boot store, he explained he was diagnosed with a heart condition and had had strict instructions to do exercise every day. He was amicable, and softly spoken, and I felt at ease with him.

"Do you want to go to my favourite place in the whole wide world?" his silvery voice asked using the same words as Nik. My first impression was confirmed. I was going to enjoy getting to know Nik's papa.

He cleared his throat; I thought it was all too good to be true. He had probably been through this before. My heart tightened like someone was squeezing it. I had known Nik for twenty-three weeks, but it felt like I'd known him all my life. I braced myself for the news, telling myself I shouldn't show any emotion. I ran through the conversation in my head. I'm sure you're a lovely girl, but you shouldn't get ideas above your station. I recalled Sarladevi's words, 'You've certainly made a good impression.' They felt like sharp knives, piercing through my heart.

"I'm pleased you've come into Nikesh's life." I

stopped, startled at his words. "Ah, you are concerned with what Sarla said to you this morning. I must apologise for my wife; Sarla has always been aware of her status." A glimmer of sadness flickered in his eyes. He continued, "You'll meet many wealthy people in your lifetime, Reena. You'll definitely see some who flaunt their wealth tonight. You must not let wealth blind you to their true nature. Did you know Pushpa's family aren't wealthy? Well-educated, but not wealthy."

I hadn't. Nik's mother wasn't from a wealthy family; that explained why I liked her instantly.

"Nikesh has a wonderful soul; he cares about so many things. The only problem is he is spoilt rotten." He chortled and shook his head. "Most of it is my fault. When he was born, I wasn't there at his birth, and I regret it, so I overindulge him at times."

I thought it was a strange thing to say; most husbands of that generation wouldn't be at the birth of their child and Nik was his brother's son. I had to remind myself that they were an extended family, and it probably made no difference whose child he was to Nik's papa.

I suddenly had the impression I was being interviewed and persuaded to take the job. The job to be Nik's wife. I was not sure how I felt. A minute ago, I thought I would die, but I felt dread. I knew I wouldn't be able to fit in as easily as Pushpa Raja. We walked past the willow and headed towards the ruins. He rested and changed the subject. "What made you choose your degree? I've never met anyone who is studying film and television studies."

I started to tell him about the day Jane Cawthorne

came to make a documentary on the Gujarati community in Leicester.

"My daddy had put my name up for the BBC TV documentary to film a rangoli pattern using dyed rice flour. She was the producer and had explained they would shoot me doing the rangoli. She asked me what I used and where I had learnt the patterns. She wrote everything in a bound notepad. She made me feel at ease, and I didn't even notice the cameraman."

"How old were you?" he asked me.

"I was ten years old." He smiled at me, and I continued. "After that, I asked my daddy if I could go to the mandir to watch them film the other events. He agreed. You know, before that day, I was only interested in drawing and reading." I paused as a blush rose on my cheeks. I hadn't known why I wanted him to know that. He nodded with his kind eyes.

"Jane is this amazingly talented woman; she managed to get everyone to do what they needed to without making them feel intimidated." I said, smiling up at him.

"So, do you still keep in touch with her?" He had stopped for a breath.

"Yes. At the screening of the documentary at the mandir before they showed it on BBC Two, I asked Jane how I could become what she was doing. She laughed at first, but when she realised I was serious, she left an address and telephone number with my daddy and asked me to send her a letter. That's when she became my mentor."

"So, your father likes the career choice you've made?"

I had let out a long exhalation. "My daddy finds every

decision I make difficult."

He confirmed letting daughters go was difficult for all fathers. I thought about this and reflected on what he had said. I hadn't really thought about how my decision to go to Warwick University would affect my father. I was focusing on my career. Perhaps I should have been more sympathetic to my father's feelings.

We ambled silently and came to a scattering of stones. Six feet away, more piles of rocks revealed the outline of a medieval manor house; the only visible sign of it was the remnant of a chimney. He explained the new house was moved to its site during the reign of Queen Anne. We walked towards a wooden bench placed in the courtyard of the old house and sat watching the surrounding countryside. The arrival of spring had brought with it a patchwork blanket of green. All the creatures were beginning to wake from their long hibernation. The land was no longer barren, and the great greening had begun. We watched a pair of song thrushes chase each other in and out of the ruins of the chimney. He pointed to a field beyond, and we saw one, two, three, rabbits frolicking. I smiled up at him.

"You're the first girl Nikesh has brought home for us to meet."

I knew Nik had had a long-term girlfriend and wondered why he hadn't brought his first love to meet them.

"I know he has some bad habits; he finds responsibility difficult." He continued, "I like you, Reena. I think with you by his side, Nikesh will have nothing to worry about."

I didn't know what to say. What should you say to someone who had already married you off? I wasn't ready to be married. I was dumbfounded, yet my heart skipped and danced, then I saw her face. My reverie ended and I thought, *pity his wife doesn't think I am suitable*.

He glanced at his gold pocket watch. "What do you think about my favourite place?" he asked as he turned a full circle.

"It's lovely." I was refreshed by the countryside, and I couldn't stop the grin from drawing across my face. On our walk back, we talked about his plans to step down from the business, as Rajesh and Suresh had joined them, and he wished to persuade Anil to join the business too. His ambition was to hand over Nikesh Traders to the three younger men to take it to the next level.

***

"PAPA, GLAD TO SEE you're following your doctor's instructions," a woman shouted as she hurriedly walked towards us. I took a deep breath; I was about to meet another one of Nik's family.

Rita Parekh was a replica of Pushpa Raja, the same height, same build, same tingling laugh, the same tone of voice, only 20 years younger. She took her papa in her arms and gave him a big wet kiss on his cheek. "Happy Birthday for yesterday, Papa."

"Thank you, my dikri," he replied. She pulled away, holding his hands in hers adoringly.

"Rita, may I introduce you to Reena."

She turned and gave me a hug and planted a soft kiss on my cheek. "So, you're the girl who has stolen my brother's heart?"

I flushed. Nik had informed all his family about me. I,

on the other hand, had kept him a secret. My brother Amit and I were very close, but I hadn't been able to tell him about Nik. I was not sure telling my big brother I had a boyfriend was a good idea after only three months. Umi had introduced Nik to Amit during Navratri, and he seemed nonchalant about it, but I wouldn't bet on it that he was happy. I knew my future bhabhi had an inkling I had someone special in my life, especially after the conversation we had on New Year's Eve. This was the first Indian family I had met whose children weren't nervous about bringing their girlfriends or boyfriends home.

"Finally. That was a long walk, Papa." I felt Nik's eyes drawing an arc on my face. I locked on his eyes and gave him a small affirmation that I was okay.

He pulled out his elbow and instructed his papa and his sister he needed me to sort through some lights in the marquee.

"Niku, promise me you'll bring Reena to the swimming pool after you're done," Rita shouted. We turned around and stopped.

"Sure, Ben; just need Ree's creative flair for the lights." Nik noticed the change in my breathing and whispered, "I'll take you on the tour of Shakti Bhavan; Umi's already been." He grinned from ear to ear.

Seventeen

WE WALKED TO THE FRONT of the house. Suddenly a peacock landed on the lawn and started to strut and dance, displaying his feathers. I gawked at the peacock, and I repeated Umi's words, "What the eff, Nik? Are you an Indian prince or something?"

He laughed out loud and quietly replied, "Maybe. And you'll be my princess." He grabbed me around the waist and pulled me to the main entrance, the one I had been deprived of the day before.

The gigantic ceiling-height doors were made from dark mahogany wood; they were carved in the style of ornate temple doors. Nik pulled at the substantial antique brass handle and opened it to let me into the house. We were back in the pink and golden hallway. I surveyed the details again. There was a pair of double doors opposite the entrance, but he took me through another set on our right. Next to them was an iron gate.

"What is that?" I asked Nik.

"Oh, the lift shaft," he replied.

The swimming pool was at least twenty feet long; on

the left of the pool room, there was a set of doors that could be opened to the elements and led to a garden. I took a deep breath and counted the pool loungers one, two, three, four, five, six, to calm down. I was happy Nik wanted me to meet his family, but all in one weekend was a bit too much. I thought it would have been better if I'd met them away from Shakti Bhavan. To be honest, Shakti Bhavan probably needed to be met in small doses, too.

A head popped up from under the water; she was wearing a white swimming cap to protect her hair.

"Hello, you two. I've got two more laps to do." She smiled up at me. "Niku why don't you go sit on the chairs by the shallow end."

Rita stepped out of the pool, grabbed an aquamarine towel and wrapped it around her shoulders before she sat down. Her smile resembled her brother's. She reached across and squeezed his hand, scrutinising his face.

"Tell me one thing about Reena you like?"

"Her laugh and her quirky dress sense, but mostly I love her laugh," he replied, and I burst out laughing from the nerves to demonstrate.

Rita laughed too, "You're growing up, Niku. If I'd asked you last year, you would have said something stupid about her body."

"Come on, Ben; that's not true. I don't just like girls for their bodies."

"Yes, yes I believe you, Niku." She patted his hand. "Do you have brothers, sisters Reena?"

I prepared myself for another interview. As I talked, my eyes kept drifting to the pool and the lure of the water. I imagined how it would feel to be in the pool, relaxing and floating. I loved swimming; it was one thing we did as a family regularly.

"Do you swim?"

"Oh yes. We often go to the swimming baths. It's something my father started to do with us after my mother died."

My eyes watered, and I blinked back the tears. I didn't want to talk about my mother. The memory flooded my senses with sadness. Nik moved his hand to hold mine; he had noticed the change in my voice as I mentioned her. Rita changed the subject and teased Nik about his first experience of water.

"Hello, hello, my favourite people." Rupa stepped through a glass door.

She was wearing a pale-pink towelling dressing gown. She sat deflated on the only empty chair. "I want to go to the sauna."

Nik quickly explained there was a sauna, a steam room, a gym, a shower room and the plant room along the side of the pool room.

"You can't! You know what motaba thinks about the heat in your condition."

My eyes rested on Rupa's hand; she was stroking her belly. *Why can't you use the sauna if you're pregnant?* I thought.

"It's not for long, Bhabhi, and you know she has her customs and rituals."

Rupa stood up, slipped her gown off to reveal a floral swimming costume and walked into the swimming pool.

"At least I'm allowed to swim now," she said and dived under the water. When she emerged, she turned gracefully, like a synchronised swimmer, and shouted, "Reena, have you brought your swimming costume?" I shook my head. Rita jumped up.

"Great idea, Bhabhi. I think Jaishree is the same size. Come with me, Reena,"

"No way!" Nik gripped my hand "You've all hogged her for far too long today. I'm taking her on a grand tour." He pulled me up and headed back out into the entrance hall; he was walking so fast I had to run.

Tinkling laughter echoed through the pool room as we headed out. "You're right, Bhabhi, he's got it bad," Rita said.

NIK'S ROOM WAS PAINTED azure blue with a double bed in the centre; it was furnished in an eclectic style of modern and antique pieces. There was a 1930s walnut bedside table on one side of the bed, and a pine chest of drawers painted white with ceramic handles on the other. A small sofa was positioned opposite a Juliet balcony. He had a modern white desk and a comfortable desk chair facing the wall opposite the bed. I was examining the spines on the bookshelf next to it when I heard the key turn.

"Bahar se koi ..." His baritone sent shivers down my spine. 'Nobody can come in from the outside.'

"Nobody can go out from the inside." His eyes sparkled with gold.

It was a song from my favourite Bollywood film, Bobby. "Hum Tum Ek Kamre Mein Band Ho." He slowly stepped towards me and stopped. "Think what would happen in such a situation." He took one more step and stood in front of me. We were almost touching. He wrapped his arms around me and started kissing me all over my face, his hands in my hair, on my upper back, my lower back, drifting to my bottom. "Oh my God, Ree; I can't take this anymore." He sighed as his lips met mine; we kissed, and the strength of our kisses grew deeper and deeper. He pulled me to the bed.

"Nik," I gasped in between the kisses. He was lying on the bed and had pulled me on top of him.

"Why did you choose a polo neck? I can't get to my favourite places."

"Nik, someone might come," I implored.

"You and I are both locked in a room, and the key is lost," he sang in response.

I had moaned in reply as his tongue met mine. I hadn't realised I, too, had missed him, missed being able to touch him. His hands had slipped under my jeans; pushing them off my bottom, his fingers were gripping me with longing. My hand grabbed at his belt and touched the little tufts of hair above his pubic bone. I felt his shudder and heard his moan and then I remembered where we were.

"Please, Nik. We can't." My whole being wanted him, needed him. "Not in Shakti Bhavan," I uttered breathlessly. He stopped and pulled my jeans back up and fastened them, his actions slow and full of regret. He straightened my polo neck jumper, and he gently lifted me off him. He knelt on the floor in front of me, reaching for my hands. He lifted them to plant little kisses on my wrist, little yearning kisses on my palm, little hungry kisses on my knuckles. He fixed his eyes on mine and kissed the tips of my fingers.

"Then Nikesh will get lost in the charm of your eyes," he crooned one more time. Every single hair on my body was upright. A chill ran through me. Nik stood up, lifted me up in his arms and gave me a kiss full of longing, releasing me reluctantly, and he inhaled deeply. "Okay, I'll wait, but you should know I'm lost in those charming eyes."

✳ ✳ ✳

THE CATERERS HAD ARRIVED in three large vans and were unloading the equipment. Nik had told me there would be Punjabi, South Indian and African foods. I was impressed; most functions I attended had one type of food. You either had Gujarati catering, English catering and, lately, some Punjabi catering. I thought back to Mayur Bhai and Rohini Bhabhi's tenth wedding anniversary party I had been invited to last summer. As far as I was aware, it was an expensive function, and we had Punjabi food and hot naan made in a portable tandoor. This was on another level. If Mayur Bhai was wealthy, the Rajas were super-rich.

We had entered an enormous drawing room; this was a formal sitting room. The furniture was ornate and antique. The whole room was littered with small elegant tables, their shiny polished surfaces laden with trinkets and small photo frames. The theme for this room was cream with hints of aquamarine and jade. Heavy curtains draped elegantly from thick mahogany poles with huge carved artichoke-shaped finials above the tall windows. The floor was carpeted with exquisitely decorated cream Persian rugs placed to form three distinct areas. A formal sitting area where two large sofas with soft feather cushions, padded backs and wooden lions claw legs were positioned opposite each other with two pairs of arabesque chairs placed around a polished walnut coffee table. A cosy sitting area next to the white Regency-style Carrara marble fireplace with a green leather Chesterfield sofa facing it. To enhance the symmetry of the arrangement, a pair of buttoned-back tall armchairs covered in a jade fabric had been placed on each side of the sofa. On the wall above the chimney breast was a tall gold-framed family portrait of the Rajas. The other side of the room was designated for writing and group games, backgammon, playing cards and chess. Three small, square, dark-wood tables had been placed along the width, and a variety of chairs had been positioned around each. A writing bureau with a thin writing chair had been placed against one wall. There was a set of glass double doors leading to a formal dining room. On the side of the door was a small sofa with lion's claw feet covered in cream floral linen fabric with a jade piping. A low padded chest had been placed in front as a table or footrest. Next to it was a child's playpen. Peter, Jay, Ravi and another man were playing cards at a table with cabriole legs. I assumed the man must be Sunil, Rita's husband.

Umi was sitting by the fireplace with Suresh, Jaishree, Anil, Dick and a tall slim girl with a short bob. Nik guided me to the fireplace, and we sat down on the Chesterfield.

"Reena, meet my lovely fiancée, Ashi," Suresh said. They were sitting on one of the armchairs; the woman sat confidently on his lap.

"Hi, Ashi. You don't mind if I call you that?" I raised a wave to her.

"No, not at all, some of my friends call me Veena and some call me Ash. Most of the people who live here call me Ashi." She smiled.

Ashveena Mehta was tall for a Gujarati woman at five feet five inches tall. She had a long nose with a small hook; her eyebrows had been plucked and were arched over a pair of dark eyes. Her heavy fringe and smooth bob encased her oval face. Her hair had an auburn tint to it. When she smiled, the shape of her eyes rose upwards. She was wearing light make-up, her milky-coffee-coloured complexion was enhanced with subtle blusher, and a bright pink lipstick accentuated her full wide mouth. She informed me she was in her final year at Aston University studying public relations, and I understood why Suresh travelled up to Birmingham often and brought food for Nik.

"Come on everyone, lunch is served," Rita shouted from the double doors leading to the hallway. Nik led me to the door. As we stepped out into the hall, Rita questioned us. "Have you introduced Reena to Sunil?"

"No, Ben. Jijaji was playing cards. I didn't want to interrupt his game."

She said she'd introduce me to him later.

"Where's Sammy, Ben? I haven't seen him all morning?"

She laughed. "You've not been around." She wagged a finger at him. "He's having a nap; you'll see him later. Go, go get your lunch, I'm going to wait for Sunil." We watched her walk into the drawing room.

The breakfast bar in the family kitchen was laid out with lunch. Dick joined me when I went to get my plate of food and asked me what the dishes were.

Gujarati vegetarian food is one of the best things you can eat for lunch; it's light and, in this case, there were a couple of dishes to choose from. I pointed and told Dick what each dish was called and what was in them. He began to load the ceramic plate with one of each. "I'm not taking the sandwiches or chips," he whispered. "I know what they taste like." He threw his toothy smile in my direction. I didn't take the chips or the sandwiches either and picked up a fresh orange juice from where the drinks were placed on trays.

Ramprakash's Birthday Weekend
Saturday Lunch

Palu Bhaji
fried bread rolls with mashed spiced vegetable and butter

Mattar kachori
fried plain flour pastry encased balls of masala peas

Bombay sandwiches
toasted sandwich made with tomatoes, cheese, onions, boiled potatoes and coriander chutney and special spice blend

Ambli khajjur ni chutnee
tamarind date chutney

Dhana, marcha ni chutnee
fresh coriander and green chilli chutney

Kapali dungari
chopped onions

Cheese and salad sandwiches
fried potato chips
Fruit juices

I loved what we were eating; so much food, so many choices. I felt sorry for the ladies who worked in the kitchen, Anu Masi and Bhavini, until I overheard Suresh comment his mother's peas kachori was the best ever when Peter commented on how good it was. Nik had said his motaba was a great cook, but I hadn't expected her to cook these meals. I thought of my Divya Ba and how she could cook for so many people without flinching and felt admiration for these fantastic matriarchs.

Relief washed over me when I had finally met Sunil. I had never liked being the centre of attention, preferring my own company most of the time. We were all sitting in the drawing room with Rita, Sunil and their son, Sameer. Jay had sat down near Nik; throughout the day, he had glared at me with his beady eyes and had made me feel like I was not welcome. Jaishree and Ashveena had gone to have their nails done for the party. Suresh, Anil and Rajesh were dealing with the caterers, in their sports clothing, prepared to hit the gym once they had finished the remaining chores. We had one more job to do before we could relax too. Rajesh had instructed us on our final task to make up the temporary beds in the cinema room.

Rita had brought Sammy into the drawing room, placing him in the playpen. The little boy was happily playing with wooden bricks and bright plastic toys. Nik had moved closer and closer to the playpen, his eagerness visible on his face. He laughed and ruffled the baby's curly black hair, as they played a game of passing toys to and fro. It seemed that Umi had fallen in love with Sunil's voice and maybe even Sunil. She couldn't stop asking him questions about his work, and what he was going to specialise in once his registrar stint in hospital was over. I understood what was appealing; he had an excellent bedside manner, and his voice was deep and calm. He had a prominent jaw and an oblong face with high-defined cheekbones. He had large expressive eyes and the longest eyelashes I had seen on anyone. What added to the distinguished look was a streak of white hair in the middle of his forehead. His hair was cut short at the sides and long at the top, slicked back with a low side parting. Rita watched and smiled with her eyes. I was confident that she knew the effect her husband had on women. Peter and Ravi had sat down at the card table and were playing cards again. Dick had closed his eyes, his arms supporting his head and his legs stretched out, listening quietly. Jay had drifted to Sameer and Nik and was also playing with him. I took a sneak peek at Nik and saw how he loved to spend time with Sammy. I added another reason to my list of why I loved Nikesh Raja.

***

WE WERE ALL UPSTAIRS TAKING out the bedding, the only job we hadn't done yet. Nik called the lift and opened the metal gate; once the bedding was loaded, he pulled me inside and quickly closed the gate.

"Whoa, let us in Nik," they had all chimed.

He scowled at them and quietly replied, "No, I want Ree in here." He pressed the button for the basement, and, as the door closed, I saw a fleeting look of disdain on Jay's face.

Ravi chortled, "Have you no shame?"

They were waiting at the lift doors in the basement. Nik had pressed the ground floor to lengthen the time for kisses in between each level. I was blushing when the door opened. Peter came into the lift, picked me up and carried me fireman-style to the cinema room. Nik yelled in protest at Peter, shouting he'd kill him if any harm came to me. We laughed and joked and then fell in a heap on the soft armchairs.

The cinema room had seats in the centre and large banquettes on three sides. We quickly made up the beds on the banquettes, and Nik took us through to a secret door to a dark room. The walls here had exposed stone. It was an old wine cellar; there were bottles of wine in the dark recesses, but, where we had entered, there was a bar with a drinks fridge, a table-football table, two old brown leather sofas and tub chairs. It smelt of cigarette smoke and alcohol.

"A secret smoking room!" Dick howled, as he slapped Nik on the shoulder.

"Do you have cigarettes here, Nik, I'm dying for one?" Umi grabbed at his arm. He reached behind the bar and pulled out a tortoiseshell cigarette box. Everyone except Dick and I reached for a cigarette or cigarillo. We sat down on the sofa, our stomachs full, happy to spend our last weekend before the exams in this house that resembled a posh hotel.

Eighteen

JAISHREE'S OLD ROOM WAS very much a sanctuary for her artistic talent. There was a French armoire and a matching dressing table placed against one of the walls. A bookshelf full of art books ran along one wall, and I wished I had the money to have some of them on my bookshelf. Above the bed was a set of posters from French Impressionist art exhibitions from around the world. On the opposite wall was a large print of Monet's 'Water Lilies'.

Umi and I had a couple of hours to spare before the party and were gossiping about the people we had met so far and Nik's exceedingly posh house. Our outfits for tonight were displayed on the bed. Most of my clothes were second hand; they were either hand-me-downs from family friends, or I found them from charity shops, my favourite being Oxfam. Umi's were new, except she had agreed to wear an outfit I had adapted for her tonight.

"What have we done? It's like being in *Dynasty*," Umi said.

I reminded her of her insistence on coming to the

party. Umi and Dick were so excited about the invitation to the party that they had convinced us all to say yes. Dick and I had trawled all the charity shops to find outfits and Umi had reluctantly agreed she, too, wouldn't mind wearing something old.

One of the advantages of volunteering at the Oxfam shop on Hereford Street was that the volunteers got a first glance at some of the items sent to the shop. Mrs Jackson had set aside a bag from Mrs Spanswick, a wealthy banker's wife. She had expensive taste. However, she only gave away clothes that were damaged. That's how I found my designer scarves. I don't know what she used to fasten them, but she gave a lot of those away. The shop also had a sewing machine set up in the back room to fix minor damage. My home economics classes at school covered sewing and developed my love of making clothes from old dress patterns. I had found the '70s style full-sleeve black crepe silk jumpsuit in the bag. The seam had loosened on the left leg, and the bottom edge of the right leg had a slash. I had opened up the seam to above my knees on both legs, and, as Mrs Spanswick was taller than me, the tear on the bottom edge could be cut away. I had bought some pearl beads to sew on the collar and had taken the sleeves off and had made a red-silk tie belt from scraps I had collected from my job at Roop Lila to bring in the waist. Dick was going to wear a maroon jacket and black slim-leg trousers that Mrs Jackson had given him. It had belonged to her son, who had tired of it. The jacket was long, the trousers narrow, in the style of Teddy boys. I'd sewn on a black ribbon down the outside of the legs. I had found a pair of satin silk bright-yellow flares for Umi, and we had gone to C&A to buy a freesia-pink vest top to wear with them. I'd made some big roses from the floral print silk from my stash of useful material, created a bunch, and sewn it on one shoulder.

Umi was helping me with pinning my hair up when there was a knock on the door. Rupa Bhabhi was dressed in a black silk dressing gown; she had curlers in her hair and had applied party make-up. "Hello, girls. I just thought I'd bring my jewellery over to see if you want to wear any of it." She was holding a large carved sandalwood box that she placed on the dressing table. "Show me what you're wearing," she asked. "I love these trousers, Umi." She felt the material. "Let's get you sorted first." She picked up a pair of long earrings with huge pink stones. "Are you wearing your hair down? They'll only work if you're wearing it loose." Umi's face was full of apprehension. She preferred to wear studs but nodded. Rupa Bhabhi commented on my hair. She held a pair of pearl cluster studs the size of a penny in one hand and huge red stone studs in the other and asked me to choose. I chose the pearls. "Good choice," she confirmed. "You'll look stunning in these clothes, girls. I'll see you later." She picked up the box and headed for the door. "Thank you, Bhabhi," we said in unison.

***

UMI AND I WERE SITTING on a pair of chairs placed together in the opulent entrance hall. We had been staring at the photographs resting on the shiny black Steinway, trying to work out which baby photo belonged to which Raja; they were all identical, wearing white smocks, shot in a photographic studio with a painted backdrop. It was too tricky, so we had decided to sit and wait. We heard them before we saw them; they were laughing and joking as they climbed up the stairs. We stood up; Peter blew a wolf whistle. The hair on my arms bristled.

"Sorry, couldn't help it. You look amazing."

We both raised a smile. Peter and Ravi were wearing black tuxedos and had decided on red bow ties instead of the black. Dick was dashing in his maroon jacket and trousers and paired it with a frilly shirt and cravat instead of a bow tie. To add to the bohemian look, he wore a pair of black winklepickers and had scrunched the hair he wore longer at the top in the style of David Bowie. Nik and Jay were wearing black tuxedos with black bow ties and cummerbunds with patent leather shoes. Jay was whispering something in Nik's ear. Nik's brow furrowed, and he threw an angry look at Jay. My heart raced when I saw him, and I had to let out a slow breath to calm down. His eyes had fixed on mine as he came forward and picked up my right hand and raised it to his lips. I shuddered slightly.

"I missed you, my darling." His eyes turned to Umi and he said, "Wow! You look stunning, Umi!"

"You're such a flirt, Nikesh Raja," she chortled.

"Come on, let's go find the bar, I'm thirsty." Peter slapped Nik on the shoulder, and we all agreed an alcoholic drink was in order.

Nik lingered in the entrance hall allowing the others to walk ahead. He drew an appreciative eye over my outfit. His voice lowered and was full of longing. "I could ravish you here and now, but I won't. I promised … I'd wait." I felt the heat rise in my body. "Oh, you smell delicious. May I have one kiss."

Panic surfaced in my eyes; he dragged me to the room on the right of the entrance. He took me in his arms and kissed the tops of my shoulders, neck and then my lips. I returned the kiss. When I pulled away for a breath, I saw that we were in a home temple with an ornate cream full-length curtain across one of the walls. I saw a large photograph of a portly man with an orange turban and a fresh flower garland. Behind him were paintings of Sita and Ram and Radha and Krishna. I pushed him away. "We're in a mandir!"

"Now you've seen every room in the house. Motaba and Kaki were preparing things for tomorrow's puja earlier," he replied nonchalantly.

We have a small shrine in my house that sits on a shelf in the dining room. My father usually lights a divo on special days and birthdays. I shook my head; *what else should I have expected*. Everything about the weekend had been excessive. I inhaled and prepared myself for the party, remembering Nik's papa's words from the morning walk.

There was a fleet of cars parked in the driveway. I noted the makes. Mercedes, BMW, Jaguar and a couple of Rolls-Royces. People dressed in their finery were heading to the marquee; some nodded hello to Nik. I pulled my hand out of his, and he chuckled. "I don't care who sees us, Ree."

"But I do," I told him under my breath.

At the entrance to the marquee stood two waiters holding drinks trays. Nik picked up two champagne glasses and placed one in my hand. I searched anxiously for our friends. There was a band playing instrumental versions of Indian Bollywood songs in one of the corners. In the middle down one side, there was a long table decorated with balloons. Behind the table were the lights we had arranged earlier. They twinkled 'Happy Birthday'. The dance floor was in the middle of the marquee, and round tables covered in white tablecloths had been placed around it. The air was thick with the scent of flowers from the centrepieces.

Rajesh walked slowly towards us. "You are beautiful tonight Reena, and with your hair up you look like Mumtaz." He stood in front of me and pulled out his arm. "I'm taking her to meet some of my friends, Niku. You can come along if you want." He glanced at his younger brother. I resigned myself to another session of introductions. I gulped back my champagne and handed the empty glass to Nik; he placed it on a passing drinks tray and gave me another one. Meeting Rajesh's friends wasn't as daunting as Nik's family; they were all very charming and easy-going, jokingly warning me to run away from Nik as fast as I could. Nik took their ribbing with good grace and was enjoying himself. He knew everyone present including some of his parent's business associates and was polite and charming and thoroughly enjoying himself. I had always thought my brother could work a room with his confident stride and secure manner. But he was nowhere near as sure as Nik. I suppose your upbringing does make a big difference. Amit had had to deal with a little sister, a drunken father and money worries. Nik had had the support of his family and the privilege that comes with money.

"Let them enjoy the evening," Rupa interrupted. She had put her hair up in a high ponytail, and the soft curls tumbled down her back. She was wearing a maroon silk-chiffon saree with silver filigree cutwork. She wore a ruby and diamond necklace and a pair of large ruby teardrop earrings that just brushed her jawline.

Nik's father was at the microphone. "Ladies and gentlemen. Thank you for coming to celebrate the birthday of my hero, my friend, my mentor and my big brother. Motabhai, Bhabhi, can I ask you to come to the table please."

Nik's papa and motaba walked across the floor to stand behind the table. The lights dimmed, and a big cake with sixty candles was brought in by two of the serving staff. The band's male singer started to sing.

"Baar baar din yeh aaye," the usual song sung by Indians at birthday parties.

Ramprakash beckoned his brother and his wife to share the cake with them. All the children gathered behind the table, and the photographer asked them to smile.

"They all have the same smile," Umi remarked, and I acknowledged that even though they were from two different mothers, the Raja gene was certainly dominant. The children's partners joined them for a family photograph. Jaishree and Ashveena had opted for evening gowns in the latest fashion, balls of taffeta in the style of Lady Diana. Jaishree was wearing a teal one-shoulder gown with black velvet trim around the waist and Ashveena was wearing a black mutton-sleeved gown with bright pink and green sculpted flowers on the plunging neckline. Rita was wearing a cream lace saree with a high-collared sleeveless blouse. She was wearing her hair loose, and I admired the cut; its long layers emphasised her round face. She pointed to me and urged me to join them in the photograph. I shook my head and stayed steadfastly in my chair. Nik also waved at me to join them. I threw him a look of annoyance, and he shrugged his shoulders.

When Nik walked back to our table, he beckoned the photographer over to take a photograph of us. As the photographer instructed us to get closer, I felt the disapproving eyes from the room.

Nik had placed me on one side and Umi on the other. I had noticed he had done this quite often that evening. I think he felt he needed to protect Umi from the attention she was getting. She had been inundated with a stream of admirers. I thought he had nothing to worry about as I had seen Umi in action and knew for a fact she could take care of herself.

As soon as the cake had gone back to be sliced, a hoard of staff came with starters. "Excuse me, Sir, do you want non-veg or vegetarian?" the waiter asked Nik.

"We'll have both," he informed him.

Three large chargers were placed on the table, each filled with dishes from the Punjab, South India and East Africa. I had to ask about the starters. I hadn't come across, coconut fried shrimps, red spice chicken, or Ugandan rolex. The food was excellent. I knew for a fact the men in Nik's family ate meat and fish, as there was a kitchen for them in the garage complex. I also knew that in traditional Hindu Gujarati families, the women were expected to be vegetarian as is the case in Nik's family.

For the main meal, we were directed to the different food stations that had been dotted along the paved area of the back garden. There was also a demarcation of meat and vegetarian stations, too. As we headed to the meat queue, I felt everyone scrutinising Umi and me. I heard their voices. 'Did you see that girl eating meat, drinking? Wonder what else she does?' Umi had huffed and puffed about how it's one rule for men and another for women. We had decided we would get plates of each type of food and share it at the table. I was queuing at the Punjabi meat station when a familiar voice from the vegetarian station said, "I don't believe that girls need education. They develop a sense of worth you cannot manipulate. Look at Rupa: instead of learning our ways, she is working on her business."

The other woman laughed. "Can I have a garlic naan?" I was shocked at what Nik's motaba had said. Nik's mother was educated. Did she feel that way about her, too? Perhaps I'd got it all wrong. I thought she liked her.

The first song the band played was a Swahili song, "Jambo Bwana," that had just come out. I thought of my father and how he would love it and reminded myself to ask if it was available on a cassette. Suddenly I missed him. Everyone including Nik's papa and motaba were on the dance floor; they had obviously heard of the song before, and I was impressed they were singing along with the band.

The band played a mixture of Indian Bollywood and Western songs. We danced as a group until I tired and sat it out for some of the dances to observe the party. Nik had gone to the crowded bar to get some more beer for our table. I was desperate to go to the toilet again. I had indicated to Umi I was going, and she had mouthed to me, asking if I needed company. I shook my head. She was dancing with Peter, who had decided that if he kept dancing with her, none of her increasing number of admirers would dare to approach. I had smiled at his protectiveness and thought how he, too, couldn't keep his eyes off her.

I was climbing back up the stairs from the basement cloakroom when I heard a woman ask, "Who is that beautiful girl in the trouser suit?"

"My Nikesh's university friend," I heard Sarladevi reply. She said friend in English and I could detect a sneer in her voice.

"Pretty and clever," concluded the other woman.

I was glued to the step. If I climbed up, they would know I had heard. I waited, hoping they would leave soon. I could not listen any more; inadequacy washed over me. I had been feeling buoyant before the encounter, and the alcohol had loosened my nerves. I was back to my first day at Loudwater.

"Haan, haan, but what use is a degree, when all they want to do is get married and have babies?" Sarladevi added.

"You're right, Sarla. So what does her father do?"

"Nothing, he's a factory worker." Nik's motaba replied with contempt.

I felt the breeze as the door opened and heard the faint sound of their voices as they stepped outside. My eyes stung, and I tried to push back the angry tears. 'Nothing … factory worker,' resounded in my head. She was never going to like me. Nik was wrong. *I was not a snob, his motaba was.* The whole weekend had been surreal. I was staying in a house that could easily be a stately home. I knew this because I had seen photographs in posh magazines at the doctor's surgery. The amount of money needed to run the house was probably more than my brother and father's combined annual income. People like me worked for people like them; they didn't have stupid dreams about happy ever after. Besides, it was the first year of university, and I had read in an article that very few university relationships survive. I took a deep breath and told myself to get a grip. As I climbed back up to the lavish hallway, the door opened and I brushed the edge of my eyes, glancing at the many mirrors.

"Here you are. I've been looking everywhere. I have something special to show you." He held the door open. I walked hesitantly towards it, head bowed. He tried to catch my eye and reached out his right hand. I held my hands behind my back. His steps matched mine, and he pointed to the opposite direction to the marquee.

The waxing moon was low on the horizon, and there was a chill in the air. The scent of the camellias filled my nostrils as we walked towards the tennis courts. Nik took his jacket off and put it around my shoulders. Our bodies bumped into each other periodically. Although I was making an effort to keep a gap, I couldn't help but be drawn to him. My head told me this would never work, but my heart, my heart had already leapt out of my chest and nestled next to his.

"I need some heavy petting, before we go back in for the slow dance."

I laughed, not at his choice of words, but to relieve the tension. He knew I was upset; he had a sixth sense when it came to me. I was always surprised he was always there when I needed him most.

"I bet you say that to all the girls," I teased.

"No, only you, Ree." He stopped and turned me to face him. "Only you."

He pulled me towards him. He felt my body tense. "The place is too big for us to bump into anyone." He pulled at me, walking backwards to the big oak tree.

I insisted Nik stayed outside as I walked back into the marquee. I watched for him. He stepped in nonchalantly, his hands in his trouser pockets. The lights dropped; his face filled with a grin. He slid next to me and whispered, "Now we're inconspicuous. Most of the old people here can't see very well in the dark."

The band said goodbye and the DJ started to play a slow song. The first song on the turntable was by The Commodores, "Once Twice Three Times a Lady."

I was surprised to see Nik's father had brought his mother onto the dance floor. They started to dance, gliding elegantly in a slow waltz. By the time the second song came on, even Sarladevi had been persuaded onto the dance floor. Their children had managed to manoeuvre the couple together, and they were also dancing a slow waltz.

By the third song, "Sau Saal Pehle", Nik was grinning like a Cheshire cat as his parents and family danced. He stood up, leant in; my heart jumped to my mouth.

"I'll be back soon," he whispered. I was relieved. I watched him stride to his sister and tap Sunil on the shoulder. She smiled radiantly up at her brother. I didn't know why I was surprised Nik could waltz. I had danced a slow dance with him before, but never the waltz. At student discos there just isn't room for a waltz. I wondered what else he hadn't told me about himself. Halfway through the song, he deftly swapped his sister for his mother; she smiled up at him and kissed him on his cheek. I was filled with the warmth of love between the parents and children. I hadn't seen this before, not in real life anyway. I'd seen films where the parents danced with grown-up children. At the functions I usually attended, the parents sat at the tables waiting for their children to finish dancing.

I went to the bar to get a jug of water. When I returned, he was waiting for me. The DJ put on my favourite song by Barry Manilow. Nik put his hand out to me, raised his left eyebrow, and I knew we would be dancing the slow dance until the music stopped.

We walked into the main house, arm in arm. I was a bit drunk and didn't care anymore if anyone saw us. Nik's siblings were saying goodnight to our friends as they headed to the family room for tea and coffee. The guys dragged Umi and me downstairs to the cinema room. I peered at my watch; it was 1.30 a.m.

"Come on, let's watch my favourite film," Jay shouted. We all shushed him and giggled. Peter and Dick fetched more beers from the drinks fridge, and we settled down to watch the film on the gigantic TV screen. Jay was sitting in one of the armchairs.

"Turn the lights off, someone. Nik, Nik, come sit next to me," Jay shouted.

Nik sat down on an armchair next to Jay, pulling me to sit down on his lap. Jay glanced sideways at us. His face was unreadable.

"I know this film," Peter exclaimed. "I love it." He started to sing. "Ye Dosa Tea Ham Na Hee."

The Indians in the room gawked like goldfish. Umi and I laughed out loud at his version of the Hindi film classic. We settled down to watch Amitabh and

Dharmendra and remembered our childhood days of going to the cinema with our family. Dick was the only one who didn't have the shared experience. Luckily there were English subtitles on this version, and he, too, would understand the Western-inspired, buddy movie, *Sholay*.

As the song started, Jay got to his feet, pulling at Nik as he pushed me away. Nik's face darkened, and I shook my head and smiled at him. Jay held Nik around his waist and swayed while singing the song. I exchanged a look with Dick; we had had a conversation about his possessiveness and his abruptness with me. I was not sure what was going on. Peter joined in and began to sing, too, so we all stood up and sang holding each other around the waist.

When the song finished, we laughed at Peter, a Nigerian who grew up watching Bollywood films, and felt how amazingly small the world was and how we had had the good fortune to meet each other, even though we came from different parts of the world and different social classes.

Nineteen

March 6th, 1983

FOR THE PUJA, I had decided to wear a grass-green kanjivaram-silk saree of my mother's with a high necked, long-sleeved saree blouse I had made from a golden and maroon silk brocade piece of fabric. given to me by Rohini Bhabhi when I worked at Roop Lila. In my ears, I had small gold studs that I have had since I was ten and a thin gold chain around my neck that my Divya Ba had given me as a present for my 18th birthday. I could never be as elegant or as well dressed as the women in Nik's family, but I knew I had a talent for combining old and new.

Umi was wearing a saffron yellow chaniya choli with silver embroidery that brought out the golden hues in her dark complexion. I knew she would look stunning in the outfit when she had shown it to me. I smiled up at her as she acknowledged all the admiring eyes she was getting as we walked into the family room.

Nik was talking to his jijaji, who was returning his

empty plate to Bhavini. I loved him in traditional Indian clothes, the pale peach and cream raw-silk jabo pyjamas sculpted his broad chest and back. Butterflies awoke in my stomach. He hastily walked over to us, his eyes admiring Umi's ensemble and then, slowly, his eyes roamed over my body.

"How was your sleep?" He paused. "Did you dream about me? I dreamt we danced the slow dance all night in my bedroom." His voice was low, his warm breath wafted in my ear. I quickly glanced around to make sure no one else had heard. The butterflies settled in my mouth, and I forced the blush down. Dick was heading towards us, his plate loaded with food, a cup of coffee in his other hand.

"Nik, your family knows how to feed people. I've probably eaten more this weekend than I do in a month. Reena, do you have a recipe for this one, it's amazingly tasty?" He turned to me, pointing to the farali khichdi.

I nodded to Dick and, as I filled my plate, I agreed with him that the food had been amazing.

Nik said, "I'll pass on your compliments to Motaba."

Ramprakash's Birthday Weekend
Sunday Breakfast

Farali khichdi
a dish of boiled potatoes, peanuts and tapioca made on fast days

Theekhi puri
*deep fried small rolled flatbread made from wheat and gram
flour and spices*

Dahi
natural yoghurt

Gaur keri nu athanu
sweet mango pickle using spices and raw cane sugar

Khati keri nu athanu
*raw mango pickled with crushed mustard seeds, salt, chilli,
turmeric and lemon*

Dhana marcha ni chutnee
fresh coriander and green chilli chutney

Talela marcha
fried green chillies

Farfar
fried tapioca or rice flour crisps

Toast
Butter, jam, marmalade
Masala chai, coffee with cream
Chopped fruits
Fruit juices

303

The three of us headed to the huge dining table to sit with the remaining stragglers.

"Good morning, Reena, Umi." Nik's mother was making her way to the small kitchen. She took my hand, "What an amazing colour. It really suits you. Did you manage to get any sleep last night?"

We all cast our eyes down sheepishly at our plates. We had gone for a walk around the grounds at four in the morning.

She laughed and scuffed Nik's hair, "My Niku is such a party animal." Sarladevi shouted across from the door to the small kitchen.

"Stop talking to the young people, Pushpa. We need to get the puja thali sorted." Nik's kaki rushed to her side and I observed they were wearing identical bright-red silk sarees and had their hair tied in loose buns.

The large family portrait had been taken down and replaced with a painting of Ram, Laxman, Sita and Hanuman. A low wooden stool with a small statue of Ganesh sat underneath. Various pots and plates were placed around the puja area, filled with flowers, rice, mung beans, wheat, and a selection of different coloured powders. The thali for the aarti was painted with a rangoli; a divo was ready for lighting. The warmth of the March sunshine brought out the scent of beeswax, incense and roses; the smell reminded me of a childhood memory I couldn't quite place.

Sitting cross-legged at the front was a stout man in an orange turban, murmuring Sanskrit mantras as he performed the Hindu ritual. Sarladevi and Ramprakash were sitting next to the man. Behind them sat the rest of the family in regimented rows, each couple sitting next to each other. The women all wore red sarees and the men had jabo pyjamas in various pastel shades, except Sunil who wore a red jabo with cream pyjamas.

Their guests were either sitting on the floor or on the sofa and chairs that were against the walls. Sammy was sitting on his grandmother's lap, playing with her long mangalsutra chain. We tried to squeeze into spaces on the floor and Nik made his way to the front to sit next to his papa. The Guru picked up a red thread, tied it around his wrist, and placed a red tilak on his forehead.

After the Ganesh puja, a small band of musicians arrived and seated themselves at the back of the room. The singer was a young woman who had a melodious voice that vibrated through the room. She began to sing bhajan encouraging the rest of the people to join in. Little books of printed lyrics were passed around the room. Each bhajan had the words written in English as well as Gujarati script.

Dick nudged me; his jaw dropped, and he whispered, "How do you know all the words?" I smiled and continued to sing. I had sung these bhajans all my life. There had been plenty of times when Dick had heard me decline invitations to a Hindu Society function at university. He'd assumed I wasn't aware of the religion. It's not the religion I objected to. It's the Indians who claimed to be fervent followers of it. My father had exposed us to these songs on our visits to the mandir. Saturday nights and the devotional words lifted my spirit as they did my father's. The tunes and the words washed over me, and I recognised my heart had slowed down into its usual comfortable beat for the first time the whole weekend.

Once the ceremony had finished, the family took their blessings from the Guru. Nik's mother beckoned me over and introduced me to the portly man who had moved to one of the armchairs. He was wearing a long cream silk robe and had several ropes of differing holy beads around his neck. Tied around his right wrist was an orange cloth bag, which held his prayer beads. His head was covered with an orange turban.

"Guruji, can I introduce you to Reena."

I held my palms together in salutation and greeted him, "Jai Shri Krishna."

"Come and sit by my feet, Beti. I want to get a closer look," he directed me. I knelt down next to his feet and rested my bottom on my feet; he placed his hand on my head to give me a blessing. "Live long, daughter, and may God bless you."

While he was giving me his blessing, Sarladevi rushed to his side and asked, "Jagdish Bhai, do you see anything about this child's future?"

He lifted my chin with his index finger and scrutinised my face. I felt pain as he peered further into my eyes, and an uncontrollable urge to run away swept through my body. I took a deep breath to calm myself and felt Nik's breath on my shoulder.

"You have lost someone. Hari Om, the beginning of your life was difficult, Beti, and the road you'll travel is full of hardship and sorrow."

My face dropped. I didn't believe anyone could tell your future by looking in your eyes, but he had said it in front of Nik's parents, and they believed in this man's predictions. He sensed my misery and added.

"I can also see happiness, wealth and success too, Beti." He turned to Sarladevi, "I can get her janam kundli prepared if you want, Sarladevi?"

"Na, na, Guruji, your opinion is enough for me."

As soon as it was humanly possible, I excused myself from the people surrounding the Guru and rushed to the bathroom. Their sympathetic words scorched my eardrums. I'd heard it so many times before, it was like water off a duck's back. But that day with Nik's family and friends it felt like sharp knives of inadequacy stabbing at my heart. I wanted them to like me. I wanted their approval. I scolded myself. You've only been seeing him since December. *It was far too soon to imagine a life with him.*

I saw him as I opened the door; he was standing nervously by the candelabra. His eyes locked with mine, and he took long strides towards me and stopped inches away from me. He saw the hurt in my eyes.

"Are you all right, my love?" I raised a thin smile in reply. I needed to get some fresh air to clear my head. "Come on." He grabbed my hand and led me out to the garden.

We ran to a nook; bees were buzzing around the flowers, and their scent filled the air. I finally allowed the tears to flow.

"I'm sorry, my darling. Motaba just has her ways." My head rested on his chest. The rhythmic thump-thump of his heart was soothing. I began to count the beats one, two, three, four, five, six … and slowly the sadness and pain seeped away.

"Are you ready to go get lunch?" I nodded and Nik's forehead touched mine as he reassured me of his love. We entered the marquee and searched for our friends. I surreptitiously peeped at the head table and saw

Sarladevi glare reproachingly at us. Nik shrugged his shoulders and continued to stride with a purpose to our seats. I had been placed between Dick and Peter, and Nik was seated between Umi and Ashveena's cousin. The girl introduced herself as Nita. She had round eyes, a matching round face and an air of elegance only found in the privileged. Her make-up was immaculate, not too much to make her look made up but enough to bring out her best features. She covered her mouth as she tittered and fluttered her eyes sideways to Nik during the conversation around the table. I began to resent the seating arrangements and my mood darkened.

"How are you feeling Reena?" Peter enquired.

"Better," I replied quietly, unable to control the sudden envy in my voice. Nik beckoned to one of the women and asked them to fill our plates.

"I'm not too fond of this one, what is it?" Dick asked me.

"Oh, that's bitter gourd. I thought you'd like it considering the amount of bitter you drink." Peter's loud chortle stopped the girl from tittering. I saw the hurt on Dick's face and sheepishly apologised. He good-heartedly laughed it off.

"I don't mind drinking the stuff, but eating it is another matter."

The celebratory meal was placed before me, and I avoided looking at Nik and the girl who was obviously besotted by him. I tried to ignore the conversation they were having, but my ears kept homing in on snippets.

"Law? You must be so smart. What do you think of public relations, Nikesh? I love America; have you been, Nikesh?"

Dick squeezed my hand and quietly said, "Eat, you must be starving."

Ashveena was moaning that the date of their wedding had been pushed back to May. Umi asked her why and she began to recount the story of how Guruji had looked at Suresh's janam kundli and hers and had advised the best time for them to marry would be in May.

"What is a janadally?" Peter asked.

Ashveena and Suresh laughed in unison. "Janam kundli, Peter! It's a chart of how the stars were aligned on the day of our birth."

"Do you believe in it?" Peter questioned.

"Sure, it's our tradition," Ashveena replied. "Everything we do is approved by Guruji."

"Do you feel the same Suresh?" Umi asked. "My dad doesn't believe in all that stuff."

"Yes, I suppose and if it keeps Motaba and my future wife happy, I'll tag along."

I could feel Nik watching me, but I kept my head down as I ate.

"Do you want another puran puri, Ree?"

I glanced into his magnificent eyes and saw they were also displeased at being placed away from me. The golden shards glowed like burning embers ready to ignite.

I nodded and then questioned, "Is that your third?"

He nodded guiltily, "It's my favourite food. How can I not have a third?"

"How many favourite foods do you have, Nik? I fear you are a glutton," Dick interjected, flicking his hand at him. Everyone except the girl laughed. Her eyes

Ramprakash's Birthday Weekend Puja Lunch

Puran puri
flatbread stuffed with pigeon peas split lentils, sugar and cardamom paste cooked in ghee

Karkeri karela
crispy fried spiced bitter gourd curry

Ringda valor nu shaak
aubergine and hyacinth beans curry

Bateta nu shaak
potato curry

Osaman
thin broth made with cooking water of pigeon pea split lentils

Mattar baath
fried and steamed rice and peas

Roasted papad
thin crispy bread made with lentil flour dry roasted on a flame

Kachumber
a salad made with cabbage, cucumber, carrots, onions and tomatoes

Fruit juices

finally acknowledged me, and she scornfully glanced away.

***

LATER THAT AFTERNOON, I was in the bedroom, picking up our bags. Umi and I had changed earlier and had gone down to laze by the swimming pool. As I was about to leave, I felt a soft breeze from the Juliet balcony doors and went to close them. I could hear the chinking of china as they put their cups down.

"Since the day he was born, this boy is here to drink my blood. Did you see that girl last night drinking and eating meat like the men?"

I stepped back from the double doors afraid I might be seen. I heard my father's angry words when someone sidled over and tried to listen in on his conversation. But I wanted to know what Sarladevi thought of me. I had a sense she was essential to whether this relationship survived.

"Do you remember the summer party we had two years ago? Nikesh with that tthoydi. You remember the one who kept kissing him. Those people have no shame. What was her name?"

"Julie, Julie Ramsbottom."

"Hai Bhagwan, thank you for sending her away. Where did she go to, do you know?"

"Yes, I met her mother at the hair salon last week; she went to work in Spain. She's back, working at a hotel in the Midlands now." I had heard the name before and tried to recall where. "I like her, Bhabhi. Did you see her at this morning's puja. She knew all the prayers and bhajan off by heart and didn't once look down to read the sheets. Even our children don't know all of them."

"I had Nita lined up for Nikesh. They would make a good couple."

"I don't think Motabhai will approve of the marriage. You know how he feels about Makund Bhai. You do know Nita drinks, too, I've seen her."

"They all drink these days, even our daughters and daughters-in-law drink wine and champagne."

"Have you heard?" Nik's mother continued conspiratorially, "Poor Jaya Ben, her daughter-in-law, the one from Kenya, Maya, has started to cook eggs in her main kitchen. She says she needs to eat them now she's pregnant."

"Tut tut, what is this world coming to? They are losing all their culture in this country." She sighed, "We will lose our children to the British."

"We have to change, Bhabhi. We've educated them, and education opens minds."

"Haan, haan, we know what education does to these girls."

I could sense the tension in the inaudible silence. I should have stopped listening; it was becoming too personal, but I couldn't help myself.

"Bhabhi, give her a chance. You'll like her, too. Don't you think her father has raised her well? Niku won't find any better."

The warmth of Nik's mother's opinions filled my heart with hope. I had an ally. I silently closed the doors and almost danced out of the room.

A thought flickered to the forefront of my mind. I frowned and pushed it back; *I was happy. I wanted to savour the moment.* Nik's mother actually thought he wouldn't find anyone better than me. I shook my head; that was the second time that weekend someone had mentioned marriage and Nik.

Twenty

"REE, REENA, LOOK AT ME."

I was interrupted from my recollection by Nik's words and I focused on him.

"I want Kaka and Kaki to be the first to know you've said yes."

"But, I'm not sure I'm ready."

"What do you mean? Have you changed your mind?" He turned his face to mine.

"No, never. I'm just not sure how your motaba will take it." I caressed his arm as he held the gear stick.

"She'll be fine. I've asked my parents, and they've approved."

The car's cassette player played Kishore Kumar's The Golden Collection on a loop, and Kishore sang "Pyar Diwana Hota Hai." It struck me that love is crazy and wonderful. It is unaware of happiness and sadness.

He opened the passenger door for me. "Ready?" I looked up; my heart was in my mouth and my stomach was in knots. The last time I came to Shakti Bhavan was before Nik and his family went to India in the summer break, before the dreadful summer I had to make a difficult choice. He lifted me up.

"Don't worry," he said and he squeezed my hands.

Nik knocked on the door to the study, poked his head through and said, "Kaka, Kaki, I've brought someone to meet you." He walked in and pulled me into the room. "Please may I introduce my fiancée."

I stood awkwardly as he grinned at his father who was sitting behind a large walnut desk with his wife sitting opposite. They had several buff folders in front of them. Nik's mother turned towards us and swiftly lifted herself off the comfortable black leather office chair, holding her arms out.

"I'm so glad you've forgiven my crazy son and agreed to marry him." She used the Gujarati word for crazy. She pulled me to her and gave me a kiss on my cheek. She put me at arm's length and surveyed me and then added, "You are a bit thin. I hope you're not forgetting to eat from studying too much."

"Jai Shri Krishna, Kaka." I placed my palms together and looked at Nik's father who was sitting at the desk, busy tidying up the folders. Nik had already sat down on the chair vacated by his mother, and I was directed to the other chair. I sat down, my head lowered, and gazed at his father's face through my fringe. He lifted his eyes up at the wall opposite; Nik's mother placed her hand on my shoulder.

"Motabhai was a wise man." I turn my head to follow his gaze. Hanging on the wall was the portrait of Ramprakash Raja I'd given Nik as a late birthday present. "You make Niku very happy. We're glad you sorted out your differences. Welcome to our family, Reena. You are a very talented artist. You've captured his personality very well."

I had chosen warm hues for the portrait, to reflect the personality of the charming, witty, confident man, who was easy-going and relaxed in his dealings with people. I let out a soft breath; my body relaxed a little. Nik's mother squeezed my shoulder. His father's eyes moved to Nik.

"Have you spoken to Reena's family, Niku?"

"I spoke with Reena's bhai and bhabhi last week. I might need your help with her father … I don't think he approves of me," he laughed nervously.

"What do you mean you spoke with my bhai and bhabhi?" I was surprised by what he'd said. I'd spoken to Amit and Smita Bhabhi on Monday, and they'd said nothing about Nik calling them. He laughed. "Besides, how could you be sure I'd say yes?"

"I know every inch of you better than you do, Reena Solanki," he said, lifting his wicked eyebrow, his eyes sparkling. A blush rose on my cheeks, and I tried my hardest to keep it down.

"See, they love you like I do," Nik said as we headed to the stable block to see Anousha until dinner time when I'd have to meet Nik's motaba. I was relieved I didn't have to deal with her yet.

"Hello, anybody home?" Nik shouted as we entered the kitchen.

"We're in here, Niku," Rajesh called to us, his baritone very similar to Nik's except with a hint of an accent. The couple were on the sofa with their daughter sitting between them. A large colourful book was on Anousha's lap and she pointed to illustrations of objects. She saw Nik and slid off the sofa, her face lit up, her arms raised. Nik quickly lowered himself to greet her.

"Hello, little princess, did you miss me?" She gave him a sloppy kiss.

I was at the door, nervous to see them again. Nik had Anousha in his arms and turned to guide me into the room. Rajesh lifted himself up and helped his wife get up from the sofa.

"Lovely to see you again, Reena." He leant in to kiss my cheek.

Rupa smiled at Nik and queried, "You look pleased with yourself?"

"Reena said yes, Bhabhi." He lifted my left hand to show off the ring.

She pulled me to her and gave me a hug. I felt the bump against my stomach and realised Rupa Bhabhi was pregnant again.

"Congratulations let me see your ring. Did you get it from the jeweller in Hatton Garden?" she questioned, holding my left hand up to admire it. "It's lovely, Niku. Do you like it?"

"Yes, Bhabhi; he was excellent, and sent someone to deliver it to me on Friday."

I suddenly had the vision of the blonde woman at the hotel reception and grinned up at Nik and said, "I love it, Bhabhi. It's perfect."

Anousha pulled at Nik's face as he talked to his bhai and bhabhi. "Neenu, Neenu."

"No, Anousha, Nikukaka, Nikukaka."

Nik reprimanded his brother. "I like being called Neenu. Come, pumpkin. Neeno, Neeno." He had her on his back and ran around the room pretending to be a police car. I laughed at his antics; he's wonderful with children.

"You better not get married this summer," Rupa said to me.

My jaw dropped; I hadn't even thought about when we'd get married. Engagement was one thing. Marriage was very different. Our families' ideas about weddings were very different; Suresh's wedding had been very different from my brother's wedding.

April 2nd, 1983

SMITA AND AMIT HAD TOLD me to invite some friends for their wedding, and I'd asked Peter, Ravi, Dick, Umi and Nik. I didn't know many people from my course so early in my first year to invite them. The wedding took place at a secondary school and community centre in Woolwich. Smita parents, who own a small supermarket, had managed to get their staff to cover for the whole day. We had set off from Leicester in different cars and a minibus. My father's boss had agreed to drive Amit in his jaguar. My father had filled his car with Divya Ba and a couple of the older ladies from the mandir. I was in the car with Mr and Mrs Robson and had arranged to come back with Ashwin in his car when Amit brought Smita home. We had agreed to meet at Toddington Service Station to regroup before we travelled from north London into south-east London.

I saw him waiting by the steps leading to the entrance of the school; he was wearing a cobalt-blue jabo pyjama. The butterflies in my stomach rose up; the sight of him took my breath away every time. We spoke every day on the phone, but I had only met him once in the Easter break. However, last week had been difficult because of the ceremonies and relatives staying with us. I had escaped to a phone box to speak with him last night, and he'd asked if he was going to be introduced to my father. He had been upset when I said I wasn't sure.

As soon as my father's car pulled in with the minibus, the other guests from the groom's side moved to greet us. Everyone gathered by the minibus and I stepped out of the jaguar. I had watched his face searching for me. Umi leant towards him and said something; he tried to raise a smile. As soon as he saw me, his face lit up, his eyes locked on mine, and he smiled, tilting his head. I held back the urge to run into his arms and strolled to my friends, smiling and waving.

"Hello, when did you guys get here?" I asked, just in case someone was listening.

Umi held my hand and whistled. "Wow! You look incredible in orange."

I was wearing a mango-orange silk saree with silver zari work. I had decided to wear it Gujarati-style to show off the silver brocade design of peacock feathers on the pallu. My hair was tied into a low plaited knot. Tiny silver bells adorned my head. Around my neck was a long silver filigree-work necklace with matching drop earrings that had belonged to my mother.

Nik was standing by my side. He said, "I agree," and added, "I could ravish you here and now," his voice husky in my ear.

"We have to decorate the car." I pointed to the cream jaguar and pulled at Umi's hand as I waved at Amit in the car.

"Hello, guys, have you been waiting long?" Amit asked.

I had re-introduced Peter, Nik and Ravi to Amit when

he had come to pick me up from university. He had already met Dick and Umi several times. Mr Robson opened the boot and handed the keys to Amit, and he and his wife joined my father and the rest of the wedding guests. I took out a carrier bag, and we unravelled the garland I'd made to decorate the car.

"These are beautiful," Umi said. "Did you make them?"

We draped the garland of red and white paper flowers in swags around the car and admired our work. My father approached the car and said.

"Hello, you must be Reena's friends," holding his hand out. I stood by his side and introduced them by their names, adding what subjects they were studying. "Nice meeting you. Enjoy the wedding," he told them, and he headed to where Jane was pulling up in her red MG.

Smita's family came out to invite us in for breakfast. Amit sat back in the car and waited for his to be brought to him. We walked up the steps to a reception area. The dining hall had long rows of tables covered with white paper tablecloths. On the left, there was a buffet with jalebi, ganthia, tea and coffee. I was given a steel plate of fruit, farali chevdo, barfi and saffron milk to take to Amit, who couldn't eat whole grain until after the wedding.

Nik and my friends were just entering the hall when I was heading back out to Amit's car. "Where are you going?" He reached for my arm and stopped short of touching it.

"I'm going to take Amit's breakfast to him," I told him. He frowned. I felt his eyes on my back as I walked down the corridor.

When I came back into the building, he was waiting for me by the trophy cabinet.

"What are you doing here?"

"Come with me." He walked to the other corridor, opened the door to a broom cupboard and pulled me in. He took me in his arms and inhaled. "I've missed you so much."

"What if someone sees us?"

"Not in here, they can't," he told me. "No windows." He kissed my ears, my neck, my collarbone; he lifted up my pallu and kissed my exposed belly, kneeling down in front of me. "Can't kiss you on the mouth, your lipstick will smudge," he said as his eyes rested on my lips. My body shivered; I wished he would put his soft lips on my mouth.

After breakfast we fetched Amit. The Gujarati wedding ceremony consisted of many parts. Firstly, the bride's family met us at the entrance to the hall where the wedding would take place. Smita's mother greeted Amit by placing a tilak on his head. He then stepped down and broke two clay pots filled with mung beans and loose coins. We followed him in and were escorted to our places. The wooden-panelled hall was laid out with rows of chairs on either side of a central aisle; two small plant stands with Ganesh statues had been placed by the steps either side of the stage where the mandap had been erected.

Amit was welcomed under the mandap where Smita's mother washed his feet and fed him panchamrut, a drink made from ghee, honey, sugar, milk and yoghurt. Ashwin had been given the task of keeping his shoes safe, but failed miserably, as a younger cousin of Smita had cut the bottom of the carrier bag he'd placed the shoes in and stole them. We all laughed and protested that the little imp was too smart. I had been placed in a chair behind Amit, with a small bowl filled with bells, and had been instructed to shake it and brush it along Amit and Smita's backs throughout the ceremony. This was another ritual my father had disapproved of; he said that as the Gods were present, there was no need to ward off the evil eye. But Bharat Kaka, his cousin had overruled him.

The groom's guests were supposed to sit on the right side of the room, but Nik and my friends had placed themselves on the left so they could watch the ceremony. Dick had brought his camera and was taking pictures at the bottom of the stage. My father had called him to the stage and told him he could come up any time to take closer shots.

A cloth was pulled in front of Amit when it was time for Smita to come to the mandap. He gasped when they lowered the red shawl. She was stunning in her red and white silk panetar and crimson bandhani silk garchoru. He leant into her and whispered something, and she giggled.

Throughout the ceremony, I felt Nik's smouldering eyes watching me, catching my eyes and raising a smile. The rhythmic bells and chanting of the priest lulled me into a daydream. Instead of my brother and his future wife, images of Nik and me filled my mind.

"Reena, come and tie the cheda chedi?" asked the priest. I jumped when he called me, missing the kanyadan, and Nik smiled and turned to Umi, who laughed.

After the hastamelap, the fire was lit, and the couple walked with the blessing of Agni Dev around it four times, each circle representing Dharma, Aarth, Kam and Moksha. At the beginning of each round, Smita's brothers gave them a blessing that was witnessed by all. I saw my father's eyes fill with tears as he watched his son getting married. It was hard for him, as my mother was no longer with us to perform the ceremony. He had asked his cousin, Bharat, and his wife Anju to sit in the service as representatives of Amit's parents.

Once the saptapadi, the sindoor and kansar ceremony were observed, Amit and Smita took the blessings of my daddy, and he hugged them both, tears rolling down his face. My kaka and kaki comforted him, and Amit and I exchanged glances; we, too, missed our mother.

After the wedding ceremony, we all ate our lunch in the dining hall; I sat with my family on the main table and everyone else picked a spot on some of the vacant tables laid out in rows. As soon as I had finished my lunch, I headed to the table where Amit's friends were sitting to speak with them and then walked to where Nik was seated; he pulled out an empty chair next to him. I sat down; he moved his leg to touch mine.

"I loved that the priest explained everything in English. I've got it written down in my book and have taken lots of photographs of the beautiful women who are here." Dick took his book out of his jacket pocket. He smiled at us; we all knew he'd also taken phone numbers in his little notebook, too.

"He's been writing in that and bugging us for spellings." Ravi pointed at the notebook. We all laughed. Whenever we asked Dick what he wrote in his book, he always replied, "research" conspiratorially.

By the end of the wedding, no-one was sitting in rows. Most people were milling around, talking to friends and family they hadn't met since the last wedding.

"What's the matter?" Nik sat next to me, his face ashen, as I watched the photographer finish taking photographs of Amit and Smita under the silver mandap. His eyes cast down to his lap.

"Your dad's just confronted me in the toilet."

My heart stopped. "What did he say?" I quizzed in a hushed voice.

"He asked if I was Ramprakash Raja's son and told me a close school friend of your mother's used to work for him in Nairobi."

"What? Does he know your family?" I turned to ask him, no longer caring if anyone heard me.

"No, I don't think so, but your mother knew of my papa."

I found myself thinking about how Divya Ba talked about how people from East Africa know each other in some way or other. I heard her words in my mind. 'The lives of the people in Africa are interwoven like the threads of a saree pallu.'

May 28th, 1983

WE HAD ALL BEEN GIVEN an invitation on thick card with gold-embossed lettering, which shouted of money and privilege, for Suresh and Ashveena's wedding reception at Grosvenor House, Park Lane. Nik drove us down in his car and had dropped me off at Umi's. I had insisted on staying in Harrow and not at Shakti Bhavan. He had argued that his family knew I was his girlfriend and wouldn't mind. I wasn't convinced everyone was okay with me being his girlfriend.

On the evening of the reception we took the tube to Marble Arch station; it had felt a bit awkward walking to the hotel dressed in a saree, but I told myself I had to get used to it if I was going to move down to London for work.

I was wearing a silk chiffon saree in royal blue with a parrot-green border and pallu in silver brocade that Rohini Bhabhi had discarded, and I paired it with a parrot-green three-quarter-sleeved chiffon blouse with a transparent back that was tied in a knot at the front. Umi had lent me a small silver necklace and earrings to wear with it. She was wearing a mustard yellow and maroon silk salwar churidar with a mandarin collar.

"Effing hell! Look at all this!" She waved her arms at the tall Georgian facade.

"Good evening. Welcome to the Grosvenor Ballroom." A footman in a grey morning suit and top hat opened the door for us. We entered a large foyer which had a huge crystal chandelier and steps leading up to the ballroom. There were two colossal flower displays with orange and red flowers on both sides of the stairs and an easel holding a large portrait of Suresh and Ashveena; underneath a gold sign announced, 'Raja Mehta Wedding Reception.'

"May I take your coat?" A footman stepped up to us. Umi and I handed him our coats.

I filled my lungs with oxygen and released a slow breath and Umi took my hand.

"You'll be fine. He'll be waiting."

Suresh and Ashveena were standing at the top of the steps to greet the guests; next to them, on either side, were both sets of parents: on Suresh's side was

Ramprakash, Sarladevi, Anant and Pushpa, and on Ashveena's side was her parents, Dolat and Savita. Nik was loitering beyond and strode towards me and then stopped, clenching his fists, worrying his bottom lip. My stomach filled with butterflies. I cast my eyes towards the parents and saw Sarladevi glare at me and then at Nik. Her smile dropped slightly; she quickly raised a fixed, polite smile. We shook hands with everyone in the line-up and then entered the reception area; Nik took mine and Umi's hands. He walked us towards an elderly bespectacled couple standing with Rita and Sunil. "Faiba, Fua, can I introduce my friends Reena and Umi." His fua nodded at us.

Nik lifted the hand that was holding mine. "Reena, this my Fua, Purushottam Mehta; he and Vijaya Faiba have come for Suresh's wedding."

I took my hand from Nik's, put my palms together and said, "Jai Shri Krishna."

He nodded and he gazed at Umi and said, "So you must be Umi, very nice to meet you," in perfect English. Umi also put her palms together.

Rita said something to her aunt, and she nodded and smiled, my ears burnt. Nik's faiba took my hands and said, "You are beautiful, Reena. Pleased to meet you. I've heard some great things about you from Motabhai."

Nik was smiling, but on hearing this, his grin spread from ear to ear. When I'd built up the courage to look at her face, she was smiling. She looked remarkably like her older brother. She had salt-and-pepper hair, tied in a simple knot and wore a pale carnation-pink silk saree that showed off her toffee-coloured complexion. She wore minimal makeup, some kohl in her eyes and a thin layer of pink lipstick. Her jewellery was understated, a simple gold kada on the one hand and a gold Rado watch on the other; around her neck she wore a pearl and gold long necklace with matching studs with a chain that connected to hair clips. She had a medium-sized, red-vermillion dot on her forehead, her centre parting was filled with sindoor, and she wore a small diamond nose stud.

"Kem cho?" I asked her, smiling.

"Not bad. A bit tired from the wedding celebrations. Why weren't you at the wedding?"

I recalled the conversation I had had with Nik. He'd sulked when I'd told him I couldn't take the weekend off from revising as I was going to go home for my mother's birthday. In reality, I had felt it was too soon for me to go to his brother's wedding even if I'd been given an invitation with a personal note from Suresh. He had moaned he would miss me and it wouldn't be any good without me. After a couple of days of barely talking to me, he said.

"Okay, but I'm coming straight to yours afterwards, to thoroughly quench my thirst."

"I had too much work last week," I told her, hoping she hadn't noticed the blush on my cheeks from remembering his words. The rest of Nik's family came up to us and greeted us as if we'd known them all our lives, giving Umi and me hugs and kisses.

"Sorry, you can talk to them later." He held out his hands to Umi and me and said, "Come on … the guys are already in the ballroom," and he led us further into the room. A waiter approached with a tray full of champagne glasses filled with passion fruit juice or pink champagne. He picked up glasses of pink champagne and handed them to us.

"We are sitting at the same table. I've made sure no one has messed with the seating plan this time." I remembered the puja and the Guru's words. His grip on my hand tightened as I tried to take it away. My eyes darted sideways and saw that some of the guests had turned and were watching us.

The ballroom was a vast room decorated in cream damask wallpaper. Four massive chandeliers ran along the centre leading to a set of full-length doors. The floor was covered in a red carpet and, in the centre, there was a large wooden dance floor. Circular tables covered in white tablecloths had been placed around the dance floor, each with a large red and orange tall floral centrepiece matching the flowers of the reception foyer. I counted the tables; there must have been at least six-hundred people invited to the reception. At the other end, there was a bandstand and sitting on deep cushions were Indian classical musicians playing music as the guests filled the room. Waiters and waitresses dressed in black bottoms and white shirts guided us to our table.

I was seated between Nik and Dick. Umi was sitting next to Peter on one side and Ravi on the other. Dick grabbed my hand as I sat down; I saw his small notebook and a pen placed on the table.

"Hi, you okay?" He frowned at me. I took a deep breath and made myself relax.

I studied the room. I knew there would be a mixture of people from different countries, but hadn't expected women in African, Thai, Chinese and Indonesian costumes. There were women in ball gowns, long dresses, sarees, salwar kameez. It was a genuinely multicultural occasion full of society's wealthiest and most well-connected.

"Reena, are you okay?" Dick asked me again.

"Yes, sorry, just taking in the atmosphere."

"And panicking. You're hyperventilating, slow down," Nik instructed me. I counted the glasses for each place setting, one, two, three, four, hoping the counting would help calm me down. I counted the chairs around our table, one, two, three, four, five, six, seven, eight, nine, ten.

Jay approached our table with a short, plump girl dressed in a sky-blue chiffon evening gown. Nik stood up and hugged her. Meera was Jay's younger sister; she greeted us quietly with huge expressive eyes as she told us she was in the middle of her O-level exams. Ashveena's cousins, Rahul and Nitin, who were both in their final year at school, occupied the other two chairs. We all introduced ourselves to the people on our table. Ashveena's cousins were dumbstruck with Umi's beauty. Meera's face dropped. Peter took Umi's hand as a display that she wasn't to be approached.

After the welcome address from Ashveena's father, dinner was served by our table's personal waiter, who asked us if we were vegetarians and served us our starter and main course, according to our preference; the desserts were laid out on a trolley that was brought to the table for us to choose from. The meal ended with tea or coffee and petits fours. After tea and coffee Nik, Ravi and Jay retired to the balcony to smoke, and the tables were cleared. Peter and Umi headed out of the double doors in search of a discreet place to smoke. When everyone came back to the ballroom, our waiter descended on us to ask for our drink orders from the bar. Nik's family stood up and mingled with their guests. Ashveena and Suresh came to our table, and we congratulated them on their marriage.

While we were eating, the classical musician continued to play the music that reminded me of Hindustani classical music made famous by Ravi Shankar. They stopped and were replaced by a live band. The lights were dimmed, and the lead singer announced the bride and groom wanted everyone on the dance floor to join them for the first dance. The female singer warbled: "Everybody's doin' a brand new dance now." Everyone formed a line and danced around the ballroom. The older people went back to their seats. Some of the men walked out to the bar in the foyer.

Nik and I danced together for the next few dances; he held my hand continuously. When I wanted to rest, he came with me to sit, our heads touching. "Stop worrying, it's dark, and they are over there. No one will see," he said as my eyes searched around me. "You look delicious today; royal-blue suits you, my love … is your blouse tied to the front by this?" He had managed to get his hand under my pallu. "I have a room in the hotel," he whispered in my ear. I blushed, felt my body temperature rise, and stood up.

"Where are you going?"

"I need to go to the toilet, Nik."

"'Let's Twist Again.' I love this song: dance with me."

"I'm bursting. Go and dance." I waved him off to the dance floor.

The lady's toilet was bigger than the downstairs of my whole house. An attendant was handing out towels and hand cream. While I was in the cubicle, I heard two women enter.

"Can you tell my son to control himself? He's behaving like a majnu."

"Bhabhi, he's so happy."

"I'm ashamed of his behaviour. Did you see him in there holding hands with that girl? I wouldn't mind if it were Umi. She's a bit dark-skinned, but at least her father's a teacher."

"I like her; she's a good influence on him. He's a lot more responsible."

"Well, I'm not happy. She's a Solanki, Pushpa! Doesn't that bother you? Think of the gossip, a low-caste girl in our family. Hai Bhagwan, why have you sent this boy into my life?"

"It may not come to anything, Bhabhi. You know the young."

"In the meantime, we are the talk of the kitty parties and mela mandir." She sighed. I sat rooted to the toilet seat, tears stinging my eyes.

"Hello, Mrs Abbott, are you enjoying the evening?" Nik's mother asked.

"Yes, thank you, Mrs Raja. It's a beautiful wedding reception."

I sat for as long as I could in the cubicle, waiting for them to finish and leave. *Why had I thought this would ever be anything but a fling?* I had been stupid to think I would be accepted by Sarladevi; my caste and my circumstances would never be acceptable. The tears streamed out of my eyes. I held toilet tissues up to them, praying my mascara hadn't run. When I eventually came out of the cubicle, I used a wet tissue to remove the dark mascara smudges under my eyes. The attendant watched me with a sympathetic smile;

even though the conversation was in Gujarati, she understood it was about me.

I walked back to the lobby; my instinct was telling me to get out of the place as quickly as possible. I had been too busy thinking of what excuses I could use to leave early and hadn't seen him by the steps.

"What took you so long?"

"Stop following me like a lost puppy Nik … people have noticed," I told him through gritted teeth. I avoided looking at him; my eyes focused on the steps leading to the ballroom.

"What people, Ree?" He pulled at my arm and stopped me from walking up the steps. I tried to hide the pain in my eyes. He gripped my hand and pulled me back into the foyer. "Come with me." He took long strides, and I saw heads turn as I urged him to stop.

We were in the main lift foyer of the hotel. Anger rose in me as we waited for the lift. What was it about these people and their prejudices? I had been brought up not to think of caste or for that matter, social class, as a barrier. After all, Smita's family were of a higher social class than ours. Her parents had not objected to their marriage. We lived in England, and we lived in the twentieth century, these old-fashioned ways were no longer relevant.

When the lift door closed, he turned to face me. "What happened?" I kept my head down. "Look at me, please." I remained resolute, my jaw clenched, staring at his patent leather shoes.

We entered the vast hotel room. He stood so close I could hear his heart pounding in his chest.

"Tell me what happened." His voice was harsh, and he pushed me down to sit on the edge of the bed. He sat on his haunches on the carpeted floor and took my hands. "Look at me, Reena." He frowned, his eyes darkened, and the golden embers burnt brightly. "Did someone say something to you?"

"I heard them, Nik." My throat hurt from the sound.

"Who, who did you hear?"

"Your motaba and kaki. I heard what she thinks of me." The words 'low-caste' and 'Solanki' filled my ears again, and I instinctively covered them. "They don't like me, Nik; she prefers Umi. She told your mother to tell you to stop behaving like a majnu. She doesn't want a Solanki in her family. Do you understand Nik? I'm not good enough for your motaba. Please, we have to stop before it hurts too much. I don't want to see you anymore." I gulped back a sob. "This isn't going anywhere, please let me go home." I cried sad and angry tears, not caring that dark tracks would appear on my face.

He sat silently on the floor holding my hand, letting me cry until every drop of moisture was wrung out of my eyes. "Better?" he asked, lifting my chin so I had to look at his chiselled face; his jaw was clenched. "It doesn't matter what she thinks. I love you and would give all this up for you, in a heartbeat."

"It's not as easy as you think, Nik. Money makes everything easy. Without it, life is a struggle. We live very differently from you."

"It won't be the same for us. Look at your bhai and bhabhi; things have changed for your family since they got married. Besides, she did the same when Jaish and Jiju started seeing each other. It's just her way of coping with change. Trust me, I won't hurt you, I promise, I love you." He stood up and pulled me up into his arms, lifting my face, planting small kisses on my wet cheeks, on my eyes, on my lips, soft and pleading, I succumbed to his caresses, and slowly my heart returned to its normal rhythm.

"Do you have lipstick and mascara in your bag?" He smiled at me, and I stepped into the bathroom to apply my lipstick and wipe the mascara off my face. Nik walked in, wrapping his arms around me, and began to sing.

"Do badan ek jaan thi – two bodies one soul. I think Motaba might be right: my heart and soul are yours, always have been." His eyes smouldered at me in the reflection of the mirror.

Twenty One

I PULLED MYSELF BACK to the living room of the cottage, and the word 'wedding' resounded in my head. I began to panic and thought about my father's reaction to the news. *What have I done?* I've said yes. My bhai and bhabhi are okay with the idea of me marrying Nik, but two people can veto this. A little bit of bile rode up to my throat.

"Are you okay?"

I gulped back the anxiety and willed myself to calm down, taking deep breaths. I dared not say anything until my heart returned to normal.

"Oh no, we haven't even thought of a date," I told Rupa Bhabhi.

"Enough excitement. We were trying to calm Anousha down for a nap. Let me have her, Niku." Rajesh took his daughter in his arms. "Say bye bye to Niku Kaka and Reena Kaki." The little girl waved at us and blew a wet kiss as he took her upstairs.

The word 'Reena Kaki' sunk into my mind; five days ago, I wasn't even ready to take our relationship to the next stage.

The intercom rang and Rupa picked up the phone. "Hello … Okay, I'll send them to the house."

She turned to us. We were sitting at a beautiful old antique table in the kitchen drinking tea.

"You've been summoned." She laughed. "Good luck. I remember when Raju and I got married." She gave me a quick hug as we left through the kitchen door.

Instead of walking towards the arched gate to the walled garden, Nik pulled me towards the boot store.

"Nervous?" I nodded. "Don't be. Kaka and Kaki have said yes. Do you remember me telling you I'd give all this up for you, when Motaba said we were like Laila and Majnu?"

I frowned at him; he must have been thinking about that night too.

"How can you forget Rishi Kapoor all bearded and love-struck?" He knew I idolised Rishi Kapoor.

He sang, "Laila majnu … should I grow a beard and moon around to convince you of my love?"

I raised a small smile. "Wait, I think I've already done that." His eyes glinted mischievously. "One kiss." His soft lips touched mine and I was lost in his arms. My heart calmed.

They were in the family sitting room, Sarladevi in her usual place on the sofa, with Nik's mother by her side. The chair that belonged to Ramprakash remained empty, and Nik's father was reading a newspaper in his armchair; the fire was throwing amber flames of warmth into the room. Anu Masi collected the tray that had the remains of their afternoon tea.

We walked from the side kitchen door, and I let go of Nik's hand; he didn't resist like he usually would but looked briefly down as I hide my ring hand in my coat pocket.

"That's not going to work," he whispered. I stared at him, panicking.

"Jai Shri Krishna, Motaba," he shouted as he pulled at my coat and then at his and dumped them onto the long ottoman on the side.

She put down the book she was reading and glared at us, her eyes invisible under the gold-rimmed glasses; neither Nik nor I were in any hurry to traverse the vast room. It felt like wading through treacle. I pressed my palms together in subjugation and said, "Jai Shri Krishna."

"Jai Shri Krishna, Reena. I see you've come back into Nikesh's life." Her tone reminded me of Jay's words at Peter's party, and I wished the floor would open up and swallow me. This wasn't going to be easy; every pore in my body was telling me to run. But I could hear Nik's heart, thud thud, thud thud, in his chest and felt the urge to stay put. He sat down on the sofa and patted the space next to him.

"Motaba, I have to tell you something … Reena has agreed to marry me."

"Haan, and are you asking my permission or opinion?" Her face was stern; I still couldn't get used to the missing red dot on her forehead and the large nose stud. She was a lot frailer than when her husband was alive. Nik's father deliberately folded his newspaper and stared at his bhabhi. Nik's mother gave us a sympathetic smile.

"I … just wanted you to know … " His voice trailed off at the end.

"So, you've broken all family customs and decided to

do it your way." She sighed. "You've come to eat my brain, Nikesh. I haven't had an ounce of peace since you were born." I wondered why she said this, it seemed odd as he wasn't her son. "Your mother and father know how I feel about this match."

"You've said yes, Reena." She glared at me. "In the Gujarati community, weddings are between families, not children. You seem to have no knowledge of this."

"Bhabhi! You will respect my decision," Nik's father interrupted. His voice was clipped.

We could feel the electric charge in the air as the two elders glowered at each other. Nik's body stiffened, and he gripped my hand tightly; we both gazed at the coffee table.

"I'm sure Bhabhi didn't mean anything by it." Pushpa's soft lilting voice pacified the standoff.

"Your motabhai wouldn't have approved … she's a factory worker's daughter, doesn't that offend you? Our name will be mired. At least the other children have found partners from suitable families. How will we show our face? Nikesh, you're making a big mistake. Don't come running back when this all goes wrong." She held her head in her hands; the silence was like a chasm between us.

"I support my son's wishes, and I'm following Motabhai's instructions. He would have been delighted; he told me Reena was the ideal match for Niku." Nik's father broke the silence; he turned his face and smiled at us as he told her this. "You should start thinking less about the community's opinion and spend more time on your children's happiness."

"I was only concerned with our reputation … do as you wish. This country is worse than Africa. At least there, the children showed some respect for traditions." She stood up, putting her book in her bag. "I have some work to do in the kitchen before dinner," she informed us and left the room.

"That went well." He smiled, shaking his head as he glanced at his wife.

"Don't worry, Beta. She'll come around. Do you remember when Jaishu and Anil wanted to get married?"

Nik nodded and let out a small laugh, and the grip on my hand loosened. I pulled it away and shook it. He saw the action.

"Sorry, Ree. Didn't mean to hurt you." He took my hand and kissed it. I blushed with horror that he'd just done that in front of his parents.

Sarladevi was probably right; you wouldn't dream of doing what he just did in the Gujarati community.

***

"YOU'RE VERY QUIET TODAY. Relax, it can't be as bad as telling Motaba."

He wasn't aware of my father's outbursts. I'd told him very little about his drunken stupors and the violence that followed. There was a weight in my stomach that wouldn't shift. I recalled the anger in his eyes after the comments made by Dolat Mehta.

He pulled off the motorway and instead of heading straight down Narborough Road, he turned left at the traffic light and pulled up at a pub car park.

"Right. What's the matter?" He separated my hands; he pulled my left hand up and said, "Do you want to take it off?"

A tear made its way down my cheek. I didn't want to take it off, but I knew how my father would react when he saw it. My stomach clenched, and I felt nauseous. I couldn't speak. I didn't want Nik to come in and eat dinner with us. I wanted him to drop me off and go. But then again, I did want him to speak with my father. Keeping my secret engagement from my father had haunted me. I had woken with night sweats at the thought of him finding out from his boss or someone else who was a friend of the Rajas.

"My love, my love. I didn't mean to make you cry. I'm sorry." He grabbed a tissue from the box and dabbed at my cheeks. I took another one and blew my nose.

"I don't know?" My voice came out as a croak.

"He'll see it and get cross, and then he'll walk out. Take it off and give it back to me. I'll keep it safe, and when he says yes, I'll get it out and ask if I can put it on your finger."

I took his face in both my hands and kiss him, and then I took off my ring, and he put it in his breast pocket.

My anxiety built up steadily as the hour for my father's return approached.

"Sorry, I'm late, Smita. Went for a drink with Mr Robson. We got a big order from Marks and Spencer's today." He walked through from the kitchen and saw Nik, and his lips thinned.

"Daddy, we've asked Nik to stay for dinner," Smita smiled up at him as she stood up. "Can I get you anything?"

He approached Nik and held out his hand. Nik stood up awkwardly from the settee.

"Good evening, Kaka. How are you?"

"I'm well, haven't seen you in a long time." My

father's eyes searched mine.

Throughout dinner, my father hardly spoke, his face stern, his eyes darting angrily at Nik. The food on my plate tasted like ash; my body told me to run away from this place. Amit and Smita Bhabhi delivered small smiles at me periodically and exchanged sympathetic looks.

Nik sat opposite my father and Smita was doing her best to lighten the atmosphere with tales of her final year. Nik hardly ate anything; he politely refused second helpings and his natural charm seemed to have escaped him.

After dinner, my father invited Nik to sit and have a drink with him in the front room.

"Thank you, Kaka. A small one please, I'm driving home tonight."

"Ah yes, home. Where did you say you lived?"

I sighed, thankful for my father's good manners. He had never allowed anyone to leave our house without food or drink and polite conversation. I took some ice and water in for them. Nik sat on the settee, and my father was in his favourite chair; he took out three glasses and a new bottle of Black Label.

"How do you want your whisky, water or ice?"

"Ice, please," Nik replied.

He put some ice in the three glasses and poured the golden liquor. I was frozen to the spot, my eyes fixed on the deliberate slowness of the ritual. Amit nudged me with his foot, and I held back a yelp. I headed back into the kitchen. Smita Bhabhi had already started the washing up and threw the tea towel at me.

"So, Daddy, this new order is good news for Mr Robson?" Amit tried to break the silence.

"Yes, it's a trial contract, but if we deliver on quality and on time, we'll get a repeat order. Seems a bit complicated, but the designer and cutter are happy they can do it."

Smita put a wet hand on my arm. "Don't worry, it will be fine." She is always so upbeat and optimistic, and I stared in wonder at her.

"Kaka … I have come to ask you … a question." I heard Nik's halting voice. He had built up the courage to ask. I put the tea towel down on the kitchen worktop, silently walked through the dining room and stood outside the front room door.

"May I ask for Reena's hand in marriage?"

"I know you are seeing each other, but I cannot watch my daughter suffer again. I assume your family found out and told you to stop last time. I was told as much by Dolat Mehta."

"No, that wasn't why … " Nik's voice trailed off; he couldn't tell my family what really happened.

"Listen to me, Nikesh. You and Reena are from very different backgrounds. This idea of marriage won't work. When your family cut you off … and, you have to work for a living. This thing you call love won't be enough. I won't say yes, you do not have my blessing."

"Kaka, my parents already know I want to marry Reena and they've approved. We have the blessings of my family. Please give us your permission."

"Do you and Smita know about this, Amit?"

At the mention of her name, Smita squeezed my arm. I hadn't heard her approach the door.

"Yes, Daddy. I give my full support to my sister in her decision to marry Nikesh."

"Oh, I see, brother and sister are together on this." His

voice was barely audible.

"Reena, can you come in here!"

I jumped at the mention of my name, took a deep breath and walked into the room. Nik eyes were downcast. Amit's eyes met mine as I walked in and it felt like old times when we would go as a pair to ask permission for something we knew our father would disapprove of.

My father's gaze was fixed on mine, his dark eyes give nothing away. "Do you want to marry this boy?"

"Yes, Daddy. I've always known I wanted to marry him. Please approve." I lifted my chin and held his gaze. I hadn't realised I had the strength to say that to my father and the tension I'd been holding released.

"It will be difficult for you to fit into his family; they are very different. Can you handle the conflict?" He confronted me.

"There will be no conflict, Kaka — " Nik stood by my side. " — I'll make sure of that. I promise to always protect your daughter. She will never be unhappy."

"Yes, yes, you say that, Nikesh, but there will always be conflict. Not everyone in your family will accept my daughter. She is stubborn." As he said this, a hint of a smile lifted the corner of his lips.

He had approved. Smita rushed in and took my hand, leant in and whispered, "Told you it would be fine."

My father sighed, sat back in his chair and lit a cigarette.

Nik took out the ring from his breast pocket and asked, "May I put this on your daughter's hand, Kaka?"

"Yes." He waved his hand. "I see you've already bought the ring. My children are far too clever for me." He slipped the ring back on my finger; this time, my family were witnesses to the ceremony.

We left my father in the front room and sat back in the dining room a little more relaxed. The night closed in, and Nik reluctantly got up to go home, back to Loudwater.

"Before you leave, Nikesh, can I have your parents' phone number?" My father had come into the dining room. "My daughter will not be coming to see you at your home until you are officially recognised as a couple. I will not have her reputation ruined. Certain protocols will need to be observed." I stood transfixed as he said this; Nik's face dropped.

Smita's girly laugh interrupted, "Oh yes, I forgot the guar dhana ceremony."

"What's that, Bhabhi?"

"When Daddy and Divya Ba came with Amit to my house to officially ask for my hand in marriage."

"Where was I?" I quizzed them " … I can't remember this."

"You were on an Oxfam volunteers' trip," Amit said, "Besides, it wasn't a big thing."

Twenty Two

March 30th, 1985

IT HAD FELT STRANGE being back home and everyone knowing when the phone rang at 8 p.m. that it was Nik. They moved discreetly out to allow us to talk freely. It reminded me of the time when Amit and Smita were engaged, and my father and I would sit in the dining room, me with my sketchbook and my father with his newspaper, teasing him when he came out about all the TV we were missing. Amit and Smita had done the same, giving me the TV guide highlighting the TV programmes they wanted to watch. The plan was that they would be coming in the morning for the gaur dhana. I'd spent the days leading up to it cleaning and tidying everything: washing the net curtains, cleaning the windows until they sparkled, washing the front door and step.

I was lying awake, afraid the house would not be good enough. For lunch, I was cooking Nik's favourite food and adding my parents' favourite foods, too: karela for my father and waatidall na bhajia to remember my mother.

Reena & Nikesh's Gaur Dhana Ceremony

Puran puri
flatbread stuffed with pigeon peas split lentils, sugar and cardamom paste cooked in ghee

Batata nu shaak
potato curry

Karela nu shaak
bitter gourd curry

Osaman
thin broth made with cooking water of pigeon pea split lentils

Waatidall na bhajia
ground black-eyed pea and split mung beans fritters

Baath
plain boiled rice

Topra ni chutnee
freshly grated coconut chutney

Roasted papad
thin crispy bread made with lentil flour dry roasted on a flame

Kachumber
salad made with cabbage, lettuce, cucumber, carrots, onions and tomatoes

They were due to arrive at twelve, and I'd changed into a turquoise kanjivaram silk saree with a bright-pink border; it had belonged to my mother. I paired it with a bright-pink blouse with three-quarter-length sleeves. I was wearing the gold necklace Nik gave me as a Valentine gift in our first year, a square pendant with my nickname engraved on it. I smiled when I thought of what he'd said, 'When you wear it you'll know that I'm always with you.' On the other side, the side next to my skin, was his nickname.

The doorbell rang and my father opened the door and welcomed the Rajas into our home. Nik introduced his motaba and his parents to him, and they were asked to sit down. I brought in some soft drinks and placed them on the coffee table, handing the glasses to everyone. As I gave the glass to Nik, his hand touched mine, and his smouldering eyes lingered on my face; I tried to hold back the sensation to gasp.

"Can I introduce Divya Masi. She is like a mother to me." My father took Divya Ba's hand and was speaking to our guests.

Nik's father and my father fell into an easy conversation about politics and cricket, and the women sat and listened. Divya Ba explained to the women the significance of the guar dhana ceremony, and they talked of the difference in the traditions for different communities. I could sense that Sarladevi didn't approve of what we did; her mouth held a thin smile. She hardly said a word.

The clock on the wall read twelve-thirty, and Nik's motaba said, "It's time. Do you have everything prepared?"

Smita moved to the sideboard to pick up a small

stainless steel puja dish with some sindoor, rice and gaur dhana and stood with it in her hand.

Nik and I were prompted to sit next to each other; he moved his leg to touch mine, his mischievous eyes glinting. I tried my hardest not to blush, but failed. Divya Ba instructed Nik's mother to put a tilak on Nik's forehead, and on mine, and fed us the small pieces of jaggary and dry coriander seeds.

His mother gave me a hug and said, "Welcome to our family, Reena."

I glanced at my father and saw his eyes glisten. Smita was instructed to do the same, and when she hugged Nik, she whispered something in his ears; his smile disappeared for a split second. The family exchanged hugs and handshakes. We were now officially recognised as a couple that wished to spend the rest of our lives together.

"Kaka, can I take Reena from here for a couple of minutes?" He asked my father, who nodded in reply.

"These young people," Nik's father laughed, as we walked into the dining room.

"You are ravishing today, my love," he told me as he kissed my left hand. "Did you deliberately wear my necklace today? 'Nik' touching your beautiful neck?" I blushed at the implications of what he said.

"Nik … everyone's here … " I implored.

"Come here then." He pulled me out of the back door to the other side of the bathroom. "Just one kiss, please." He grinned at me.

"No … I … can't."

"No one's watching. I won't smudge your lipstick, I promise." The last two words sounded like a moan and he kissed me softly on my lips.

"Welcome to my family, Reena Solanki. I look forward to spending the rest of my life with you." He took out a handkerchief from his pocket and wiped his mouth, "See?" He turned it to me. "No, smudges. It's still intact."

I checked my lips in the mirror in the bathroom as he waited for me, and we walked back into the front room.

Nik's father was standing and admiring my mother's portrait. "Your daughter is very talented, Naren Bhai. She could make a living out of selling these paintings if she chose to."

My father smiled. "Yes, she has her mother's creativity. I'm very proud of her."

That was the first time I'd heard him say something personal about my mother without being drunk.

"You're back. Shall we eat, so the young people can go somewhere?" Divya Ba said as she stood up. We pulled the dining table to the centre of the room and sat the elders down first. Our dining table could fit six, at a push. Nik was sitting on the settee waiting to eat with us. Smita and I still had the task of making the puran puri for when they sat so that everyone had them hot off the stove. Amit was hovering around the table, serving food as the plates became empty.

"The food is delicious, Divya Masi. You are an excellent cook. You must tell me how you made the karela nu shaak."

"Reena has made the food, Motaba," Nik informed her.

"Oh, I suppose she's had to learn. How old was Reena when her mother died, Naren Bhai?"

"My children were very young when their mother left

us, Sarla Ben. Reena has learnt her cooking from Divya Masi and me."

"No, no, no, my Reena has surpassed me a long time ago; she has the talent to put just the right amount of masala. Did you know, she has been helping in the mandir kitchen since she was ten years old," Divya Ba informed Sarladevi, shrugging off the compliment. "Naren's children are both very talented. He has done an outstanding job, raising them on his own," she added. "Do you know Reena sews her own clothes too, and you've seen her paintings. She is a very clever girl, but not the type who boasts. My dikri is modest and very loving."

My ears burned, and I felt the blush rise. I told Smita Bhabhi to take the next batch of puran puri to them instead of me. Nik noticed and moved to lean against the wall and turned his head to give me an approving smile.

"It will be good to have someone who can fill Bhabhi's shoes in the kitchen. I'm afraid our other daughters-in-law have no idea what to do in the kitchen, except peeling potatoes," Nik's mother added. They all laughed at the comment.

"Haan, haan, but what is the point? From what I hear about the work Reena wants to do, she will be roaming around the country and coming home too late to help in the kitchen."

"I've educated my daughter, so she doesn't have to spend all her time in the kitchen, Sarla Ben. Even my Smita doesn't cook for us every day. We are quite capable of cooking our own food."

"Ah, but in our family, the men don't cook."

"Bhabhi, we have you and Anu Ben to do the cooking.

It isn't a problem Reena will have to face," Nik's father interrupted.

After lunch, Divya Ba asked them to visit her house, and they left our house to walk up the street. As they exited through the front door, for the first time that day I noticed the sun was out and it was a pleasantly warm spring day.

They came back to the house later in the afternoon. I brought in the tea, trying very hard not to shake. I knew these people, so my body shouldn't have reacted in this way, but the level of adrenaline in my body had increased and my nerves were on edge. The conversation with the elders had been halting with moments of awkward silence, broken by Divya Ba's attempts to lighten the mood. Although Nik's parents had been kind and gracious, his motaba had sat upright and stern-faced. My father's face had darkened as he watched the family's matriarch examine our tiny homes with derision.

"Come and sit down, Reena. We'll need to discuss when you two want to get married." Nik's father instructed me. Nik cleared a spot on the settee next to him and took my hand. Amit took the other for reassurance.

"First, we need to match their janam kundli, Anant Bhai. Naren Bhai, do you have one prepared for your daughter?" Sarladevi said.

"I don't believe in astrology, Sarla Ben. Planets, and where they are in the sky don't make a difference to how we live in this world."

"It's our way, Naren Bhai. All my children have had their janam kundli matched to find the best day for the engagement and wedding. Can you tell me Reena's birthdate, time and place of birth?"

"Bhabhi, I want to know from the children when they want to get married. This year? Or do they want to wait until they are settled into work?" Nik's father said.

"This year, Kaka," Nik replied, his eyes questioning me. I nodded. "This year," he repeated.

Smita had gone to pick up a small book that my father keeps in our temple, and he took out his glasses and read out the details of my birth.

"Wednesday 25th September, 1963, at 3.50 in the afternoon at the Leicester Royal Infirmary. The Gujarati calendar date is Ashvin 8."

"September 25th, Navratri ni Adham?" she asked, the latter words in Gujarati.

"Yes, Motaba. Reena and I share the same birthday. We are meant to be together." Nik's face lit up with a beaming smile. Nik's mother smiled back at him, and Divya Ba nodded. His motaba turned; her eyes drifted from me and then settled on Nik's.

"Not all couples have the same birthdate, Nikesh. It is just a coincidence you are born on the same day." Her voice was clipped. He cast his eyes downwards. The beaming smile that was on his face gone. "Thank you, Naran Bhai. I'll get Jagdish Bhai to find a suitable date. Do you have any idea of when you'd be prepared for the wedding?"

"We will need some dates, and I'll see when the mandir is available. I know my daughter, and she won't want to get married anywhere else. As for the engagement, we are flexible. I'll leave that for you, whatever suits you. I believe we are coming to you for that?"

"What are you doing, Nik?"

He pulled me towards the back door. Our parents were bidding each other goodbye at the front door. Smita waved for me to go with him. He took me in his arms and inhaled. I held him tight until my heart returned to normal. We were in the small lobby. He kissed my forehead, my cheeks, my neck, and then my lips. I pulled away. "Someone will see," I whispered in his ear.

"No one will, they're too busy saying goodbye," he pleaded as he pulled me to him and continued our kiss. We walked hand-in-hand through the alleyway onto the street, and I stopped.

"The house is so small; it's smaller than Rajesh's house. How do they manage to live?" Sarladevi asked Pushpa as they walked past. Nik turned me to him and took both my hands.

"Shall we go to Gretna Green for a long weekend?"

I was confused and frowned at him. He smiled. "We could elope. I love you, and all I want is for us to spend the rest of our lives together."

"I love you too. But I'm not sure your motaba will ever like me." Tears stung my eyes.

"She's set in her ways, but she'll love you just as much as I do." He brushed his thumb under my eyes and pulled me to him.

"I'll call you tonight. Persuade your father to allow you all to come down for the barbecue," he whispered in my ear as he held me tight.

We walked out in the street, and he kissed my hand. I watched as the car drove down the road.

Twenty Three

Easter Sunday Barbecue Shakti Bhavan

THE DOOR TO THE MANDIR opened as I lifted my foot to climb up the stairs.

"Reena! I was hoping to speak with you alone."

I turned, Nik's motaba was standing at the door.

"Can you come in?" she asked me.

I took a deep breath. Amit, Smita and I had come for the barbecue that Suresh and Anil had arranged for Easter Sunday, and I was heading upstairs to fetch a cardigan from the bedroom.

She sat cross-legged on the floor and turned to a small silver trunk on the side of the family deities. I sat opposite her, knots developing in my stomach. She handed a small A5 notebook, wrapped with red threads, to me. I opened the cover; inside there was a rectangular sketch, divided diagonally with lines into segments. Each section was filled with spidery handwritten words in Gujarati script. I was confused; she let her fake smile slip for a split second, and a look of contempt fleetingly passed her eyes. "That's yours and Nikesh's janam kundli, put together."

"I can't read Gujarati," I said, knowing this would be another notch on the stick she held to tally all my shortcomings.

"Then, let me explain." She raised a thin smile, locking my gaze with her dark eyes. "It shows you are not suitable. Guruji has not been able to find a date suitable for your engagement or wedding. Your janam kundli shows that in your marriage you will bring pain and suffering. You will ruin my son's happiness. When I first heard about your mother and grandmother dying when you were young, I knew it. You bring a burden of unhappiness and bad luck with you, Reena. I haven't shown this to anyone yet. You can save my son from the suffering." She grabbed my hand.

I gulped back the lump that had risen in my throat. All my fears about being the cause of my mother's death resurfaced again. Perhaps she is right. I have seen the sadness in my father's eyes when he looks at me. The pain that surfaces when he cannot cope with living.

"I know my son is besotted with you; you have cast a spell on him. I saw the suffering he felt when you left him last summer. Why did you come back to him? I am asking you as a mother, leave him. I cannot see him marry you and endure that kind of life. I will find a nice wife for him who will look after him and make him happy."

She used my silence as an affirmation and continued.

"You can use your career as an excuse, find a job away from here. It will be best for both of you. Reconsider, Reena. Give my son up for his sake. Can you watch him suffer?" She paused. "We haven't done anything yet that cannot be undone."

I gave her the notebook back, nodded and got up. My legs were weak, and my throat burnt. I turned my gaze towards Radha Krishna, the eternal lovers, and walked out, leaving the woman placing the notebook back into the trunk.

'Guruji has not been able to find a date suitable for your engagement or wedding. Your janam kundli shows in your marriage, you will bring pain and suffering.' Her words resounded in my head. We won't get married, then what she believes won't come true. But we'll have to. We could just disappear. I'll apply for a job somewhere far from here, and Nik can find a position with a law firm. We'll live in sin; so many people are beginning to do so. But he loves his family. I would have to make him choose. He'll be miserable. His eyes light up when he talks about his family business and how he wants to grow it.

I stopped. I was in the walled garden, and I walked to the alcove to sit. She had proof and would use it to take Nik back. I have no choice but to give him up. The wretched tears welled out of my eyes and my world fell apart. The brief time, when both our families approved of our pairing, was all I had to cling to for my happiness.

"What are you doing here? I've been looking for you everywhere … weren't you fetching a cardigan?" I kept my head down. I didn't want Nik to see the pain and hurt. He sat down next to me. "What's the matter?"

I buried my head in his chest and held him tight and thought about what I should say to him. *How am I going to end this relationship without hurting him?* I remembered how gaunt and thin he became last autumn. He stroked my head.

"Come on, tell me what's wrong."

"It's all a bit too fast, Nik." My voice was a whisper; if I spoke any louder, I knew it would give me away.

"It's just nerves. I can't wait for you to be my wife."

"I just … I think we should slow down, perhaps think about getting married next year. I haven't found a job yet. I might have to work in Birmingham or Bristol. How can we be married if I live somewhere else?"

He laughed. "You're worrying about stuff that hasn't happened yet. Look at me." He lifted my chin and gasped as he saw the pain I was unable to hide in my eyes. "Did someone say something to you? This isn't just about nerves."

I pressed my lips tighter. "You can't keep this from me, Reena. Tell me who did this! What did they say?" His anger was palpable. "Tell me! I will not have it, do you understand? If you don't tell me, I'm going to take you with me and ask everyone who's here." He pulled me off the seat and gripped my hand.

"Nik, please … please," I implored, struggling to keep up with his long strides. We walked back into the house through the door of the kitchen. Nik's mother was preparing some vegetables and glanced at him.

"What's the matter, Niku?" She stood up, putting down the vegetable knife she was holding.

"Do you know anything about this?" he asked her, and she saw my red-rimmed eyes and understood.

She touched Nik's arm and quietly commanded, "Go to the study."

"Hello, you two. Fed up of the barbecue already?"

Nik's father said as Nik pulled me in. His mother walked in behind. "Sit down." She pointed to the sofa. "Why are you upset, Reena Beti?" Nik's father walked around the desk and pulled the two office chairs closer to the sofa. They were staring at me. I could not breathe, and I looked anxiously at Nik, my eyes begging.

"You have to tell us, my darling. Who has upset you?" Nik said.

"Janam. Kundli." The words came out as a sob, and the tears burst out of my eyes. Nik's mother pushed him away. Holding me tightly in her arms, she murmured, "Everything will be fine. We'll sort it."

Nik's father stood up, almost toppling the chair, and stormed out into the hallway.

"You're crying about a janam kundli?" Nik laughed nervously.

"It's not what is in it. It is what has been asked of Reena that is upsetting her, Niku." His mother added.

The door opened, and Nik's motaba was ushered into the study and guided to the chair positioned opposite the sofa. His father took the other. Her black eyes darted from Nik's face to his mother's, avoiding mine.

"Bhabhi, did you speak with Reena today about her janam kundli?" Nik's father asked his sister-in-law calmly.

"Haan, I picked it up from Jagdish Bhai this morning. It isn't good news, Anant Bhai. They do not match at all. We can't find a date, and all the signs show she will bring pain and sadness in Nikesh's life. I have explained it all to Reena. She knows what she must do."

"And what did you tell her to do, Bhabhi?" Anant

asked disappointedly.

"I told her to leave Nikesh."

"What? Why would you say that, Motaba?" Nik asked; he was gripping my hand.

"She is bad luck. It would be better for both of you to end this before it gets too far."

"Don't leave me, Ree. I couldn't bear it. I can't live without you." He then uttered the wretched words, "I'll … I'll kill myself."

"Stop! I'm unlucky, Nik; you have to let me go." I raised my hand to his cheek and made him look into my eyes, telling him in that exchange that I could live separated from him. Even if living without him would be like serving a life sentence, the thought of him leaving this earth was unbearable. His eyes glistened and turned to a dull brown. Tears burnt tracks down his cheeks.

"Motaba, I will not leave Reena; she is my heart." He pulled me to him and choked back his tears.

"Reena isn't going anywhere, Bhabhi." Pushpa's voice was calm. "Are you?" Her kind eyes were pleading. "You will ask Jagdish Bhai to find a solution. We found one for Suresh and Ashveena, and you'll find one … for my son." Nik's mother's voice was authoritative.

Sarladevi's lips curled up. "Haan, haan, Pushpa. I am sure we will find a solution. I wanted Reena to know the truth of her birth. Just that."

"If Motabhai were here, he wouldn't have liked what you've done to this girl, Bhabhi." Anant stared longingly at the portrait on the wall. "Once you move beyond your community, you will find you will like her, like her very much. Niku, can you take Reena to the kitchen and get her some water? We have some things to discuss."

Sarladevi's head bowed at the mention of her husband, and she clasped her hands tightly, holding them in her lap. Nik took my hand, and we walked out into the cavernous hallway with its gigantic chandelier. Instead of the kitchen, we walked down the stairs to the basement.

Nik picked up a bottle of The Famous Grouse, poured out two glasses and added ice. He sat down on the soft leather armchair and patted his lap. I sat down; he chinked my glass. "I love you, Reena; always have, always will."

I let the liquor slide down my throat.

"No one is ever going to keep us apart. We are meant to be together. Remember that my love. I've known it for a long time," he added, his golden eyes on fire.

Twenty Four

AT THE END OF THE EASTER HOLIDAYS, when Nik came to take me back to Warwick, he went straight away to deliver a note from his motaba to my father. His motaba had given Nik and me instructions on the days we had to fast, and Nik had a ring with a gemstone to wear until our wedding day. I was also going to perform a ceremony where I would be married to a tree so my bad luck would be attached to the poor tree. I had decided not to tell my family. I knew they would disapprove of my actions. I didn't believe it either, but I knew Nik did deep down, even though he joked about not allowing the tree to lay its wooden hands on my body. I was sure Sarladevi would hold it against me if I didn't comply.

Smita and I were eavesdropping, although in our house it wasn't really eavesdropping; you could be in the kitchen and hear a conversation in the front room without straining your ears.

"A winter wedding. Couldn't you get it any earlier?"

"No, Bhabhi," I replied. "Besides it will give me time

to find a job."

"Are you going to look in London? Daddy's going to be upset if you are."

Three weeks after the end of final-year exams I got a phone call from a production company. Mitchell & Leonard, a small television production company specialising in documentary making, had liked the fly-on-the-wall approach that Dick and I had taken when we filmed and produced the story of the comings and goings of the Oxfam shop in Coventry. They had asked me to help create a pitch for Channel Four. I was reluctant and nervous to tell my daddy, especially as my father seemed to be enjoying my time at home.

One evening when my father and I were the only two at home, we discussed the awkward subject.

"So, you've got a job?"

"Yes, Daddy. Who told you?"

"Your brother. When do you start?"

I told him the date, and he asked, "Are you going to live with the Rajas?"

"No, I'll stay at Umi's at first then find somewhere to rent."

"Good, I'm not happy having you stay at … what do they call it?"

"Shakti Bhavan."

"My daughter, the TV producer. Let's celebrate. Go get some ice."

I hugged him. I'd expected an outburst, but instead, he was calm. Bit by bit, my father was letting go of his responsibility. I wondered if I would ever see the man Divya Ba talked of before my mother died.

August 24th, 1985

NIK AND I WERE PRACTICALLY LIVING together;

he moved in some of his clothes at the flat I shared with Anne-Marie, a lively Irish graphic designer, who Jane knew. She is a couple of years older than me and had been working for the BBC for a year. I was not sure what he told his family when he was at mine, but I didn't care. Anne-Marie didn't mind either; she is bubbly and generous, but Nik insisted on paying for his share of the costs.

I woke up to a gloriously hot Sunday morning. The sky was blue. My joy-filled heart sang; today we would be officially engaged in the Hindu tradition. I dreamt of Nik, dressed in his jabo pyjamas, smiling, his magnificent eyes glinting and sparkling as we sat together while members of his family and mine blessed our union. I bought a carnation-pink silk saree from Roop Lila, and Rohini Bhabhi gave me an ornate silver tika as a gift, as a consolation for not attending the engagement. As I dressed, I thought of the reaction I would get from Nik. The blouse I had sewn had a low neck and an open back, with cap sleeves. The ornate-silver brocade border wrapped around the bottom of my rib cage.

This was the first time my father would visit Shakti Bhavan; he had declined to attend many functions at the house. He was nervous and hardly said anything as we drove down the motorway. When we buzzed at the gate, Nik's father came up the drive, waving at us. "Hello, hello, welcome, welcome to Shakti Bhavan."

Nik and his brothers were waiting by the stables; he was wearing a pale-peach embroidered jabo with matching pyjamas and had a red scarf over his shoulder; his brothers were wearing similar outfits in pastel shades, but theirs were less ornate. Nik's father took my father, Smita's father and Bharat Kaka away with him. They went into the house through the elaborate, gargantuan hallway.

"So, let me see you?" Nik leant into the car as the door opened.

Smita laughed at him, "Behave yourself, Nikesh Raja."

"I can't, Smita Bhabhi," he told her. "Today, we tick another day that will bring my beloved closer to becoming my wife." I smiled up at him when he said that and held out my hand.

"No running off with Reena, Niku," Rajesh interjected as he saw Nik helping me out of the car.

Nik clasped my hand to his chest, "Bhai you kill me, just a little time."

His brother shook his head, smiling, as he walked towards us. "We are sticking to a tight schedule this morning; you'll have time to yourself after the ceremony. Welcome, can I ask you to follow Niku and Reena, please?" He directed the remaining group.

We were served breakfast in the family room. The elders were already sitting at the huge dining table; sets of square tables had been arranged to provide everyone somewhere to sit. Breakfast was being made in the kitchen. Bhavini and another lady were busy restocking the serving dishes.

As I sat down at the table with my bhai and bhabhi and Nik, Anu Masi approached with a teapot. "Especially for you, Beti. No masala." She asked Amit, "Can I give you the same?"

"No, no, I like masala chai. My sister is the only one who's crazy," he replied in Gujarati.

We were instructed to sit on two low silver stools, and Nik was handed a coconut and an envelope of money by my bhabhi after she put a vermillion tilak on his forehead, and then his part of the ceremony was over. He sat patiently by my side, making sure his leg was touching mine, and he occasionally stroked my stomach with his hot hands. I urged him to stop with my eyes; he just grinned. I wished I had worn a chiffon saree so his hands would be visible. I concentrated on keeping my blushes down. The ladies of Nik's family performed the next part of the ceremony; they approached me to add a vermillion tilak on my forehead and then proceeded by putting a letterbox-red, crepe silk saree with silver booti work over my head. My silver jewellery was removed, and his sisters replaced it with the jewellery they had brought me, bangles, anklets, earrings and a necklace.

"The set is similar to the ones I gave my other daughters-in-law," Sarladevi commented to Divya Ba and Jane. "It is diamonds on white gold. I don't know what it is about these modern girls. They don't seem to like yellow gold anymore." Divya Ba translated the conversation to Jane. I recalled the conversation I had with her about not wanting any diamonds, let alone the colour of the gold. I was thankful my father was at the back of the room and hadn't heard her boasting.

OUR FRIENDS HAD ARRIVED after breakfast; they were the first to celebrate our unofficial engagement and were with us to witness our engagement; Nik's eyes were full of disappointment when Jay came to say goodbye after lunch.

"Are you some kind of lord from India, Nik?" Anne-Marie asked him, as she finished her tour of Shakti

Bhavan. "And I don't understand why'd you want to live in Hanwell above a Spar when you can live here?" "But my heart doesn't live here and without it how can I function?" he replied.

She stared at him with her piercing eyes, and muttered, "You old romantic."

For the rest of the afternoon, we sat listening to the soft rustle of the willow and the chirping tweets of the songbirds. We talked about our new jobs and where we would like to be in five years.

When it was time for my family to go back, we gathered at the stable block. I hugged Divya Ba, Amit and Smita, then stopped in front of Daddy. He pulled me in his arms.

"You look just like your mother in this saree." I had changed after lunch into the red saree Nik's family had given me. "I'm going to miss you, my daughter." He burst out crying.

A lump grew in my throat, my eyes stung, and hot sorrowful tears rolled down my eyes as I held him tightly.

Nik's father put a hand over my father's shoulders and said, "Naren Bhai, you haven't lost a daughter, you have gained a whole new family. This is your home as much as ours now."

Nik's mother took me in her arms and kissed my wet cheeks, "Now, now, Reena, you're my daughter. I promise I won't treat you any differently."

My father stood, his fist clenched, and Nik rushed to hug him. "I'll bring her home next weekend, Daddy." My father raised a thin smile at his words. Nik hugged Divya Ba, Amit and Smita, too, who had also become teary after seeing my father and me crying.

We drove behind them in Nik's car as they left Shakti Bhavan and I think if this is how my Daddy feels at the engagement, what will he be like when I actually do get married.

***

WE WERE ON THE M1 heading up to Leicester; Nik had picked me up from work at Mitchell & Leonard production office in Soho. I had travelled up to Leicester several times since our engagement. Nik would drive me home, and Amit would drive me back down.

By the time we came off Junction 21, it was ten o'clock. My father had become more and more depressed after our engagement, and although I had spent at least a part of my weekend at home, his mood had not lightened, and he had resorted to drinking heavily again, halting the progress he had made after Smita's arrival.

I could hear the turntable as it whirred round and round, the needle lifted, no longer playing the song that was ingrained in my head. It was a familiar sound. My heart sank. It would be the first time Nik would see what life was like for me and my brother when we grew up. He had made us dinner and waited for us to arrive to eat. But as the time of our arrival slipped, he had turned to drink to drown his sorrow, disappointed we hadn't come.

He was dishevelled, his hair standing on end; his jacket had fallen in a heap by the chair. At his feet, there was an empty bottle of Black Label, and the ice he brought in a bowl had melted to water. Nik stopped the record player.

"Daddy, Daddy!" I tried to wake him by shaking his shoulder.

"Come on, Daddy. Let's get you upstairs." Nik lifted him up off the chair.

"I'm fine, I can go to my room on my own, Amit." As he focused his eyes, he realised it wasn't Amit.

"Oh, it's you, Nikesh. When did you come?"

"Sorry we're late, Daddy. There was too much traffic today," Nik replied.

He pushed at Nik, who was taken aback by the strength.

"So, you think you can come to my house and take my daughter away from me, Nikesh Raja?" It sounded like a threat. "I don't need your help. I can make my own way to my room." He patted Nik's chest. "You sit, come, eat, drink, take it all, what's mine is yours." He staggered. I tried to grab him to steady him. "You! Why did you abandon me? What did I do wrong? I tried my best. Go, go and leave me alone. Stop haunting me." I was confused. I didn't think he was really talking to me. "Go!" he shouted, and he pushed me.

I lost my balance and fell on the coffee table. Nik was instantly by my side, his arms pulling me upright. My eyes filled with tears. My father's expression changed. "I'm sorry, Reena. I'm sorry. I miss you." He slumped on the floor. We lifted him off the floor and took him upstairs to his bedroom. Nik took off his slippers and his belt and guided him into the bed, lifting the covers over him, and we closed the door.

"Are you okay, my love?" Nik's eyes were full of concern as he held me. I sobbed into his chest. We stood on the landing until the beat of my heart returned to normal.

"I'm going to warm the food up. Sit down," he instructed as he headed for the kitchen. I walked back to the front room to tidy up. I picked up his jacket, and that's when I saw the yellowing sheets of paper, folded and worn.

"Where have you gone, Ree?"

Nik recognised the significance of my posture and sat down, holding me to him as I read.

My Dearest Naren

Why have we come to this land? Do you remember how happy we were to get the navy-blue passport, to get the plane ticket to begin our life in the country of our Queen? How wrong I was to think the people here like us, want us. You don't hear what I hear. They think I'm one of them, with my light complexion, and talk about how we smell and don't wash and worship false idols. Then when they hear my voice, they realise I am one of the smelly, unwashed idol worshippers. They look me straight in the eye with no apology as they refuse to take money from my hand, slam doors in my face, sell me rotten fruit and vegetables. What makes me most unhappy is the disappointment in your eyes when you go to work. The boss, who has promoted you, doesn't see the bright business student who impressed the authorities in Kenya. Instead, you work as a translator, telling the ladies at the clothing factory what needs to be done. I don't understand your stubbornness; we could go back, back to the smiling people, back to the hot sun, back to the life we had, back to the land of our birth. I hate this country, this dark house, the dirty streets, the people who smile with their teeth and not their eyes.

Yesterday when I came back from the mandir in my saree, a young man looked into the pram, and I was expecting the usual reaction, 'isn't she fair, look at the colour of her hair,' but he spat at Reena. I was shocked at the way he did that, and he then walked away, swearing and telling me to go home.

This morning was the hardest. You hurt me with your words, 'sort yourself out and get out of bed.' I was devastated. I thought you understood. You know what the ladies at the mandir have said. A witch has given our daughter the Evil Eye. How can anyone not envy the dark curls around the beautiful porcelain-skinned face? How else can you explain the crying in the evening, the fretful periods of sleep and waking up with the shrill cries? Tell me how can you explain the inability for me to function normally since the birth of our child? There must be a grain of truth in it.

When Amit was born, he was so quiet and stared at me with wise eyes and saw me fumble through motherhood. But our little girl cries all the time; she is so angry at the world and shows her frustration at every opportunity.

I thought I was a good mother. Our little boy is bright and happy, but I have felt useless with Reena. My mother would have known what to do. Even she isn't here in this cold and grey land with cold and grey people. I have no one to turn to. My new life is intolerable. The ladies at the mandir help, but they too suffer from the grey skies and the cold rain that soaks into our bones.

I have to confess to you before I leave you. I hope it will bring you some peace and explain why I am doing what I plan to do.

Do you remember the year after Reena was born and it snowed for days in April, the north wind was bitingly cold?

*The recently fallen snow had melted to sludge and turning
to ice rapidly, but I had to take the washing to the laundry.
I put both of the children in two layers of clothing and
wrapped them in a double layer of blankets and put them in
the old pram we'd bought from Mrs Davis. I put the bag of
dirty washing on top of the hood.*

*The journey to Narborough Road was awful. I had no grip
on my shoes and I was wearing a flimsy coat that was not
suitable for cold winters and my hands and feet had gone
numb after a few minutes outside. Amit started
complaining he was cold and wanted to go home.*

*Pushing the pram with the bag on top was so difficult, it
fell many times. Amit was so angry to be taken out in the
biting wind he started bawling as loud as he could. I lost
your favourite shirt then. You were so upset. I couldn't tell
you how I'd lost it.*

*By the time I reached the laundry, Amit was still crying,
Reena was screaming at the top of her lungs, and I too
could feel hot tears rise up. I sat and cried and cried, Amit
cried and cried, our daughter cried and cried. Lucky or
unlucky for me, no one was at the laundry.*

*I was useless, what was a ten-minute walk turned to thirty
minutes. Many people gave me disapproving stares and
tutted as I walked past them.*

*What was I supposed to do, not go to the laundry? Let my
family wear dirty clothes?*

*The next part is still difficult to recollect. I put the washing
in the machine, Amit had calmed down in the warmth, I
gave him a packet of crisps, I gave the baby a bottle of milk
and I walked out.*

I left our children in the laundry!

I walked to the park by the river. I couldn't stay with our daughter. I was angry at our little girl, who cried for food, cried for sleep, cried for a wash, cried for attention, cried for no reason but to make my life hell. I was angry I was in this cold foreign country, having no one to help me. Even Divya Masi, who has been like a mother, chides me for not keeping the house and the children clean.

I walked numbly in the cold and thought of how easy it would be for me to jump into the river and wait for the cold water to soak through my limbs and slowly stop my heart. No one would know. Who would go to the park on a cold, windy day? That was the first time the draw of water beckoned me. It has called to me a lot lately, the soothing voices beckon me. That's why I've stopped going to the park.

But something made me come back from the dark thoughts. My hair caught on a low hanging branch and the memory of Amit wrapping his fingers round and round on a loose strand of my hair to soothe himself came to my mind. I remembered our beautiful daughter; whose rare smile fills the room when I sing to her.

I ran back to the laundry, my heart in my mouth, not knowing how long I was away, worrying someone would have taken our children and I would have to go to the police to tell them what I had done.

As I approached the laundry, I saw a little girl playing with Amit. Sitting on the bench to the side was an old woman. I stepped through the door and she greeted me. She knew I left the children, but she was so friendly and smiled at me with genuine concern.

She opened up a bag of pear drops, offered me one and patted a space on the bench next to her. I sat down and she explained her daughter was resting as she too struggled with looking after her little girl and sometimes, you just have to ask for help.

Do you remember Mrs Jenkins who lived on Jerome Street? She was a very wise woman and was always helpful to me, one of the few people of this land that see me as a human being. She listened to me when I needed help. I miss her now she has moved away.

When I relive the day, I am so scared. What would you say when you hear what I did? Would our children ever forgive me for abandoning them?

I resolved to fight the urge to end it all, to be stronger, but lately, I keep thinking about my mother's death. The world is full of sadness. Naren, can you imagine what her death would have been like, all alone in the small flat? She didn't have any family with her. You know it's been difficult for her since Amrut went away.

I know what I'm doing is going to cause you hardship and pain. But I'm afraid I'll hurt our children if I don't do this. I'm sorry, my husband. I've tried to be a good wife and mother. The demons that possess my soul are calling me. I cannot control them anymore. Believe me, when I say I've tried so hard to keep going for our children. Some days I weep for their life without me.

Tell my children I love them, but it was my life and the world I hated. Tell them about all my inadequacy as a wife and mother.

Goodbye, my darling husband, I hope to be a better wife and mother in our next life.

Usha

The sob I was holding onto broke free, and I howled with the guilt. My head ached with my thoughts; my mother killed herself because of me, because of how I was. She left us because I made her life a misery. My birth had caused my family pain, and I was now going to inflict it on Nik.

Nik turned me towards him and kissed me. I yielded to his soft kisses, clinging to him for comfort. Then the Guruji's words resounded, 'The beginning of your life was difficult, Beti.' He was right. He saw I had killed my mother.

"It's my fault, Nik. I killed my mother. They are right … I'm bad luck. I will bring you pain." I handed him the letter. He read it, holding me close.

"This is not your fault." He lifted the letter. "It's sad your mother had no one to help her. But you are not responsible. You were only a child, and I didn't expect you to be placid. You are not that type of person. You are not bad luck, in fact, it is my good luck to have found you. I love you, Reena Solanki, and nothing, nothing is going to stop me from loving you."

✳ ✳ ✳

"Mummy, Mummy, Mummy."

I didn't know why she wouldn't come. I'd asked for her, and no one would tell me where she had gone. I knew I slapped her, but sometimes I got cross. She still didn't get up.

"I'm sorry. I'm sorry I won't do it again. I'll be a good girl. I promise I'll be a good girl. Mummy, where are you?"

Someone bent down and pulled me onto their hip.

"Daddy! Where's Mummy? I want Mummy."

"Shush, Reena. Come let's wipe your tears." He took a handkerchief and dabbed it to my eyes. "Shush, I'll get you an ice lolly."

I watched his face and gulped back my tears. "Where's Bhai, Bhai!"

"He's right here, look down, Reena."

"Bhai, we're getting a lolly." My brother was looking down at his feet. "First you have to be a good girl. Come and say goodbye to Mummy."

"Why? Where's Mummy going?"

Mummy was wearing her red saree. She was beautiful. Her head was covered, and she had dark-red lipstick on her lips. I didn't like the dark-red lipstick; she looked more beautiful in the colour she usually wore.

"Why is Mummy still sleeping? Wake up Mummy, wake up."

"Shush, Reena. Remember the ice lolly. Give Mummy the water, there's a good girl. Let's walk around. I'm going to give you to Kaka, be a good girl."

"Kaka, why won't Mummy get up? I didn't mean to slap her, but she wouldn't get up. Is she angry with me, is she pretending? Bhai pretends to sleep all the time."

"Shush, dikri. Look how peaceful she is."

"Stop, stop, why are you covering her face?"

"Stop. Stop. Stop. Mummy wake up, Mummy, please wake up, Mummy."

"Ree, I have you, you're safe my love."

The small bedside lamp was on, and Nik was holding me in his arms. I put my face in his chest, and the miserable, bitter tears soaked his T-shirt.

"It's just a dream, you're safe. I have you, my love."

I took a deep breath. "I remember, I remember it all Nik." I burst into tears again, holding on tightly for comfort.

When I woke up again, I searched for Nik and a lump closed my throat. "Nik." My voice choked. Thoughts formed in my foggy head, he's sleeping downstairs, and we're at my house. My father wouldn't allow us to sleep in the same bed, but he was with me last night. How would he allow that? The letter. I remembered it all.

Nik was sitting at the dining table with a mug of masala tea in his hands. "Good morning my love." I walked up to him and gave him a kiss on the lips. His eyes sparkled as he pulled me down. "Did you miss me?"

"How was the settee, comfy?" I pushed his hair off his face as I sat on his lap. He placed his hand on my lower back, and I winced.

"Sorry. Let me see." He turned me to examine my back. He took a deep breath and I turned back to him. His eyes grew darker.

"Is it big?" My voice came out husky as I remembered how I got the bruise.

"I don't think you should come home anymore. I won't watch and do nothing as you get hurt. Yesterday was the first and last time that will happen." His voice was stern.

"He just needs to adjust to us, Nik."

"Has it happened before?" I nodded. "And you didn't think I should know?"

"It's happened … before I came to Warwick. He hasn't been as drunk since Smita and Amit got married." I felt pain for my father, knowing that his wife killed herself.

"Does he hurt only you or does he hurt Amit, too?"

"I just got in his way, that's all." I said.

"Did you get in his way last time?" I told him, yes, and

I felt the hot tears roll down my cheek. "You didn't answer my question. Is it only you or Amit, too?" His voice could not hold back the anger.

"Whoever he finds first." I replied with resignation.

"Never again, do you hear me, Reena? He will never hurt you again. If you want to come see him, I will come and stay with you. Come here." He pulled me closer, and I continued to cry on his shoulder.

My father climbed down the stairs at ten o'clock in the morning. He was in his pyjamas and dressing gown. His face darkened as he saw us sitting on the settee. His mood for the rest of the weekend would be bad; it always was after his drunken outbursts, the guilt of hurting us gnawing at him. Amit and I usually behaved as if nothing had happened to lighten the mood and to make him forget. I wondered if Nik would be happy to play this game with me, after what he witnessed last night.

"Are you still here, Nikesh?" he said.

"Yes, I'm here for the weekend. We'll go back down to London tomorrow evening."

"Just remember, you might be engaged, but you will not do anything inappropriate with my daughter."

"I will never hurt your daughter, sir. She is my heart," Nik replied, curtly.

He left us in the house for the afternoon, telling us he had arranged to meet up with friends on Narborough Road. Nik and I went for a walk in Bede Park, and I told him what I remembered about my mother's death. He listened to me quietly, reassuring me with kisses, allowing me to mourn my mother properly. When we returned to the house, I put the letter back where I had found it, hoping when my father returned, he would think he just mislaid it for a while. I didn't want him to know we had read it.

At four o'clock my father returned. I could smell the tobacco and alcohol on his breath and knew he'd been to the pub. "I went to the butcher's and got some chicken," he told us as he placed the carrier bags on the kitchen counter. "Have you had Reena's methi ni murgi, Nikesh? Will you make it for us?"

I sighed with relief; at least he wouldn't be grumpy for the rest of the weekend. Having Nik here had changed his usual behaviour.

Twenty Five

I WAS IN THE PRODUCTION OFFICE at Mitchell & Leonard, listening to my brother tell me the twins had arrived early. We'd all been excited when the scan revealed Smita Bhabhi was pregnant with twins and teased her incessantly that she would be the size of a whale. Nik had even bought her a soft toy whale as a joke present.

***

WE ENTERED THE SPECIALIST neonatal unit and were taken to a large glass window. The room had six incubators placed against the walls holding varying-sized babies. Along the left-hand-side of the room was Amit. He was standing next to a plastic incubator where two tiny babies were nestled. The smaller one had a blue hat on and the slightly longer one had a pink hat on. Both of them had a tube inserted in their mouths, pads taped over their eyes and a blue light shining on them. I burst out crying when I saw the tiny babies; they were the size of small dolls. Nik was holding my hand, and he pulled me to him. "They're just small; you heard what Amit said. They have jaundice and need help with oxygen. They are fighters."

Our parents were in the waiting room, and when we entered, they stopped in mid-conversation.

"What were you talking about?" Nik asked his father as we sat down.

"The doctors are saying the twins will need to stay in the hospital for at least six weeks."

"Six weeks. But that's until after the wedding." Nik said.

"Haan, at least Smita will be out by then," Nik's motaba interjected " … these things happen. The date is set. It must go ahead."

A lump formed in my throat, and I couldn't speak. I fiddled with my engagement ring and kept my head down. I let the enormity of the news sink in my brother and his wife would be far too worried about their children to enjoy my wedding day. They wouldn't come to London for the wedding reception. I wanted my family to be at my wedding. The only people who mattered to me would not be there to celebrate the start of my new life with Nik. The silence in the room expanded like a cavernous hole.

"What did you think? Aren't they great?" Amit said as he walked into the room. His face dropped as he saw the expression on everyone's faces. "What has happened?"

"Sit down, Amit." My father's voice was hushed, "We have to discuss Reena and Nikesh's wedding."

I listened to them discuss our wedding day: how Smita and Amit would need to be there for the ceremony but wouldn't be able to sit in the puja to give me away;

how Smita would need to be careful because of the caesarean and Amit would have to take her home to rest; how it would not be possible for them to come for the reception unless they felt happy to be far away from the babies. Nik tried to gauge my reaction to the conversation, his eyes darting sideways at me.

"Reena Beti, you're very quiet?" Nik's father said.

I glanced at my brother, whose face was sad. He was looking forward to giving me away: he was more like a parent than a sibling to me.

"I … I want Amit and Smita Bhabhi to give me away … " I began to say.

"That's not possible. Smita can't sit in any religious ceremony," Sarladevi interrupted.

"Can't we do something," I pleaded.

"Na, it's been difficult to find a suitable date. You will be given away by your kaka and kaki," she replied.

I stood up. Nik held my hand and looked questioningly at me and released it. "I have to go for a walk," I said to the elders.

"I'm coming with you." Amit took my hand.

"Do you think it's a sign, Anant Bhai?"

"What sign, Bhabhi?" asked Nik's father.

"You know the trouble with the janam kundli?"

"Bhabhi, you must learn to hold your tongue. These children have enough to worry about," he reprimanded.

My brother and I halted, shocked at what we heard. He squeezed my hand, and we walked out of the ward and out of the hospital. The cold of the November night slapped my face and tears welled up in my eyes. My thoughts jangled with all the information I'd been given. Nothing about getting married to Nikesh Raja had been easy. *Would it have been easier if I had walked away as Sarladevi had asked me to do that day?*

"Do you have to get married this year?" Amit asked tentatively. A glimmer of hope filled my heart.

"No, we don't. We see each other practically every day. We could postpone it until next year." I let my words sink in.

"How would Nik feel about it?"

"I don't know, Bro. He'll probably be upset, but … I'm sure he'll understand." Then the thought of cancelling the mandir and the hotel reception filled me with dread. "We can't. Think of the money. Daddy has saved up for this; he will lose all the money."

"It's not a cancellation, Sis, it's a postponement. I'm sure we can speak with the caterers and the mandir. This sort of thing must happen all the time."

I smiled up at my brother, the rescuer; he had always been there for me, buoying me along when I lost hope. Cheering me up when I was down. When I told him about our mother's letter, it was he who asked my father to show it to him. It was he who had helped him deal with his loss as he should have. He is like a calming balm in my family. My mother was right when she said he was wise.

"What do you mean postpone the wedding?" Nik paced up and down the hospital corridor, his eyes throwing sparkly arrows in my direction.

"Please, Nik, please understand. I want Amit and Smita Bhabhi to give me away, and if we get married on the twenty-first … " I covered my face with my hands. I couldn't contemplate what being married without them would be like.

"They'll be there. Be reasonable, Reena. Your kaka and

kaki sat in the puja for Amit's wedding."

"Yes, but I have an older married brother now!" I tried to control my voice from rising.

"I can't … it will take ages for us to actually be married." He paced silently, his fist clenched, working the problem in his mind. The creases deepened as he concentrated. Eventually, his fists loosened. "When do you think would be the right time for us to marry, Ree?" He stopped pacing and stood in front of me, his eyes glistening, chewing at this bottom lip. I took his hand.

"I love you. Thank you for agreeing to it."

"I'm still not happy about it, but I know why you'd want this. Let's go and see Smita Bhabhi." He lifted me up and kissed me.

Smita Bhabhi was asleep, and Amit was sitting in an armchair. "How is she?" I whispered to my brother.

"She's sleeping. I thought I'd wait for you to give me a lift home."

"I'm not sleeping, Amit, just closed my eyes. How are the babies?"

"Shall we go and see them? Can you walk?"

Amit helped his wife climb out of bed. She walked slowly and tentatively along the corridor to the neonatal unit, Amit holding her up. While we watched them, Nik pulled me to him and kissed the side of my head.

"You know, it must be hard for them. Putting our wedding back will help won't it?"

"Yes, it will only be until the new year, Nik."

***

"YOU DON'T LOOK GOOD. What's happened?"

Dick stood up and gave me a hug. I sat down, clutching my hands; the gnawing ache that was in the pit of my stomach was growing more and more, as I waited for any news from Nik.

"Have you heard from Nik?" I quizzed him.

"No, why?" He poured me a glass of white wine, and I took a gulp and told Dick why I was worried about him. "So, how far is the wedding date?"

"30th November next year. It's the only weekend suitable, but we've asked for a weekday."

"Ouch, I can understand why he'd be upset."

"When do you find out about the new date?"

"I rang his motaba. She's found a couple, he knows of them. I don't understand him. We're practically living together anyway. Why does moving our wedding upset him?"

"Ah, but you're not living together. It's not the same; he has to keep going home. Are you sure he's not at some Expo you don't know about?"

"He calls me every day if he doesn't see me. What if … "

"Stop speculating and letting your imagination run away with you."

We ate our meal in silence, the noise of the chatter in the restaurant becoming a barrier for conversation. After dinner, we rang Peter, Ravi and Umi and asked them to meet us at my flat.

"Is he holed up in that hotel?" Umi asked me, and I frowned. "You know, the one we found them at last time."

"Why would Nik do this, go on a drinking binge with Jay?" I voiced my concern and she took my hand. Peter picked up the phone and asked directory enquiries for the phone number.

"Hello, can you put me through to Nikesh Raja's room? Oh … do you have a Jayesh Dattani staying there? Thank you." He put the phone down, and a fleeting look of sympathy appeared on his face before he resets his expression.

"Jay was there last night, checked out this morning. He's probably home now. Call his house, someone." Dick picked up the phone to ask for Nik and left a message on Jay's answer phone. Every cell in my body was screaming that something terrible had happened. I rushed to the bathroom and threw up, clutching at the toilet bowl, spitting and retching, expelling the carbonara I had eaten earlier. Umi rubbed my back. As we came out of the bathroom, Peter and Ravi were stepping out of the door.

"We think we know where they might be," Ravi shouted.

Two hours later, there was no sign of Peter, Ravi or Nik. Anne-Marie had come home, and we were drinking tea, waiting for any news of Nik or Jay.

The doorbell rang. I rushed to open the door and found Jay with Peter and Ravi.

"Hello, Reena." He looked sheepishly at his feet, slid his thin body past mine and walked into our sitting room.

"Go on, tell her, Jay," Peter scolded.

Jay recounted how Nik was upset and had come to his office on Monday afternoon; how they'd gone drinking and clubbing in their old haunts in Watford.

He asked accusingly, "Why would you move the wedding day? He's hurt, really hurt by it all. Don't you want to marry him?"

I shielded my face with my hands. I didn't want him to see the pain those words had inflicted on me. Dick put his arm around my shoulder, and Umi squeezed my hand. He was hurt and instead of telling me, he'd gone to speak with Jay, the only person who would not or could not talk through the options. The only person who thought the best way to deal with emotional issues was to get drunk and go to nightclubs.

"You do know that Amit and Smita have had the twins early?" Anne-Marie barked at Jay. "The wedding or Nik is the last thing Reena needs to worry about. Why didn't you just send him home, Jay?"

He stared back at Anne-Marie, scorn in his eyes. "No, I didn't know about the twins." His voice was barely audible.

Jay left as soon as he'd recounted his story, his thin chin pointing defiantly in the air. He did not have any regrets for his actions and had made it clear to us that what he'd done was in the best interest of Nik.

* * *

PETER, RAVI AND UMI had already left. Dick and Anne-Marie were sure Nik would come to the flat and had insisted on waiting up with me for his return.

The latch turned; I walked slowly to the door as he stepped into the entrance hall. His face was gaunt, his eyes were bloodshot, he had a two-day stubble on his face. The relief flooded through my body and the tension I'd held diffused. I grabbed the door to steady myself. His arms hung limply by his side.

"I'm sorry Ree, I've been stupid. I should have called you."

He walked tentatively towards me; my legs felt like

jelly, and I swayed a little. I grasped onto the door handle, and he had me in his arms, as the tears flooded my face.

"Nik, you're an idiot. Why would you put someone you love through this?" Anne-Marie poked her head out from the kitchen, holding up a kettle.

"Bloody hell, Nik! Where have you been? Ree's been worried sick."

"Sorry, Dick. I don't have any excuse for what I did."

He pulled me to his chest, and I was engulfed in his arms. He pulled me at arm's length, scrutinising my face. "Please forgive me. I just couldn't cope with the wait."

"Go and sit down. I'm making tea. Do you want a hot drink, Nik?" Anne-Marie shouted from the kitchen.

He apologised to Dick and Anne-Marie as she walked in with the tray. *What is it about Jay that draws Nik to him. What hold does he have over him?*

"I should've been stronger. I thought I was okay. But even the new dates are too far away. Why aren't you saying anything, Ree?" I shook my head. I wanted to hide the hurt in my heart. I knew who I would turn to; it would always be Nik and no one else. Dick answered for me.

"Ree would have come to you, Nik. So what if you can't get married until next year? Find a way to spend more time together with your parents' consent. She loves you more than you can imagine. I've seen how she suffered last time. Get your priorities right; either you protect her from the hurt, or you give her up and continue living the life you're drawn to. I've told you if you hurt her again, I won't be responsible for my actions." Dick stood up, took Nik's hand off my shoulder, and drew me to him. "I'm going home, call me if you want me to come back."

His stance showed he was too angry to stay. His steely blue eyes were dark and threatening. He gave Anne-Marie a hug and glared at Nik before he picked up his coat and closed the door behind him.

"Right, that's my cue to say goodnight, too." Anne-Marie headed for her bedroom. "You two need to talk. I mean, a serious discussion on where your relationship is heading."

We sat in silence. Dick had moved me to the armchair away from Nik. He struggled to say something; the gap between us widened. He pushed his hair off his forehead with both hands and leant forward.

"We have to get married on the 21st December. I can't wait for a whole year. All this sneaking around is killing me. I want to spend time with you openly."

"I won't have a wedding without Amit and Smita Bhabhi." I rubbed my forehead, trying to keep the tears at bay. "I love you, Nik, but it's not fair for you to ask me to do this."

"Let's just have a register marriage; we'll have them both present. Amit can be your witness. It doesn't have to be complicated." A glimmer of hope presented in his eyes. He was kneeling in front of me, his head dipped. He lifted my chin with his thumb and kissed me. My eyes filled with tears. "Why are you crying?"

I wondered why I was upset. We'd found a solution to our dilemma. We would be married; there would be no reason why Amit couldn't give me away. But I wanted to get married under a mandap, walk around the havan blessed by Agni Dev. The whole Hindu ceremony I had dreamt about and seen in Bollywood movies. I pulled his hand away from my face, and held it in my lap, and watched as teardrops fell uncontrollably on the back of my hand.

"Please, Ree, tell me what you are thinking." He lowered his head and looked up at me.

"I … I'm sorry Nik … this isn't how I'd imagined marrying you."

"But … we have a solution … have you changed your mind? Have I ruined it for us by doing this?"

"I want to marry you Nik, I really do. It isn't my family who insists on astrology and mumbo jumbo to pick a date. Your motaba insists, so either we accept this, or we get married any date we want as soon as we can. The choice is yours. I'm upset too. I'm upset that I have to fast. I'm upset because as far as your Guru is concerned, I'm the problem and not you. Why is that Nik? Why do I have all the bad planets and none of the good ones in my chart? Do you know what I did when I found out about the dates? I don't want to wait either. It's hurting me as much as it's hurting you to be apart. I called my daddy and pleaded with him to find an alternative that was sooner. Do you know what he said Nik? He said he didn't believe in janam kundli and if he went to find a closer date, he'd be condoning it." I rubbed away the tears from my face and locked eyes with his. "When you asked me to marry me, I … I thought you could talk to me about your fears, about your hopes. Do you know what was going through my mind? Do you? You promised, Nik. You promised you wouldn't hurt me."

"I'm so, so, sorry. I'll change. I'll never do it again. Please forgive me, my love. Please."

He stood up and pulled me to him. I yielded to his

embrace; the tension I had been holding on to as I spoke about the injustice of the customs and rituals his family practise washed away.

I felt his heart thudding and I said, "I love you more than you can imagine, Nik." We eventually went to bed, neither of us wishing to speak anymore, both of us wanting to forget the ache and pain of our separation, entwined in each other's arms.

We were woken by BBC Radio 1's Breakfast Show in the kitchen as Anne-Marie prepared her breakfast. Nik was resting on one elbow.

"Good morning, my darling." He kissed me softly. "I have an idea." His golden eyes glinted. "But it's a surprise. Keep the weekend of the 21st December free." He pulled off the bedcovers and was on top of me, his arms holding his weight.

"What time do you have to go in today?"

"Late start. Client meeting at 6.30 tonight." I smiled up at him.

"Oh, plenty of time, then." He began to slide down my body, planting kisses as he progressed.

Twenty Six

"GOOD MORNING, MY LOVE. Ready for this weekend?"

I was awoken with warm kisses. As I kissed Nik back, I asked, "Can you give me a hint?"

"No, no, no hint. Just make sure you have what I asked you to pack."

We are in the car by 10.30 a.m. and Nik put on *Mohammed Rafi's Greatest Hits* as we drove up the motorway to the Midlands.

"Why are we going to Coventry?"

"Just have to pick something up from the house. You don't mind, do you?"

I shook my head. My anxiety had built up; I was not sure he was telling me the truth. He had been unusually quiet today on our car journey up, looking anxiously at his watch. When I told him the funny stories about the twins and how they got cranky when Amit and Smita held them separately, he was unable to raise a smile; it resembled a grimace. Even his usual singing to the tape hadn't happened on this drive.

Mohammed Rafi started to sing my favourite song "Likhe Jo Khat Tujhe" from the mixtape, I smiled and raised an eyebrow, expecting him to start, but he stayed silent. When we stopped off at Newport Pagnell Service Station for a break, he declined his mid-morning snack of sandwiches. I wondered what was making him so nervous. *It wasn't normal for Nik to be like this.*

"What's the matter?" I smiled at him. "Don't you like it?" I pointed to the half-drunk coffee.

"Too excited about tonight's big dinner," he told me, smiling. "You'll love what we're eating."

He pulled into the garage and rushed to open the passenger door. He took my hand and kissed it, his head bowed as he leant into the car. "Reena, do you still want to marry me?" He pulled me out of the car, and I wrapped my arms around his neck and kissed him telling him in the kisses there was no one else I would want to marry.

"I thought you'd need something nice to wear," he said as he drew me to his side. We sat down on the sofa, and I carefully removed the wrapping paper from the gift box. I lifted the lid and inside there was a vermillion chiffon silk saree with a gold brocade border. I looked at him quizzically. "You know I said I wanted to marry you today?"

My mind went back to the conversation in the alleyway. 'Shall we go to Gretna Green for a long weekend?'

"Yes, but I'm not eloping with you, Nik." My eyes stung.

"Ree, my love!" He took my hands and started to kiss them. "It's not what you think, my love. I didn't mean to upset you." He embraced me. "I love you. I wouldn't do that to you. Reena Solanki, will you take seven vows around the sacred fire with me today?"

"Can we come out now?"

Anne-Marie walked in from the dining room, dressed in a chaniya choli. My jaw dropped as Umi, Peter and Dick walked in from the dining room, dressed in traditional Indian outfits. Umi put on a cassette of romantic Hindi film songs on the music player.

The doorbell rang.

Dick walked to the entrance hall. Jay and Ravi arrived carrying big bunches of flowers and a rectangular cardboard box.

"You haven't got much time. Go and get ready," Ravi instructed us.

Nik picked up the box and took my hand. "You'll have to get ready in Ravi's old room," he said. "My room's out of bounds for the time being." He took the box and placed it on the bed. "Do you like the surprise?" I nodded, still unsure what he had planned. "Trust me, my love." He kissed the soft sensitive underside of my wrist.

I opened the box again and lifted the saree; underneath there was a red underskirt and a matching blouse. Nikesh Raja was full of surprises; it looked like the blouse would fit me perfectly.

There was a tap at the door. The door opened, and Anne-Marie and Umi walked in.

"Well, how's that for a surprise?" Anne-Marie grinned, her eyes twinkling. "Do you like my chan yah cho lee?" She twirled. She was wearing a forest-green chiffon silk chaniya choli with gold appliqué paisley design; she had pulled her curly strawberry-blonde hair up, and some curls loosely framed her round cherub-like face.

"How did you manage to keep such a big secret?" I quizzed; we'd always laughed at how much of a gossip she is, and how we could never trust her with anything confidential.

"It has been killing her. When she let slip she was going to Southall shopping last weekend … I thought the cat was out of the bag," Umi added. She was wearing a shocking-pink silk saree, with gold, blue, green and yellow flower work; the colour made her complexion glow. She was wearing her gorgeous ebony hair loose and curled.

The door opened, and Nik walked in with my bag. He grinned at them and sat down on the bed and took my hand.

"Please, indulge me, my love. I know it's not the same as an actual wedding. This is the day I'd been looking forward to, and then we … " He paused. " … please, take the seven steps to eternal life with me today?" I thought of the obstacles that had been put in front of us to keep us apart, and it dawned on me that I didn't need any of it. I was already his forever; I couldn't imagine life without him.

"Say yes. He'll moan for the rest of the year if you don't," Anne-Marie impatiently interrupted. Nik smiled up at her. I thought about what marriage means to a Hindu; I'd seen the seven steps performed at Gujarati weddings, the vows the couple take in front of everyone to announce they are husband and wife.

"Yes," I nodded and then whispered in his ear, "Always and forever." A grin from ear to ear drew across his face at my words.

He stood up, and glanced at his watch, planted a kiss on my wrist and said, "You'd better help my fiancée get ready," to Umi and Anne-Marie.

I changed out of my clothes, and they helped me put on my saree. I had brought with me a pair of gold sandals Nik insisted I should bring. I put my hair up into a long plait and Umi helped me put on my makeup, using iridescent-copper eye shadow on my eyes. "You're getting married; you can't look like your usual self," she admonished as I protested that my eyes were even more prominent than usual.

There was a soft knock at the door.

"Can I come in?" Nik shouted from behind the door.

"No!" they both shouted. "You can't see her until she comes down the stairs," Umi added.

"But I have something I want to give to Ree."

Anne-Marie opened the door slightly. "I'll give it to her."

She held a rectangular red velvet-covered jewellery box that she handed to me. Inside there was a gold filigree bead necklace with matching drop earrings and four thin kada.

Umi whistled, "He certainly has good taste in jewellery. Do you have your red glass bangles?" I reached into my bag and handed her my bangle pouch.

"Wow, you are stunning in that colour," Anne-Marie said, "You should wear it more often."

The butterflies in my stomach were fluttering so much I imagined that as soon as I opened my mouth, they would fly out. I kept my jaw clenched, unable to smile.

"Smile, Ree," Umi urged, "It's a good day." I parted my lips slightly and let out a short breath.

Dick was waiting with his camera. He frowned, "Are you nervous?" He wrapped his arms around me.

"Don't be. It's a good surprise, besides I'm here for you, Ree."

I walked down the narrow stairs, and as I reached the bottom, Nik came out of the sitting room. He was wearing a cream jacquard sherwani with cream churidar and a red scarf on his shoulder. He took both of my hands and groaned, "You're sumptuous in red. I think it might become my favourite colour. Will you be my wife, Reena Solanki?" I nodded. "I won't smudge your lipstick, yet." He bowed as he raised his left eyebrow. His smouldering eyes looked up at me as he kissed the back of one and then the other hand.

The sofa and the armchairs were against the walls, and the coffee table had been placed in the centre of the room. There were two large vases of flowers on the sideboard. Jay walked in with a large clay divo and placed it on the coffee table. My heart skipped a beat. We were taking our marriage vows witnessed by our friends and Agni Dev, and the thought filled me with joy.

Nik lowered his head, and he said, "I love you, Reena Solanki." Jay took out his lighter and glanced at his watch.

Lata Mangeshkar sang "Tere Mere Beech Mein" from *Ek Duuje Ke Liye*. Ravi and Umi took out the flower garlands and handed them to us. Someone switched the music off.

"Sita chose her husband Rama by placing a Jaimala around his neck. Rukhmani did the same with Krishna. Will you choose me?" Nik asked.

Jay told us it was time as he lit the sacred divo. The clock on the wall showed that it was two-thirty, the time Guruji had explained was the most auspicious time for our marriage ceremony to begin.

I placed the flower garland over Nik's head and said, "I choose you always."

He placed the flower garland over my head and said, "No one but you. My heart is empty without you."

Umi picked up some A5 cards, and handed one to Nik; he grabbed my right hand, took one step and said, "My first vow is to provide for your welfare and happiness and also the welfare and happiness of our children,"

He handed me the card and I read my vow. "I promise to happily shoulder your responsibilities with you."

Umi handed Nik another card and I gave my card to Ravi.

We took another step, and he said, "My second vow is to protect and provide security for our family, and I ask you to stand by me."

I took the card off him and said, "I promise to be your strength, giving you my eternal love and support in your duties."

We took our third step. The divo flickered in the dimmed room. Dick was taking photographs of our steps, and the only sound we heard was the clicking of the camera.

"My third vow is to work hard and provide wealth for you and our children to make sure our children are educated." His voice took on a sombre tone; his head turned to me.

"I promise to look after your wealth and support our children in their education."

Then we said together, "We promise to be loyal and faithful to each other." He stopped; his eyes sparkled like a firecracker.

He paused and turned to pick up the card from Umi, and we took our fourth step around the sacred flame.

"My fourth vow is to keep you happy and thank you for walking around this sacred fire with me."

"I promise to take care of you and support you with our religious duties."

I squeezed his hand as we both said, "We promise to share in our happiness and sadness and to take care of and respect the elders in our family."

We took our fifth step.

"My fifth vow is to take care of our children and bring them up as strong and noble human beings." He smiled at me.

"I promise to look after our children and support you in your duty to look after all living things."

"We vow to take care of our parents," we said in unison

Our sixth step together reminded me of the vows in a Christian marriage ceremony, and of the time when I used to play weddings with my friends.

"My sixth vow is to be with you in sickness and in health and pray that your life will be filled with joy and peace."

He kissed my hand. I could hardly breathe. I walked behind him as we walked around the divo and the scent of tobacco, citrus, sandalwood and musk filled my nostrils.

"I promise to be with you through thick or thin and will support and comfort you in your hour of need." My voice came out as a croak.

"We vow to be together forever."

He turned to me and asked me to lead, and we took our seventh and final step around the sacred flame. The ceremony was not the same as the one we would perform at our wedding in front of our family, but the meaning sent a shiver through me, as he said, "I tell you that this last vow means I am your husband and you are my wife."

I replied, "With God as my supreme witness, I am your wife and will love and cherish you."

I turned to him, and we both said, "We vow to be lifelong friends," facing each other. A dome appeared on Nik's eyelashes. I brushed it away with my fingers. I took a deep breath to prevent the tears that welled in my eyes. He enveloped me in his arms. The world stopped briefly; all I could hear was the thud thud thud of his heart, and I waited until my heart synchronised with his and returned to normal. And they all cheered, and whooped, throwing confetti over us.

"Come on, you guys. You're embarrassing us. Let go of each other," Umi interrupted. Our friends pulled us apart.

***

"SEE YOU BACK HOME on Sunday night." Anne-Marie gave us a hug, as our friends left in the cars they had arrived in.

I didn't know how they did it, but they kept all of it a secret including getting an outside caterer to provide a vegetarian meal packed full of our favourite foods that we ate at the large dining table in the house in Coventry. The house that was filled with fond memories of our time at Warwick. Jay was the only one who wasn't buzzing and happy. He was subdued, and I began to wonder what I could do to make him like me. I knew he had a bond with Nik that went back a long time. He needed to accept that Nik wanted to spend the rest of his life with me. He was the last to leave and held onto Nik a little bit longer than necessary. Nik frowned questioningly at him as he pulled away.

He closed the front door, turned me to him and lifted my chin with his thumb. I gazed into his smouldering eyes, and he brushed his soft lips against mine and groaned.

"I've been patient, dear wife. Time for some kissing and a lot more." He pulled me to his side, and we walked up the narrow stairs. "Close your eyes."

My breath caught with apprehension. I wondered what surprise he had in store for me. The room was filled with flickering lights, tiny fairy lights radiating from the central ceiling rose, and candles had been placed on the desk, shelves and bedside tables. The flickering lights danced on the dark-red flower petals that had been strewn on the white bedsheet. He pulled me to him and kissed me with a passion that took my breath away.

"I haven't taken one of these off you before." His golden eyes sparkled, and he pulled at my saree pallu. "Wait, it's pinned up," I told him, and he turned me around and searched for the safety pin on my blouse that held it in place. I could feel his hot breath on the back of my neck; he lifted my plait out of the way and kissed my exposed back. He unhooked the blouse and wrapped his hot hands around my waist. My stomach flipped. I pressed my back into him, as he stroked my exposed belly. I kept my eyes closed as he turned me, luxuriating in the sensation of his fingers on my skin. It appeared as if he was drawing a pattern on my back. He pulled at the pallu; I spun around slowly, as the saree unravelled. I heard the soft silk cloth flutter to the floor.

"Come here." He pulled me to him, his hands on my

bottom. He put his index finger under the waistband and slowly untied the tie of my petticoat; it, too, dropped onto the floor. "Lift your arm." He pulled at my blouse. "Open your eyes, my love." His eyes were like firecrackers, the shards highlighted by the candlelight. "You wore my favourite underwear. Promise me, you'll never stop wearing red." He sighed. "Now it's your turn." He raised his left eyebrow.

I started at the hook on his Nehru collar and slowly unbuttoned the sherwani; I put my hand inside and felt the warmth of his chest. I ran my fingers through the hair on his chest; he sighed and shivered. I rested my hand on his heart. I slid one side of the long coat off his shoulder and pulled at his sleeve. "Turn around," I whispered, my eyes drifting to the tuft of hair appearing just above the waistband of his trousers. His back was exquisitely broad. I ran my hand from one side to the other and pulled the cream coat off. I pulled him to face me, raising my eyebrows, smiled, and I dropped the sherwani on the floor. I pulled at his waistband, loosened the ties. It slipped to the floor. He pulled me to him and kissed my neck and slowly kissed the tops of my breasts. I pulled his head up and kissed him longingly, unable to control my urge to possess him; he pulled away reluctantly and lifted me in his arms. He shuffled towards the bed. We fell on the rose petals, his feet tangled in his churidar. He lifted himself up to sitting, pulling off the tangled silk trousers. I lay on my side, raised on my elbow. He flopped back onto his back and turned to face me. The rose petals surrounded our nostrils with their sweet scent as our hot bodies crushed them.

"I am your husband, and you are my wife." His voice was hushed.

"I am your wife, and you are my husband."

The enormity of our vows sank in and I gazed at his smiling face. We were married for this life and all our future lives. His lips touched mine and I pressed my body against his, telling him in kisses I would always be his for now and eternity. He pulled at my hair to loosened it and ran his fingers through it, my scalp tingling at his touch. My head leant back into his hand, and I longed for the feel of his warm hands on my body.

He lifted himself on top of me. "I love you," he groaned.

I put my hands on his waistband, sliding them under his boxer shorts. "Nik … please, I need you."

"All in good time, wife." He ran his finger lightly down my neck. I shivered; little bumps rose on my breasts. I held my breath as his fingers lifted my breasts out of my bra, his thumb lightly brushing my nipples. His lips caressed the line from my belly button towards my tuft of hair as he moved down my body. His warm breath teased me; he wrapped his fingers in the side of my knickers and pulled them down. I closed my eyes to concentrate on the burning sensation of his soft lips.

We lay entwined with each other, our bodies hot from the slow passionate act of fulfilling our vows as man and wife, surrounded by the sweet smell of roses. He lifted my arm off his waist and jingled my glass bangles; I opened my eyes and saw them sparkle in the candlelight. "I should take them off, or there won't be any left."

"I'll buy you new ones, keep them on. I like you naked except for your jewellery."

He lifted me up on top of him. I pulled my legs apart and straddled him. "Oh, are you ready again, husband?" I smiled and leant in to kiss his luscious lips, his chin, his cheeks, his eyes.

His voice was a whisper. "Yes, ever ready for you, my wife." He nuzzled his face into my breast.

Our first night as husband and wife was spent in a passionate embrace, our bodies and souls bound forever. When I woke up, Nik's legs were entwined with mine; his arm was pinning me down. I hadn't realised how taking the vows would make me feel. All our time together led to this one day, this one night. Nik and I belong together. We are destined to be together forever. I am no longer scared.

"You're staring at me with those intoxicating eyes, wife."

"How can you see through your eyelids?" I whispered.

"I feel you here." He tapped his chest. He opened his eyes and the golden shards radiated like a Catherine wheel; he tucked my bottom to him. "I want to lose myself in those eyes, my dearest wife." His lips brushed mine and I lost myself in his golden eyes.

My head was resting on his shoulder when I woke up. I thought of all the stolen moments, all the time we had been apart since our engagement weekend. Although Nik had moved in with me, it was still a flat we shared with someone else. I missed spending day and night together. I finally understood what Dick meant about our arrangement not being the same as when we were at university. I was not sure I could survive one more stolen moment with Nik again. I wanted everyone in his family and mine to know that we slept together and no longer wanted fleeting secret meetings. The thought of leaving Nik that night overwhelmed me. Tears welled in my eyes, and I started to cry.

"What's the matter?" He lifted my chin with his fingers, the creases on the edge of his eyes appeared, and he kissed me until my tears stopped then he said. "I can't bear the thought of leaving you tonight. I can't carry on living the way we do after today, these fleeting meetings, a night here, a full day there. May is just too far away. Let's spend more time here, my love." I kissed him and I realised that he had been thinking the same as me; it's like our minds are linked. He pulled himself up on one elbow as he worked through the problem; the creases by his eyes deepened. He chewed his lower lip and I searched his chiselled face. A smile drew across his face. "We can be one of those couples that work away from home and come up to Coventry on the weekend. I'll pick you up from work on Friday night, and we'll drive up and spend Saturday and most of Sunday together, just you and me. I know you'll have to go see your father, and I'll have to spend the odd weekend at home, but we can do it."

"What will you tell your family?"

"I'll think of something." The golden shards in his eyes twinkled as his mind hatched a plan. I let go of the breath I had been holding, and my eyes filled with tears again. I buried my face in Nik's chest and he enveloped me in his arms until my tears dried up and my heart returned to normal. "Let's have something to eat. You'll feel better, my love." He slid out of bed, his back covered with rose petals.

"Wait." I leapt out of bed and ran my hand down his back; he turned, and I showed him my fist full of rose petals. His eyes twinkled. He picked a rose petal from my hip.

"Turn around." His voice came out gravelly. He sighed, "So many petals," and he started lifting the petals off slowly. My heart leapt and the pit of my stomach lurched, as our desire to be one increased again.

Twenty Seven

I'D BEEN UP WITH THE BIRDS. The excitement of the day had permeated through my core.

"Reena, phone for you!" my father shouted. I knew who it was, no one else would dream of ringing at seven in the morning.

"Good morning, Mrs Raja. Ready to marry me again?" I smiled. We were already legally wed and had been for two weeks. We'd arranged to have our closest family and friends attend the register marriage that was lawfully required and we'd had lunch in Sharmilee on Belgrave Road.

"Are you, Mr Raja? Can you cope with another wedding?" I teased.

"Anyone else in the room with you?" I told him no, "good. Did you dream about me?"

I blushed at the delicious dream I'd had last night. "Oh, from the silence I guess it must have been very salacious. I want details."

"Nik … " I laughed. "You're so wicked … I'll tell you later."

He sighed, "I'll have to wait, I suppose, but remember the details."

"Niku, what are you doing in here?" his father asked.

"Sorry, Kaka. Just talking to Ree … Looking forward to being married to you, Reena Solanki. I just wanted to say, I love you, Ree, always have, always will. My heart is empty without you. See you at six o'clock."

"I love you more than you can imagine, Nikesh Raja. Love you, always and forever."

That was how my wedding day began; it was like being in a Bollywood movie. People were coming in and out of the house, carrying baskets of flowers, fruits and mithai. A small marquee had been put up in the garden and the men hung out on the street. The early summer sky was cloudless, and Bollywood music played loudly from a sound system rigged by Amit's friends. As the wedding was not going to take place until the evening, everyone was relaxed. Divya Ba and the ladies from the mandir had taken over the sitting room and were singing Gujarati wedding songs. As was the custom for the bride and groom, I was fasting, so instead of a typical lunch, Divya Ba had come up with a special lunch menu for everyone. It reminded me of my time in the mandir kitchen when we created a meal for Janmashtami, the day of Krishna's birthday.

Reena's Special Wedding Day Lunch

Sabodana magfali ni khichdi
a blend of steamed tapioca, potato and peanuts

Singhara ni puri
fried round flatbread made with water chestnut flour

Tameta ne mogo nu shaak
tomato and cassava curry

Sukha betata jeera nu shaak
dry curry made with potato and cumin seeds

Rajigro no sheero
sweet dish made from amaranth flour, sugar and ghee

Arbi ni Tikki
shallow fried colocasia root flour and potato patties

Sabodana ni farfar
tapioca thins fried crisps

Tameta ni chutnee
fresh tomato chutney

Dahi
natural yoghurt

Chaas
natural yoghurt drink blended with water

Chopped fruits

I gazed at my reflection in the mirror as Smita Bhabhi helped me put on my sandals. I had chosen a cream crepe silk panetar with dark-green and red daisy booti. The brocade border was a wide antique-gold that glistened with small specks of crimson, saffron-yellow and emerald threads. My hair had been put up in a high bun and was covered in cream and dark red roses. On my forehead I had an ornate pattern of white and red dots; the centre tilak was big and red.

"I hope you don't mind, but I wanted to get you something special for your wedding day, Reena." Jane was holding a square jewellery box in her hand. She was wearing a magenta evening dress, with boxy shoulders and ruched bodice; we had tried to convince her to wear a saree, but she declined, and just like at Amit's wedding, she had come in an evening gown instead of her usual trouser suit. The box had two small gold kada with multi-coloured semi-precious gemstones. "Smita helped me choose them." Tears welled up in my eyes and I took a deep breath. "Jane, they are beautiful, thank you." I pulled out my wrists as she took off the pins and fastened them to my wrist. The kada matched my mother's set perfectly. I felt honoured and privileged to have someone like Jane in my life.

* * *

HE LOOKED DIRECTLY AT ME as soon as he stepped out of the white Rolls-Royce. "Oh, God, you are beautiful," he mouthed when our eyes met.

This part of the ritual was different from our own. In Nik's family, the bride placed a flower garland around the groom. Smita and the ladies welcomed the jaan at the main entrance to the mandir. I waited nervously at the top of the stairs, holding the flower garland, my hands sweaty. I walked down with Umi, Anne-Marie, and my distant cousins Minakshi and Hina by my side.

As I climbed down, I took in the splendour of his wedding outfit. He had kept his outfit a secret from me, as I had kept mine from him. He was wearing a cream and silver brocade sherwani, with silver buttons with a thin red silk edge, a pair of red silk churidar and, on his feet, a pair of handmade silk shoes made from the same material as the sherwani. On his head, he wore a red turban, with a pearl and peacock feather brooch.

"Make sure you keep your head up, Niku. We don't want to make it easy for Reena," Ashveena teased.

He was standing on a low stool, and as I raised my arms to put the garland around his head, instead of keeping his head up, he bowed and said, "I bow my head to the most beautiful woman in the world."

"I knew he couldn't resist," Rita said. "I know my brother well." Everyone laughed. I was taken away to the room that was set aside for me and told to wait until I was called.

The younger women of the Raja family came in with my garchoru. Nik and I had gone shopping with Motaba and Kaki to choose the traditional dark-red silk chequered saree. The one his motaba insisted we bought had fifty-two zari-bordered squares with intricate bandhani patterns of flowers and dancing girls. They helped drape it partially over my flower-covered head and draped one end on my right shoulder; the remaining material of the six-yard saree was pleated, tucked and pinned on top of the panetar. "Your set is beautiful." Rita was holding up the necklace in her hand. "Did it belong to your mother?" I nodded in reply.

"Doesn't it match the panetar's booti perfectly, Ben?" my bhabhi added. I gazed at my reflection in the mirror; my mother's set was made up of petal-shaped ornaments linked to a large central daisy with red, green and yellow enamel work. The jhumbar earrings had the same daisy and petal ornaments. The tika and a panja I was wearing were found by Rohini Bhabhi as a close match from her costume jewellery makers.

Time had stopped and the wait for the priest to say "kanyia patharon sawthan" was the longest I had experienced in my life; the seconds dragged to hours. My anxiety built as the wait prolonged. When Smita Bhabhi's cousin popped her head through the door, my heart started to race. Smita Bhabhi took my hand, and we approached the entrance to the mandir. Mayur Bhai, Amit, Dick, Ravi, and Peter were waiting to escort me to the mandap. This was usually a ceremony performed by the maternal uncle, but as we had no idea where my mama was, we decided my closest friends and my brothers would do the job. A cream shawl with a maroon embroidered border was used to shield Nik's view, and when the barrier was lowered, Nik held his right hand to his heart, leant towards me and whispered, "My heart is full to bursting. Finally, you are mine, my wife, my life." My heartbeat returned to normal as I concentrated on his face.

The wedding was small compared to Amit's or any that would happen in Nik's family, but it was precisely what I wanted. The priest told everyone to be quiet during the ceremony as he explained the various rituals: the kanyadan, where I saw my father shed a tear; the hastamelap; the exchange of flower garlands by the bride and groom; and the four phera, as is the tradition of Gujarati weddings; the septapadi, the seven steps and the vows that unite us as a married couple; the sindoor and mangalsutra. When Nik pinched some sindoor and drew a line on my centre parting, he whispered, "We've taken the vows twice, my love, so you are my wife, and I am your husband for eternity."

When it was time to say goodbye, my heart ached. I was standing with a handful of rice and was told to throw it as high as I could over my head, aiming for the intricate cloth canopy of the ornate sandalwood four-post mandap. The music system started to play, "Bena re … sasariye jata." I began to cry. The song always sets me off; its meaning filled with pain: the protective hand of your father is gone, and the walls of your childhood home cry; you were a temporary deposit for our safekeeping, daughter.

My father stood in front of Nik and me, took me in his arms and said, "So you're leaving me." His eyes filled with tears and I held on tightly, afraid he would suffer more this time because I would no longer be his responsibility.

Nik put his hand on his shoulder and said, "No, she isn't, Daddy. She'll never leave you. I'm just moving her to another home."

He tried to raise a smile, and said to Nik, "You're a good boy, Nikesh. Keep her happy."

My tears soaked my father's suit jacket. I didn't want

to leave my family. I knew this new one had many who loved me, but it wouldn't be easy making the one person who doesn't like me, love me.

SHAKTI BHAVAN WAS BATHED in light, the hedges and trees lit up with torches. The drive down on the M1 wasn't long; we left Leicester when the night had drawn in and were given instructions to arrive at the front door by twelve-fifteen. As soon as we hit the motorway, the adrenaline that had fuelled me through the day drained from my body and I fell asleep immediately, my head resting on my husband's shoulder. Nik had asked the driver to stop at Chiltern Hills before we head to our new home. He woke me up, and we stepped out to gaze at the stars; the sky was clear, the place was magical, and he kissed me softly and longingly. I tasted the salty tears and pulled away.

"Finally, my love, always and forever, never leave me, Ree," he haltingly requested.

I wiped his tears and kissed him. "Why would I? You are my husband, and I am your wife."

The women of the family led us to the large, ornate front door.

"Welcome to our family, Reena." Nik's mother was holding a small silver puja dish with sindoor, rice and flower petals; she put a tilak on our foreheads and threw rice and flower petals over our heads. On the threshold, there was a bulbous copper pot, and, as I kicked it with my right foot, the white rice grains scattered across the pink marble. "Welcome, Laxmi, to our home." Her voice was lilting and soft.

We were directed to the mandir, and a divo had been lit by the small statue of Ganesh. A large silver shallow bowl with water, milk, flower petals and sindoor was placed in front of us, and we sat on low silver stools, Nik on my right, my place next to his heart. Nik's mother opened a ring box and held up a solitaire diamond ring. "Whoever wins this ring will rule the marriage." Her eyes twinkled. Rita threw in a handful of mini conch shells.

We played aeki beki; in the days of arranged marriages this was a light-hearted way to allow the bride and groom to get to know each other before the first nuptials. The game is simple: whoever wins the ring four times out of seven will rule the marriage. We both won the ring three times each. His mother smiled at me, "You'll need to win this time if you want to rule over my son." During the last play, Nik grabbed my hand under the water and wouldn't let go.

"Come on, Niku!" Jaishree shouted, "Let Reena's hand go."

He grinned up at them, "If I let her hand go, you're going to take her away from me, Jaish." He turned to me, and I smiled at him. "Should I let go?" I nodded.

We searched and searched through the water, and I couldn't find the ring; we sought, and Nik grabbed my fingers intermittently; my anxiety rose, as I felt for the ring among the conch shells. Sarladevi frowned and looked at her watch. "Have you got the ring, Nikesh?" He laughed and revealed his little finger. As I lifted my hand out of the water, he pointed his little finger down, and the ring fell onto my palm. I closed my fingers.

"That's cheating. You won that one, Niku," Ashveena rebuked him.

"My wife will always rule my heart, so why would I want to rule our marriage?" Nik turned to me and his eyes sparkled. Everybody laughed at his romanticism, and then I was pulled up and taken away from Nik by his sisters.

Twenty Eight

NIK'S BEDROOM HAD BECOME a guest bedroom, and we had been moved to the suite, a small sitting room, bedroom, dressing room and bathroom at the front of the house. Rita and Jaishree led me up the stairs, laughing and joking about not waking up until at least mid-day. I knew my face gave me away, my cheeks glowing from what they were implying. The king-size bed had red and white flower garlands draped around the headboard and around the base. The bed sheets were white, and, in the middle, there was a red rose petal heart.

I was told to wait in the room; the anticipation of Nik entering the room made my stomach flip. I told myself off. Calm down, Reena; it's not like this is your first night with Nik. He knows every inch of your body, and you know every inch of his. The door opened, and Nik was pushed into the room by his brothers. I could hear them laughing outside. I was sitting on the padded stool at the art deco dressing table; it was positioned opposite the door. He stopped and walked towards me. I looked up at his reflection in the mirror. He ran both his hands through his hair; he was nervous, too. *How strange we both felt the same.*

He pulled me up and took off my Jaimala, and I did the same to his, and placed them on the dressing table. He searched for the pins on the shoulder of my saree and took them out, putting them on the dressing table.

"Are there more?" I nodded and pointed to the waist on my left-hand side, he took them out. I pointed to my pleats in front. He ran the back of his index finger over my belly and the nerves on my skin jumped, as he took the last one out and untied my petticoat. He took my hand and kissed my palm. "Does this hand have my name hidden in it, or is it this one?" He kissed the palm of my other hand. I lifted my eyebrows and smile up at him.

"You have to find it, no clues," I could only whisper. Any louder, my voice would have broken. He pulled at my sarees as he slid the waistband of my underskirt over my bottom. My breath slowed.

"Oh God, Ree." He helped me step out of the heap of material on the floor and pulled me to him. I could feel his arousal. Our lips met, and our kisses built to a crescendo. I pulled at the button on his sherwani. Nik's bare chest was exposed, and his churidar was tied loosely. My yearning could not be controlled. I pushed him on the bed and pulled at his trouser bottoms and threw them and his shoes on the floor.

He was on the bed resting on both of his elbows, his eyes smouldering, his lips slightly parted, breathing heavily. I started to take the flowers out of my hair, throwing them at him.

"My heart, what are you doing to me?" I longed to be

on top of him. Our bodies merged with each other, but this time I wanted to make love to him, totally naked. I pulled at my hairpins to loosen my hair and pulled off my jewellery. He licked his lips, his eyes resting on mine. I felt a flutter and touched my lips. Nik sighed. I walked back slowly to him and turned my back to him, holding my hair away from my neck.

"Can you take off my necklaces?" My voice was hushed, and he kissed the back of my neck. An electric current ran down my spine. He turned me to face him, holding the necklaces in his hand. "Nik" I pleaded. My body was aching, and I could not wait any longer. He dropped them on the floor, took my face in both his hands and kissed me hungrily. I responded with my kisses claiming him, possessing him.

He pulled away and said, "Do you remember our first time, your white bikini?" He ran his finger in the lace cup of my white bra. I blushed at the thought of that day. The hair on my body stood on end. "Got you, Mrs Raja." He grinned as he scooped me up and lay me down in the middle of the rose petal heart. His golden eyes explored my body. My breath caught. I pulled at his neck and kissed him. Our desire to be one overwhelmed us, and we slowly and deliberately joined together. This time, no one will keep us apart. Finally, we can tell everyone we are together forever.

✳ ✳ ✳

SOFT KISSES ON MY EYES, my cheeks, my neck, woke me up and I opened my eyes to his magnificent eyes staring at me. "Hello, husband. What time is it?"
"It's twelve-thirty, my love. I'm hungry. Shall we shower and go and get some breakfast?" A gurgling

sound came from my stomach; he lifted his eyebrow and grinned. He picked me up in his arms; I placed my head on his shoulders and kissed his neck; he smelled of roses and sex. I inhaled him, and he walked to the en-suite bathroom. He turned on the shower, lathered the soap he squeezed from the bottle, and we washed the rose petals off our bodies. The water was warm, but my body was hot; I held onto him, pulled his face down to mine, and my kisses told him the depth of my love.

* * *

NIK WAITED ON THE ARMCHAIR; he was wearing a peppermint-green jabo pyjama. We had taken the blessings of the Gods at the mandir after our wedding and the family shrine last night. Later in the afternoon we were going to go to the Hindu mandir in Watford. I put on a parrot-green chiffon silk bandhani saree with gold border. The blouse had transparent elbow-length sleeves and a low back. It was one of the five new sarees my father insisted on giving me as part of my wedding trousseau. My father didn't believe in dowry and made it plain to Nik's family he would not be providing any to me. He had, however, given me my mother's gold set that I wore on my wedding day. I was sitting at the dressing table and putting on the earrings from the gold filigree beaded set my husband had given me on the day of our vows. There was a knock on the door; Nik opened it, and Jaishree was grinning and holding a tray with our breakfast.

"Good afternoon. Thought you'd want to eat your breakfast in your room today."

"We were just coming downstairs, Jaish." Nik took the

tray off his sister.

"Didn't think you'd be dressed, after all, it is your honeymoon. Spend a bit more time with your wife, Niku," she teased. I felt the heat rise on my cheeks.

"Can I help with your necklace, Ree?" She fastened the beaded necklace as I lifted my hair away. Our eyes met in the mirror. "You look happy; marriage suits you." Nik walked back to the dressing table, and she turned to him. "You were right, this set is stunning."

Jaishree had been in on the secret of our marriage vows. My jaw dropped and my eyes darted from brother to sister. She placed her hand on my shoulder, and squeezed it, "I know what it's like to be on the other end of Motaba's tradition. I'll tell you all about it when I can drag you away from my brother for a spa weekend." He took my hand and led me to sit at the walnut table and chairs that were placed by the Juliet balcony in our sitting room. Nik opened the door, and mild breeze entered our rose-infused rooms. Breakfast or brunch was bateta nu shaak, puri, papad, fruit salad, a bowl of roasted salted nuts, two small glasses of orange juice, a small pot of masala chai for Nik and a small pot of chai for me.

We could hear the chatter from the drawing room, as we walked down the stairs hand in hand. "Hello, Niku, Reena. Ready for the darshan?" Kaki smiled. The dimples were more pronounced today, her eyes more sparkly. She lifted herself up from the armchair and walked towards us, her arms outstretched. Everyone was dressed in Indian clothes, the men in jabo pyjamas and the women in sarees. The Rajas were presenting the newest member of their family to the mandir community in Watford and my stomach clenched as the enormity of meeting everyone dawned on me.

She released me, and Motaba was waiting to hug me. Her eyes drew an arc around my face. "You've remembered to fill your parting with sindoor. I didn't think you'd know about it." I raised a small smile. *Why would I forget such a meaningful sign of my status, especially today?* I had been brought up to understand the significance of this custom and had also put on my mangalsutra. I had picked a long black beaded mangalsutra with a simple gold filigree-work pendant which rested between my breast, as all my sets were short and fitted snugly around my collarbone.

"Come on everyone, let's go. I have to pick up Reena's dress at seven o'clock from London." Nik voice was loud and abrupt. He had heard the tone of contempt in Motaba's voice. He tucked me into his hips and turned to the enormous entrance hall.

"Haan, haan, stand up, chalo, chalo," Motaba instructed everyone in Gujarati.

We headed to waiting cars and Nik and I were instructed to sit in the back seat of Suresh's red BMW M3. I finally took a breath to let go of the hurt.

He turned my hand, kissing my palm. "Are you all right, my love?" His eyes were embers ready to ignite. I rested my head on his shoulder and slowly inhaled to stop the tears forming in my eyes. "I still can't find my name, Ree. You have to tell me. Which hand?" he asked to lighten my mood.

"What have you been doing, Niku?" Ashveena teased. "Suresh found his in the first hour."

"Yes I did, but you kept thrusting the hand in my face all the time, darling," Suresh laughed. "Give him a clue, Reena. He'll be a laughing stock if he can't show everyone at dinner tonight," he continued. I lifted my left-hand palm up to Nik.

"It's my favourite place to be kissed," I whispered. He peered at the cuff of the henna gloves that had been piped onto my hands by Rohini Bhabhi at my mehndi night a few days before. He whooped with triumph when he found his name.

"Rohini Bhabhi is very clever." He ran his index finger from his initial backwards. "She's written your name in mirror writing here, too." He brushed his lips on my vein. Our eyes met and he said, "Do you remember I told you to come to me when you're upset, and I'd make it go away." I nodded. "I promise I'm here for you always, my wife, my life." We approached Bhaktivedanta Manor through a pair of metal gates.

May 31st, 1986

WE BOTH STOOD at the double sink in the en suite bathroom. I was wearing the scarlet silk dressing gown and nightdress, a wedding present from Nik, and he was wearing the silk paisley-print dressing gown with matching pale-ultramarine pyjama bottoms from Liberty I'd given him. I still couldn't believe I was living on a set from *Dynasty*. The bathroom was white Carrera marble with gold fittings. There was a big bathtub with gold claw feet in the centre and double shower enclosure against the back wall.

The family had all gathered at the house ready for the weekend, reminding me of the first time I had come to Shakti Bhavan. My family were arriving that afternoon, and Motaba was preparing the rooms for our extra guests.

"Shall we have a bath this morning?"

"No, quick shower." I grabbed my husband by the waist and stood on my tiptoes to kiss his luscious lips; he tasted of toothpaste. He returned the kiss.

"Can we have a bath before we get ready for tonight?" I nodded and pulled him to the shower.

Breakfast had been laid out on the breakfast bar in the family sitting room. The dining table was full, and some of the people were heading with their plates to the formal dining room.

"Jai Shri Krishna." I held my hand in salutation to the elders, the Rajas and their in-laws, who were at the dining table.

"Jai Shri Krishna, Beta," Nik's father smiled up at me, "Didn't expect you two to join us."

"Haan, Haan, I was just going to get a breakfast tray ready for you." Her dark flint-like eyes scrutinised me. I was wearing a magenta silk blouse and a pair of blue jeans; the black beads of my mangalsutra lay on top. Her eyes darted to my wrists: on the left I was wearing the gold Seiko dress-watch my father gave me as a graduation present, and on the right hand, I had a set of multicoloured glass bangles. I had been warned what was expected of a new bride in the Raja household by Rupa Bhabhi. She had told me about how she had received a dressing-down in front of her parents on the traditions and customs of a Hindu household for not adorning both wrists with jewellery. Nik had even added a small pinch of sindoor to my parting.

"Jai Shri Krishna, everyone. Thought we'd join you for breakfast today." He squeezed my hand and pulled me towards the breakfast bar.

Breakfast was upma with coconut chutney and spicy yoghurt.

"Jai Shri Krishna, Anu Masi. Can I have some brown toast and a cup of tea please?"

"Nothing else?" Nik turned to me questioningly. He knew I loved upma, but I was too nervous to eat. I grabbed a banana from the fruit bowl.

"I'll bring you your chai, Beti. Where are you sitting?"

"Thank you, Anu Masi, we're going to the dining room," Nik informed her as he balanced his mug of masala chai on his overly-filled plates. I put the banana on the plate I was holding and took his mug. He slid his hand on my lower back, and we headed to the dining room.

We were sitting with Nik's siblings and their partners at the dining table with our refills of tea or coffee.

"Where are you two planning to go, so we can set up?" asked Suresh, holding his cup to his mouth.

"We are going to go to the stream and having a picnic lunch. Ree is desperate for some fresh air," Nik informed him.

"No peeking mind you. You can't come back until three."

"Yes, we know. I don't understand the secrecy. It's not as if we haven't had a marquee before."

"Stop being a spoilsport, Niku," Ashveena said petulantly. "Jaish and I have been organising this for ages, and we want it to be a surprise. No lingering by the main house after eleven; you can only come up to the garages," she continues.

Ashveena and Jaishree had taken it upon themselves to arrange the reception after Nik and I had both shown little interest. They asked us our preferences.

Nik asked for a live band, and I asked for Punjabi food and fried mogo with chilli garlic sauce. My mind recollected the conversation.

"We're here to help if you're worried about costs. You know you should have your heart's desire for your wedding, Ree," Ashveena said, with concern in her eyes.

"Yes, I know, but a small wedding at the mandir is all I've ever wanted," I replied.

"You are a simple soul, Ree." Jaishree patted my hand, "But we have to have a reception. Think about it: anything you want. Don't worry about the money."

"We have to be at the hairdressers by three-thirty. You'll be first, Ree. Make sure you're ready to pick up by four-thirty, Niku." Jaishree's instruction broke my thoughts.

After breakfast, we packed for our honeymoon. We were going to go for a week to Italy. To satisfy my thirst for art, I suggested Rome and to satisfy Nik's thirst for me he suggested the Amalfi Coast. We were flying into Rome and driving down to Sorrento. I was very excited at the thought of the narrow Roman streets and the outdoor cafes. My only reference was the film *Roman Holiday* with Audrey Hepburn and Gregory Peck. At ten-thirty Nik and I both came down again to head out for our picnic. He released my hand and gave me a quick kiss. "I'll go and get the cassette player, you go and see what's happening in the kitchen."

"In our family, a new daughter-in-law does not help in the kitchen until her mehndi washes off." Motaba was standing at the door from the family sitting room, her arms crossed. "Anu Ben, you should have told Reena to go away." I saw the hurt in Anu Masi's eyes fleetingly and sympathised for the woman who had to work with the matriarch.

"Bhabhi! I told Reena to sit with us while we prepared sandwiches for their picnic," Kaki informed her sister-in-law as she walked back from the larder holding a tray full of ingredients.

"Reena you will not be helping in the kitchen for at least a month," Motaba added sternly as she sat at the preparing table. During my visits to Shakti Bhavan, since our engagement, I had spent a great deal of time in the kitchen. There was a reason for this: cooking and preparing meals helped keep my anxiety at bay and I wanted to keep some distance from Nik who thought it was fine to grab me for a kiss and a cuddle at the most inappropriate times.

***

"Are you going to cut this?" Nik was pushing back the long fringe that had come away from my high ponytail.

"Why? Don't you like it?" I smiled up at him.

We had made love by the brook, listening to songs from Rishi Kapoor films. He was up on one elbow, his other arm curved around my naked waist under the blanket. He pulled a face.

"No, I don't. Prefer you with a full fringe. I want my wife back." He leant in and brushed his soft lips on mine. Asha Bhosle sang "Mil Jaaye Is Tarah."

"Promise me you'll meet me here, like two waves that cannot be separated, Ree, no matter what happens?" His eyes glistened, and I pulled him to me and gave him a kiss. I loved coming to Nik's favourite place in the world; sometimes we kissed and cuddled, sometimes we talked, most of the time we sat on the blanket in silence listening to the brook.

"I promise, husband. I'll never be separated from you, always and forever," I replied in between the kissing. After our picnic lunch we practised our first dance to "Pal Pal Dil Ke Paas"; it was our song, since the day he gave me the mixtape and told me how he felt on New Year's Eve. 'My heart sings your song.' The words made my heart sing.

"Relax my love," he whispered in my ear. I exhaled.

"Can we go for a walk and practise later?" I kissed his favourite spot on his neck to thank him for the confidence he had in my ability to dance gracefully.

When we came back to the house, through the walled garden, we were surprised that the lawns showed no sign of a metal framework.

"Bhai, why isn't the marquee up?" Nik shouted anxiously, as we walked to the outdoor seating area where Rajesh, Rupa Bhabhi, my brother Amit and Smita Bhabhi were sitting with tea and plates of food.

"Don't worry, Niku," he reassured him. "Everything is on time and on schedule."

"Hello, Sis." Amit held me in his arms; he pushed me at arm's length, smiling down at me. "You look happy." He bowed his head and added, keeping his voice low, "What's it like living in a palace?" I laughed. He pulled me to his side. "Daddy's inside. Go and say hello and get your tea."

I gave my bhabhi a hug and asked after the twins. Once Nik had greeted them and made Smita Bhabhi promise to bring the twins to see him, we stepped through the kitchen to the family room. Even before we stepped out of the door, my father was waiting to greet us, his arms outstretched. Nik bowed down and touched his feet; my father was taken aback, "No, no, Nikesh. Give me a hug." He pulled him up. I could see in his eyes he was touched by the gesture. His eyes focused on me, and I flung my arms around his shoulders, trying to gulp back the lump in my throat. He stroked my head. "How are you, my daughter? Isn't your husband keeping you happy?" he teased.

We got our tea and nasto and headed back to sit outside. Nik stood up to fetch some water and said, "Where is everybody? I thought the guys were coming early?" trying unsuccessfully to control the tension in his voice.

"Everyone's here. Don't worry, they're just busy," Rajesh informed him.

"Finished? Everyone's gathered at the garages." Jaishree fixed her eyes on Smita Bhabhi. "Are you sure you don't want to come with us, Smita Bhabhi?"

"No, I'm good thank you. Rupa Bhabhi and I plan to help each other with our hair, besides, my two will need feeding soon."

Nik handed me my glass of water, and I gulped it down quickly. He took my hand, and we walked to the garages where the other ladies were waiting to take me to the hair salon in Loudwater.

Twenty Nine

"CAN I SEE MY DRESS NOW?" I said, holding up my lipstick. Nik was lounging on the armchair in his dressing gown, staring at the front lawn. When we came back from the hairdressers, we were mesmerised by the huge circus tent on the front lawn. I walked to my husband. "Maybe we should have had some say. I'm not sure if Jaish has had much control over Ashi's ideas."

He pulled me onto his lap. "Peter tells me it's elegant and sophisticated." He kissed me. "What did you say, my love?"

"And so, it begins, in one ear and out the other. I thought it would be at least a year before you stopped listening to me, husband."

"Just a temporary lapse, please forgive me." He kissed the palm of my left hand.

"Can I see the dress?" I asked again.

He lifted me up to standing and walked to our dressing room. Nik and Suresh had picked up the dress after our visit to Bhaktivedanta Manor, but I had not yet seen it. I waited by the door as he pulled out a scarlet off-the-shoulder chiffon evening dress from the white canvas dress bag. The bodice was ruched and long, and there was a layer of chiffon for the skirt; on the right shoulder strap, there were fabric flowers in differing sizes leading to the top of the bodice. I felt the fabric and pulled myself up on my tiptoes to give my husband a kiss.

"Oh Nik, it's beautiful, thank you." He held the dress away from us with his right arm extended and wrapped me up in his left. We heard a knock on the door.

"Come in!" Nik shouted, reluctant to let me go.

"I thought I'd bring my rubies to show you." Rupa Bhabhi was dressed in an indigo silk chiffon saree with a silver crystal border. Her hair was loose and curled down her back. She had a small diamond-encrusted choker and a pair of long diamond earrings to add to the elegant ensemble. She placed her sandalwood jewellery box on my dressing table and looked admiringly at the dress. Nik took it to the armoire and hung it up on the door. "Amanda is a talented designer. I'm glad you chose her dress. The shape of the bodice will really show your figure off, Reena." She paused. "I wish I could wear something like that but … " She patted her belly.

"You knew Bhabhi?" I shook my head, and she smiled at me. I turned to Nik, who was standing with his hands behind his back.

"Thank you, Bhabhi, but can I give another wedding present to Ree? She can decide then if she wants to wear your rubies." He grinned and held up a velvet jewellery box. I was stunned. He took my hand and guided me back to the dressing table. "Breathe, my love. It's a good thing. If a husband can't buy gifts for his wife on her wedding day, then, when can he?"

"But I already have too much jewellery," I told him.

Rupa Bhabhi's low and rumbling laugh filled the room, "One can never have enough jewellery, Reena." Inside there was a gold thin link bracelet; in the middle of each alternate link there was a red stone. There were two sets of earrings. "It's Victorian, and the stones are garnets. I had it adjusted, and the jeweller suggested the earrings from the leftover links. The larger ones were on display. They will work so well with this dress; they are garnets, too."

Rupa Bhabhi reached for her jewellery box. "Your husband, like mine, has exquisite taste. I don't think you'll like my rubies." She planted a kiss on each of my cheeks and gave my shoulder a squeeze.

"Thank you for the compliment, Bhabhi, but I'm nowhere near as good as Bhai. He did choose you."

She gave him a quick kiss on the cheek and a hug. "We'll see you at the marquee at 7 p.m." She glanced at the clock. "Relax, you've got plenty of time to get ready." I could hear the subdued giggle in her voice as she hurried out of the room.

"What are you doing?" I was scooped up in my husband's arms.

"You heard Bhabhi. She said we should relax. I'm going to need some help relaxing." I thumped him playfully on his forearm.

"I don't want my hair messed up," I protested as he took me to the bed.

"I'm sure you know of a way to do both." His golden eyes twinkled, and a wicked grin drew across his face. He knelt against the bed and kissed the tops of my breasts, reaching for my bra clasps. The hair on his head brushed my nipples as his lips worked to the waistband of my black lace knickers. My skin tingled and a soft sigh escaped from my mouth. "Oh God, Ree," he groaned. His hands worked to bring me pleasure. I pulled him up, untied his dressing gown and pushed his boxer shorts off his pert bottom, unable to pull my eyes away from his arousal. He moved me and fell backwards onto the bed, pulling my legs apart, and I straddled him. He lifted himself up and kissed my breasts. I could feel his arousal as he slowly gyrated his hips. My body wanted him.

"Nik … please." I pulled his mouth to mine, and we became one. This is where I belong, with him, part of him, never to be separated. Slowly and deliberately, our rhythm matched until we were fulfilled. I slumped on top of him, my husband, my one and only love, always and forever.

He lifted me off him and walked me to the dressing table. "See not a hair out of place." He ran his index finger under my fringe, the smoulder in his eyes sending a shiver down my spine. When would the shock of those eyes stop making my heart skip?

Nik walked back from the dressing room in his black tuxedo trousers; his crisp white dress shirt was unbuttoned. I had put on my underwear, my three-inch high heeled gold sandals, and retouched my makeup. I turned to reach for my dress.

"Wait, my love." He was by my side, lifting the hanger off the door. He smiled, holding it up for me. I slid it off the hanger and stepped into it. "I hope you've packed more of these strapless lacy bras for our honeymoon." He lifted his left eyebrow; my cheeks felt hot as he stroked the cup.

"Stop!" My eyes implored him. "We're going to be late."

"You didn't answer my question." A lopsided smile appeared on his face.

"I thought you preferred me underwear-less, my husband?"

He took a deep breath as I shuffled the dress up over my breasts and shrugged my shoulder into the single strap.

"Yes, I thought so, too, but I'm enjoying taking this new lingerie of yours off, wife." I turned to my side and lifted up my left hand; he pulled the zip, kissed my armpit and took a deep breath. "Freesia, roses and sex," he groaned and kissed my armpit again.

"Nik, please." I deliberately made myself take a deep breath.

"It's my honeymoon." He grinned at me.

I raised my eyebrows and said, "Only your honeymoon?"

He pulled me to him by my bottom. "Our honeymoon." He kissed me longingly. He opened the door of the French armoire; Rupa Bhabhi was right: the bodice of my dress sat just below my hips; the balconette bra I was wearing revealed the tops of my breasts. The ruched fabric disguised the little hump of my belly that no amount of sit-ups had been able to reduce. The chiffon skirt parted to reveal my right leg from my thigh, elongating my legs. Nik stood behind me, holding my hips. "It fits like a glove," he murmured, his eyes roaming from my exposed ankle to the tops of my breasts in the mirror. A shudder crawled across my body.

"How did you get my exact measurements?" I

quizzed, taking a deep breath.

"A husband has to keep a few secrets from his wife." He turned me around. "You are the most beautiful woman in the world, my love, my heart." This time his kiss was soft and caressing.

I held my hand on his heart and said, "Thank you, it's beautiful." *It's probably expensive, too,* I thought.

"Can you help with my buttons?" He twirled me to the dressing table. I picked up the jet and gold buttons and inhaled him; he smelled of tobacco, citrus, musk and sex. My cheeks coloured. "No one will mind, they expect us to smell of sex." He kissed the top of my head.

I had asked the hairdresser for a high chignon and a small beehive, in homage to Audrey Hepburn. It is a hairstyle Nik loves. She examined my thick waist-length hair and said it would be difficult. I told her to cut my hair just below my shoulder blade and saw the colour drain from her face. She went to speak with the manager, a small plump woman with immaculately cut silver hair who asked if she could donate my hair to a charity that makes wigs for people who've lost their hair through radiation treatment. I hadn't even thought about what hairdressers did with the hair.

"How much have you taken off?" he asked. I told him about the hairdresser's suggestion of taking off at least twelve inches for a good cause. "I'm glad. You were beginning to look like those masibas. Even Kaki has shorter hair than you." He picked up my silver sindoor pot and added a small pinch just above my fringe, visible for the people who would search for it. "Now, everyone will know you're married, and you're mine." Our friends were waiting as the lift door opened, all dressed in their evening dress splendour. Dick whistled, Ravi released a growl and Peter stepped forward and bowed. "Nikesh Raja, you have good taste in women and clothes. Where did you get the dress?" His eyes ran appreciatively down my body, and I felt hot. "See." He turned his head to Ravi, "Easy to blush." I slapped him on his arm.

"I thought you'd be on my side today, of all days." I feigned a look of hurt.

"No need, you have Nik, now and forever." Jay leant against the one of the mirrors, his eyes only focused on Nik.

"Yes, and don't you forget it." Nik pointed to Ravi, Peter and Dick.

Umi and Anne-Marie stepped though the black and white honour guard and took my elbows, one dressed in freesia pink to go with her sultry dark complexion, the other dressed in emerald green to go with her Celtic complexion.

"You'll get her back," Umi reassured Nik, and he let go of my hand.

We stepped towards the covered arch that led to the entrance to the circus tent, the men following behind. The heady smell of roses hit my senses, as we stepped into a foyer. The rose arch led to two sandalwood columns with a display of pink and red roses. Our family was sitting on two sandalwood sofa sets placed on either side. Jaishree and Ashveena rushed up to us. On the walls were large painted groups of Indian girls, in different dancing poses, the black background emphasising the vibrant colours of their costumes. I put my hand to my mouth to suppress the sound of the gasp. My eyes prickled with tears. Ashveena grabbed my hand, and Jaishree grabbed Nik's.

"Come, let's show you inside," Jaishree said. The black velvet curtains were pulled apart and tied back by two men in cream jabo pyjamas and black waistcoats. The circus tent ceiling was adorned with tiny fairy lights resembling stars; the wooden dance floor was in the middle, and at the end, there was a raised stage where the musicians were setting up. The round tables were set for twelve, each set with a tall candelabra-style light, a wreath of pink and red roses circling the base. The setting was pure white porcelain, with silver cutlery.

"Do you like it?" Ashveena asked apprehensively. My mouth was dry, and I croaked a yes.

"It's beautiful, Ashi, Jaish." Nik pulled me into his side as we both gazed up at the starry canopy. "Thank you so much, you two are geniuses. Just enough glamour, thank you." He pulled his sister to his other side and kissed her on her cheek. I stepped away, and he grabbed Ashveena and did the same to her.

I hugged them both. "I love it, where did you get the stars?" We admired the stars in silence.

"Can you take Ree back? I need to speak with the musicians." Nik walked towards the musicians.

Both families lined up under the arches to meet our guests, and everyone was welcomed with a glass of champagne or orange juice. The musicians played Hindi film song instrumentals as we ate our Punjabi meal.

Reena & Nikesh's Reception Dinner

Starters

Mutton cutlets
shallow fried minced lamb patties

Tandoori paneer kebabs
spiced fresh Indian cheese cooked on skewers

Aloo mattar samosa
triangular shaped pastry stuffed with potato and peas

Lasun mogo
fried cassava wedges with garlic and chilli powder sauce

Main Course

Butter chicken
mild creamy chicken curry flavoured with ghee and spices

Sabzi korma
mild creamy mixed vegetable curry

Aloo gobi
potato and cauliflower curry

Rajma
slow cooked kidney bean stew

Sides

Navratan pilau
fried rice dish made with dry fruit and nuts and seasonal vegetables

Naan
leavened flatbread cooked in a tandoor oven

Tandoori roti
unleavened flatbread made with wheat flour cooked in the oven

Boondi da raita
natural yoghurt blended with fried gram flour balls

Kachumber
salad made with cabbage, cucumber, carrots, onions and tomatoes

Assorted papad
Roasted and fried thin crispy bread made from lentil flour

Desserts

Rasmalai
fresh Indian cheese and thickened sweetened milk

Gajjar ka halwa
carrots, sugar and milk powder cooked with ghee

Garam gulab jamun
deep fried milk powder and dough balls in sweet sticky rose syrup served hot

Alphonso aamb with vanilla ice cream
Alphonso mango served with vanilla ice cream

Nik and I sat at the centre table facing the band; all the important people in our families were placed on our table, including Jane, who was sitting next to Nik's father and Divya Ba. After dinner, Nik's father took to the stage to welcome everyone and asked them to raise a toast. When it was my father's turn, he was happy but nervous. "My dear wife would have been proud to see our daughter find happiness, and I want to thank you, Raja family, for welcoming us. I love you, Reena. We love you, Reena." He nodded towards Amit and Divya Ba. "We wish you a long and happy marriage, my daughter. When Nikesh asked for Reena's hand in marriage, I was reluctant, but I have learnt to love him. He is a fine young man. Welcome to our family, Nikesh." He raised his glass. As he came back to the table, he squeezed Nikesh's shoulder, gave me a kiss on my cheek and sat down.

The male singer took the mic and announced, "Ladies and gentlemen, can I ask the groom to come to the stage?"

"Stay here, my love." Nik squeezed my hand. "I'll come for you." He kissed my lips. I felt the colour rise on my neck. He walked casually up to the stage. "Thank you, Ajay and Bharti for the wonderful music so far. I haven't told Ree this, but for my whole life, I felt I was missing something. When I found her, the day she crashed into my life, I knew she was a piece of my heart that was missing. You make me whole. You are the reason for me to live. You are the reason for me to breathe. Reena Raja, my wife, my soul mate, my heart, this song is for you." He walked to the keyboard and Ajay adjusted the mic in front of him, and he started to sing.

"Yeh Reshmi Zulfein." The song from *Do Raaste*. My heart was in my mouth. My father squeezed my hand and smiled. My husband was full of surprises; I knew of the piano lessons, but I didn't know he played so well. I concentrate on his smiling face and his sparkling eyes. My heart stopped, and then everyone and everything faded. All I saw and heard was Nikesh Raja.

Everyone clapped their hands in applause. He stepped off the stage, locked eyes with me and took me to the dance floor. The band started to play "Pal Pal Dil Ke Paas."

"Keep your eyes on mine and follow my lead. No one cares if we miss the steps, my love." His arm was on my lower back, my right hand engulfed by his and I let him glide me across the dance floor. The words 'my heart sings your song' filled me with joy as we twirled and dipped. My heart calmed and I focused on him and only him.

NIK INSISTED ON COMING UP to our room with me when I told him I wanted to change my sandals. He also used the time to quench our desire to kiss. We were climbing down the stairs from our bedroom, our footsteps muffled on the carpet, when we heard two people talking.

"Your new daughter-in-law is like a beautiful doll. Her skin is so light. I heard you had trouble finding a good day." A hushed voice was talking in the grand hallway. He stopped at the middle landing, pulling me towards him, away from the sightline of the women below.

"Yes, it took a while for Guruji to find a good day for

the wedding. The best day for my Nikesh to take his vows in front of Agni Dev was the 21st of December, but with Reena's brother's children arriving early, we found the second-best day was last Thursday. Hai Bhagwan, why do all the men in my family prefer light skinned women?" The last sentence sounded like a reproach and then she sighed. "Yes, you are right, Manjula, my son's wife is beautiful, just like a china doll," Motaba added as they stepped out of the large front door.

I smiled; little did Motaba know that we did have the blessings of Agni Dev on the day of our intended wedding. *Maybe I'll tell her one-day*. Usually, I felt inadequate when I heard these conversations, but my heart sang as I recalled her words, 'My son's wife is beautiful.' Nik lifted my face, his thumb on my chin. I gazed into his sparkling golden eyes; he brushed his lips on mine. "My wife is beautiful," he repeated, "I'm the luckiest man in the world."

But I heard those words again, the words that haunted me, the words that had some truth in them.

'You bring a burden of unhappiness and bad luck with you, Reena. Your janam kundli shows that in your marriage, you will bring pain and suffering.'

The End?

Want to find out if Reena and Nikesh get their Happily ever after?

Read Where Have We Come Book Two - University Series Reena and Nikesh.

Glossary

Gujarati words

Aarth – one of the four objects of human pursuit in Hindu Scripture meaning material prosperity

Aarti – a worship ritual with the lit flame known as a divo

Aeki Beki – a ceremony to find a ring performed by the bride and groom after the wedding

Agni Dev – God of fire

Avatar – incarnation of a Hindu deity in human form

Ba – mother or grandmother

Bapu – a respectable name given to a wise elder

Bandhani – specialist intricate tie dye technique originated in Gujarat

Ben – sister

Beta – child usually boy but can be used for either male or female

Beti – daughter

Bhabhi – brother's wife

Bhai – brother

Bhagwan – God

Baheno – collective word for sisters

Bhajan – Hindu hymn

Booti – silk or thread embroidery

Chaniya choli – traditional long skirt and blouse worn with a long scarf

Chalo – let's go / walk

Cheda chedi – tying of the groom's and bride's clothes during the wedding

Chundadi – a scarf worn with chaniya choli or salwaar / churidar kameez

Churidar – tight silk / cotton trouser worn under kameez or sherwani

Dada – paternal grandfather

Dadima/Dadi – paternal grandmother

Dandiya – short pair of wooden sticks used in Gujarati folk dance

Dandiya Raas – traditional Gujarati folk dance using short wooden stick

Dharma – one of the four objects of human pursuit in Hindu scripture meaning moral duty

Darshan – an opportunity to see a deity at a temple

Dikri – a pet name for a daughter

Divo – a lamp created using a cotton wick and clarified butter

Durga – Goddess of divine energy

Faiba – paternal aunt

Fua – paternal aunt's husband

Ganda – meaning someone who is crazy

Ganesh Prathna – prayers to Ganesh the god who removes difficulties and obstacles Ganga – River Ganges

Garba – traditional Gujarati folk dance performed during Navratri

Garchoru – unique wedding saree given to the bride by the groom's family

Gaur dhana – pre-engagement ritual to announce an intention to marry, the couple are fed jaggery and dry coriander seeds

Guruji/Guru – a spiritual teacher

Haan – yes

Hai Bhagwan – Dear God

Hai Ram – Dear Ram

Hastamelap – placing together of the bride's and groom's right hands

Jaan – Gujarati word for groom's entourage; also means life or soul

Jabo pyjamas – long shirt and trousers worn by men

Jaimala – fresh flower garland placed on bride and groom's necks by each other

Jai Shri Krishna – Glory to Krishna, a common greeting in Hindu household

Jai Siya Ram – Glory to Sita and Ram, a common greeting in Hindu household

Janam Kundli – horoscope chart prepared at birth

Jhumbar – chandelier-type earrings

Jijaji / Jiju – sister's husband

Kada – a thick bangle

Kadia – a round wok-style pan used for frying

Kaka – paternal uncle

Kaki – paternal uncle's wife

Kam – one of the four objects of human pursuit in Hindu scripture meaning love and pleasure

Kameez – long shirt / dress worn over trousers traditionally worn by women

Kanyadan – the ceremony of giving away of the daughter at marriages

Kanyia patharon sawthan – call for the bride to enter the mandap

Katha – religious story

Katoris – small stainless-steel bowls

Kem cho – Gujarati greeting meaning how are you?

Laxmi – Goddess of wealth

Majnu – meaning demented, someone who is besotted

Mandap – a four-posted canopy under which a Hindu marriage ceremony is conducted.

Mandir – Hindu temple

Mangalsutra – meaning sacred thread: gold and black bead necklace given to the bride by the groom

Masa – maternal uncle

Masi – maternal aunt

Masiba – a term for a group of elderly ladies

Mehndi – paste of crushed leaves of the henna plant used to create intricate body art during wedding and festivals

Moksha – one of the four objects of human pursuit in

Hindu scripture meaning spiritual liberation from the cycle of life and death

Motaba – eldest mother

Motabhai – eldest brother

Na – no or of, in the case of food

Nana – maternal grandfather

Nanima – maternal grandmother

Nasto – savoury snacks

Navratri – nine-day festival to celebrate the divine power of the goddess Durga

Navratri ni adham – the eighth day of Navratri

Omkara – the Aum symbol

Panetar – white and red saree worn by Gujarati bride given to her by a maternal uncle

Panja – hand ornamental jewellery with rings

Pari – angel

Pallu – the decorated end of a saree that is left loose or displayed at the front

Puja – worship

Ram Katha – religious tale of Ram from the Ramayan

Rangoli – pattern and design made using rice flour or coloured powder

Saree – traditional garment worn by Indian women

Salwaar Kameez – wide trousers and a long dress that is worn by women

Sanskrit – ancient classical language of India

Septapadi – seven vows performed at a Hindu wedding

Seva – service

Sevaks – volunteers who conduct service

Shakti Bhavan – home of divine energy

Shradh – days when Hindus pray for their deceased ancestors

Sherwani – a long coat that is worn by the groom

Sindoor – a vermilion red pigment used in Hindu ceremonies and worn by a married Hindu woman

Sunderkand Paath – recitation of the tale of Hanuman, the first devotee of Ram

Tandoor – cylindrical clay oven used for baking using wood or charcoal.

Thali – a metal plate used to serve a variety of foods as a set meal

Tilak – auspicious mark on the forehead using vermilion or sandalwood

Tthodya – white people

Tthoydi – white woman or girl

Tulsi – holy basil used in Hindu houses; the beads are worn for spirituality.

Vishnu – one of the three main deities in Hinduism – God the preserver

Foods

Aloo gobi – potato and cauliflower curry

Aloo mattar samosa – triangular shaped potato and peas stuffed fried pastry

Alphonso aamb – Alphonso mango

Amba hurdar – green yellow and white turmeric root pickled in salted water and lemon

Ambli khajjur ni chutnee – tamarind date chutney

Arbi ni tikki – shallow fried colocasia root flour and potato patties

Baath – plain boiled/steamed rice

Barfi – sweet made with milk powder and sugar

Bateta nu shaak – potato curry

Bateta tameta shaak – potato and tomato curry

Bateta ni chips – fried potato chips

Bhajia – fritters made using gram flour and vegetables

Bharela bhinda – spicy masala stuffed okra

Bhinda – okra

Bombay sandwiches – a toasted sandwich made with tomatoes, cheese, onions, boiled potatoes and coriander chutney and special spice blend

Butter chicken – mild creamy chicken curry flavoured with ghee and spices

Chaas – diluted natural yoghurt drink

Chai – brewed tea with milk, sugar and spices

Chevdo – a fried savoury snack made from gram flour noodles, nuts and potato chips also known as Bombay mix

Chuti mag ni dall – split yellow mung stew

Coconut fried shrimps – dry spiced desiccated coconut coated fried shrimps

Crispy betata na bhajia – fried thinly sliced potato coated in gram flour

Crispy bhajia – thinly sliced vegetable fried fritters coated in gram flour batter

Dahi – natural yoghurt

Dahi phudina ni chutnee – mint and yoghurt chutney

Dal makhani – matpe beans (black gram) slow cooked stew with cream speciality of the Punjab

Dall – split lentils soups and stews

Dhana marcha ni chutnee – fresh coriander and green chilli chutney

Dhudhpak – thin and creamy milk dessert with rice, sugar and spices

Farali chevdo – fried snack made with tapioca flakes, nuts and potato crisps

Farali khichdi – a dish of boiled potatoes, peanuts and tapioca

Farfar – fried tapioca or rice flour crisps

Farsi puri – crispy fried savoury flatbread made with plain flour, black pepper and cumin seed

Flaky chapati – rolled flatbread with buttered layers cooked on a dry griddle pan.

Fried mogo – fried cassava roots cut into chips

Gajjar ka halwa – sweet made using ghee, carrots, sugar and milk powder

Gajjar no sambharo – Gujarati-style stir fried carrots and

green chillies

Ganthia – spicy a fried gram flour noodles

Garlic naan – Indian leavened flatbread made with flour and garlic cooked in a tandoor oven

Gaur – raw cane sugar also known as jaggery

Gaur keri nu athanu – sweet mango pickle using spices and raw cane sugar

Ghee – clarified butter

Gulab jamun – deep fried milk powder and dough balls in sweet sticky rose syrup

Jalebi – sweet dish made with coiled batter fried and steeped in sweet syrup

Kachumber – a salad made with lettuce, cabbage, cucumber, carrots, onions and tomatoes

Kadhi – a thick broth made from gram flour and yoghurt

Kapali dungali – chopped onions

Karela nu shaak – bitter gourd curry

Karkeri karela – crispy fried spiced bitter gourd curry

Kesar – saffron

Khati keri nu athanu – green mango pickled with crushed mustard seeds, salt, chilli, turmeric and lemon

Kitchi – steamed rice flour dumplings

Lal marcha lasun ni chutnee – red chilli powder and garlic chutney

Lasun mogo – fried cassava chips with garlic and chilli powder sauce

Limbu sharbat – fresh lime juice made with sugar and water

Makia na Pawa – Gujarati-style steamed spiced sweet corn and flaked rice

Masala Chai – brewed tea with milk, sugar and spices like cardamom, cinnamon, ginger

Mattar baath – fried and steamed rice and peas

Mattar Kachori – fried plain flour pastry encased balls of masala peas

Methi ni murgi – fenugreek leaves and chicken curry

Methi na thepla – griddle fried wheat flour, gram flour with fenugreek leaves, rolled thin bread

Mithai – generic name for traditional Indian sweets

Mug baath – rice with mung bean curry

Mug ni dall – yellow split lentil stew

Mutton kebab – spiced cubed mutton cooked on skewers under the grill

Naan – leavened flatbread cooked in a tandoor oven

Navratan pilau – fried rice dish made with dry fruit and nuts and seasonal vegetables

Osaman – thin broth made with cooking water of pigeon pea split lentils

Papad – thin crispy bread made with lentil or rice flour eaten either fried or dry roasted on flame

Patra / timpa – steamed colocasia leaves stuffed with gram flour and masala

Pau bhaji – fried bread rolls with mashed spiced vegetable and butter

Penda – traditional Indian sweet made with milk, sugar and spices

Puran Puri – flatbread stuffed with pigeon peas split lentils, sugar and cardamom paste cooked in ghee

Puri – deep fried small rolled flatbread made from wheat flour

Rajma – slow cooked kidney bean stew

Rasmalai – sweet made with fresh cheese and thickened sweetened milk

Riawala murcha – green chillies pickled in crushed mustard seeds

Ringda valor nu shaak – aubergine and hyacinth beans curry

Sabji dall – mixed vegetable and assorted split lentil stew

Sabodana magfali ni khichdi – steamed tapioca, potato and peanut dish

Sabodana ni farfar – tapioca thins fried crisps

Sabzi korma – mild creamy mixed vegetable curry

Shaak – any vegetable curry

Singhara ni puri – deep fried small rolled flatbread made from water chestnut flour

Sukha Bateta jeera nu shaak – dry curry made with potato and cumin seeds

Talela murcha – fried green chillies

Tameta ne mogo nu shaak – cassava and tomato curry

Tameta dungali kachumber – tomato and onion salad

Tameta ni chutnee - fresh tomato chutney

Tandoori paneer kebabs - spiced fresh Indian cheese cooked on skewers

Tandoori roti - unleavened flatbread made with wheat flour cooked in the oven

Tel - cooking oil, sunflower or vegetable

Theekha gathia - spicy chilli powder savoury fried gram flour noodles

Theekhi puri - deep fried small rolled flatbread made from wheat and gram flour and spices

Thepla - griddle fried wheat and gram flour rolled thin spicy bread

Topra ni chutnee - freshly grated coconut chutney

Ugandan Rolex - East African specialty of rotli roll stuffed with omelette

Umpa - savoury semolina and vegetable porridge from South India

Undiyu - mixed vegetable curry especially eaten in Gujarat, made with a combination of root vegetables and green vegetables with fried fenugreek and gram flour fritters

Waatidall na bhajia - ground black eyed pea and mung split lentil fritters

Acknowledgements

I want to thank all the people who've helped me write this book; without your help and support, it would never be what it is now.

To my first readers, who told me that they liked my story and that it was worth telling. Hassy, Rani, Milo, Natasha, Nadia, Aman, Jes, Uma, Femi and anyone else who I bored with my writing journey. Thank you for your support and love.

To Rani, who gave me one of the best compliments ever, by telling me that my book was like a Yash Raj film. Who hasn't seen *Daag, Kabhi Kabhie, Silsila, Chandni*, and some of the later ones, *Dil To Pagal Hai, Dilwale Dulhania Le Jayenge*, to name a few of my favourites. If you haven't seen these films, you must. For those of you who are experts in Hindi and Urdu, please forgive me, I have taken liberties with the translation of the lyrics in the songs that I've quoted.

I have referenced the recording of Sibelius's Seventh Symphony at Butterworth Hall at Warwick Art Centre; most of it was recorded in the mid '80s, but I'm not sure if there was a compilation available at the time

To Niall who read my first chapters and gave me the confidence to carry on.

To Hassy who has been through thick and thin with me and is always there for me when I need her. I love you loads and loads and am so glad you were the girl who already had a room in the house I moved into so, so long ago.

To Marina and Sarah, your draft editing have helped me make my writing better.

To Claire for your excellent editing and proof reading.
To Mita, your designs are awesome and without your help, I wouldn't have beautiful book covers.

To my family: my constant – you've been through my life's tribulations and helped me tremendously. I don't say it often enough, but you are my rock and I love you.

To our son, whose name is apt: his strength to survive against all odds has given me strength. I am who I am now because you came into my life.

To my precious boys, I am so proud to be called your mother; you have made me so happy. I love you: without you, my life would be empty.

To my husband, who has helped me become who I am. I am thankful for the day I met you. You are my friend, my love and the father of our sons. I will always love you, forever.

Finally, and most importantly to you my readers, THANK YOU so much for reading my story, I hope you liked it. I am always interested in connecting with you all.

Please leave a review; it will help other readers find new stories and help self-published author like myself to reach new readers.

About the Author

Saz Vora was born in East Africa and migrated with her family to England in the 60's to the Midlands, where she grew up straddling British and Gujarati Indian culture. Her debut duet My Heart Sings Your Song and Where Have We Come is a story in two parts about love, loss and family, the second book in the series is based on true events that has shaped her outlook on life's trials and tribulations.

Before she started writing South Asian romance she held down successful jobs in Television Production and Teaching...But her need to write stories has led to what she is doing now – writing.

She lives in London, England with her husband in an empty house as her two beautiful sons have began their own life journey.

Saz's hobbies are listening to music, cooking and watching Bollywood, Hollywood and Independent films.

Please visit her website, where you can read her blog and sign up to her newsletter where she will share, missing scenes, recipes, playlists and all things book related.

Website **www.sazvora.com**